THE WAR OF THE PROPHETS

STAR TREK
DEEP SPACE NINE®

MILLENNIUM

BOOK II OF III

THE WAR OF THE PROPHETS

JUDITH & GARFIELD REEVES-STEVENS

POCKET BOOKS
New York London Toronto Sydney Singapore

An *Original* Publication of POCKET BOOKS

POCKET BOOKS, a division of Simon & Schuster Inc.
1230 Avenue of the Americas, New York, NY 10020

This book is published by Pocket Books, a division of Simon & Schuster Inc., under exclusive license from Paramount Pictures.

ISBN: 0-671-02402-7

First Pocket Books printing March 2000

10 9 8 7 6 5 4 3 2 1

Printed in the U.S.A.

For Herman Zimmerman
and all his talented artists and designers in the
Deep Space Nine Art Department
who took "a strange, intriguing object
in orbit of Bajor"
and made it the best-looking series on television.

There is linear in the nonlinear, so that neither exists one without the other. So it was with ANSLEM, *and all the multitudes that he held within himself, myself among them, in that place that was no place, obtained only by knowing the absence of hours in the hourglass. An* hourglass *as the entryway? Was there ever such a joke to make even a Vulcan laugh at those immensities and contradictions of meaning? Yet caught in that sea of sand, drawn toward the neck of that hourglass where both the Temples at last were aligned—well, what else could we do in those vast temporal currents but race time. . . .*

—JAKE SISKO, *Anslem*

PROLOGUE

In the Hands of the Prophets

"THIS DOES NOT HAPPEN," Captain Jean-Luc Picard says.

The Sisko walks with him by the cool waters of Bajor. "It does *not, but it* did," *the Sisko says. "Look around and see it for yourself."*

They stand together on the Promenade, the Sisko and O'Brien and twelve-year-old Jake with his bare feet and his fishing pole, and with Kai Winn and Vic and Arla Rees and all of them, and they watch the Promenade die exactly as it dies the first time, deck plates buckling, power currents sparking, debris and trailing strips of dislodged carpet spiraling into the singularity that is Quark's bar—where the Red Wormhole opens the doors to the second Temple.

"There is no second Temple," Admiral Ross says.

He sits across from the Sisko in the Wardroom of Deep Space 9. Behind him, the casualty lists scroll end-

lessly as the war with the Dominion begins, ends, begins again.

The Sisko stands at the center of B'hala, in the shade of the bantaca *tower.*

"But there was,*" the Sisko says.*

"There is no was," Kira protests.

"Then explain this," the Sisko replies.

He is with them on the bridge of the Defiant *as Deep Space 9 is consumed by the Red Wormhole and the ship is trapped in a net of energies that pull it from that time to another yet to be.*

In his restaurant in New Orleans, the Sisko's father says, "That time is meaningless."

On the sands of Tyree, the Sisko's true mother says, "And another time yet to be is more meaningless still."

*In the serene confines of the Bajoran Temple on the Promenade the Sisko's laughter echoes. "You still don't understand!" It is a marvel to him, this continuation of a state of being that should not exist without flesh to bind it. "*I *am here to teach* you, *am I not?"*

"You are the Sisko, pallie," Vic agrees.

The Sisko makes it clear for them. "Then . . . pay *attention!"*

The Prophets take their places in the outfield as the Sisko steps up to the plate.

"Not this again," Nog says.

The Sisko is delighted. "Again! *That's right! You're finally getting the idea!" He tosses his baseball into the air. It hangs like a planet in space, wheeling about Bajor-B'hava'el, until there appears a baseball bat like a comet sparkling through the stars to—*

Interruption.

The Sisko is in the light space.

Jennifer stands before him, her legs crushed by the debris on the dying Saratoga, *her clothes sodden with her blood. "You keep bringing us back to the baseball game."*

The Sisko takes her hand in his. "Yes! Because now it is you*—" He looks around the nothingness, knowing they are all within it. "—*all *of you who will not go forward!"*

Jennifer is in her robes of Kente cloth, as she wears them on the day they are wed. "There is no forward."

The Sisko discovers he is learning about this place, as if when he falls with Dukat and his flesh is consumed by the flames of the Fire Caves, all resistance to the speed of thought is lost.

"If there is no forward," he argues, "then why are we not already there? Why do you not know everything that I tell you?"

"You are linear," General Martok reminds him, as if he could forget.

"So are you," the Sisko says.

And for the very first time, the Sisko now forces them *from the light space to a place* he *makes real, where from the mists of the moon of AR-558 Jem'Hadar soldiers advance and Houdini mines explode all around them.*

"What is this?" they plaintively chorus.

"This is death," the Sisko tells them. "This is change. This is the forward progression of time to an end in which there is no more forward. This is the fate of all beings—even your fate."

"Impossible," Kai Opaka says by the reflecting pool.

The Sisko leans against the bar on Space Station

K-7, smiling as he looks down at the old gold shirt he wears with the arrowhead emblem that is only that, not a single molecule of communicator circuitry within it. "This is what has gone before," he informs the smooth-foreheaded Klingons at the bar.

The Sisko stands on the sands of Mars, before the vast automated factories where nanoassemblers fabricate the parts for Admiral Picard's mad dream—the U.S.S. Phoenix. "This is what is yet to be," he informs the Tellarite engineers at his side.

And now it is he who returns them to the light space. "And you are all part of that continuum from past to future, with an end before you as surely as you had a beginning."

"What is this?" Arla asks in despair.

"It is why I am here."

"You are the Emissary," Nog agrees.

The Sisko shakes his head. "I am not the Emissary. I am your Emissary."

"How is there a difference?" Grand Nagus Zek asks.

"Think to an earlier time. The first time I came before you."

"You are always before us," O'Brien says.

"I am before you now," the Sisko agrees. "As your Emissary. As one who has come to teach you what you do not know. But before that first time—you must remember!"

The Sisko brings them all back to the baseball game. "Here—this first time—you did not know who I was!"

Solok looks at Martok. "Adversarial."

Martok looks at Eddington. "Confrontational."

Eddington looks at Picard. "He must be destroyed."

The Sisko throws a ball high in the air, swings, hits

one out of the park, and all the Prophets turn to watch the orb vanish in the brilliant blue sky.

"Do you see?" the Sisko asks. "How things have changed? *The way you were* then. *The way you are* now."

The Prophets are silent.

Nineteen-year-old Jake steps forward from them all.

"This . . . does not happen," the young man says.

"Maybe you're right," the Sisko sighs. He sits at his desk in his 1953 Harlem apartment, pushes his glasses back along the bridge of his nose, flexes his fingers, then Bennie types on the Remington: `Maybe all of this did happen . . .`

The Sisko stands on Bajor, gazing up as that world's sun reacts to the proto-matter pulse set off by the Gri-gari task force eight minutes earlier and goes super-nova, claiming all the world and all its inhabitants on the last night of the Universe.

`. . . or maybe none of it happened,` *Bennie types.*

"But still," the Sisko says as he tosses another base-ball into the air, "you want to find out what happens next because, for now, you just don't know."

"We know everything," Admiral Ross says.

"Then answer me this," the Sisko says as another fly ball clears the home-run fence. "When I first came to you, when you did not know me, why did you want to destroy *me?"*

The Prophets are silent.

"Then see this, *and answer an even greater mys-tery," the Sisko says, as he returns them all to the bridge of the* Defiant *just as Captain Thomas Riker de-livers his ultimatum.*

"What mystery?" Weyoun asks, clad in his vedek's robes.

"I will show you the fate of the people who pray to the Prophets as gods. But then you must tell me: To whom do the Prophets pray?"

The Prophets still do not answer.

But they watch as the Sisko continues his story. . . .

CHAPTER 1

LIKE THE thirty-three fragile beings within her battered hull, in less than a minute the *Starship Defiant* would die.

Wounded. Space-tossed. Twenty-five years from home. Her decks littered with the bodies of those who had not survived her journey. And for those who still lived, her smoke-filled corridors reverberated with sensor alarms warning that enemy weapons were locked onto her, ready to fire.

Beyond her forward hull, the *U.S.S. Opaka* accelerated toward an attacking wing of three Starfleet vessels. But adding to the confusion of all aboard the *Defiant,* that warship, which was defending them—inexplicably named for a woman of peace—appeared to be a Starfleet vessel as well.

The *Opaka* was almost a kilometer long, and though her basic design of twin nacelles and two main hulls was little changed from the earliest days of humanity's first voyages to the stars, each element of the warship was stretched to an aggressive extreme, most notably the two forward-facing projections thrusting out from her command hull like battering rams. Now, as she closed in on her prey, needle-thin lances of golden energy pulsed from her emitter rings. Existing partially in the other dimensions of Cochrane space, those destructive energy bursts reached their targets at faster-than-light velocities, only to be dispersed into rippling patterns of flashing squares of luminescence as they were broken apart by whatever incomprehensible shields protected the three attacking Starfleet vessels.

In response, the *Opaka* launched a second warp-speed volley—miniature stars flaring from her launching tubes. The sudden light they carried sprayed across the *Defiant*'s blue-gray hull—the only radiance to illuminate her so deep in the space between the stars, for there was no glow from her warp engines.

Wisps of venting coolant began escaping from the *Defiant*'s cracked hull plates, wreathing her in vapor. Within the ruin of her engine room, at the source of the leaking coolant, the hyperdimensional stability of her warp core seethed from instability to uselessness a thousand times each second.

The ship had no weapons. Diminished shields. No propulsion. The most limited of life-support, and even that was rapidly failing.

But seconds from destruction, caught in a battle of a war that belonged only to her future, the *Defiant,* like her crew, was not finished yet.

"Choose your side!" Captain Thomas Riker screamed from the *Defiant*'s bridge viewer.

And within this exact same moment, Captain Benjamin Sisko was frozen—twenty years of Starfleet training preventing him from making any decision under these circumstances.

Somehow, when Deep Space 9 had been destroyed by the opening of a second wormhole in Bajoran space, the *Defiant* had become enmeshed in the outer edges of the phenomenon's boundary layer and, like an ancient sailing ship swept 'round an ocean maelstrom, she had been propelled into a new heading—almost twenty-five years in her future.

The year 2400, Jadzia Dax had said.

Which meant—according to Starfleet general orders and to the strict regulations of the Federation Department of Temporal Investigations—that it was now the responsibility of all aboard the *Defiant* to refrain from any interaction with the inhabitants of this future. Otherwise, when Sisko's ship returned to her proper time, his crew's knowledge of this future could prevent this timeline from ever coming to pass—setting in place a major temporal anomaly. Thus the source of Sisko's paralysis was simple: How could his ship and crew return from a future that would never exist?

With the weight of future history in the balance, Sisko could not choose sides as Riker demanded. Whatever this War of the Prophets was—and Sisko wished he had never even *heard* Riker say that name—he and the crew of the *Defiant* had to remain neutral. Starfleet and the FDTI allowed them no other option.

Sisko straightened in his command chair. "Mr. O'Brien. All power to shields—even life-support!"

Almost immediately, the lights in the bridge dimmed and the almost imperceptible hum of the air circulators began to slow. At the same time, Sisko felt the artificial gravity field lessen to its minimum level, and understood that his chief engineer had chosen to reply to his order through instant action in place of time-wasting speech.

Then the *Defiant* was rocked by a staccato series of explosive impacts unlike any Sisko had ever experienced.

"What was that?" Dr. Bashir protested to no one in particular. He was holding his tricorder near Jadzia, checking her head wound once again.

"Shields from sixty-eight to *twelve percent!*" O'Brien reported with awe. "From *one hit!*"

Sisko had already ordered the main viewer set to a fifty-percent reduction in resolution so that no one on the bridge—especially O'Brien and Jadzia—might inadvertently pick up clues about future technology simply by seeing what the ships of this time looked like. But the display still held enough detail to show the attacking Starfleet vessels flash by. The three craft, each twice the *Defiant*'s length and half its width, were shaped like daggers, the tips of their prows glowing as if they were nothing more than flying phaser cannons.

"Worf!" Sisko said urgently. "What are they firing at us?"

"Energy signature unknown!" Worf's deep voice triumphed over even the raucous, incessant alarms. "Propulsion systems unknown!"

Now the *Opaka* streaked by in pursuit. The viewer flickered with flashes of disruptive energy as once again the hull of the *Defiant* echoed with the thumps of multiple physical impacts.

"Worf?" Sisko asked. Under the circumstances, it

was a detailed enough question for the *Defiant*'s first officer.

"Sixteen objects have materialized on our hull," Worf answered without hesitation. "They are attached with molecular adhesion. Sensors show antimatter pods in each."

"Contact mines," Sisko said, pushing himself to his feet. "Beamed through what's left of our shields."

Jadzia called out to Sisko from her science station. Her hair was still in uncharacteristic disarray. The medical patch on the side of her forehead obscured her delicate Trill spotting. But nothing could disguise the apprehension in her tone. "We're out of our league here, Benjamin. I think the mines were beamed in from those three ships, but I can't make any sense of their transporter traces. For what it's worth, they probably could've punched through our shields even at one hundred percent."

Major Kira didn't look up from her position at the helm. "The three attackers are on their way back. The *Opaka*'s still in pursuit."

Worf spoke again. "Sir, I am detecting a countdown signal from the mines on our hull. They are programmed to detonate in seventy-three seconds."

Sisko grimaced, trying to understand the logic of that. "Why a countdown? If they can beam antimatter bombs through our shields, why not set them to go off at once?"

Commander Arla Rees had the answer. "It's what the other captain said." The tall Bajoran spun around from her auxiliary sensor station. " 'Every ship is needed for the war.' He said he wasn't going to let the *Defiant* get away."

Sisko struck the arm of his chair with one fist. "Of

course! The other side wants us too, and they'll only detonate the mines if—"

He and everyone on the bridge involuntarily flinched, shielding their eyes from the sudden flare of blinding light that shot forth from the viewscreen faster than the ship's overtaxed computers could compensate for. At precisely the same instant, the deafening rumble of an explosion erupted from the bridge speakers as the *Defiant*'s sensors automatically converted the impact of energy particles in the soundless vacuum of space into synthetic noise, giving the crew an audible indication of the size and the direction of the far-off explosion.

"One of the attackers . . ." Kira said in disbelief. "It dropped from warp and *rammed* the *Opaka.*" She looked back over her shoulder. "Captain, that ship had a crew of fifty-eight."

Now at Sisko's side, Bashir murmured under his breath, "Fanatics."

Sisko tried and failed to comprehend what such desperate action said about the Starfleet of this day.

"Forty seconds until detonation," Worf warned.

"Captain," O'Brien added, "our transporters are offline. I can't get rid of the mines without an EVA team, and there's just no time."

Time, Sisko thought. And that was the end of his indecision. As a Starfleet officer, he couldn't risk polluting the timeline. But as a starship captain . . . his crew had to come first.

"This is the *Defiant* to Captain Riker, I am—"

The stars on the viewer suddenly spiraled, and the *Defiant*'s deck lurched to starboard, felling everyone not braced in a duty chair, including Sisko.

"Another ship decloaking!" Worf shouted as three

bridge stations blew out in cascades of transtator sparks. "We are caught in its gravimetric wake!"

"Dax!" Sisko struggled to his feet. "Stabilize the screen!"

The spiraling stars slowed, then held steady, even though all attitude screens showed that the *Defiant* was still spinning wildly on her central axis.

Then, with the same dissolving checkerboard pattern of wavering squares of light that Sisko had seen envelop the *Opaka,* the new ship decloaked.

Again, Sisko had no doubt he was looking at a ship based on advanced technology. But in this case the vessel was not of Starfleet design; it was unmistakably Klingon—a battlecruiser at least the size of the *Opaka.* Yet this warship's deep purple exterior hull was studded with thick plates and conduits, with a long central spine extending from the sharp-edged half-diamond of the cruiser's combined engineering and propulsion hull to end in a wedge-shaped bridge module.

"Whose side is it on?" Sisko asked sharply, even as Worf reported that he could pick up no transmissions of any kind from the vessel. But Jadzia caught sight of something on the Klingon's hull and instructed the *Defiant*'s computer to jump the viewer to magnification fifty and restore full resolution.

At once, Sisko and his crew were looking at a detailed segment of the warship's purple hull. Angular Klingon script ran beneath the same modified Starfleet emblem Tom Riker had worn on his uniform—the classic Starfleet delta in gold backed by an upside-down triangle in blue.

"It has to be with the *Opaka,*" Kira said.

Worf's next words unnerved Sisko. "And her designation is *Boreth.*"

The *Opaka* was named for a Bajoran spiritual leader—the first kai Sisko had met on Bajor. And Boreth was the world to which the Klingon messiah, Kahless the Unforgettable, had promised to return after his death. The Starfleet of Sisko's day did not make a habit of naming its ships after religious figures or places. Something had changed in this time. But what?

"Thirty seconds," Worf said tersely.

Sisko faced the viewscreen. "This is Captain Sisko to Captain Riker and to the commander of the *Boreth.* My crew stands ready to join you. We require immediate evacuation."

"Course change on the two remaining attackers!" Kira announced. "Coming in on a ramming course!"

Sisko clenched his hands at his sides. He didn't understand the tactics. What about the antimatter mines? Their adversaries could destroy the *Defiant* without sacrificing themselves in a suicidal collision.

Sisko turned abruptly to O'Brien. "Mine status?"

"Only nine left! Seven . . . five . . . Captain, they're being beamed away!"

"The *Boreth,*" Sisko said. That had to be the answer. But why?

He looked at Jadzia. "Any transporter trace?"

"Still nothing detectable, Benjamin."

"Ten seconds to impact with attackers!" Kira shouted. "The *Opaka* is firing more of those . . . torpedoes or whatever they are . . . five seconds. . . ."

Sisko reached for his command chair. "Brace for collision!"

And then, as if a series of fusion sparklers had ignited one after the other across the bridge, Dax, Bashir, and Worf—

—vanished.

One instant Sisko's senior command staff were at their stations. Then, in the center of each of their torsos a single pinpoint of light flared, and as if suddenly twisted away at a ninety-degree angle from every direction at once, the body of each crew member spun and shrank into that small dot of light, which faded as suddenly as it had blossomed.

"Chief! What happened!"

O'Brien's voice faltered, betraying his utter bewilderment. "I . . . some kind of . . . transporter, I think. It—it hit all through the ship, sir. We've lost fifteen crew. . . ."

Sisko strode toward Jadzia's science station, but Arla reached the Trill's empty chair before he did.

"The attackers have gone to warp, sir. The *Opaka* is pursuing. The *Boreth* is holding its position."

With an arm as heavy as his hopes, Sisko finally allowed himself to touch his communicator. "Sisko to Jake."

No answer. Sisko's stomach twisted with fear for his boy.

Arla looked up at Sisko.

"My son—he was in sickbay," Sisko said in answer to Arla's questioning glance.

"Communications are down across the ship," Arla offered.

And then a far-too-familiar voice whispered from the bridge speakers, with pious—and patently false—surprise.

"Captain Sisko, I cannot tell you what a privilege it is to see you once again."

Sisko forced himself to raise his head to look up at the viewer, to see the odious, smiling speaker who sat in a Klingon command chair, a figure clad in the unmistakable robes of a Bajoran vedek.

"*Weyoun . . . ?*"

"Oh Captain, I feel so honored that you remember me after all this time," the Vorta simpered. "Though I suppose for you it is only a matter of minutes since you were plucked from the timeline and redeposited here."

Sisko stared at the viewscreen as if he were trapped in a dream and the slightest movement on his part would send him into an endless fall.

No, not a dream, Sisko thought. *A nightmare. . . .*

Because Weyoun's presence as a Bajoran religious leader on a Klingon vessel with Starfleet markings meant only one thing.

Sometime in the past twenty-five years, the war had ended.

And the Dominion had won.

CHAPTER 2

THE INSTANT the sirens began to wail, Captain Nog was out of his bunk and running for the door of his quarters, his Model-I personal phaser in hand. Then, barefoot, wearing only Starfleet-issue sleep shorts and no Ferengi headskirt, Nog slammed into that door. It hadn't opened in response to his full-speed approach.

Coming fully awake with the sudden shock of pain, he slapped his hand against the door's control panel, to punch in his override code and activate manual function. But before he could begin, the lights in his cluttered quarters dimmed, alarm sirens screamed to life and, with a stomach-turning lurch, Nog felt the gravity net abruptly shut down, leaving him bouncing in natural Martian gravity, still with all his mass but only one-third his weight.

Reflexively Nog slapped at his bare chest, as if his communicator badge were permanently welded to his flesh, then swore an instant later in an obscure Ferengi trading dialect. He darted back to his closet to get his jacket, only to pitch forward as the first shockwave hit Personnel Dome 1.

His cursing reduced to a moan of frustration, Nog jumped to his feet—and banged his head on the ceiling because he'd forgotten to compensate for the suddenly diminished gravity. Dropping to the floor once more, he yanked open his closet door, then ripped his communicator from the red shoulder of the frayed uniform jacket hanging inside.

He knew exactly what had just happened. The four-second delay between the loss of gravity and the arrival of the ground tremor made it obvious. The main power generators for the entire Utopia Planitia Fleet Yards had been sabotaged. Again.

Nog squeezed his communicator badge—a scarlet Starfleet arrowhead against an oval of Klingon teal and gold—between thumb and forefinger as he turned back toward the door. But all the device did was squeal with subspace interference—jamming, pure and simple.

Nog tossed the useless badge aside, then punched in his override code for the door. When the door still didn't open, he abandoned caution and protocol and blasted through it with his phaser.

A moment later his bare feet were propelling him with long, loping strides along the dark corridors of the shipyard's largest personnel dome. Multiple sirens wailed, all out of phase and echoing from every direction, a sonic affront to his sensitive ears. Flashing yellow lights spun at each corridor intersection. More shockwaves and muffled explosions rumbled through the floor and walls. But Nog ignored them all. There was only one thought in his mind, one goal as important as any profit he could imagine.

The Old Man.

As he reached the main hub of the dome—a large, open atrium—he could see thin columns of smoke twisting up from the lower levels, as if a fire had broken out at the base of the free-standing transparent elevator shafts.

Nog rushed to the railing, leaned over, and peered down to the bottom level. Glowing lances of light from rapidly moving palm torches blazed within the heavy smoke that filled the central concourse five floors down. Though he could see nothing else within the murk, his sensitive ears identified the rush of fire-fighting chemicals being sprayed by the dome's emergency crews. He could also hear the thunder of running footsteps, as other personnel bounded up the stairways that spiraled around the atrium, fleeing the fire below.

To the side Nog saw a disaster locker that had automatically opened as soon as the alarms had sounded. He ran to it and took out two emergency pressure suits, each vacuum-compressed to rectangular blocks no larger than a sandwich. As swiftly as he could, he tugged the carry loops of the compressed suits over his wrist, then charged up the closest stairway himself, pushing coughing ensigns and other Fleet workers out of his way while automatically counting each one, even as he also kept track of each set of twenty stair risers that ran from level to level. He was a Ferengi, thank the Great River, and numbers were as integral to his soul as breathing—fourteen times each minute, or approximately 20,000 times each Martian day.

Torrents of statistics flooded his mind as he ran, triggered by the people he passed. In this dome, he knew, most of the personnel were either Andorian (42 percent precisely) or Tellarite (23.6 percent), supplemented by a few dozen Vulcans (48) and Betazoids (42) who had been unable to find rooms in the respective domes set to their environmental preferences.

Of the six main personnel domes in this installation—hurriedly constructed after the attack of '88—none were set to Earth-normal conditions. After '88 it just hadn't made sense.

The Old Man's quarters, however, as befitted a VIP suite, had individual gravity modifiers and atmospheric controls, enabling flag officers and distinguished guests to select any preferred environmental condition, from the Breen Asteroidal Swarm frigid wasteland to Vulcan high desert. Those quarters were on the ninth level, just one below the topmost ground-level floor, with its common-area gymnasium, arboretum, and mess hall.

By the time he reached that level, Nog's feet were stinging from a dozen small cuts inflicted by the rough non-skid surface of the stairs. But mere discomfort had no power to slow him. He looked up once just long enough to see that all the clear panes of the dome's faceted roof were still intact, then headed away from the stairs to charge down the corridor leading to the VIP units.

Nog swore again as he saw the bodies of two guards sprawled on the floor by the shattered security door. Absolute evidence, he feared, that the sabotage of the generators was just a diversion, that the real target was alone and defenseless at the end of this final corridor.

Nog launched himself like an old-fashioned Martian astronaut over the knife-sharp shards of the shattered door. At the same time, like a twenty-fourth-century commando, he thumbed his phaser to full power. The pen-size silver tube bore little resemblance to the weapons he had trained with when he entered the Academy more than twenty-five years ago. But at its maximum setting this new model had all the stopping power of an old compression phaser rifle. For ten discharges, at least.

Nog finally slowed as he rounded the last corner before the Old Man's quarters. The sirens were quieter here, and only one warning light spun, presumably because security staff were always on duty here. But none of those alarms was necessary, because there was no mistaking the distinctive ozone scent of Romulan polywave disruptors—and that was warning enough that a security breach was under way.

He had been right about the true target of this attack, but the knowledge brought him no satisfaction. The Old Man was ninety-five years old—in no condition to resist an attack by Romulan assassins. The best Nog could hope to do now was to keep the killers from escaping.

Two more long strides brought him to the entrance of the Old Man's quarters. As he had expected, both doors had been blown out of their tracks, sagging top and bottom, half disintegrated, their ragged edges sparkling with the blue crystals of solidified quantum polywaves.

Phaser held ready, Nog advanced through the twisted panels, into a spacious sitting room striped with gauzy tendrils of smoke. The only source of light came from a large aquarium set into a smooth gray wall. The aquarium obviously had its own backup power supply, and undulating ripples of blue light now swept the room, set in motion by the graceful movement of the fins of the Old Man's prized lionfish.

Nog paused for a moment, intent on hearing the slightest noise, certain the assassins could not have left so soon. The shields that protected the shipyard's ground installations were separately powered by underground *and* orbital generating stations, and not even the new Grigari subspace pulse-transporters could penetrate the constantly modulating deflector screens. However the Romulans planned to escape, their first step had to be on foot.

Nog had no intention of letting them take that step—or any others.

As methodically as a sensor sweep, he turned his head so his ears could fix on any sounds that might be coming from the short hall leading to the bedroom, or from the door to the small kitchen, or from the door to the study.

He concentrated on the hallway. Nothing. Though that didn't rule out the possibility that someone might be hiding in the bedroom.

Next, the kitchen. Nothing.

Then the study. And there Nog heard slow, shallow breathing.

He began to move sideways, still holding his phaser before him, aiming it at the study door. There was just enough light from the aquarium to avoid bumping the bland Starfleet furniture. He flattened himself against the wall beside the study door, silently counting down for his own—

—attack!

His absolutely perfect textbook move propelled him through the study doorway in a fluid low-gravity roll, smoothly bringing him to his feet in a crouch, thumb already pushing down on the activation button of his phaser as he targeted the first Romulan he saw—the one on the floor by the desk.

But when the silver phaser beam punched its way through the Romulan, the Romulan gave no reaction.

For an instant, Nog stared at his adversary in puzzlement. Then reality caught up to him. His shot had been unnecessary.

The first Romulan was already dead.

So was the second Romulan, slumped on the couch. The gold shoulder of his counterfeit Starfleet uniform was darkened by green blood seeping from the deep, wide gash that scored his neck.

Then a tremulous, raspy voice came from the direction of the room's bookcases. The ones filled with real books. "There's a third one in the bedroom."

Nog slowly straightened up from his crouch. "Admiral?"

The Old Man stepped from the shadows, into the light spilling through the doorway behind Nog. He was a *hew-mon,* slightly stooped. His bald scalp was flushed a deep red, and his long fringe of white hair, usually tied back in a Klingon-style queue, sprayed across his bare shoulders. Only then did Nog realize that the Old Man was naked, his sharp skeleton painfully evident through nearly translucent, thin skin. The only object he carried was a *bat'leth.* It dripped with dark and glistening green blood.

But the Old Man's eyes were sparkling, and the creases around them crinkled in amusement as he also took a closer look at his would-be rescuer. "It appears you're out of uniform, Nog."

Nog laughed with affection. "Look who's talking, Jean-Luc."

Fleet Admiral Jean-Luc Picard—the beloved Old Man to his staff—joined in the laughter. "I was in the sonic shower when—" He doubled over, coughing.

Immediately, Nog pulled from the couch a blanket untouched by Romulan blood, and draped it carefully around the Old Man's sharp-boned shoulders. Fittingly, Nog saw, the blanket was woven with the old Starfleet emblem and the name and registration of Picard's last ship command: the *U.S.S. Enterprise,* NCC-1701-F.

Nog reached for the *bat'leth.* "Maybe I should take that."

The Old Man stared at the weapon for a few moments, as if wondering how it came to be in his hands.

"That's the one Worf gave you, isn't it?" Nog asked gently.

The Old Man seemed relieved. "That's right." He handed the *bat'leth* to Nog. "How is Worf? Have you heard from him on Deep Space 9?"

Nog kept his smile steady. He had already conferred with Starfleet Medical on this: The Old Man was in the secondary stages of Irumodic Syndrome, a degenerative disorder linked to a progressive and incurable deterioration of the synaptic pathways. The doctors had told Nog that the Old Man's short-term memory would be first to show signs of disruption, and that's just what had happened. It had become common this past year for the admiral to forget the names of the newer researchers who had joined Project Phoenix. But now, as the project drew nearer its absolute deadline and the unrelenting pressure mounted, it was distressing to see that the Old Man also seemed to be having more and more difficulty recalling events that had occurred years, even decades, before.

"Worf is dead, Jean-Luc," Nog said quietly. "When Deep Space 9—"

The Old Man's eyes widened. "—was destroyed.

That's right." He licked his dry lips, pulled the blanket of his last command more tightly around his shoulders. "That's when it all started, you know."

Nog understood what the Old Man meant. Everyone in what was left of the Federation did. With the destruction of Deep Space 9 and the discovery of the second wormhole in Bajoran space, all the conditions that had led to this terrible state of siege had been set in place.

"I was there when it happened," Nog reminded him.

Late at night, the memories of that last day, that last hour on DS9, that last minute before he had been beamed out to the *U.S.S. Garneau,* were as vivid to Nog as if they had happened only hours earlier, as if he were still in his youth, still only an ensign.

Back then, back there, he had been working in Ops with Garak and Jadzia, painstakingly restoring the station's computers. Then something had happened in his uncle's bar. Captain Sisko had asked for Jadzia's help, for Chief O'Brien's help, even for Nog's father's help. But he had not asked for Nog's.

Less than an hour later, the gravimetric structure of space had suddenly distorted, and every warning light and siren in Ops had gone off at once as the order came to abandon the station. Even now, Nog was still unable to make sense of the readings he had seen at the time. Only after the fact had he learned that a wormhole had opened unnaturally slowly in his uncle's bar on the Promenade. After the fact, he had learned that a few survivors from the Promenade had been beamed aboard the rescue flotilla, with stories describing how the three Red Orbs of Jalbador had moved into alignment by themselves, somehow triggering the wormhole's appearance.

But in the confusion of those final moments, Nog had been left with the mystery of the sensors, watching uncomprehendingly as transport indicators showed the start of mass beam-outs, and—inexplicably—a handful of beam-ins.

Then, only seconds from the end, when the station's power had failed, plunging all of Ops into momentary darkness before the emergency batteries came on-line, Nog had heard Jake Sisko's voice as if he were calling out from far away. He remembered spinning around, already so close to panic that only Garak's eerily calm example had kept him focused on his work of dropping shields according to emergency evacuation procedures in order to permit as many transports as possible.

But when he had turned in answer to Jake's call—that was when Nog had screamed as only a Ferengi could. Because Jake was only centimeters behind him.

Jake had reached out to him then, silently mouthing Nog's name as if he were shouting as loudly as he could. To his perpetual regret, Nog had drawn back from his friend in fear. His abrupt move caused him to stumble back over his stool, begin to fall, and when he landed, he was on a cargo-transporter on the *Garneau*.

Two muscle-bound lieutenants had dragged him off the array so quickly, one of his arms had been dislocated, the other deeply bruised. And by the time a harried-looking medical technician had finally gotten to him, everything was over.

Deep Space 9.

The *Defiant*.

His father, his uncle, and his best friend, Jake.

Gone. Snuffed out. The void within him the equal of the one that had swallowed everyone he had loved.

"I was there when it happened," Nog said again. "When everyone died."

That sudden flash of a smile came to the Old Man again. "Oh, no. They didn't die, Nog."

But Nog knew that theory, too. And he didn't accept it. If there was any hope for the Federation, for the galaxy, for the universe itself, that hope rested instead with Project Phoenix and the brilliance of Jean-Luc Picard, however much that brilliance was compromised. What needed to be done now—the only thing that *could* be done—was something that only the Old Man had accomplished before; at least, he was the only starship captain alive today who had accomplished it. And Nog, and everyone else who had sacrificed and struggled to make Jean-Luc Picard's *Phoenix* a reality, continued to believe he could do it again. They had to believe.

Fifteen more standard days, Nog thought. All he had to do was keep the Old Man calm and stress-free for 360 more hours. Keep the Old Man's peridaxon levels up. Make sure he slept and ate as his medical team determined was necessary, and the *Phoenix* would fly and the nightmare would end. Failure was unacceptable—and unthinkable.

"Jean-Luc, Captain Sisko was lost with the *Defiant.* They were *all* lost. And now the Federation is counting on *you,* and science. Not some ancient prophecy."

The Old Man stood in the middle of his sitting room, shaking his head like a patient teacher addressing a confused student. "You know . . . you know people used to fight over whether or not a photon was a wave or a particle. Centuries ago they used to think it had the characteristics of both, and depending which characteristic an experiment was set up to find, that's the characteristic that was revealed."

It might have been a long time ago, but Nog still remembered the science history classes he had taken at the Academy. He was familiar with the muddled early beginnings of multiphysics, when scientists had first encountered quantum effects and had lacked the basic theory to understand them as anything more than apparently contradictory phenomena. He knew that the old physicists' mistake had not been in trying to determine the nature of light as particle or wave, but in thinking it had to be only one or the other. Fortunately, the blinding simplicity of the Hawking Recursive-Dimension Interpretation had taken care of that fallacy, and all apparent quantum contradictions had disappeared from the equations overnight, opening the door to applied quantum engineering for everything from faster-than-light communication to the Heisenberg compensators used in every transporter and replicator system to this day.

"The debate over the nature of light is ancient *history,*" Nog said kindly. "Not science. Certainly not prophecy."

Another tremor shook the floor beneath them. Longer and more sustained than the others that had preceded it. Nog looked away from the Old Man as his ears picked up a distant, high-pitched whistle, something he doubted any *hew-mon* would be able to hear. To him, it could mean only one thing: The atmospheric forcefields were down.

"But the way the question was *resolved,*" the Old Man insisted. "That's what's applicable today."

Nog quickly slipped one of the vacuum-compressed emergency suits off his wrist, tugged on the loop to break the seal, and in less than a second shook out a crinkly, semitransparent blue jumpsuit. "Here, Jean-Luc. We'd better put these on."

"Y'see," the Old Man said, as he stepped agonizingly slowly into one leg of the suit, then the other, "the conflict between particle and wave was resolved when it was discovered that the real answer united *both* aspects. Different sides of the same coin."

Nog slipped the blanket from Picard's shoulders and helped pull both the Old Man's sleeves on, making sure the admiral's hands reached to the mitt-like ends.

"Same thing with ancient prophecy and science," the Old Man explained.

Nog smoothed out the flaps of Picard's suit opening, then pressed them together so the molecular adhesors created an airtight seal. All that remained now was to pull up the hood hanging down the Old Man's back, seal that to the suit, then twist the small metal cylinder at the suit's neck, which would inflate the face mask to provide the admiral with ten minutes of emergency air while at the same time transmitting a transporter distress beacon.

Though he estimated the atmospheric pressure in the personnel dome would hold for the next minute or two, Nog didn't want to take any chances with the Old Man. Swiftly, he positioned Picard's hood, sealed it, then twisted the cylinder so that a clear bubble of micro-thin polymer formed around the Old Man's face.

"Science and ancient prophecy," the admiral shouted through the mask, undeterred by all of Nog's ministerings. "Look deeply enough, and who's to say both aren't different aspects of the same thing? Just like particle and wave!"

Even as Nog shook out his own suit, quickly donning and sealing it, the admiral's words had a chilling effect on him. The Ascendancy's propaganda had won it dozens of worlds already—fifty-two to be exact, according to the latest intelligence estimates. If those falsehoods were to reach the workers of Project Phoenix, perhaps the project would survive. But if they infected Admiral Picard . . . Nog didn't even want to think of the consequences.

Nog hesitated before pulling his own hood over his head. Fortunately, the pressure suits were designed to fit up to a 200-kilogram Tellarite, so there would be ample room even for a Ferengi head and ears. "Jean-Luc, you can't allow yourself to be distracted by Ascendancy lies. You have to concentrate on finishing the *Phoenix*."

"But they're not lies," Picard replied indignantly.

Nog put his hands on the Old Man's shoulders, and their suits crackled like a blazing campfire. "Jean-Luc, please. Remember what you've been telling us since the project began. The Ascendancy will do anything, *say* anything, to divert us from our course."

Picard patted Nog's hand on his left shoulder. "But that was *before*, Will."

"Before what?" Nog didn't bother to correct the Old Man. When he was tired or confused, the admiral often thought Nog was his old first officer from the *Enterprise-D* and *E*, Will Riker. Another casualty of '88.

"Before this attack!" The Old Man spread his arms grandly, and Nog noticed that both his suit and Picard's had begun to expand slightly, obviously in response to reduced air pressure in the dome.

Nog checked the ready light on the small metal cylinder on his own suit. The emergency beacon was transmitting. The automatic search-and-rescue equipment installed throughout the Utopia Planitia Fleet

Yards was designed to be activated by the first sign of falling air pressure. By now, Nog knew, sensors throughout the domes should be locking onto emergency beacons and activating automatic short-range transporters to beam personnel to underground shelters.

"What's so special about this attack?"

"It's fifteen days!" the Old Man said. "Don't you see? It's no coincidence they're attacking now! It's a diversion. To keep us from the truth."

"What truth?" Nog shouted. The air outside his suit was thinning rapidly, and the Old Man's voice was fading.

"They've come back!" the Old Man said. "It's the only explanation."

Then, before Nog could offer an alternate explanation of his own, he was relieved to see the Old Man begin to dissolve in a transporter beam, followed a moment later by the transformation into light of the admiral's quarters. They were both being beamed away.

But as their new location took shape around them, Nog realized with a start that they hadn't been beamed to safety in the underground shelters.

Martian gravity had been replaced by Class-M normal.

He and the Old Man were no longer in the shipyards, and the people surrounding them were not Starfleet emergency-evacuation personnel.

They were Romulans.

And this close to the end of the universe, Nog knew that Romulans could only want one thing.

The death of Admiral Jean-Luc Picard.

CHAPTER 3

SOMETIMES, Julian Bashir remembered what it was like to be normal.

But such bittersweet memories were suspect, because they were invariably mixed in with disjointed recollections of his early childhood, from his first faint glimmerings of self-awareness to age six. For the rest of his childhood—that is, everything beyond age 6 years plus 142 days—there were, of course, no disjointed recollections, only perfect recall. Because on the one hundred forty-third day of his seventh year of existence he had awakened in the suffocating gel of an amino-diffusion bath, with an illegally altered genetic structure. On that day everything had changed—not just within the boy he had been, but within the universe that had previously surrounded him.

In fact, sometimes it seemed to Bashir that the innocent male child who had been born to his parents thirty-four years ago had perished in that back-alley gene mill on Adigeon Prime, and that he—the altered creature who now called himself Julian Bashir—was in fact a changeling of old Earth legends.

Little Julian—the terrified boy who had been immersed in the diffusion bath with no idea what he had done wrong to make his parents punish him in such a way—had been undeniably slow to learn throughout his entire, brief life. His environment had been a constant marvel to him, because so much of it was simply beyond his natural capacity to comprehend. His beloved stuffed bear, Kukalaka, had been no less alive to him than his mother's cruelly nipping and yipping Martian terriers. To little Julian, it had been obvious that the various computer interfaces in his home contained little people who could speak to him. And he had only been able to watch in wonder as the other children at his school somehow answered questions or accomplished tasks with abilities indistinguishable to him from magic.

One recollection that most often resurfaced when least wanted from those blurry, half-remembered days of dull normalcy, was of standing in his school's playroom listening to Naomi Pedersen chant the times table. To little Julian there had been absolutely no connection between the numerals that floated above the holoboard and the words that his classmate sang out. The disconnect had been so profound that Bashir clearly remembered his early, untransformed self not even attempting to understand what was going on: Naomi was simply uttering random noises, and the squiggles above the holoboard were only unrelated doodles.

From his present vantage point, Bashir regarded those days of simple incomprehension as the peace of innocence. They marked a time when he was unaware that life was a continuing struggle, a never-ending series of problems to be overcome by those equipped to recognize and solve them.

Now he recognized that same peace of incomprehension in most of the fourteen others with whom he had just been transported from the *Defiant,* and he envied them their unknowing normalcy.

But, incapable of giving in to what he suspected was their hopeless situation, Bashir still studied his surroundings. He and the others were standing together in what appeared to be a familiar setting: the hangar deck of a Starfleet vessel, complete with the usual bold yellow sign warning about variable gravity fields, and the stacks of modular shipping crates marked with the Starfleet delta and standard identification labels. Other than the fact that the lighting was about half intensity, and the air unusually cool, Bashir could almost believe he was on a standard Starfleet cargo ship in his own time. Only the Starfleet emblem on the crates confirmed that he and the others from the *Defiant* were still in the future.

Interestingly enough, that emblem, though understandably different from the one used in his time, was also different from the emblem Captain Riker had worn on his uniform, and that had been emblazoned on the Klingon cruiser. That identifying mark, Bashir recalled, had placed a gold Starfleet arrowhead against an upside-down triangle of blue. But here on this ship, the arrowhead was set within a vertically elongated oval, its width matching the oval's. The arrowhead itself was colored the red of human blood, the lower half of the oval teal and the upper half gold—as if the colors of the *k'Roth ch'Kor,* the ancient Klingon trident that was the symbol of the Empire, had been merged with the more recent symbol of Starfleet.

But rather than give himself a headache trying to fathom the political permutations that might have led to the two different versions of the Starfleet emblem in this future, Bashir set that particular problem aside. Instead, he directed his attention to the conversations going on around him—five now—and his mind was such that he could effortlessly keep up with each at the same time. In all except one of those conversations, Bashir heard relief expressed, primarily because of the familiar surroundings.

The single conversation that was more guarded was that between Jadzia and Worf. Klingon pessimism and the Trill's seven lifetimes of experience were obviously enabling the two officers to come to the same conclusion Bashir's enhanced intellect had reached: They were in more danger now than when the *Defiant* had come under attack.

Bashir wasted little time contemplating what might happen in the next few minutes. His primary responsibility was to his crewmates, and to the few civilians who had been evacuated from Deep Space 9 to the *Defiant* and then beamed here.

He rapidly assessed the fourteen others for obvious signs of injury or distress. Nine of them were either *Defiant* or DS9 crew members, six in Starfleet uniforms, three in the uniforms of the Bajoran militia. The other five, including—Bashir was surprised to see—the unorthodox archaeologist Vash, were civilians; three of these human, the other two Bajorans.

He also noted, without undue concern, that the medical patch on the side of Jadzia's forehead was stained with blood and needed to be replaced. Without a protoplaser he had been unable to close the small wound; the dense capillary network beneath a Trill's spots made them prone to copious and unsightly—though not life-threatening—bleeding as a result of any minor cut or scrape in the general area.

Close by Jadzia's side, Worf was uninjured and unbowed. His uniform was soiled by smoke, and one side of his broad face was streaked with soot. His scowl was evidence not of any wound to his body, but rather to his sense of pride and honor—outrage being his people's traditional response to captivity.

Bashir also observed that Jake Sisko, who was currently engaged in listening carefully to Worf and Jadzia's conversation without taking part, also seemed unharmed. The tall, lanky young man had been helping out in the *Defiant*'s sickbay when the group transport to this ship had taken place. It was a blessing, Bashir thought, that at least none of the *Defiant*'s surviving crew or passengers had required critical medical attention before their doctor had been kidnapped.

Then again, the last he himself could recall from his own final moments on the *Defiant*'s bridge was that there were still some antimatter contact mines attached to her hull, so there was no way of knowing if the ship or any of the crew and passengers not transported here still survived.

Then a hoarse female voice interrupted his thoughts. "This isn't good, is it?"

It was Vash, and automatically Bashir reviewed her condition. The last place he had seen her had been in Quark's bar, when the three Red Orbs of Jalbador had moved themselves into alignment and somehow triggered the opening of a second wormhole in Bajoran space.

Vash, an admittedly alluring adventurer and archaeologist of questionable ethics, was still in the same outfit she had worn in the bar—no more than an hour ago in relative time—as if she were prepared to trek across the Bajoran deserts in search of lost cities. She no longer toted her well-worn oversized shoulder bag, though. Bashir guessed it must be either back on the *Defiant* or left behind in the mad rush from Quark's and the subsequent mass beam-out to the evacuation flotilla.

Vash waved an imperious hand in front of his face. "You keep staring at me like that, I'm going to think one of us has a problem. And it's not me."

"Sorry," Bashir said, flushing. "I didn't see you on the *Defiant*. There were some injuries from the evacuation, and . . ." He shrugged. It was pointless to say anything more. It was quite likely Vash was used to people staring at her, for all the obvious reasons.

"I was hustled into the *Defiant*'s mess hall right after I was beamed aboard." Vash frowned. "What the hell happened?"

Bashir told her as succinctly as he could. The old, apocryphal legends of the Red Orbs of Jalbador had turned out to be correct, at least in part. A second Temple—or wormhole—had opened, though since they were now twenty-five years or so into the future the part of the legend about the opening of the second Temple causing the end of the universe was clearly and thankfully not correct. Bashir was about to describe the attacking ships and what Captain Thomas Riker had said about the War of the Prophets, but Vash interrupted.

"Twenty-five years? Into the *future?*"

Bashir nodded. "It happens."

"Not to me."

"Think of it as archaeology in reverse."

Vash's eyes flashed. "This isn't funny, Doc. The longer we stay here the more likely it is we'll learn about the future, and the less likely we are to have someone let us go back." She looked over at the crates. "Especially if some bureaucrat at Starfleet has anything to say about it."

"That's true," Bashir agreed. He glanced at the main personnel doors leading into the interior of whatever vessel they were aboard—one of the two surviving attack ships, he had concluded. "But on the plus side, no one from this ship has attempted to communicate with us. That could suggest they're also following Starfleet regulations, and want to keep us isolated for our return."

"You don't really believe that."

"And why not?"

"If they wanted to keep us isolated, why beam us off the *Defiant?*"

"We were under attack. The *Defiant* might have been destroyed."

"Attacked by who?" Vash asked, and Bashir told her the other half of the story, about Thomas Riker in the *Opaka* and the three attacking Starfleet vessels.

"That makes no sense," Vash said when Bashir had finished.

"Things change. Twenty-five years is a long time."

"How things have changed has nothing to do with our current situation," Vash told him. "If this is a Starfleet vessel, how long do you think it would take some technician to run a search of the service record of the *Defiant?*"

"Your point?"

"C'mon, Doc. Did that strange transporter scramble your synapses? If the historical record shows the *Defiant* disappeared with all hands when DS9 was destroyed, then we're not going back. It's that simple."

Bashir bit his lip. Vash had reached the same conclusion he had. There were a few unresolved issues, however. "This ship we're on was probably one of the ones involved in the attack. If it's been damaged, the *Defiant*'s service record may not be available. The delay in any attempted communication could be a result of having to wait to hear back from Starfleet Command."

Vash looked skeptical. "I never took *you* for much of a dreamer."

Before Bashir could reply, Jadzia, Worf, and Jake had joined them.

"Julian," Jadzia said teasingly, "a dreamer? Like no other, complete with stars in his eyes."

Bashir did not respond to Jadzia's banter. She had been trying to act as if nothing had changed between them since she had married Worf. But it had. Though until these last few weeks, when Jadzia and Worf had sought his counsel on the likelihood of a Klingon and a Trill procreating, Bashir had almost convinced himself that Worf was only a temporary inconvenience, not an insurmountable barrier. In time, he had reasoned, Jadzia would tire of her plainspoken Klingon mate and begin to seek more sophisticated company. But knowing her as he did, even he could not fantasize a time when Jadzia would tire of her child-to-be, or deny that child a chance to know its father.

So there it was. His heart was broken, and his success at hiding his misery from Jadzia was one of the few advantages of having an enhanced intellect: Only his ability to master advanced Vulcan meditation techniques was sparing him public and personal humiliation.

"Vash is concerned that the longer we wait here," Bashir explained, "the less likely it is we'll be allowed to go back to our own time."

"Allowed?" Jake asked in alarm.

Jadzia put her hand on the young man's shoulder. "To go back, Jake, we're going to need access to advanced technology."

Jake looked confused. "What about temporal slingshot?"

Jadzia shook her head. "We didn't get here by slingshot, so we don't have a Feynman curve to follow back to our starting point. Any attempt we make to move into the past will result in a complete temporal decoupling."

Jake stared at her, not a gram of understanding in him.

Worf took over. "It would be like entering a planet's atmosphere at too shallow an angle. Our craft would skip out, away from the planet, never to return."

"Though in our case," Jadzia continued, "we would skip out of our normal space-time and . . . well, then it becomes a question of philosophy, not physics. But if you think about it, if anyone with a warp drive could go back in time wherever and whenever she wanted, half the stars in the galaxy wouldn't exist. I mean, a century ago Klingons would have gone back in time a million years and dropped asteroids on Earth and Vulcan to eliminate the Empire's competitors before they had ever evolved."

Jake glanced at Worf. "Really?"

Worf shifted uncomfortably. "It was a different time. But yes, I have heard rumors of the Empire dispatching temporal assault teams to destroy . . . enemy worlds before the enemy could arise."

"What happened to them?" Jake asked.

"We do not know."

But as Bashir anticipated, Jadzia found so simple an answer unacceptable. "As far as we can tell," she said, "the physics of it is pretty straightforward. Any given time traveler moving from one time to another at a rate greater than the local entropic norm, or on a reverse entropic vector, *has* to move outside normal space-time along a pathway called a Feynman curve. Now, if the past the traveler goes to is not disrupted, the Feynman curve retains its integrity and, provided the traveler can find it again, the way is clear to return to the starting point. However, if the timeline is significantly disrupted, the Feynman curve collapses, because its end point—that is, the traveler's starting point—no longer exists. It's like cutting the end of a rope bridge."

Bashir was curious to see how Jake's imaginative mind would tackle Jadzia's elegantly defined problems of temporal mechanics. Though strict causality did not exist at the most fundamental levels of the universe, it *was* the defining characteristic of macroscopic existence. Indeed, that was one of the chief reasons why the warp drive and time travel took so long to be discovered by emerging cultures. Even though both concepts were rather simple, requiring little more than a basic atomic-age engineering capability to demonstrate, the ideas of faster-than-light travel and time-like curves independent of space could not easily be grasped by minds narrowly conditioned by primitive Einsteinian physics—any more than Newton could have conceived of relativistic time dilation.

Jake's young face wrinkled in concentration. "Hold it . . . it sounds as if you're saying that the Klingons *could* have traveled back in time and destroyed the Earth."

"There's no reason why they couldn't," Jadzia agreed. "In fact, several of the temporal assault missions Worf mentioned could have succeeded. It's just that if they did destroy the Earth in the past, the present they came from—in which the Earth had not been destroyed—no longer existed, so they could never return to it."

"But . . . ," Jake said uncertainly, ". . . the Earth *does* exist."

"In this timeline," Jadzia agreed. She smiled indulgently at Jake. "What you're struggling with is what they used to call on Earth the grandfather paradox. It was a long time ago, before anyone thought time travel possible. Yet early theorists imagined a situation in which a time traveler could go back in time and kill his grandfather before his father was conceived. No father meant no son. No son meant no time traveler. But no time traveler meant that the grandfather hadn't been killed, so the father was born, the son became the time traveler, and . . ." Jadzia smiled as Jake finished the paradox.

". . . and the grandfather was killed." Jake's expression was thoughtful. "But . . . you're saying that *can* happen?"

"There's nothing to prevent it. The difference between what the Einsteinian-era physicists thought and what we know today, from actual experimental demonstrations, is that no paradox results."

"How's that possible?"

"Two solutions are suggested, but neither is testable—so both have equal validity. One solution is that if you, say, went back in time and killed your grandfather, a temporal feedback loop would be established that would collapse into a hyperdimensional black hole, cutting the loop off from any interaction with the rest of the universe. The end result would be as if the events leading to the feedback loop never happened. The second solution states that the instant you killed your grandfather, you'd create a branching timeline. That is, two universes would now exist—one in which your grandfather lived, and one in which he died."

"But if he died, then how could I go back and kill him?"

"You can't, Jake. Not from the new timeline. But since you came from the old one, there's no paradox. However, because the Feynman curve you followed no longer exists, you are trapped in the new timeline you created, with no way to get back. In effect, you're a large virtual particle that has tunneled out of the quantum foam."

Jadzia put her hand on Worf's shoulder, a gesture of familiarity that caused an unexpected tightness in Bashir's throat. "A few years ago," she said, "when Worf was on the *Enterprise,* he encountered a series of parallel universes that were extremely similar to our own. Some researchers suggest that those parallel dimensions have actually been created by the manipulation of past events by time travelers."

Vash put her hands on her hips and sighed noisily. "Do the rest of us have to know this for the test? Or does *any* of this hypothetical moonshine have anything to do with *our* situation, right here and now?"

Bashir sensed Jadzia's dislike of Vash in the Trill's quick reply, though her words were polite. "It has everything to do with our situation, Vash. From *our* perspective, we've traveled into our future. But from the perspective of the people who live here, we're intruders from the past who—if we return—could prevent this future from ever existing."

"It wouldn't just be a split-off, parallel dimension?" Jake asked.

"It might be," Jadzia allowed. "But then again, this present might just wink out of existence, along with everyone in it. Remember what happened on Gaia, to the people who were our descendants? If this was your present, would you be willing to risk nonexistence for the sake of a handful of refugees from the past?"

As Jake thought that over, Worf added, "Several years ago, the *Enterprise* encountered the *Bozeman*—a Starfleet vessel that had been caught in a temporal causality loop for almost a century. Once we broke the loop, the crew of the ship was in the same situation we face now."

"What happened to them?" Jake asked.

Worf frowned. "Historical records stated that the *Bozeman* had disappeared without a trace. Since it had never returned home in our timeline, Starfleet could not risk sending it back. Under Starfleet regulations, her captain and her crew were . . . resettled in their new time."

"And that's what's going to happen to us?" Jake said, dismayed.

"That appears to be the most likely outcome," Bashir said, when no one else offered an answer to Jake's question.

"Not for me," Vash said. "I'm not Starfleet. I'm going home."

"Really? How?" Jadzia asked. Bashir could tell she

intended her challenge to reduce Vash to inarticulate silence.

But Vash merely issued her own challenge. "I thought *you* were the big expert on the Bajoran Orbs. You've never heard of the Orb of Time?"

"She's right!" Jake said.

Vash smiled dazzlingly at Jake. "Okay. I've got one partner. Anyone else?"

Bashir shook his head, refusing to play Vash's game.

"Too dangerous," Jadzia said. "We didn't get here through the Orb of Time, so there's no Orb-related Feynman curve connecting back to our own time."

Vash rolled her eyes. "C'mon! You're a scientist—think outside the warp bubble. Let's say you hadn't reached this time period on the *Defiant.* You could have lived through the past twenty-five years, easy. Are you telling me that under those conditions you couldn't use the Orb of Time to slip back twenty-five years?"

"Of course I could," Jadzia said, and Bashir could hear the growing annoyance in her tone. "Because the subatomic chronometric particles bound within my molecular structure would be in perfect synch with the current universe's background chronitronic radiation environment. I would *belong* in this time. But all of us are out of phase, Vash. We can't establish a second Feynman curve in this time because we're already connected to the first curve, stretching from our own time. Either we go back the way we came—by traveling through the boundary region of the wormhole that brought us here—or we don't go home at all."

Vash groaned in frustration, her expression becoming almost that of a wild creature held against its will.

Bashir leaned forward, lightly touching Vash's arm.

"We're still simply speculating," he said in his most reassuring tone. "Starfleet might send us back at any moment."

"And if they don't?" Vash retorted.

Bashir took a deep breath and said what he knew someone had to say. "Then considering all the possible timelike curves we might have followed, perhaps twenty-five years isn't all that bad."

"What?!" Vash exclaimed.

"You said it yourself. This time period is within our natural lifetimes. People we know will still be alive. The places we know won't have changed all that much. It will be easier for us to adapt than it was for the crew of the *Bozeman.*"

This time Vash grabbed his arm, and her tone was not at all reassuring. "Is it that easy to make a quitter out of you?"

Bashir peeled her hand off his arm. There were larger issues at stake. "Are you that willing to risk the lives of the billions of beings alive in this time who might be wiped from existence by a single act of selfishness on your part?"

Vash's cheeks reddened as her voice rose in anger. "I didn't ask to be beamed to the *Defiant.* I didn't ask to . . . oh, I *hate* you Starfleet types. The good of the many . . . it makes me sick!" Then she whirled around and marched off toward the main personnel door leading from the hangar deck.

Bashir resisted following, but he called out to her, "Vash! If you go out that door, you only increase the odds they won't send you back!"

Vash's pace did not lessen.

"Don't worry," Jadzia said. "The door will be sealed."

Just then the status of the door ceased to be important, because Vash suddenly collided with—nothing.

Bashir saw her come to a sudden stop, as if she had run into a slab of transparent aluminum, undetectable in the dim light of the hangar deck. Vash stepped back and rubbed at her face, then reached out and slapped her hand against something that was solid, yet absolutely invisible.

"She's hit a forcefield," Jadzia said.

"Unusual," Worf commented. "Most forcefields emit Pauli exclusion sparks when anything physical makes contact."

"Whatever it is, I don't think it's anything to worry about," Bashir said. He watched Vash turn and begin to walk across the deck, sliding her hand as she moved along the forcefield's invisible boundary. "I mean, even if it's a forcefield, it's not delivering a warning shock. I think it's further evidence that they want to keep us from interacting with . . ."

He stopped as a throbbing vibration began to sound through the deck, and he heard the rest of the *Defiant*'s crew begin talking excitedly as—

—the main hangar door slid open to reveal stars streaming past to a vanishing point.

Bashir reflexively held his breath. The ship was traveling at warp, and only the hangar deck's atmospheric forcefield was preventing the fifteen of them from being explosively decompressed into the ship's warp field.

"I think someone's trying to get our attention . . . ," Jadzia said lightly.

Bashir turned as he heard the quick hiss of an opening door.

Three Vulcans stood in the corridor beyond, two females and a male, their impassive faces offering no clue as to their intentions.

One after the other, the three Vulcans stepped onto the hangar deck, and Bashir took some solace from the fact that the uniforms they were wearing reflected Starfleet traditions. Their trousers and jackets were made of a vertically-ribbed black material, with the entire left shoulder of each jacket constructed of a block of contrasting fabric in a traditional Fleet specialty color, in this case red on two of them and blue on the third. In the center of each colorful shoulder was what could only be a communicator badge, identical to the modified emblem on the crates and complete with the colors of the Klingon *k'Roth ch'Kor.* Only one element was completely new to Bashir: Two of the Vulcans—those with the red shoulders—were wearing large clear visors over their eyes, like some kind of protective shield.

As the three figures halted at the boundary of the forcefield, Bashir took the chance to study their uniforms more closely for rank markings. He found them on small vertical panels, a centimeter wide by perhaps four centimeters long, centered on their jackets just below their collars. Instead of the round pips that Bashir wore, these uniforms used square tabs, though he felt it was likely the number of tabs would carry the same meaning.

"The woman on the right, with the blue shoulder," Bashir said quietly to Jadzia and Worf. "The captain?"

The Vulcan in question had four square tabs in her rank badge, and seemed older than her two companions. Her skin was a warm brown, almost the same shade as Jake's, and a few strands of gray ran as highlights through her severely-cut black hair. Since the specialty color on her shoulder was blue, Bashir guessed that either blue was the current color signifying command or this was a science vessel with a scientist for a captain. She was also the only one of the three not wearing a visor.

Bashir looked at Worf. "Commander, we should probably follow the temporal displacement policy to the letter, and you are the ranking command officer."

Worf gave Bashir a curt nod, then stepped toward the silent Vulcans.

"I am Lieutenant Commander Worf of the *Starship Defiant.* I have reason to believe these people and I have been inadvertently transferred approximately twenty-five years into our future. Under the terms of Starfleet's temporal displacement policy, I request immediate assistance for our return to our own time."

The Vulcan captain put her hands behind her back as she began to speak. "Commander Worf, I am Captain T'len, commander of this destroyer, the *Augustus.* You and your people have been positively identified by your DNA signatures, obtained from transporter records. As you have surmised, you have traveled in time almost twenty-five years from what was your present. The current stardate is 76958.2."

She paused, and Bashir concluded it was to let her confirmation of their fate sink in. "As I suspect you have also already surmised," she then continued, "the historical record shows that the ship on which you made this temporal transfer was lost with all hands on stardate 51889.4, concurrent with the destruction of the space station Deep Space 9. Under these circumstances, Starfleet regulations are clear. Do you agree?"

Worf's voice deepened. "I would like to examine the historical record myself."

Captain T'len raised an eyebrow. "That would be a waste of time and resources. If you do not believe me, logic suggests you will not be able to believe any historical transcript I provide."

Bashir was slightly surprised that T'len wasn't aware that Klingons preferred physical proof to logical inference. "Then I wish to be put in contact with officials from the Federation Department of Temporal Investigations."

T'len's deep sigh—a most atypical expression of emotion, unless Vulcans in this future were somehow different—strongly suggested to Bashir that the Vulcan was under some undisclosed yet incredible strain.

"Commander," she said almost wearily, "your personnel records indicate you are a reasonable being. Indeed, the records available for most of the other non-Bajorans with you indicate a high degree of probability you can still be of use to Starfleet in this time period. All you need to know now is that the Federation Department of Temporal Investigations no longer exists. Twelve years ago its responsibilities were assumed by Starfleet's Temporal Warfare Division. I assure you that under current conditions the personnel of the TWD are most unlikely to expend any effort in trying to convince you that this present is everything I say it is. You must either accept my word, or not."

Worf's grim expression betrayed his struggle to maintain composure in the face of what he obviously considered a threat, though it was as yet of an unspecified nature.

"What *are* the current conditions?" Worf asked, immensely pleasing Bashir. That was exactly the question he would have asked first, to be quickly followed by inquiries about the exact nature of the ominously named Temporal Warfare Division and what the Vulcan captain meant by her cryptic reference to the Bajorans among them not being useful.

"The Federation is at war with the Bajoran Ascendancy. And my crew and I have no more time to waste with you than does the TWD. Therefore, I put it to you and your people as straightforwardly as I can. The non-Bajorans among you may now take this opportunity to reaffirm your loyalty to the Federation and to Starfleet, and to join us in our war. Those who comply will be allowed to leave the hangar deck and will be assigned to suitable positions within the fleet. Those who do not comply will remain on the hangar deck with the Bajorans until the atmospheric forcefield is dropped, in . . ." T'len tapped her communicator badge twice. ". . . three minutes."

Immediately, yellow warning lights spun across the deck and bulkheads as the familiar Starfleet computer voice announced, "*Warning. The hangar deck will decompress in three minutes. Please vacate the area.*"

All around Bashir, the other captives began to talk in groups again, their mutterings and exclamations full of anger and shock. But Worf, interestingly, seemed only to become calmer, as if now that he understood the challenge he faced, he could focus all his energy on overcoming it.

"Am I to believe," the Klingon growled, "that in only twenty-five years Starfleet has degenerated into a gang of murderers?"

"Believe what you will," T'len replied crisply. "We are fighting for more than you can imagine. Logic demands that we waste no time or resources on anything—or anyone—that does not help us in our struggle. Commander Worf, your choice is simple: Join us in our war against the Ascendancy, or die with the Bajorans among you."

"Warning, the hanger deck will decompress in two minutes, thirty seconds. Please vacate the area."

Worf turned to face the fourteen others who looked to him for leadership. He was about to speak when it suddenly came to Bashir what the Vulcan was actually doing. He held up his hand to stop Worf from saying anything more.

"She's bluffing, Worf."

Worf's heavy brow wrinkled as he considered Bashir's emphatic statement, but T'len spoke before he could.

"Dr. Bashir, Vulcans do not bluff."

Bashir's response was immediate and to the point. "And Starfleet doesn't kill its prisoners—war or no war."

The captain held his gaze for long moments, then without a sign, suddenly wheeled and walked back toward the personnel door. "You know what you have to do to survive," she said without looking back. "The prisoner containment field is now deactivated. This door will remain open until five seconds before decompression." Then she and her two companions stepped through that door and were gone.

"Warning, the hanger deck will decompress in two minutes. Please vacate the area."

Vash started for the unseen edge of the forcefield. "Hey! You didn't ask me! I'll join up!"

But Bashir moved forward and pulled her back. "Get back here!"

Vash twisted out of his grip, slapped his hand away. "Look, all due respect to your Bajoran friends, but I don't plan on getting sucked out into hard vacuum!"

"We are in no danger," Bashir said forcefully. He looked around at the others. "Captain T'len will not decompress the hangar deck!"

"How can you be sure?" Worf asked.

"Because she is a Vulcan, and there is no logic to . . . to killing Bajorans, even if somehow they are enemies of Starfleet in this time. And there is absolutely no logic in killing *us.* We're completely contained on this hangar deck. We're no threat to anyone. And you heard what she said about confirming our identities through DNA scans—she knows that none of us is involved in . . . current conditions."

"Then why is she threatening us?" Jake asked.

"Warning, the hanger deck will decompress in one minute, thirty seconds."

Bashir registered Jadzia's and Worf's matching expressions of less-than-full confidence in his argument, as well as the outright look of fear on the five Bajorans, now standing apart from the others. "She's testing us."

"Where's the logic in that?" Jadzia asked.

Bashir knew he lacked a definitive answer. "Maybe what she said about DNA scans wasn't the truth. If they really don't have a way of confirming our identities, they don't really know who we are."

"And why would that be important?" Vash snapped.

But then Jake snapped his fingers. "Founders can fool a DNA scan, right?"

Bashir nodded, equally impressed by and grateful for the young man's quickness. "That could be it. If this . . . Bajoran Ascendancy is a result of the Dominion establishing a foothold in the Alpha Quadrant, Starfleet could still be at war with the Founders. For all Captain T'len knows, we might all be shapeshifters who've impersonated the lost crewmembers of the *Defiant*."

Jadzia narrowed her eyes. "Then why didn't they just strap us down and cut us to see what happened to our blood?"

Bashir winced. She was right. Though the Founders could mimic almost any living being down to the level of its DNA, once a single drop of blood escaped from that duplicated form, it immediately reverted to the Founders' normal gelatinous state. As his Trill colleague had just pointed out, there were easier, more direct methods of being certain Worf and the others weren't changelings.

"*Warning, the hanger deck will decompress in sixty seconds. Please vacate the area.*"

"T'len!" Vash shouted. "I'm on your side! Beam me out!"

"If this is a test," Bashir said sharply, "*you* are most certainly failing."

"Me?" Vash hissed. "I'm the only one acting like a human being. I want to live!"

"*Forty-five seconds to explosive decompression,*" the computer warned.

"Commander Worf!" Everyone turned to the Bajoran who had called out. He was an ensign no older than twenty, face pale with fear, the looped chain of his silver earring trembling. "You can't all die because of us." Bashir saw the other four Bajorans beside the young ensign nod nervously. Apparently they had discussed this act of sacrifice and he spoke for them all. "Do what the captain wants. Save yourselves. We . . . we'll trust in the Prophets."

"Thirty seconds to explosive decompression."

"Y'see?" Vash urged. "Even they don't want any false heroics!"

"It is not false!" Worf barked at her. Then he faced the Bajorans and stood at attention. His words were calm and deliberate. "Ensign, your courage brings honor to us all. But as a Starfleet officer and a Klingon warrior, I cannot abandon you to an unjust fate." Worf placed his arm through the ensign's, taking his stand beside the Bajorans. Jadzia promptly followed his example. Then Bashir, Jake, and all the others, except for one, stood together on the hangar deck, their fates as inextricably linked as their arms.

Only Vash stood alone.

"Fifteen seconds. . . ."

"Captain T'len!" Worf's voice rang out across the cold, dark hangar deck. "If Starfleet has forgotten the ideals for which it once stood, then let our deaths remind you of what you have lost."

Bashir watched Vash rub a hand over her face, almost as if she was more embarrassed than afraid to be so obviously on her own.

"Oh, for . . . ," she muttered, then hastily crossed the few meters to link her arm through Bashir's.

"Ten seconds . . . ," the computer announced.

"Happy now?" Vash asked Bashir.

"We're in no danger," Bashir answered. "I don't know why, but I'm still convinced this is a test."

"I'm convinced you're insane."

With a loud bang, the personnel door guillotined shut.

"Five seconds."

Bashir detected an instant increase in his heart's pumping action at the same time as beside him he heard Vash say, "Oh, what the hell," and he felt her hands on his face as she pulled him around and kissed him as deeply as he had ever been kissed, just as the computer announced, *"The hangar deck will now—"*

Then the rest of the warning was swept away in the sudden roar of rushing wind and the hammering of his heartbeat—and for all his enhanced intellect, Bashir couldn't tell if he was reacting to the threat of sudden death, or to Vash's thrillingly expert kiss.

CHAPTER 4

NOG JUMPED in front of the Old Man to block whatever weapons the Romulans might have, but before he could do anything else, the ribbon-like discharge from a polywave disruptor smeared across his chest.

Instantly Nog felt his entire body numb, then he collapsed to the floor, slightly puzzled by the fact that he was still alive. At maximum power, polywaves could set off a subatomic disintegration cascade that was far more efficient than disassociation by phased energy. He had seen Starfleet's sensor logs of the aftermath of polywave combat—the ghastly scattering of limbs and partial torsos left behind by the tightly-bound polyspheres of total matter annihilation.

Yet at the moment, whether he himself lived through such an assault or not was of no importance to him. Because if the Old Man had been hit with even the same type of low-intensity paralysis beam, it was extremely doubtful that the elderly *hew-mon*'s fragile body would survive the shock.

Nog lay absolutely still on the floor—he could do nothing else, no matter what had happened to the admiral. Unlike a phaser stun, the polywave version left its victims completely alert but completely immobilized.

His vision began to blur. He was incapable of blinking, and the flow of air through his emergency breathing mask was drawing moisture from the surface of his eyes. His hearing was also becoming less acute, as if the small muscles connecting to both his primary and secondary eardrums were losing their ability to function. The only sound he could hear clearly was the slow thud of his own heart.

But . . . there. Somewhere in the increasingly indistinct background noise, Nog thought he heard the Old Man speaking. Though how could the *hew-mon* do that if he'd been paralyzed as Nog had?

Suddenly, Nog's field of vision shifted and shook as someone raised him up, ripped open his emergency hood, and peeled back the air mask. At once his vision cleared, and the first thing he saw was a young Romulan woman in the bronze chainmail of the Imperial Legion waving a small device in front of his face. The device, Nog realized, was a dispenser that sprayed a moisturizing mist, to keep his eyes clear.

"Ferengi," the Romulan said, her voice distorted and muffled as if she spoke from behind a door. "I am Centurion Karon. You are on board the Imperial cruiser *Altanex.* Though you cannot respond, I know that you can hear me. Your paralysis will begin to lessen within an hour. There is usually no permanent damage."

Usually?! Nog thought with alarm.

The Centurion shot a second cloud of mist into his eyes. "To answer what I suspect are your most pressing questions, the crew of this ship are no longer allied with the Ascendancy. We need to talk to Admiral Picard. We presume you are his bodyguard or attendant. When we have concluded our discussions, if either or both of you desire, we shall return you to a secure Starfleet base."

If either or both desire? To Nog, it almost sounded as if Karon expected that he and the Old Man might be persuaded never to return to Utopia Planitia. What could she ever say that would make that even a possibility?

Karon misted his eyes again. Though Nog could still only look straight ahead, he now saw the Old Man, hood removed, being led away by two other Romulans without sign of force or struggle.

The Centurion recaptured his attention with her next words. "No matter what decision you ultimately make, neither you nor the Admiral will be harmed. Two bions will now take you to our sickbay. When your paralysis has ended, we will speak again."

Nog tried his utmost, but failed to make a single sound of protest. *He* wasn't the one who needed sickbay—the Old Man was.

Her statement delivered, Centurion Karon slipped from his view, as once again Nog realized he was being moved. And only full polywave paralysis prevented his drawing back in disgust from the . . . things that moved him.

Bions.

Starfleet Intelligence had examined captured bions, and Nog had read the classified situation assessments with horror. Bions were supposedly artificial life-forms, created by Romulan science and now used as workers and soldiers throughout the Star Empire. Though the creatures were disturbingly humanoid, the Romulans insisted bions had no capacity to become self-aware. They were simply genetically-engineered organic machines, no different from the myriad forms of mechanical devices that served the Federation, from self-piloted shuttlecraft to nanite assemblers. The only difference, the Romulans maintained, was that instead of being built from duraplast and optical circuitry, bions were self-assembled—that is, *grown*—from proteins swirling in nutrient baths. Or so, Starfleet warned, the Romulans would have the galaxy believe.

As far as Starfleet was concerned, there was a reason why bions had begun to appear shortly after the Romulans had allied themselves with the Ascendancy, and the first battles had been fought in the undeclared War of the Prophets. Bions, Starfleet's biologists had concluded, were not genetically-*engineered* artificial lifeforms; they were genetically-*altered* prisoners of war.

Nog shuddered inwardly, if not outwardly. The Romulans were now doing to their captives what the Borg used to do with theirs. Except in the case of the bions, the Borg's biomechanical mechanisms of assimilation had been replaced by strictly biological processes.

The underlying technology was, without question, Grigari. And if only for that reason—the unconscionable alliance with the Grigari Meld—Nog fervently believed the Ascendancy deserved to be wiped out.

Nog was grateful he could not see the dreadful mutants that carried him now. Without constant misting his vision had blurred again, and he was able to form only the vaguest impression of green metal doors sliding open before him, a surprisingly narrow corridor moving past him, and, finally, an oppressively small medical facility, where an angular treatment bed emerged from a dull-green bulkhead, the display screen above it glowing with unreadable yellow Romulan glyphs and multicolored status lights.

He was maneuvered onto the treatment bed, and almost immediately his vision cleared again. This time the ocular mist came from an overhead pallet of medical equipment. Just in time to give Nog a brief, shocking glimpse of a bion.

Its face—for the bions were neither male nor female—was unnaturally blank, its severe features nearly obliterated by the camouflage effect of its bizarrely mottled skin, a dizzying patchwork of Andorian blue and Miradorn white, Orion green, Tiburonian pink, and Klingon brown.

Even more disconcerting, its mouth was a tiny, lipless gash intended to do little more than ingest nutrient paste. The creature had no real nose, only two vertical slits that pulsed open and closed like the gills of a fish.

Yet the real problem for Nog was what had happened to the bion's ears. Despite years of working with *hew-mons* and Vulcans and other cartilaginously-challenged species, Nog knew he still had difficulty abandoning the old Ferengi presumption equating intelligence with ear size. And the same ruthless efficiency displayed in the bion's other minimal features had reduced its ears to mere vestigial curls of flesh that protruded from the jaw hinge like the wilted petals of a flower. On a purely visceral level, it was as if he was looking at creatures whose skulls had been flayed open and were empty—

that they could even stand upright with such minuscule ears, let alone carry out useful tasks, was unnerving.

Hostage within his own still body, Nog could only watch now as one bion reached above him. Its two fingers and thumb identified it as a common worker unit. Other versions, Nog had read, had up to seven fingers for delicate mechanical repairs or complex weapons operation. No doubt other details of the bion's specific capabilities were indicated by the markings on the front of its tight gray jumpsuit and by the pattern of green stripes ringing each of its sleeves. Perhaps even the identity of the captive species from which it had been created was encoded there.

Another spray of mist clouded the air for a moment, and at the same time the gray-suited bion moved to position its face directly in front of Nog's unblinking eyes.

The bion's eyes were humanoid in size and placement, but the portion of the eyeball that was typically white in most species was a lustrous black. Nog didn't know if that color provided a specific, engineered advantage; he suspected it was a cosmetic detail designed to remove any sense of personality from the bions. Even a Vulcan's placid eyes could convey emotion. But bions had eyes that revealed nothing. Whatever secrets the pitiful creature's brain held, its flat gaze betrayed no trace of any individuality or past life.

The bion mercifully stepped back out of Nog's sight.

Nog waited for whatever would happen next, thinking of the Old Man, worried about where he had been taken and what their captors had done with him.

Long minutes passed without sign of anything else moving in the medical facility, and Nog concluded he had been left alone. He willed peace upon his racing mind. There was nothing he could do until his paralysis ended except meditate on the Great Material River, and hope that somehow it would take from him his mental clarity—of which he had no great need right now—and, just for a few hours at least, transfer it to Jean-Luc Picard, who most certainly did.

After all the effort these Romulans had expended in order to contact the the admiral, Nog didn't want to think what would happen when they realized that their prize captive was not the great man of years past, only a man.

Nog's thoughts paused. Hadn't someone once said something about that condition? But whether it was exhaustion or the effect of the polywaves, he no longer recalled who.

Another *lost memory,* he thought, troubled, as his consciousness finally sank into the Great River. In time, he supposed, that would be the fate of them all.

CHAPTER 5

He was only nineteen, but Jake Sisko already understood the inevitability of death. And on the hangar deck of this Starfleet vessel of the future he was, in his way, prepared to die.

Or so he told himself.

But even as the computer's warning was drowned out by the explosive burst of air that rushed over him, tugging him back against the linked arms of his fellow prisoners, Jake still didn't believe that the time of his death was near.

Part of the reason for his confidence in his survival came from his half-felt suspicion that the Bajoran Prophets might intercede, or that, at the very least, their existence implied that death might not be the end of his own awareness.

But as to whether it was faith in the Prophets or faith in Dr. Bashir's logical assessment of their situation—

that they were merely being tested by the Vulcan captain of this ship—or simply the fire of his youth that at this moment made him unwilling to accept the final extinction of his intellect, Jake wasn't certain.

All he knew was that when a *second* blast of air rushed over him, and he realized that the ship's atmospheric pressure had been maintained and that he could still breathe—he wasn't really surprised.

Smiling broadly like most of the others at their close call, Jake glanced over in Bashir's direction. What he saw then *did* surprise him. The doctor was engulfed in an embarrassingly passionate embrace with Vash. Jake couldn't help gawking as a handful of excited conversations began around him and he saw Vash draw back from the doctor, look around, and he heard her say, "Guess you were right, Doc." Bashir was looking decidedly flustered, and Jake felt himself experiencing an unexpected pang of jealousy. Vash was extremely attractive, in a dangerous, older sort of way.

Then his and everyone's attention was diverted to the personnel door as it opened once again and Captain T'len reappeared, accompanied by her two visored officers in the black Starfleet uniforms with red shoulders.

"Is the test over?" Bashir asked. Jake appreciated and mentally applauded the defiance in his tone.

"It is," T'len replied.

But the doctor wasn't finished. "May I ask what the purpose of it was?"

"It was necessary to see if you had been altered by the Grigari. No Grigari construct yet encountered is capable of facing a life-or-death situation without attempting to bargain for its life."

Jake vaguely recalled Kasidy Yates telling him stories of the Grigari, though she'd seemed to imply that few experts believed that the fabled lost species was real—merely a name given to an amalgam of legends that had accumulated over time.

Bashir was nodding at Vash, who was still standing beside him. "Not a very convincing test. Vash here was ready to bargain with you from the beginning."

Jake regarded Bashir anxiously, wondering if it was a good idea to say anything that might provoke the captain, but the Vulcan seemed unperturbed by the doctor's identification of a logical flaw in her test.

"Vash is not a Starfleet officer. Her reaction was in compliance with historical records of her personality."

At that the archaeologist broke away from the group of captives, heading straight for T'len. "Yeah, well what about *this* reaction?" she said threateningly, leading Jake to half-expect she'd try to deck the Vulcan captain when she reached her.

But before Vash could cross more than half the four meters that stood between her and T'len, what looked to be a phaser beam shot out from the visor worn by the officer on the captain's right. The silver beam hit Vash dead center, and she immediately crumpled to the deck as if stunned.

"Whoa . . . ," Jake whispered. Then, as Bashir, Worf, and Jadzia rushed to Vash's aid, he took a closer look at those special clear visors of T'Len's officers, what he had at first thought were a type of safety eyewear. After a moment, he realized that if he looked slightly away from the two officers, he could just make out a pattern of glowing lights on their visors' surfaces, as if the visors were generating some sort of holographic display for their wearer. On the officer nearest him Jake also noticed a narrow black wire that ran from the arm of the visor and hooked over the Vulcan's pointed ear. The wire disappeared into the collar of the officer's uniform.

Not bad, Jake thought. *A phaser that doesn't require anyone having to waste time to draw and aim it.* He had no idea how the odd silver phaser beam could have been generated in such a thin device, but he decided it was reasonable to assume that twenty-five years could have led to at least a few technological breakthroughs. He reminded himself to be on the alert for other hidden marvels of the day. They'd make for interesting details in the novel he planned to write after he returned to his own time. Because, just as he had not been ready to believe he was going to die, he was somehow sure that eventually he *would* return. All he needed to do was work out the details—or be sure that Dr. Bashir, Jadzia, and Worf worked them out.

For now, the doctor and the Trill were helping Vash to her feet. From what Jake could see of her, the archaeologist was unharmed, though the way she staggered made it clear she was still suffering from the effects of the stun.

Captain T'len continued coolly as if nothing unusual had just happened. "As I explained, your identities have been confirmed by DNA analysis. But do not think that changes your status on this ship."

"Just what is our status?" Bashir asked. He had his arm firmly around Vash's shoulders to support her.

"Refugees," T'len answered. "But that can change."

"How?"

"The decision is not up to me." The Vulcan captain then went on to explain that they would be taken from the hangar deck and given quarters, to which they'd be confined until their arrival at Starbase 53. During their confinement they would be provided with limited computer access in order to familiarize themselves with their new time period. "Make no mistake," T'len concluded. "This time period will be your new home."

As the refugees fell silent in the face of that blunt statement, Jake took advantage of the moment to shout out, "What happened to the *Defiant?*"

Captain T'len's dark eyes immediately sought him out, and Jake surprised himself as he held her intense gaze. "Your ship was captured by the Ascendancy. To answer the rest of your questions which must logically follow: So far as we know, the *Defiant* was captured intact. Though we do not have definitive knowledge, it is logical to assume that the crew has been captured. Whether or not they are subsequently harmed will depend on the degree of resistance they offer."

"Then we should attempt to rescue them," Worf said bluntly. "It is unacceptable to retreat."

T'len's gaze shifted from Jake to Worf, but her next words had the teenager's full attention. "I can assure you that a rescue attempt will be made. Starfleet has no intention of letting the Ascendancy keep Benjamin Sisko in custody."

Jake experienced a huge upswell of relief upon hearing the captain state Starfleet's objective so authoritatively, though he couldn't help also wondering why his father would have such importance in this time. But before he could get up his nerve to ask for clarification, one of the Bajorans changed the subject.

"Who are the Grigari?"

The captain's enigmatic response was ominous.

"You'll find out." She gestured to the open door, and Jake followed the rest of T'len's prisoners as they began their long march.

To Jake, T'len's ship, the *Augustus,* seemed half-finished. The dull-gray floors of the cramped corridors had no carpet—the decks were simply bare composite plates. And no attempt had been made to hide the ship's mechanical components. The cluttered ceilings were lined with so many differently colored pipes and conduits that Jake doubted there was a single Jefferies tube on the vessel. ODN conduits were everywhere, running along bulkheads and punching through decks and ceilings almost at random. At least, Jake *assumed* they were ODN conduits. Who knew if optical data networks were still being used in this future?

The ship appeared to have no turbolifts either. He and the other fourteen prisoners from the *Defiant* had to change decks by using steep and narrow metal staircases that rattled alarmingly as so many pairs of feet pounded down them. For a ship of the future, the *Augustus* was reminding Jake more of the old walk-through exhibit of the *U.S.S. Discovery,* a *Daedalus*-class ship more than 200 years old, at the Starfleet Museum in San Francisco. But even that old veteran, one of the first ships commissioned by the newly formed Starfleet, had had more room.

The environmental controls also seemed to be less precise than the ones Jake was used to. The hangar deck had been cool, but the first corridors the refugees had been led through were uncomfortably hot. On their enforced march they had already encountered a few more of T'len's crew, and they had all, without exception, been Vulcan. That made the heat make sense to

Jake: It reflected the crew's normal and preferred ambient temperature.

But then, trudging along in the line of captives, Jake stepped off a stairway into a corridor that was so cold its gray metal walls were rimed with frost. With a shiver, he abandoned his earlier theory of acclimation for a Vulcan crew, and decided that the unsettling changes in temperature merely meant that the ship's environmental controls were faulty.

Finally they reached the end of their march, and their destination turned out to be a series of personnel cabins—they certainly didn't deserve to be called quarters. Jake was assigned to one that was little bigger than his bedroom on DS9 but which was crowded with two bunks, a fold-down desktop, what seemed to be a limited-capacity food replicator, and—crammed into one corner with no privacy screen—a small toilet-and-sink unit that appeared to be able to double as a sonic shower enclosure. Everything was in the same depressing shade of muddy gray.

Jake's roommate was Ensign Ryle Simons, a young human from Alpha Centauri with an almost pure white complexion topped by a startlingly bright-red crewcut. Simons was fresh from the Academy and had been on Deep Space 9 for only two days, waiting to join the crew of his first ship, the *Destiny.* After taking less than a second to assess the cramped nature of their room, both Jake and Simons peppered the Vulcan lieutenant who stood in their doorway with questions.

"How long will it take to get to the starbase?" Simons asked.

"And where's the computer terminal?" Jake added.

The Vulcan stepped past the two young men and

folded down the desktop so that it blocked the doors of the storage lockers that took up one bulkhead. "Our transit time is classified," she said, then busied herself with the desktop.

The surface of it was a large control surface, and the Vulcan swiftly tapped in a series of commands that quickly created what Jake recognized as a Starfleet computer input tablet not too different from the ones he was familiar with. What was different, though, was that the computer had no physical display. Instead, a holographic screen appeared a few centimeters above the desktop. For now, the modified Starfleet emblem appeared in the center of it.

No time like the present, Jake thought. "Lieutenant, why did the ship from the Bajoran Ascendancy also have a Starfleet emblem?"

The Vulcan frowned as she assessed him, shaking her head once. "The explanation is in the history briefings that will be made available to you."

"Then the explanation isn't classified?"

"No."

Jake refrained from showing amusement at the Vulcan's poorly disguised impatience. "So there's no reason why you *can't* tell us, is there? It would be more efficient."

"Then the efficient answer is: propaganda." The Vulcan abruptly stood up and moved toward the open door.

"I don't know what you mean by that," Jake said truthfully.

The Vulcan hesitated on the threshold, then looked back at Jake and Simons. Apparently she made some sort of decision, for she then delivered her explanation rapidly, without pause. "At the time the Ascendancy was formed, it initially sought new members from those worlds waiting to accept admission to the Federation, just as Bajor had been. One of the chief advantages to Federation membership is the opportunity to take part in Starfleet operations and to benefit from its defensive forces. Thus, in its attempt to sway the governments of the nonaligned worlds, the Ascendancy claimed to be the new political master of Starfleet. Since many Ascendancy vessels had been pirated from our fleet over the years, in a limited sense the claim was correct."

"Now I *really* don't understand," Jake said seriously. "How could any group simply *say* they're the ones responsible for Starfleet?"

"Following the destruction of Earth," the Vulcan said, her expression remaining completely neutral, "Starfleet's lines of command and control took several weeks to be reestablished. In some regions where political turmoil further complicated communications, some task forces and battle groups were cut off from command for months."

Jake couldn't speak, let alone think of any new question. Which was just as well, because the Vulcan had no intention of answering further inquiries.

"Use your computer," she said. "All your questions will be answered." Then she stepped back into the corridor, and the narrow door slipped shut and locked.

Jake looked at his roommate. The Centaurian ensign's white cheeks were splotched with red, while the rest of his face was almost luminescent in its paleness. "That . . . that can't be true," Simons said faintly.

But Jake knew better. The Vulcan had had no problem refusing to answer a question when the answer was classified. Thus, she had no motive for lying to them. "Let's check the computer," he said. He went to the desktop and placed his hand on the flashing yellow panel labelled USER IDENTIFICATION. At once the panel turned green, and the holographic display switched from a static image of the Starfleet emblem to that of a Bolian in the new version of the Starfleet uniform. Jake checked the square tabs on the Bolian's rank badge and saw that the blue-skinned alien was an admiral.

"This briefing," the Bolian admiral began, "has been prepared for the refugees rescued from the *Starship Defiant.* It consists of a twenty-two-minute presentation of the key events that have occurred since the destruction of Deep Space 9 and the loss of your ship until the present day, focusing on those events which have led to what is commonly known as the War of the Prophets. At the end of this briefing, you will be given an opportunity to examine files detailing the current status of any relatives you may have in this time period. The briefing will commence on your verbal request."

Jake stared at the image. "I don't get it," he said, turning to Simons. "We only showed up here less than two hours ago. How did they have enough time to make a briefing tape for us?"

Simons shook his head, puzzled. "Their computers are faster?"

Jake wasn't convinced. But he folded his arms across his chest and prepared himself for the worst. "Computer: Start the briefing."

The image of the Bolian admiral disappeared, replaced by that of a Starfleet sensor-log identification screen announcing that whatever images were about to be shown had been recorded by the *U.S.S. Garneau* on stardate 51889.4, in the Bajoran sector.

Jake felt his chest tighten even before the sensor log began.

He recognized the date.

He was about to see the events that, according to history, had led to his death.

CHAPTER 6

"WHAT'S WRONG WITH HIM?" Centurion Karon demanded.

Nog awoke with a start. He instantly moved his hand to the side of his head in response to a dull pain in his temple. Then he reacted to the shock of realization that the little finger of his right hand was broken. And then to the fact that he could move at all. Until he remembered where he was and how he had come here.

The Romulan centurion's voice was insistent. "Admiral Picard. Has he been injured?"

Nog pushed himself up on the medical bed. He rubbed at his head again, this time careful to keep all pressure off his broken finger. "Irumodic Syndrome," he said. His throat was painfully dry. He started to cough.

But Karon wasn't interested in his discomfort. "*Tash!*" she snarled.

Nog didn't know what that word meant, but from the

way the sharp-featured Romulan had said it, he could guess. And he could also guess that it meant she knew very well what Irumodic Syndrome was.

"Does that mean Starfleet's not serious about Project Phoenix?" Karon asked.

"I am not answering any questions until I see Admiral Picard."

Karon's dark eyes considered him. Their highlights seemed to shine out at him from the shadows of her deep brow and precisely-cut black bangs. "Who are you?" she asked.

Nog hesitated. Considering his present circumstances, he could be a prisoner of war, which meant he should say nothing, even though he knew his eventual fate would be to become a bion. Then again, it was possible that Karon had been truthful when she said the crew of this ship no longer supported the Ascendancy. Romulans had been the Federation's allies in the war against the Dominion. Was it possible they could be allies again? More to the point, Nog wondered, this close to the end, was there really anything to lose?

"I'm the Integrated Systems Manager for Project Phoenix," he said. "Captain Nog."

Karon looked gratifyingly impressed. "So you're in charge," she said with a slight incline of her head.

"I *manage* the project," Nog replied. "The Admiral is in charge."

Karon pursed her lips and nodded. "I understand personal loyalty. Odd to see it in a Ferengi, though. Perhaps our mission hasn't been wasted after all."

"What mission?" Nog said, deliberately ignoring her insult. It was the fate of the Ferengi to be misunderstood by all but their own kind.

Karon's cool gaze swept over him. "Perhaps you'd prefer getting dressed."

Nog looked down and felt his ears flush. He was still in his sleep shorts. His pressure suit had apparently been removed as he slept. "Yes, I would," he said stiffly. "But more than that, I would appreciate having someone look at this." He held up his little finger, trying not to grimace as he saw the strange angle it took from his hand.

It required an agonizing twenty minutes to get his finger straightened and set in a magnetic splint, and Karon apologized for the *Altanex* carrying no tissue stimulators suitable for Ferengi biology. Her explanation for his injuries seemed quite reasonable—that he'd broken his finger and bruised his temple when he fell to the deck after being paralyzed.

Once he'd been treated, Karon offered him a change of clothing, and Nog quickly pulled on a Romulan utility uniform—gray trousers, a tunic unfortunately intended for a taller person, and black boots that were, surprisingly, the perfect size. Then the Romulan centurion escorted him to Admiral Picard's guest quarters.

To Nog's relief, the Old Man was asleep, not in a coma or dead. And in response to his pointed questioning, Karon assured him that Picard's interrogators had not used any force or psychological pressure, especially—here Karon paused and fixed Nog with a measuring look—when it had become so quickly apparent that the admiral was not in full command of his legendary faculties.

With the Old Man's condition confirmed, Nog allowed Karon to lead him to a situation room three decks up. As he followed the Romulan, Nog studied what few details the short passage revealed about the vessel he was in. He wasn't certain what class of ship the *Altanex* was, but it was obviously cramped and confined, and the paltry number of crew members they passed suggested that it was also extremely small.

Lacking any other ready source of information, Nog had no reservations about directly asking his escort about her ship.

"We're a listening post," she explained, as she adjusted the replicator in the small situation room to display its menu in Ferengi tallyscript. "Our current position is within this system's main asteroid belt."

"Ah, a spy vessel." Nog glanced around the spartan room, trying to identify any obvious recording sensors. But all he saw was a blank tactical screen, a conference table with nine chairs, and on the table a small packing crate with reinforced locking clamps.

Karon didn't confirm or deny his definition of her term. "High-speed multiple transmorphic cloaks. But limited shields and weapons."

Nog was impressed. "With transmorphic cloaks you don't need shields. I had not realized you had perfected them."

A grim expression flashed across Karon's stern features. "Our engineers found they could solve their impasse with certain . . . biogenic components."

Nog understood and shared her distaste. The Romulans had again employed Grigari technology. Which meant the ship's state-of-the-art cloaking device was controlled in part by engineered tissues taken from captives.

Then, without preamble Karon said, "The Star Empire is collapsing."

Startled, Nog attempted to hide his shock the only way he could. He looked away from her, to the replicator.

"Are you surprised?" Karon asked.

"By the news? Or by the fact that you are telling me?" Nog concentrated on the replicator's talleyscript. There were no Ferengi selections available. The only non-Romulan food and drink he recognized were Vulcan, and he wasn't enamored of Vulcan cuisine. There were never enough beetles.

"You don't believe me." Karon folded her arms and drew herself up, making her posture even more erect than it had been. She was a few centimeters taller than Nog but very slight, even in chainmail. Nog had grown to his maximum height as a teenager on DS9, but he knew a decade of desk work had added more than a few kilograms of bulk to his small frame, giving him a much more substantial presence than Karon.

Nog saw little risk in answering her truthfully. "I haven't decided," he said. "For a collapsing power, you did not seem to have much trouble overwhelming Utopia's defenses."

"It was a Tal Shiar operation. They are the last to feel the deprivations of the Empire's eroding capabilities."

Nog allowed his face to reveal a slight degree of interest at her mention of the feared Romulan intelligence service. But the revelation was a calculated one, to make her think that he appreciated her candor. The centurion might believe she was engaged in a frank conversation with a fellow warrior, but to Nog, he and she were engaged in negotiations—everything was always a negotiation. And sometimes—most times—it was best not to let the other party know it.

"Why did the Tal Shiar want to kidnap Admiral Picard?"

"They didn't," Karon said. "The Utopia Yards are

your last major shipbuilding center. The Tal Shiar wanted to cripple them. My . . . group saw a chance to make contact with Admiral Picard during the confusion."

Nog made a note of her hesitation at mentioning whom she was working with. That could mean she hadn't yet determined if she could trust him. It could also mean that there was no group, and that she and the handful of crew on this ship made up the whole of the Romulan resistance.

"Two questions," he said. "First, if the Tal Shiar accepts the Ascendancy's teachings, why bother attacking the yards this late?"

Just for a moment, it seemed to Nog that Karon sensed he was hiding something from her, but if so, it did not stop her from answering him. "This was one of fifteen attacks scheduled to . . . to keep the Federation off-balance. We know about Project Phoenix and Project Guardian. Even Project Looking Glass. But we can't be sure you don't have other last-moment operations planned."

Now Nog really was impressed. For obvious reasons, Project Phoenix had been impossible to completely hide. But Guardian was one of the most highly classified operations in Starfleet's history. Even he had been told only a few details about it, and those only because of how they might relate to the timing of the *Phoenix*'s mission. As for Looking Glass, that was a code name even he had never heard before.

Karon seemed to understand that Nog wasn't going to order anything from the replicator, so she reached past him to punch in some selections of her own. "As to what the Tal Shiar does or does not believe, I don't know anymore. I think at first our politicians considered the Bajoran Ascendants to be fanatics. The reason the Star Empire supported them was because the Ascendants' goal was to destabilize the Federation—always a worthy endeavor in Romulan eyes."

"But now?" Nog asked, trying not to let his voice sound too eager for details.

A tray with two tall glasses of brown liquid appeared in the replicator slot. Each glass was topped by a froth of foam.

"I don't know how much access Starfleet Intelligence has to events on Romulus, but as the Federation and the Klingon Empire suffered outright acts of terrorism and overt military strikes, we ourselves suffered from key politicians succumbing to mysterious diseases and accidents."

The centurion handed him a glass. "You were being attacked from without. We, from within."

Nog sniffed at the drink in surprise. Root beer. It smelled delicious. "By the Ascendants?"

"You said you had a second question." Karon held up her glass in an age-old gesture of salute, drank deeply from it, then wiped the foam from her upper lip.

Nog took a tentative sip from his glass. The subtle interplay of sarsaparilla and vanilla was missing, of course. In years of study, he had yet to find a replicator version of the drink that could match that made on Cestus III. In fact, he had been surprised to learn that root beer had not been invented there, considering that the versions from everywhere else were but a pale imitation.

But he wasn't here to discuss brewing methods. He set his glass down on the tray. "Why did you want to speak to the admiral?"

Karon sighed. "We know about the *Phoenix*."

Nog made his shrug noncommittal. Such knowledge was not surprising. Almost everyone knew something about the ship. "You said that."

"We know its mission."

Perhaps in general, Nog thought, still unconcerned. It was unlikely even the Tal Shiar had managed to uncover all the details of the audacious plan the Old Man had put in motion almost five years ago.

"And we know that mission will fail."

Nog picked up his glass again to cover his shock and took another quick sip of its aromatic liquid. Swiftly, he considered all the possible reasons Karon might have for telling him this. His first thought was that she was also part of the Tal Shiar and it was an attempt to sow disinformation. But then, he reasoned, why hadn't she just killed him and Picard? Surely their deaths would have a greater chance of disrupting Project Phoenix than would their being swayed by her influence.

"For whatever it might be worth to you," he said carefully, "there are those in Starfleet who believe the same."

Karon shook her head. "You misunderstand. I did not say we *believe* your mission will fail. I said, we *know* your mission will fail."

Nog drank the last of his root beer and regretfully placed the empty glass on the tray. "How is it possible to *know* the fate of something which has yet to happen?"

He meant his question to be a challenge, and expected the Romulan centurion to respond in kind. But instead—surprisingly—Karon pulled out one of the chairs and sat down at the conference table. Her whole being seemed to Nog to be enveloped in an air of inexpressible sadness.

"Captain Nog, twenty-five thousand years ago, three Bajoran mystics set down their visions: Shabren, Eilin, and Naradim. All except the tenth of Shabren's prophecies have proved true, and that one can be read as a warning and not a firm prediction. The Books of Eilin unequivocally describe the rediscovery of the Orbs of Jalbador, just as it occurred twenty-five years ago. And Naradim's Eight Visions—"

"Are ancient poetry," Nog interrupted, as he took a chair facing her. "All the writings of the mystics are. Written with allusions and veiled references that every generation has reinterpreted and applied to their own unique circumstances."

Karon's gaze settled on Nog so intently he had the unsettling feeling that she had some alien power to read his mind. "You really *don't* believe that any of what's happened this past quarter-century has been foretold?"

Nog emphatically shook his head. "Of course not," he said firmly. "What has happened is the result of secular fanatics who have appropriated obscure religious writings in an attempt to justify brutal oppression and bloody conquest. The so-called War of the Prophets is a war of politics—not religion."

Karon's hands betrayed her inner tension as she twisted them together tightly, and she leaned forward, urgent. "But you work for Admiral Picard. *He* understands what's happening."

Nog spoke with pride. "Admiral Picard is a scientist. An explorer. A historian. Of course he understands."

"Perhaps not, it seems, in the same way you do. Captain Nog, are you aware that Naradim's Third Vision has been fulfilled?"

Nog groaned with impatience. He'd thought his presence here might give him a chance to launch a new attack against the Ascendancy. But instead, it appeared even the Romulan resistance was as caught up in religious nonsense as the fanatics who had enslaved Bajor and now threatened the universe.

"To be honest," he said, "I can't keep that drivel straight. What *is* Naradim's Third Vision?"

"It's the reason why the Tal Shiar launched fifteen attacks against the Federation and Starfleet in the last five hours."

Nog frowned. "To keep us off-balance, you said."

Karon drew back, studying him, puzzled, as if amazed that he still didn't understand her. "Captain, Admiral Picard understands even if you don't. He *told* us that he told you what had happened."

"What?" Nog rubbed at his aching temple. The centurion wasn't making any sense at all.

"The *Defiant,* Captain. It reappeared in deep space near the border of—"

"What!" Nog suddenly had trouble breathing.

"—the Bajoran Central Protectorates."

It was as if she'd shot him with a polywave all over again. "Is . . . is anyone on board?"

Karon's hands were still now. They lay flat on the table between them. "You know there's only one person who counts. And yes, *he* is on board. Benjamin Lafayette Sisko. Emissary to the False Prophets."

Nog felt the sharp heat of anger in his cheeks and ears, compounding the shock he felt. "Captain Sisko was one of the greatest beings I have ever known."

"For the False Prophets to have chosen him—indeed, if the new findings from B'hala are true, for them to have *arranged* his birth—how could he be anything else?"

Nog gripped his splinted finger in an effort to use the distraction of pain to regain his focus. "Who else?" he asked. "Who else is on the *Defiant?*"

"We haven't been able to intercept a complete list. Apparently, there's at least one Cardassian—"

"Garak?"

"I wasn't given names. Also a changeling—"

"Odo!"

"Eighteen in all."

"Eighteen . . . ?" Nog took a deep breath. The number was appallingly small. More than two hundred people had been reported missing when Deep Space 9 was destroyed. "Are there . . . are there any Ferengi on the ship?"

"I don't have that information."

"What about Captain Sisko's son?"

"Captain Nog, how do you know these people?"

Nog told her.

"That explains a great deal," Karon said when he had finished. "You served under Sisko. You traveled many times through the false wormhole. You even have experienced a temporal exchange on your trip to Earth's past."

Her tone made Nog uncomfortable. "What does that explain?"

"I apologize in advance, Captain. But by your own admission, you have had several encounters with the forces of the False Prophets. I believe that could explain why you remain so resistant to the truth."

Nog clenched his fists, despite his splinted finger. "My mind is open!"

"Captain Nog, given the power of the Prophets, true or false, how would you know if it were not?"

Nog jumped to his feet, knocking his chair back. "This discussion is over. I want you to return Admiral Picard and me to the closest Starfleet facility."

"You haven't heard my proposition," Karon said, looking up at him.

"I am not interested."

"Are you interested in stopping the Ascendancy? Saving the universe? Preserving the memory of the great Jean-Luc Picard?"

That last question stopped Nog. Twenty-four years ago, just after the destruction of Cardassia Prime, he had been assigned to the *U.S.S. Enterprise* under then-Captain Picard. That was when the Old Man had become his mentor, and had given him the new direction he had so badly needed after the loss of so many people who had been close to him. In truth, Nog admitted to himself, his career today was as much dedicated to Picard as it was to Starfleet.

"How can you do all that?" he asked the centurion.

"By myself," Karon said, as she pushed back her chair and got to her feet, "I cannot. But together, we can accomplish all that and more."

Nog held her gaze. "My question stands. How?"

The centurion spoke slowly and deliberately, as if the words she were about to say were the most important she had ever spoken. "Give us the *Phoenix*."

Nog stepped back in shock. "Never."

He saw Karon's lips tremble, as if she were restraining some great emotion. Then she turned sharply away from him and tapped her finger on the keypad of the small packing crate. With a hiss of mechanical movement, the thick locking clamps released and the crate opened to reveal a battered, discolored sheet of coppery-colored metal, a hand's breadth high and slightly wider.

Nog leaned closer. The metal sheet was supported in a nest of semi-transparent packing gel. Two of its edges were smooth, and a jagged break showed where it had been shattered, so that it seemed that at least half of it was missing.

Karon reached into the crate, lifted out the metal, and gave it to Nog. Even as she did so, he realized he was looking at a starship's dedication plaque.

"Read it," she said quietly.

Nog turned the metal over, and felt as if the gravity web had failed again.

He had seen this plaque a thousand times before. The last time—three days ago—was when it had been pristinely mounted on the bulkhead beside the primary turbolift on the bridge of Jean-Luc Picard's greatest achievement. U.S.S. PHOEN . . . the remaining letters read.

Beneath that, in smaller type: FIRST OF ITS CLASS.

Beneath that, a list of the engineers and designers Nog had worked with every day.

And then, at the bottom, the ship's simple motto, chosen by the Old Man himself: ". . . *Sokath, his eyes uncovered. . . .*"

Nog spoke without thinking. "It's . . . a bad forgery."

But Karon's next words seemed to come to him from a terrible distance. "Captain Nog, that plaque is twenty-five thousand years old."

The plaque shook in Nog's hands. How could anyone know the target date? "Where . . . where did you. . . ."

The Romulan centurion completed his question. "Find it? At the bottom of a methane sea on Syladdo."

Nog shook his head. The name was unfamiliar.

"Fourth moon of Ba'Syladon."

Nog's pulse quickened. "The Class-J gas giant. . . ."

"The largest planet in the Bajoran system. Correct." Karon's eyes remained fixed on him. She was making no attempt to take back the plaque. "And twenty-five thousand years ago, the *Phoenix* died there, *before* her mission could be completed."

"You can't know that. Not . . . absolutely."

"We can know that. We *do* know that. We can show you sensor records of all the wreckage recovered to date. Wreckage that includes enough of the deep-time components to know they were never deployed as planned."

Nog looked down at the evidence in his hands. The metal plaque burned his fingers, froze them, the confusion of sensations occurring all at once.

"Don't let the *Phoenix* die uselessly, Captain. Don't throw away Jean-Luc Picard's greatest dream on a mission that cannot succeed."

And then he finally understood. "You want the ship for another mission."

"When the ship is completed. Yes. We do."

Nog looked up to meet her gaze. Realizing that what he held in his hands was the proof that everything he had struggled for in these past five years on Mars, everything he had sacrificed, had been for nothing. Nothing.

He could barely speak the words. "You are asking me to betray Starfleet, the Federation—everything I believe in."

"No, Captain, I am offering you a chance to save those very things. The only chance you have. We came here to put this question to Admiral Picard, but his time has passed. So I put it to *you,* Captain Nog. In all the universe, you are the only one who can save it now. Will you join us?"

It took Nog a long time to make his decision.

And time was the one thing he no longer had.

CHAPTER 7

IF SISKO CLOSED his eyes, he could almost believe he was on Bajor, in the kai's Temple, in his own time. The gentle splash of water on stone in the meditation pool. The sharp peppermint-cinnamon smell of the *b'nai* candles. Even the cool breeze that brought with it the rich, loamy scent of the contemplation gardens. All these sensations brought back to him the world he had hoped someday would become his adopted home.

But even these sense memories faded when he opened his eyes and looked out through the curving viewports of the *Boreth*'s observation deck to see the *Defiant* being pulled through the stars at warp speed, ensnared in the purple web of a tractor beam and trailing half a kilometer behind the angular engineering hull of the advanced-technology Klingon battlecruiser.

At his right, he saw in Kira a reflection of his own distress at the sight of their ship—so distant, so powerless. At his left the tall, lean form of Arla Rees stood rigid, tense, though Sisko knew the defeat of the *Defiant* could not inflict the same emotional toll on her. The Bajoran commander had only served on Deep Space 9 for a few weeks, and she had not served on the *Defiant* before the events of the station's last day—or of the last twenty-five years.

"How do you think it happened?"

Sisko knew what Kira was really asking him. His conclusion—that the Dominion had won its war with the Federation—had been shared by all the others on the *Defiant* once they saw or heard of Weyoun's appearance in vedek's robes. And now, the fact that they had been been transported to Weyoun's Klingon ship and had discovered a Bajoran meditation chamber reconstructed to the last detail in its observation lounge was more proof. There could be no doubt that in this future the Dominion had won the war, and had assimilated the cultures of the Alpha Quadrant as omnivorously as had the Borg.

"Maybe it was Deep Space 9," Sisko ventured. "Once the station was gone, Starfleet had no forward base to guard the wormhole."

Kira sighed. "So we really were accomplishing something. This isn't the way I'd like to find out, though."

Arla turned away from the *Defiant*. "I thought the wormhole was no longer an issue in the war, because the aliens kept Dominion forces from using it."

Sisko saw Kira stiffen at the Bajoran commander's casual use of the term "aliens" to describe the beings in the wormhole.

"The *Prophets,*" Kira said emphatically, "chose to stop *one* fleet of Jem'Hadar ships from traveling through their Temple. But if the Bajoran people failed in their duty to protect the Temple's doorway, then it is entirely possible that the Prophets withdrew their blessing—just as they did when the Cardassians invaded."

Arla persisted. "Major, if the wormhole *aliens* are gods, how could they let the Cardassians inflict such evil on our world?"

Kira's smile was brittle. "I won't pretend to understand the Prophets, but I know everything they do is for a reason."

Before Arla could further escalate what was for now merely a discussion, Sisko intervened to keep it at that level. This argument could have no end between the two Bajorans of such dissimilar background and belief.

Kira had been born on occupied Bajor. She had grown up in relocation camps, and had fought for the Resistance since she was a child. The only thing that had enabled her—and millions of other Bajorans—to survive the horrors of the Cardassian Occupation of their world was a deep and unquestioning faith in their gods—the Prophets of the Celestial Temple.

But Arla Rees, only a few years younger than Kira, had been born to prosperous Bajoran traders on the neutral world of New Sydney. She had enjoyed a life of privilege in which the Cardassian Occupation, though an evil to rally against, had never been experienced firsthand. For Arla, now a Starfleet officer, as for many Bajorans of her upbringing, the Prophets were little more than an outmoded superstition perversely clung to by her less sophisticated cousins on the old world.

Sisko knew that as fervently as Kira believed in the Prophets and their Celestial Temple, Arla held an equally strong belief that the Bajoran wormhole was inhabited by aliens from a different dimensional realm, and that their involvement in the history of Bajor had been more disruptive than benevolent.

He himself had been wondering of late if reconciling these two opposing beliefs was one of the tasks that he, in his ill-defined and unsought role as the Emissary to Bajor's Prophets, was supposed to be able to accomplish. If so, then he was still unable to see how one could ever be reconciled with the other.

"That's enough," Sisko said to both Kira and Arla. "This debate is nothing we're going to resolve here and now."

"Oh, but we are," Weyoun proclaimed from behind them.

Sisko and the two Bajorans turned as quickly as if shot by disruptors, to see that the Vorta had apparently beamed into the observation deck behind them, just beside the meditation pool. Across the deck, the doors to the corridor were still closed, and there was no other obvious way in.

"Captain Sisko," Weyoun purred, "Major Kira, you have no idea how delighted I am to meet you again after so many years. And Commander Arla, it is such a pleasure to make your acquaintance." The Vorta smiled ingratiatingly at his guests and clasped his hands eagerly before him. "I trust you've found your quarters to your liking."

Sisko forced himself to control his initial impulse to angrily demand an explanation for everything that had happened to them. Weyoun's irritatingly obsequious manner had simply—like everything else about him and his species—been genetically programmed by the Founders in order to better serve the Dominion as negotiators, strategists, scientists, and diplomats.

In this sense, this latest version of Weyoun had changed not at all over the past twenty-five years. The clone's thick black hair, brushed high above his forehead, showed no trace of gray. His smooth, open face, framed by dramatically ribbed ears that ran from his chin halfway up the sides of his head, showed no sign of age-related lines or wrinkles. Indeed, the only aspect of the cloned Vorta that *had* changed from the time Sisko had last crossed his path was that this Weyoun now wore a Bajoran earring, complete with a gleaming silver chain.

But at the moment none of these details was important to Sisko. There was only one thought that claimed his mind. "What happened to my people who were beamed off the *Defiant?*" He did not add that his son Jake had been among them.

"Sadly," Weyoun began mournfully, "we must consider them dead. The attackers are not known for taking prisoners. And those they do take do not live for long."

Kira's outraged question filled the terrible silence that followed the Vorta's pronouncement. "What are you doing in those robes?"

Weyoun glanced down at his saffron-and-white vedek's robes, as if to be sure his clothing hadn't changed in the last few seconds. "Why, they were a gift. From the congregation of the Dahkur Temple. I believe that's in your home province, Major."

Kira's face tightened in disbelief. "None of the monks I know would ever accept a Dominion lackey as a vedek."

Weyoun gazed at Kira in hurt sadness, as if her words had wounded him cruelly. "The Dominon," he said, almost wistfully. "A name I have not heard in many years."

Kira's quick glance at Sisko revealed her lack of

understanding, but he was unable to offer her any of his own.

"Why not?" Sisko asked Weyoun. "Did the Founders change its name?"

"Founders," Weyoun repeated, as if that word hadn't crossed his lips for a long time either. "To be honest, I don't know how the Founders reacted to their loss."

"What loss?" Sisko asked. Now he needed enlightenment.

"Of the war, of course," Weyoun answered. "With the Federation."

Kira shook her head. "Wait a minute. The Dominion *lost* the war?"

Weyoun looked troubled. "In . . . a manner of speaking."

"And what manner would that be?" Sisko demanded.

Weyoun nodded thoughtfully. "I understand your confusion, Captain. Twenty-five years *is* a long time. And I will see to it that you have access to briefing tapes that recount the thrilling historic events you've missed. But for now, simply to put your minds at rest, I will try to . . . get you up to speed. Isn't that what you say?"

"Just start at the beginning," Sisko said. "Who won the war?"

The Vorta's smile was vague. "In a technical sense, no one—but the war *is* over," he hastened to add, as Sisko took a step toward him. "In fact, it ended almost one year to the day after the loss of Deep Space 9 and the beginning of your . . . miraculous voyage."

Sisko was no longer interested in even pretending to be patient. "*How* did it end?"

The Vorta pursed his lips. "With the destruction of Cardassia Prime, I'm sorry to say. A terrible battle. A terrible price to pay for peace. But the Cardassians were a proud people. And Damar and the Founder he served refused to surrender. Then, when—"

Arla interrupted suddenly. "What do you mean, the Cardassians 'were' a proud people?"

Weyoun fixed his remarkably clear gray eyes on hers. "I don't play games with my words, Commander. At all times, you can be sure I mean exactly what I say. Today, the Cardassians as a species are virtually extinct. Cardassia Prime. The Hub Colonies. The Union Territories. All destroyed."

"Destroyed?" Sisko repeated. "We *are* talking about planets?"

Weyoun nodded. "Entire worlds, Captain. Laid waste. Uninhabitable. A death toll in the tens of billions. . . . A mere handful of Cardassians left now. Traders. Pirates." He paused, then added with unexpected anger, "Madmen."

Kira sounded as shocked as Sisko felt. "But you—you somehow escaped all that destruction?"

Weyoun's facial expressions disconcertingly flickered back and forth between an overweening smile of pride and an exaggerated frown of sorrow. "No, Major. In a sense, *I* brought about that destruction."

Now Sisko, Kira, and Arla all began to speak at the same time. But Weyoun ignored their questions and protests alike.

"No, no, no," he said, tucking his hands within the folds of his robes. "Whatever you think of me, you're wrong." He stood with his back to the observation windows and their backdrop of warp-smeared stars. "Captain Sisko, you must believe me. I begged Damar to accept the inevitable. I implored the Founder to accept that it was time she and her kind accepted their fate to be partners in a new cause, not the leaders of a dying one. Yet—"

Sisko regarded him with disbelief. "Are you saying you turned against the *Founders?!*"

"But . . . they were your gods," Kira said.

Weyoun shook his head. "The only reason the Vorta believed the Founders to be gods was because that was programmed into the basic structure of our brains. Our belief in the Founders was achieved through the same genetic engineering that raised us from the forests of our homeworld."

"But you've always known about your programming," Sisko said.

"True. And our belief, engineered or not, did sustain the Vorta—sustained *me*—through the most difficult times. But then . . ." Weyoun withdrew his arms from his robes and spread them wide, as if to embrace Sisko and the others. ". . . The day came when those difficult times ended and . . . and *I* met the *true* Gods of all creation—the Prophets." His transformed face shone with bliss.

Sisko stared at the triumphant Vorta. "You . . . met the *Bajoran* Prophets?"

Weyoun nodded, his beatific smile never wavering.

"Through an Orb experience?" Kira asked doubtfully. "Or—"

"Face to face," the Vorta said in a humble voice. "In the True Celestial Temple. I traveled through it. A desperate expedition to see if it led to the Gamma Quadrant." He laughed quietly to himself in remembrance. "The Founder herself ordered me to go. Two Cardassian warships. A wing of Jem'Hadar attack cruisers. Yet . . . I was the only one to return."

And then, an icy hand gripping his heart, Sisko made sense of Weyoun's astounding story. "You traveled through the *second* wormhole."

The Vorta held a finger to his lips. "Oh, Captain, I must caution you. I have a very devoted, very religious crew. We don't call them . . . 'wormholes' anymore."

"*Two* Temples, then," Sisko said. "Just like the legend of the Red Orbs of Jalbador."

Weyoun stared at Sisko, abandoning all traces of the false veneer of a genetically engineered negotiator he had always maintained in their previous encounters. "In your time," he said seriously, "the legend of Jalbador existed in many different forms, distorted by the inevitable accumulation of error over the millennia of its retelling. But in essence, Captain, each variation of that legend possessed a fraction of the truth. A truth which you helped bring back to a universe that had lost its way."

"And that truth would be?" Kira asked grimly.

Weyoun's response was uncharacteristically to the point. "The Prophets are the Gods of all creation, and the True Celestial Temple is their home."

Then, pausing as if to compose himself, the Vorta studied his audience of three before focusing his attention on Arla. "Now I know this is not what *you* believe, Commander. I overheard what you were saying before I joined you. If the Prophets are Gods, then how can they let evil exist? That is a valid question. And it has a valid answer."

Weyoun stepped closer to Arla, addressing her as if Sisko and Kira were no longer present in this reconstruction of a meditation chamber. "You see, Commander, the Prophets do not wish their children to be afflicted by evil. But uncounted eons ago, when the universe was a perfect ideal contained within the Temple, some Prophets rebelled. Oh, they believed they had a just cause. They thought that a universe within the Temple could only ever be a reflection of perfection, not perfection itself. And so they fought to free creation from its timeless realm. And in that great and terrible battle—beyond the comprehension of any linear being—the One Celestial Temple was—" Weyoun clapped his hands together unexpectedly, startling his three listeners, "—split asunder!"

The Vorta smiled apologetically at Arla. "The battle between the two groups of Prophets ended then. But the damage had already been done. The stars, the galaxies, the planets . . . everything the Prophets had created in their image of timeless perfection spilled out into the void created by the Temple's destruction. And in that void, perfection was unattainable. Evil was loosed upon the face of creation. And all because of the pride of one group of Prophets, who thought they knew better."

"The Pah-wraiths," Arla whispered.

Weyoun brightened at Arla's response. "Ah, so you have had *some* religious instruction, Commander. Yes, of course. But the Pah-wraiths you know from your time are those poor beings who spilled from the Temple at the time it was torn in two. They could not carry on the fight in the False Temple, neither could they join their fellows in the True Temple. Instead, they sought shelter near the entrance to both shards of the One Temple, deep in the Fire Caves at the core of Bajor, lost and abandoned by both sides."

"This is all blasphemy!" Kira protested. "There was no battle in the Temple! There are no fallen Prophets! There is no second Temple!"

Undisturbed, Weyoun pointed an accusing finger at the livid major. "Then how do you explain your presence here *and* now, exactly as foretold by Naradim's Third Vision as recorded on the tablets of Jalbador?"

"What do you mean 'our presence' was foretold?" Sisko asked quickly, before Kira could interrupt Weyoun again.

"Behold," the Vorta intoned as if reciting from some ancient text, "you shall know the final prophecy of Jalbador is fulfilled when the False Emissary shall rise from among those that did die in the destruction of the gateway, to face the final battle with the True Emissary of the Prophets, and to bow before his righteousness at the time the doors shall be opened and the One Temple restored."

Weyoun's voice trembled with ecstasy as he concluded, "And by his return, and by his defeat, this shall you know as the True Reckoning, which shall come at the end of all days, and the beginning of that which has no beginning."

Sisko was unable to restrain Kira from another outburst. "More Pah-wraith heresy!" she exclaimed. "The Reckoning took place less than a month ago! And Kai Winn stopped it!"

Weyoun regarded her with pity. "Major, do you really believe any corporeal being could defy the will of the Prophets? Especially a nonbeliever such as Winn?"

Sisko could see the conflict in Kira. Winn was not the religious leader she had preferred, but neither did Kira doubt that the Kai had faith. "Kai Winn is not a nonbeliever. She is . . . sometimes misguided in her attempts to reconcile her spiritual duties with her political ones."

"Was," Weyoun corrected her. "Winn *was* misguided."

"She's dead?" Kira asked in a disbelieving voice.

"One of the first to be hung."

"Hung?!"

Weyoun sighed and bowed his head. "You missed so much. The end of the war. The Ascendancy of Bajor. The collapse of the Federation—"

Sisko, Kira, and Arla all said, "What?" at the same moment.

"*Near*-collapse," Weyoun amended. "Oh, there's still a council that meets . . . somewhere. Ships here and there that claim to be part of Starfleet. But all of it is little more than the twitching of a corpse, I'm afraid."

"What about those ships that attacked us?" Sisko asked.

"Oh, they weren't attacking you, Captain. They were attacking Captain Riker's ship in order to capture yours. Or, more to the point, to capture *you*."

"Why me?"

"Isn't that obvious? Without you the True Reckoning can't take place."

Sisko stared at Weyoun, afraid to draw the only conclusion that seemed logical.

Weyoun nodded as if reading his mind. "That's right, Captain. *You* are the False Emissary. Risen from among those who died at the destruction of the gateway to the Celestial Temple, that is, your late lamented Deep Space 9."

"But if I'm the False Emissary . . ."

"Exactly." Weyoun bowed. "*I* am the True Emissary to the True Prophets of the One Temple, now Kai to all the believers of the Bajoran Ascendancy."

"*Kai?!*" To Sisko, Kira sounded as if she were about to choke. "You're a pawn of the Pah-wraiths!"

Weyoun's smile faded. "True, I am their servant. But

consider this, Major. Even in the fringe beliefs you cling to, when was evil visited upon the universe?"

Whatever uncertainty Kira felt, it didn't prevent her from standing up to Weyoun. "Bajorans don't presume to speak for the universe. But evil came to Bajor when the people first turned away from the Prophets."

"And when was that? In your beliefs?" Weyoun added condescendingly.

"I don't think anyone knows the actual time period."

"Then *approximately* . . . how long ago?"

Kira shrugged. "At the . . . the very beginning of our time on our world."

Weyoun leaned forward, his manner suggesting to Sisko nothing so much as a spider about to complete its web. "Exactly. At the very beginning of time. And what will eliminate evil from the universe—or, at the very least, in your beliefs, from the people of Bajor?"

Sisko couldn't help feeling that the Vorta was about to spring his trap, and it seemed by the slowness of Kira's reply that she sensed the same possibility. "When . . . when all the people of Bajor return to the Prophets and . . . accept them as our Gods."

The Vorta nodded as if Kira had just answered her own question. "Then I ask you, Major, what better way to bring the people of the universe—or of Bajor—back to the Prophets than by bringing them back to the One Celestial Temple? And in all the 'blasphemous' and 'heretical' text that you refuse to accept, what is the one thing the Pah-wraiths always want to do?"

"Return to the Temple," Kira said reluctantly.

"Because by doing so the One Temple will be restored, and all the people will be returned to the Prophets."

"But the texts clearly state that the Pah-wraiths want to *destroy* the Temple!" Kira insisted.

Weyoun's reply was unexpected. "I agree. That's what your texts—inspired by the False Prophets—say. Because the False Prophets don't want the Temple to be restored. The False Prophets want to delude the people of Bajor into thinking that the Pah-wraiths are demons." The Vorta's voice began to rise accusingly. "But answer this, Major: Why is it that the Prophets you worship hide themselves in their Temple, refusing to come out, refusing to do anything except sow confusion with the Orbs they inflicted upon your world, while the Pah-wraiths—*even in your own texts*—are known to walk amongst the people of Bajor and to constantly struggle to open the Temple doors?"

"Lies!" Kira said. "I refuse to listen to more of your lies!"

"Listen to yourself, Major. Where are your arguments, your reasons? You are simply denying the truth out of habit." Weyoun was almost taunting her. "I expected so much more of you."

"Heretic!" Kira shouted as she rushed forward to strike Weyoun.

Sisko lunged after her but before he could reach her—

—a brilliant flash of red light flared from around Weyoun, and Kira was thrown back onto the flat stones that covered the deck.

Sisko dropped to his knees, supporting Kira as she gasped for breath, her dark eyes wide and unfocused. Arla moved to Sisko's side to add whatever aid she could give.

Weyoun's voice floated over them. "Forgive me. Major Kira's attack was quite unexpected, and in the years since we last met I have perfected my control of . . . telekinesis, I suppose you would call it. A little too well, it seems."

Sisko turned to Weyoun, who still stood in front of the observation windows. "Do you have a medkit or a tricorder—anything?" Kira shuddered in his arms, each hard-won breath shallower, as if her throat were closing.

"I'm afraid we have no medical equipment of any kind on board this vessel," Weyoun said apologetically.

Sisko was appalled. Klingon ships were not known for their medical facilities, but still they carried some supplies, if only for the command staff. "Then beam us back to the *Defiant!*" He felt Kira's body arch, then go rigid as she opened her mouth and made no sound, as if her airways were now totally obstructed. "She's dying!" Sisko shouted at Weyoun.

Weyoun moved away from the windows and leaned down to observe Kira. "No, she's not." He waved one arm free of his robes, then placed his thumb and forefinger on the lobe of Kira's left ear. "Her *pagh* is strong. She did not journey all this way to die so close to the end. . . ."

And then Sisko watched, uncomprehending, as shimmering red light sprang forth from the Vorta's pale hand and spread across Kira's distorted features, until suddenly her entire body trembled, she inhaled deeply, and—

—went limp, breathing easily as if she had merely fallen asleep in his arms.

Sisko looked up at Weyoun, and for just an instant saw the Vorta's eyes flash red as well.

"Yes, Captain?" Weyoun said, as his eyes returned to their crystal-gray clarity.

Sisko looked down at Kira, whose eyes remained closed. Her chest rose and fell with normal regularity.

"What did you mean . . . 'so close to the end'? The end of what?"

The Vorta smiled like a child with a secret. "Why, not the end, Captain. The beginning. Didn't you hear what I said? The reason you've been returned from the dead is so the final prophecy of Jalbador can be fulfilled."

Sisko struggled to recall the exact words Weyoun had used when he seemed to be reciting sacred text to Kira. "The end of all days, and the beginning of that which has no beginning?"

"Exactly," Weyoun said, beaming as if at his favorite pupil. "When we shall all be returned to the Temple, and this imperfect creation shall at last come to an end."

Had he heard anyone else speak in that way, Sisko would have assumed the speaker was insane. But he had seen the red glow in Weyoun's eyes. The same glow that had been in Jake's eyes when a Pah-wraith had possessed his son's body and controlled his son's mind.

Arla got to her feet, her voice uncertain, colored by fear. "You're both talking about the end of the universe, aren't you?"

Sisko felt the chill of madness fill the room, as Weyoun bestowed a smile of blessing upon the Bajoran Starfleet officer. "Oh, Commander, nothing as drastic as that. Merely the end of material existence. But at that time, you—" the Vorta smiled at Sisko. "—and the captain—" He brushed his fingers along the side of Kira's face. "—and even the nonbelievers will ascend to a *new* level of existence, wrapped for all time in the love and the wisdom of the Prophets."

Glow or no glow, Pah-wraith or no Pah-wraith, for Sisko, Weyoun had gone too far. He eased Kira onto the floor and stood up to face the Vorta. "You're insane," he said.

Weyoun merely shrugged. "Of course that's what you must think. It is demanded of your role as the False Emissary. But rest assured that even you will ascend to the Temple when you fulfill the final prophecy and acknowledge the True Prophets."

"Never," Sisko said. But even as he spoke, Sisko was aware that not even he, the Emissary of Kira's Prophets, knew what he must do next to stop Weyoun and the Pah-Wraiths from whatever terrible action they were planning. He still needed to learn more about this future before he could help anyone change it.

"Ah, but never doesn't mean what it used to," Weyoun replied. "Not when all you have left is fifteen days."

"Fifteen days . . . till what?" Arla asked.

Weyoun closed his eyes, as if at total peace with himself and the universe. "Fifteen days until the doors of the two Temples shall open together, and the final battle of good and evil shall be fought . . ." He opened his eyes, sought out Sisko as he continued, ". . . and won, and this cruel, imperfect universe shall at last pass, and we shall all ascend to the Temple for eternity."

Apprehension swept over Sisko. It was obvious that despite the complete insanity of Weyoun's proclamation, the Vorta believed every word he spoke.

And when the universe did *not* end in fifteen days, Sisko did not doubt there would be, quite literally, hell to pay.

CHAPTER 8

IN THE SMALL, low-ceilinged briefing room on the *Boreth*'s main cargo deck, Elim Garak read the sensor-log identification screen on the main wall-viewer, and felt nothing.

He didn't have to be paranoid to know that he and the seventeen other crew and passengers removed from the *Defiant* were under close observation. But from what he had already deduced about the state of this time period in general, and of the Bajoran Ascendancy in particular, being paranoid would stand him in good stead.

The large irregularly-shaped Klingon viewscreen on the far bulkhead flickered once, then displayed an image of Deep Space 9 as it had existed on stardate 51889.4, as seen from the vantage point of the *U.S.S. Garneau*. The *Garneau* was—or had been—one of two *Akira*-class Starfleet vessels dispatched when the station's computers had fallen victim to some rather clever, if disruptive, Bynar codes inserted by two vicious Andorian sisters intent on obtaining the Red Orbs of Jalbador.

At the time, as he had helped Jadzia Dax eliminate the codes from Deep Space 9's Cardassian computer components, he had been impressed by the meddlesome Andorians' audacity—though given the results of their endeavors and how they had affected him personally, he would happily eviscerate them now, very slowly.

On the viewscreen, the image of Deep Space 9 grew as the *Garneau* closed in. This moment of calm before the inevitable temporal storm to come gave Garak the chance to admire once again the stately sweep of the Cardassian docking towers and the profound balance in the proportions of its rings to its central core. To his trained eye, the station was an exquisitely compelling sculpture, majestically framed against the subtly shifting energy cascades of the Denorios Belt, and it spoke to him of his long-lost home.

None of this would he reveal to others, of course. Instead, keeping his expression deliberately blank, he checked the timecode running at the bottom of the image. In terms of his own relative perceptions—and what other perceptions could there be that were as important?—the time it indicated was barely a day ago. He had been in Ops at that moment, still working on the computer though curious about what was going on in Quark's, where so many others of the station's personnel had congregated.

Not that he would admit to being curious, either. Far better to be aloof, he knew. Far better to be unconcerned. Far better to be so unremarkable and innocuous that the passing crowd could do nothing but ignore him.

At last, something happened in the recording. A faint red glow pulsed through three or four of the observation portals ringing the Promenade level. Garak decided that must have been the moment when the three Red Orbs of Jalbador were brought into alignment in the Ferengi's bar, beginning the process of opening the second wormhole in Bajoran space—and in the middle of Deep Space 9.

The alignment had been quite a sight—or so he had been told by one of his fellow passengers, Rom to be precise. The lumpish but loquacious Ferengi repair technician had described how the three hourglass-shaped orbs, indistinguishable from the better-known Orbs of the Prophets—except for their crimson color—had levitated, as if under their own control, until they had described the vertices of an equilateral triangle. Suspended in midair less than two meters above the floor of the bar, they had proved impossible to budge.

Garak sighed as if stifling a yawn. But inwardly he was anything but bored. No wonder dear, sweet Leej Terrell had been so eager to obtain the Orbs for herself—and for Cardassia. The Cardassian scientist had been his lover once, his nemesis many times, and was one of a scattered and secretive handful of highly skilled and exceedingly ruthless operatives who had survived the Dominion's obliteration of the Obsidian Order.

With the three Red Orbs in hand, Garak had no doubt that Terrell had believed she would have the secret to creating a translocatable wormhole. If anything could break Cardassia free of its devil's bargain with the Dominion, the ability to open a wormhole connecting any two points in space would be the ultimate dealbreaker. No planetary defense force would be able to stop a Cardassian fleet that could launch from the homeworld and within seconds appear in the atmosphere of the enemy's home. Terrell's trio of orbs and that second wormhole would be the key to a *Pax Cardassia,* bringing order to a troubled galaxy.

But at the same time as Garak fully supported Terrell's passion for freedom and admired her patriotism for Cardassia's sake, he also secretly hoped for *his* own sake that this sensor log would show her vessel's destruction. In detail.

On the viewscreen, the red emanations in the Promenade's observation portals had become a constant glow, slowly increasing in brightness. Garak noted a handful of escape pods already breaking free of the habitat rings. Then, almost obscured by a docking tower, the *Defiant* released her docking clamps and began to slip back from the station, moving out of the optical sensor's field of vision.

It was just about now, Garak realized, that he had been unexpectedly beamed from Ops into the confusion of the *Defiant,* then roughly pushed out the door and toward the mess hall. And he could see that the timing of his rescue had been perfect.

Because now on the viewscreen, the red glow had infected a full quadrant of the Promenade module. Silent explosions ran along a docking pylon. And then, the habitat ring began to bend like a wheel warping out of true, as if an immense gravitational well had formed in Quark's.

As it had.

Garak continued to watch events unfold without displaying the slightest interest in or outrage at what transpired next. More escape pods shot free of the station, only to be drawn back to disappear into the opening maw of the red-tinged wormhole.

Like the mouth of the human hell, Garak thought. *How fitting. How poetic.*

And then, faster than the sensor log had been able to record, the image of Deep Space 9 shrank and was gone, replaced by what could almost pass for the opening to the Bajoran wormhole. Except that that swirling mass of forces always seemed to have a blue cast to the energies it released, and this second wormhole was most definitely color-shifted to the red half of the visible-light spectrum.

Captain Sisko's voice disrupted the silence in the briefing room. "That wasn't how we experienced the station's collapse."

Sisko, Major Kira, and Commander Arla were seated up front in the first row of hard Klingon chairs, to which they had been escorted by Romulan security guards only moments before the briefing began. Garak could understand why the captain of the *Defiant* had been separated from the other passengers and crew when they had been beamed to the *Boreth.* But he didn't know why the major and the commander had been taken with him, unless it was because they were the only two Bajorans among the eighteen. He would, however, endeavor to find out. Though Garak knew he would never admit to curiosity—at least, not in a public sense—he was fully aware that he lived his life in a perpetual haze of it.

Sisko continued his correction of the sensor log's account. "We saw the collapse of the station proceed more slowly while we were under attack by Terrell's ship."

How very *interesting,* Garak thought, only his long

years of training allowing him to keep his face completely composed.

A young Romulan who stood at the side of the briefing room, improbably outfitted in a poorly fitted variation of a Bajoran militia uniform, switched on a padd so that his angular face was illuminated from below. Then he looked over to Sisko and said, "That tends to confirm the hypothesis that the *Defiant* was caught within the boundary layer of the opening wormhole. Your ship would then have been subjected to relativistic time-dilation effects."

"Then shouldn't the same have happened to Terrell's ship?" Sisko asked.

Garak waited eagerly for the answer. But the Romulan was not forthcoming.

"There are no records of that ship as you described it—" The Romulan looked down at his padd again. "—A *Chimera*-class vessel disguised as a Sagittarian passenger liner. In any event, the *Defiant* was the only vessel to emerge into this time period."

Pity, Garak thought. He would have enjoyed one final meeting with Terrell. He would have liked to have seen her face when she learned that their precious Cardassia no longer existed. Its history, its culture, and all except a handful of its people erased from the universe, as if they had been nothing but a half-remembered dream.

He himself had learned the fate of his world just a few hours earlier from two young Klingon soldiers, also in badly tailored Bajoran uniforms. He had noted their intense interest in observing him, and upon questioning them had learned that they had never encountered a Cardassian before. Then they had told him why.

At that precise instant, Garak had to admit—if only to himself—he had felt a true pang of regret. But only for an instant. Immense relief—not sorrow—had immediately followed. In this time period, there was now nothing left for him to fight for. His struggles were over.

It was, he had decided, a quite liberating experience.

A Bajoran colonel now appeared on the main viewscreen, obviously reading from a script, droning on without much clarity of detail about the events of the few weeks that had followed the opening of the second wormhole. Apparently, the space-time matrix of the Bajoran sector had been altered in some obscure technical way by the second wormhole's gravimetric profile. Garak couldn't follow what the implications of that were, nor was he particularly interested. But supposedly the behavior of the first wormhole had become more erratic because of those changes. It had rarely opened after that, and travel through it had proved impossible.

Then, the Bajoran colonel recounted at tedious length, with the Cardassian-Dominion alliance mounting a major offensive throughout the region, a small battle group had broken through Starfleet's crumbling lines and reached the Bajoran system.

Garak covered his mouth with his hand and yawned outright. This time it wasn't an affectation. The briefing room was getting uncomfortably hot. He glanced at the unfinished metal walls, willing himself to see them move away from him and not close in. His claustrophobia—again a personal idiosyncrasy he avoided revealing to any other being—was becoming more noticeable of late. He redoubled his efforts to suppress it.

Another new sensor-log screen appeared on the viewer, and Garak welcomed it as a distraction from the heat and closeness of the room. This next recording had apparently been made by the *U.S.S. Enterprise,* also in the Bajoran system, on stardate 52145.7.

The new sensor recording began, and for a few seconds all Garak could see was streaking stars and lances of phaser fire. Then the image stabilized, and he was able to make out a tightly grouped formation of three *Galor*-class Cardassian warships surrounded by a cloud of Jem'Hadar attack cruisers, purple drive fields aglow. In the background, Garak could once again see the shifting energy curtain of the Denorios Belt, so he had a reasonably good notion of what he was watching: the departure of Kai Weyoun's expedition.

Kai Weyoun, Garak mused. He almost felt sorry for poor Major Kira, having to deal with that corruption of her deeply felt religion. *Almost* felt sorry. The major was a Bajoran, after all, and they were a far too sensitive people, regrettably quick to find fault or take offense. And judging from how they had created an entire religion around a few sparkling artifacts discarded by a more advanced species, rather easy to deceive as well.

The new sensor log continued, and Garak's conclusion was confirmed. Just as the *Enterprise* swooped in on what seemed to him to be a rather remarkably risky attack—which nonetheless resulted in the loss of a Cardassian warship—the red wormhole popped open, just as the blue wormhole so often had. At that, the two remaining *Galor*-class ships and their Jem'Hadar escorts vanished into the red wormhole, which then collapsed. Though the *Enterprise* continued on a matching course, unlike the blue wormhole the red wormhole did not open again.

Very selective, Garak noted. Which meant it was quite likely that the red wormhole was also home to an advanced species, or was otherwise under intelligent control.

The current sensor log ended, and the boring Bajoran colonel returned to the viewscreen to explain that the Weyoun expedition had been intended to traverse the new phenomenon and attempt to discover if it had a second opening in normal space, as did the existing phenomenon.

Garak's eyes began to close. Really, the colonel was almost soporific. Even he could guess that the *unstated* goal of the expedition had been to determine if the new wormhole led to the Gamma Quadrant.

But then Garak's eyes opened abruptly. The colonel had not referred to the wormholes as wormholes. He had pointedly called them *phenomena.* Why?

Listening more closely now, Garak heard the colonel go on to say that although it usually took less than two minutes to travel through the existing phenomenon, the Weyoun expedition remained in the new phenomenon for more than three weeks. At which time, of the 1,137 valiant soldiers who had made up the expeditionary force, only Weyoun managed to return. Though he brought with him new allies.

Now another new sensor log began running, this one from a Bajoran vessel, the *Naquo,* beginning with a rapid sweep across the Denorios Belt to catch the red wormhole in the process of opening. And then, from that cauldron of hyperdimensional energies, Garak saw seven ships appear.

Despite himself Garak leaned forward in his chair, as if those few extra centimeters might help him better understand the nature of the seven ships.

Are they transparent? he wondered, for certainly he

could see the glow of the wormhole and the Belt through their elongated, ovoid shapes.

But as the sensor log displayed a progression of increasingly magnified views, Garak realized that the seven ships were little more than skeletons—collections of struts and beams, each vessel slightly different from the rest but with no obviously contained areas that might correspond to crew quarters.

A sudden flash of light from one of the ships ended the sensor recording. Sitting back once again, Garak decided the flash of light had been weapons fire. Wherever the second wormhole had reemerged into normal space, it was clear that Weyoun *had* returned with allies.

Once again, the Bajoran colonel returned to the screen. This time Garak did not feel at all sleepy.

The colonel now stated that the new phenomenon had connected the Bajoran Sector to a region in the farthest reaches of the Delta Quadrant. There, Weyoun had made contact with the Grigari, who returned the Vorta when the rest of his expedition had been lost.

Garak waited for more details, but the colonel offered none. An omission Garak found distinctly amusing in its circumspection. He himself had heard rumors of the Grigari most of his life. Though he could recall no convincing report of direct contact with the species, their medical technology was often traded at the frontier, having been obtained from other, intermediary species. Furthermore, that particular type of medical technology was banned on virtually every civilized world in the Alpha and Beta Quadrants.

He recalled once reading a report outlining the results of the Obsidian Order's analysis of a Grigari flesh regenerator, which some had hoped would enable certain torture techniques to be used for longer periods of interrogation. The Order's conclusion: too dangerous.

If but one contraband Grigari device had been deemed by the Obsidian Order to be too dangerous, then it was daunting to consider the damage a Grigari fleet might be capable of inflicting. Clearly, what the Bajoran colonel was not saying in this sanitized briefing was that Weyoun's expedition—Jem'Hadar and Cardassian alike—had been utterly decimated by the Grigari. Which begged the only questions worth asking: How had Weyoun survived, and why had the Grigari come through the wormhole under his command?

Garak repressed the hope that threatened to surface as a smile on his face. *A universe of mystery to explore,* he thought. It could actually be that there would be no one here he could bribe, threaten, or seduce into taking him back to his own time. And if so, he might grow to like it here.

He settled back to see what else would unfold from this selective presentation of the past twenty-five years, and what answers, if any, might be forthcoming. So far, it seemed, for each mystery described and explained two new ones were being revealed and left enigmatic.

As the briefing continued, the ever-curious Garak was not disappointed.

CHAPTER 9

WITH SEVEN LIFETIMES of experience to draw on, Jadzia Dax recognized a dying starship when she saw one, and the *Augustus* was dying.

It obviously had been launched before completion—its environmental controls were malfunctioning. The nature of the vessel's exposed wires, pipes, and conduits also told her that redundancy and self-repair capabilities were nonexistent. And there were appallingly few signs of any attempt to make the ship a secure home for her crew. Even the earliest starships had used paint and colored lights to vary the visual environment and prevent boredom from setting in on long voyages or tours of duty. Yet even those simple grace notes were missing from this ship.

And just as the yellowing of a single leaf can indicate the failing health of a tree, Jadzia was further convinced that the decline of the *Augustus* was not an isolated event. It was a symptom of a greater disease, one that must infect all of Starfleet.

None of these conclusions had she shared with Worf, however. Even as she had walked with him through the narrow, unfinished corridors of the ship escorted by Vulcan security guards, each wearing phaser-visors, Jadzia had remained silent, as had he. Now, with little more than a look exchanged since she and her husband had been escorted to the cramped cabin that was to be their prison cell, Jadzia knew that Worf had reached the same conclusion she had.

They were under surveillance.

The fact that the Vulcan captain of this vessel could subject them to the barbaric test of their humanity on the hangar deck was proof enough that this Starfleet had deviated from the ideals that had drawn Jadzia to serve in it. The computer briefing she and Worf had watched on the holographic screen had been further evidence of whatever disease was responsible for the decay around them.

Whether the briefing had been a complete lie or not Jadzia couldn't be certain. But she was convinced that it had not been the complete truth.

She had seen that same realization in Worf's eyes as well.

Because no matter how limited Starfleet's ship construction and maintenance capacities had become, no matter how brutal and arbitrary its commanders, Jadzia could not for an instant believe that in a mere twenty-five years Starfleet and the Federation had degenerated to the point that they would take part in a religious war. It was unthinkable.

Yet according to the computer briefing, that's exactly what was under way—the War of the Prophets.

Somehow, since the destruction of Deep Space 9 a new religious movement on Bajor, centered on the beings discovered to live in the second wormhole, had become a rallying point for a new interstellar political entity—the Bajoran Ascendancy. If the briefing was to be believed, the Ascendancy had early on launched a series of unprovoked attacks against Federation territory that had resulted in years of tense negotiations and border skirmishes, each side accusing the other of ongoing acts of terrorism.

Had that been the end of the story, Jadzia might have understood how a state of war could come to exist, with the Ascendancy attempting to take over new systems and the Federation attempting to maintain its borders.

But according to the briefing that was not the point of the undeclared war.

The goal of the Ascendancy was not to acquire new territory. It was simply to prohibit the passage of non-Ascendancy ships through the Bajoran Sector, including the homeworld system and the four closest colony worlds. In Jadzia's time—in fact, throughout the existence of the Federation—Starfleet had always respected the sovereignty of independent systems. The Prime Directive permitted it to do nothing less.

But according to that same briefing, which Jadzia had found to be a particularly deplorable piece of propaganda, long on emotion and short on facts, the goal of Starfleet in this war was not to defend Federation territory, not to contain Ascendancy forces within their own boundaries, but actually to invade the Bajoran home system and destroy the second wormhole, ending the new Bajoran religion.

Even seven lifetimes had not prepared her for the

utter revulsion she felt for the Starfleet of this time. What had happened to the Prime Directive? What had happened to the Fundamental Declarations? For a moment the Trill had even found herself wondering if, in addition to traveling through time, the *Defiant* had somehow crossed over into a parallel universe, one closer to the horrors of the Mirror Universe than to the one she had lived in.

Their Vulcan captors had told them that the briefing would answer all their questions. But so many new ones had been raised in Jadzia that she had come to feel liberated. When she had entered the Academy, she had pledged herself to uphold the ideals of Starfleet and the Federation. When she had graduated, she had taken her oath as an officer to do the same. As a result, she felt no conflict in her present resolve to behave according to that pledge and that oath—both made to the Starfleet of the past and not to this hollow, dying version that did not deserve its name.

All she needed now was an opportunity to take action, and that opportunity came the moment she and Worf set foot on their third metal staircase. The ship's decks, doors, and intersections were labeled only by alphanumeric code, but Jadzia knew they were now on a deck higher than the hangar deck, which suggested they were moving closer to the bridge.

Worf and she—the tactical officer and the science officer—had been "invited" to a meeting there. And that strongly suggested that Captain T'len and her own science officer were now on the bridge, waiting for their "guests" to arrive.

Which means, Jadzia thought, *they won't be expecting—*

Two steps from the top of the staircase and the waiting Vulcan escort, she drove her fist upward into the man's stomach, and as he doubled over she smashed her other hand up against the visor he wore, seeking to damage it as much as its wearer.

Reflexively, the Vulcan guard reached out for her shoulder, seeking the nerves that would bring instant unconsciousness. But he was still off-balance, and Jadzia swept his outstretched hand aside and slammed his head against the metal handrail.

That was the telling blow, and with a groan the guard fell to the metal deck.

Only then did Jadzia turn back to see how Worf had fared, confident that he would have been looking for the same opportunity she had, and that he would have made his move in the same instant.

Sure enough, Worf was crouched at the bottom of the stairway, removing the phaser-visor from the guard who lay sprawled there. A thin thread of green blood trickled from the Vulcan's nose, which looked considerably flatter than it had a few moments earlier.

Jadzia leaped up the last few steps and pulled the phaser-visor from the guard she had felled. A thin black wire ran from the device into the collar of the guard's uniform. She pushed him onto his side and traced the wire down his back until it reached his waist. She pulled up on his jacket and discovered that the wire disappeared into a belt that was studded with various components, and which she concluded was the power supply and control mechanism for the weapon.

The belt had a twist lock that opened easily, and by the time Jadzia had donned it over her own uniform and was adjusting the visor to her head, Worf had run up the stairs with surprisingly little noise and had stopped beside her, his own phaser-visor already in place.

"Looks good," Jadzia told him. But looking through her own visor was like looking through transparent aluminum. She saw no holographic displays or any other indication of how the visor should be operated.

"Mine does not work, either," Worf said.

Jadzia tried pulling her loose belt tighter. "Maybe they're keyed to each individual user."

"Or they could require low-level Vulcan telepathy."

Jadzia realized there could be a dozen safeguards built into the visors, and even if she and Worf could get past them, they'd still not know how to aim and fire. "Okay, for now they're just fashion accessories."

Worf frowned. "This is not a time to joke."

Jadzia couldn't resist smiling at her mate. She knew that as far as Worf was concerned there never was a good time for a joke. "Good work taking out your guard. I knew you'd be thinking the same thing I was."

Something flashed through Worf's eyes that suddenly made Jadzia doubt he had been thinking the same as she had.

"Weren't you?" she asked.

"There were two earlier opportunities to attack. When you missed them both, I decided that *you* had not reached the same conclusion *I* had."

"So I took my time," she said. She most definitely intended to learn what the missed opportunities had been, but this wasn't the time for a debriefing. "But we're thinking the same thing now, right?"

"I hope so," Worf said seriously. "You are planning on locating the second hangar deck where they undoubtedly keep the shuttlecraft that were missing from the hangar deck we were beamed to."

"You want to hijack a shuttlecraft?" Jadzia asked incredulously.

"It is the best way to escape and find a source of information about this time that we can trust."

"I agree with the second part, but there's a much better way to escape than by taking over a shuttle."

Worf gave Jadzia a look she knew all too well—the one that said he was the warrior in the family and she was the scientist. "What better way?" he asked, and his tone suggested that he knew whatever she was about to say was wrong.

"We take over the ship."

"The two of us?"

Jadzia grinned. "If you'd like to go back to our quarters and rest, I can take care of it."

Worf grunted. "How?"

"First, we don't linger near the scene of the crime." She looked up and down the corridor, then started to run forward. Unlike all other Starfleet vessels she had been on, the *Augustus* had no maps or display boards in the corridors. And since the identification labels did not progress in any logical sequence, she decided to assume that the ship had been deliberately designed to make it difficult for any hostile boarding party to know where they were and where they should go.

But from what she recalled of the elongated shape of the vessel as she had seen it on the *Defiant*'s viewscreen, the odds were good that the bridge was ahead and no more than one or two decks higher.

Within two or three running strides, Worf had caught up to her, and together they ran to the next intersection.

Jadzia stopped in the middle of it, glancing port and starboard.

"How can you be sure we will not run into other guards?" Worf asked.

"Look at the ship's condition. It's filthy, poorly maintained. I bet they're running with less than half the crew they're supposed to have. That means double shifts, so everyone's either at their station or sleeping."

Worf adjusted the visor he wore—his prominent brow kept it from fitting securely across his face. "It is still dangerous to run without—"

Jadzia cut him off by pointing to a nearby door. "That one!" She ran to it, and as she looked for a control panel the door obligingly slid open before her.

"An unlocked compartment is not likely to contain critical components," Worf complained. But he dutifully followed her inside.

As the door slipped shut behind them, three small lighting fixtures flickered to life. Another sign that the *Augustus* wasn't operating at peak efficiency. The energy used to light the interior of a starship was usually negligible compared to what was required to run the warp engines or the replicators. But this ship was obviously set up to conserve even that insignificant amount of power.

"Why are we here?" Worf asked as he surveyed the room. It was almost the same size as the cabin they'd been given, but there was no furniture, and its walls were lined with conduits and cables.

"There!" Jadzia pointed to her quarry—a computer screen and control surface. "That won't have restricted access."

She went to the screen, and in only seconds she had called up a schematic of the ship. It was *Tiberius*-class, and seemed to have evolved from the *Defiant.* Almost three-quarters of its volume was devoted to warp engines and weapons systems. Only the central core of the ship contained significant life-support areas.

"This is good," Jadzia said as she made calculations based on the size of the habitable volume of the ship. "I'd say the regular crew complement wouldn't be more than fifty. So we're probably facing no more than thirty. That's just about two to one, and you're good for at least ten, so . . ." She looked back at Worf, but he wasn't paying attention to her. He was looking down at the deck. "Am I boring you?"

Worf was looking at the far bulkhead, and a sudden shaft of silver energy lanced from his visor to crackle against a bare spot between two conduits. "I have found the 'on' switch," Worf announced as he reached over to show her where her visor's activation controls were located, on the upper edge of her belt. Suddenly a rainbow collection of virtual squares appeared before her eyes, each about a centimeter across, and appearing to hover in mid-air a meter in front of her.

Then Worf touched another control on her belt and the squares seemed to float closer, until she could read their labels. Some corresponded to phaser controls. Others to tricorder functions.

"A combination phaser and tricorder?" she asked.

"Extremely efficient," Worf confirmed with approval. "It leaves both hands free to use a *bat'leth.*"

Jadzia looked past the holographic controls to give Worf a wry smile. "Exactly what I was thinking." She refocused on the controls, noticing that whichever one she looked at brightened. "How do you actually get it to fire?" she asked.

Worf quickly briefed her on the visor operating system, explaining that it appeared to be similar to the helmets worn by Starfleet warp-fighter pilots in their own time. After enabling the phaser functions, firing, it seemed, was as simple as looking at a target and blinking the right eye.

"This is better than I had hoped," Jadzia said.

Worf sighed. "Do you really think we have a chance at taking over their bridge? Even armed with these?"

Jadzia patted Worf's expansive chest. "We're not going to take over the bridge. Chances are it has defenses we can't even imagine. I had something different in mind."

This time Worf's sigh was even louder. "It is obvious we do *not* think alike, because I have no idea what you mean."

Jadzia was about to wink at Worf, then thought better of it, considering her visor's capabilities. Instead, she pointed to a spot on the ship's schematic that indicated a large cabin just down the corridor from the bridge. "What's more important than the bridge of a starship? Or should I say, *who* is more important?"

At last Worf smiled. Trill and Klingon, bound by love and duty, they were finally both sharing the same thought.

They waited in darkness—and they did not have to wait long. The door to the captain's stateroom slid open only minutes after Jadzia and Worf had easily bypassed the lock. For all the advanced firepower the *Augustus* carried, her designers had left out a considerable number of security amenities, including a weapons-suppression system, computer control of all interior locks, and a personnel-locator network. The only reason for the omissions Jadzia could imagine was that their absence made the ship simpler and faster to build. But what did the concepts of simpler and faster have to do with a construction project undertaken by robotic assemblers? All the mysteries in this time period were making her uncomfortable.

With the door opening and the lights coming on, Jadzia trusted that several of those mysteries might soon end.

As planned, the instant the door had slid shut again, Worf leaned out from his position sprawled behind the bunk and stunned Captain T'len with a blast from his triphaser.

The stun intensity was at the lowest setting, and T'len's hand fluttered toward her communicator as she slumped on the deck, semiconscious. But before the captain could report, Jadzia was at her side and removed her communicator badge. Then Worf tied the captain's hands and feet with lengths of fabric he ripped from the sheets on the bunk and carried her to the room's lone chair.

As T'len slowly regained awareness of what had happened to her, Jadzia studied the stateroom to see if she could build up a picture of what sort of person the captain was. But almost everything in it was Starfleet issue, not a hint of individuality anywhere. No paintings or framed holos. No books. Not even a Vulcan IDIC placed as a meditation aid.

Jadzia's examination ended with T'len's blunt statement. "You will not survive this attempt to take control of my ship."

"We've survived this long," Jadzia said easily. "We'll make it through a few more minutes."

Worf stood so that he was midway between the closed door and the captain, and he kept his gaze firmly on the door to challenge anyone who might come through it. "Captain T'len, what is our estimated arrival time at Starbase 53?"

"Eighteen hours, fourteen minutes."

"What will happen to us when we arrive?"

"To you? Nothing. Because you will be dead. To your fellow refugees, I cannot say. It was anticipated that they would be given a chance to demonstrate their suitability for continuing their service with Starfleet. However, if your actions are typical of what we can expect from them, they will be imprisoned."

"You knew we were coming, didn't you?" Jadzia said. It was the only explanation for how quickly the briefing program had been made available. It had been created for the crew of the *Defiant,* the Bolian admiral had said.

T'len nodded. "Several years after your disappearance, Starfleet researchers went back to the sensor logs recorded at the time of your disappearance and discovered clues suggesting the *Defiant* might have been pulled along the equivalent of a temporal-slingshot trajectory around the mouth of the second wormhole. The trajectory was calculated and the time of your reemergence into the timeline plotted."

"Why did we reemerge in interstellar space?" Worf asked.

Jadzia expanded the question. "Shouldn't we have reappeared around the wormhole?"

"You did not travel *into* the wormhole. You traveled *through* a region of space-time that was significantly distorted by the wormhole. The Bajoran system has moved on in the past twenty-five years, through a combination of its own relative motion and the rotation of the galaxy. Since the space-time distortion caused by the wormhole is not constant—as would be the case with the gravity well of a star—the absolute region of space you passed through was unbound, and moved at a different rate."

Jadzia felt vindicated. "Given your knowledge of the second wormhole, I'd say Starfleet has done considerable research into it."

"These are desperate times," T'len said, looking down at the torn sheets that bound her hands and feet together.

"A Vulcan admitting to desperation?" Jadzia asked.

"You saw the briefing that was prepared for you," the captain replied. "Logic is in short supply at this time."

"Exactly what I was thinking," Jadzia agreed. "Now tell me—what *wasn't* on the briefing?"

"That question is too broad."

"I don't believe the Federation would enter into a war against any system just to wipe out a religion."

"Perhaps not in your time."

"Are you serious?" Jadzia asked, hating the implications of T'len's answer. "This War of the Prophets *is* what the briefing described?"

T'len looked up at the ceiling, an odd gesture for a Vulcan to make. "Starfleet's objective in this war, undeclared or not, is to gain entry into the Bajoran system and destroy the red wormhole and any and all artifacts of importance to the subset of Bajoran faith known as Ascendant."

Jadzia could see that even Worf looked shocked by T'len's words. "What about the Prime Directive?"

"It is no longer operative."

Jadzia stared at T'len. "I can't believe I heard a Starfleet officer say that."

"Commander Dax, this is a war of survival. Either *we* destroy the Ascendants, or they *will* destroy us."

"Because of their religious beliefs?"

"Precisely."

Worf shared Jadzia's incomprehension. "You will have to explain to us how a belief based in personal faith can pose a danger to the Federation."

"Not just the Federation," T'len said grimly.

"Captain," Jadzia asked in sudden apprehension, "*what* exactly do the Ascendants believe?"

The captain's explanation did nothing to make Jadzia more comfortable.

CHAPTER 10

ON SIX SWIFT LEGS, the Cardassian vole scurried along the overhead power conduit mounted near the top of the bulkhead just outside the *Boreth*'s main engineering station. Visually indistinguishable in color from the stained Klingon structural panels that lined the ship's corridor, the diminutive orange creature froze in the shadows near the ceiling, almost as if to avoid being heard by the sensitive ears of the two Romulans passing by below.

But when the two stopped, and each reached out in turn for the engineering security panel, the vole's tiny head jutted forward, its spine nobs pulsing in time with its rapid breathing, the hairless flaps of its bat-like ears flattening close to its skull, its glittering, bulbous eyes focusing on each move the Romulans made as they tapped out their individual security codes.

The engineering doors slid open.

In the same instant, the vole released the opposable

claws of its two front pairs of legs and dropped from the conduit, straight for the Romulans—

—who didn't even bother to look up as the annoying buzz of a Klingon *glob* fly swerved around them, then vanished into the cavernous upper levels of the largest open area on the *Boreth.*

Seconds later, before the Engineering doors could close, the Cardassian vole gripped the edge of a second-level safety rail with its claws, then vaulted to engineering's upper deck and slipped through the narrow gap between two heavily shielded quantum-wave decouplers, both aglow with flickering status lights. Just then, an exhausted Romulan technician who had been working all shift to trace the source of an intermittent photon leak near the decouplers glanced away from her padd toward the gap. And saw a dim orange blur streak by.

A momentary frown creased the technician's face. The *Boreth,* however, was a vast ship and contained a veritable secondary ecosystem of parasites and vermin, so the sighting of the occasional pest was not worth reporting. Thus duty won out over curiosity. The photon leak was real. The technician dismissed the fleeting sighting.

And far back in the twisted labyrinth of barely passable access paths that ran behind the wall of power relays that supplied the ship's Romulan-designed singularity inhibitor, the vole stopped, and after looking all around took a deep, squeaky breath and began to *expand.* . . .

In the shadows of engineering, Odo watched carefully as his humanoid hands sprouted from the sleeves of his Bajoran constable's uniform. Unlike the other, more common shapeshifting creatures in the galaxy, changelings such as he had the ability to alter their mass as well as their form. Though it was a completely instinctive process, Odo's first mentor in the world of solids, Dr. Mora Pol, had theorized that Odo's ability to alter the shape of his molecular structure actually enabled him to form four-dimensional lattices in the shape of hyperspheres and tesseracts—geometric shapes that could not exist in only three dimensions.

In effect, this allowed Odo to shunt some of his mass into another dimension, depending on the requirements of the form he assumed. Odo acknowledged that as a scientific problem his innate ability was interesting, and that Pol's theory, if true, made some sort of sense. Yet because of Dr. Pol's belief that changelings faced the risk of inadvertently pushing too much of themselves into that other dimension and disappearing altogether, Odo still experienced unease when attempting to reduce his mass to a matter of micrograms. As a result he had seldom dared push his shape-changing ability to the extremes of becoming anything as small as a Klingon *glob* fly, a creature only half the size of a Terran mosquito.

Since learning more about his true nature from his fellow changelings in the Great Link, Odo had learned that Dr. Pol's fear resulted from his misunderstanding the shapeshifting process; still, old habits died hard, and Odo still felt uncomfortable transforming himself into anything smaller than voles or creatures of similar size.

Relieved at his uneventful reversion to normal humanoid mass and size, Odo now turned to the one or two details still requiring his attention.

On his reconnaissance mission he had observed that almost all crew members of the *Boreth* wore uniforms apparently modified from something similar to the one he had customarily worn on Deep Space 9. Except that the *Boreth* crew uniforms featured slightly different shades of brown-and-tan fabric and had a single swath of a contrasting color running across the chest from shoulder to shoulder, instead of the two seemingly separate shoulder pieces his own uniform displayed. Also for some reason, Odo recalled, the *Boreth* crew uniforms were an invariably sloppy fit, as if the ship's clothing replicators no longer had accurate measuring capabilities.

Still the changes were simple, and as he now formed a mental picture of himself wearing a new uniform, Odo sensed the familiar rippling and shifting of his outer self as his external uniform updated itself to the new standard appearance, its surface even sagging and bunching to suggest a bad fit. Then, just to further the illusion should he be seen in engineering, Odo gave his head a shake, and his sleek, brushed-back hair—a near duplicate of Dr. Pol's own style and color—slithered forward to become black Romulan bangs. At the same time his simply shaped ears elongated slightly to form Vulcanoid points, and his brow became more pronounced. Odo knew that under normal lighting conditions there would still be an unfinished look to his features (despite his ability to duplicate every vane of every feather on an avian species, the far less demanding details of a humanoid face had always remained such a difficult challenge for him he sometimes wondered if his people had engineered a sort of facial inhibition into him when they'd adjusted his genetic code, to make him long to return to his homeworld). At least, he reasoned, his new Romulan form would offer some protection during his passage through engineering, while he committed the acts of sabotage so painstakingly planned by O'Brien and Rom.

Captain Sisko, of course, had given his express approval for the operation. From the briefing the survivors from the *Defiant* had received only a few hours ago, it had become obvious to all that despite the Starfleet emblems that adorned this vessel, the institution served by the crew of the *Boreth* bore no allegiance nor resemblance to the Starfleet of twenty-five years past. The emblems, in the captain's judgment, were a lie. Odo and the other survivors suspected the briefing was also.

Odo directed his attention to an exposed bulkhead between two large and unidentifiable cylindrical housings, where he found a power-relay switching box surrounded by a nest of conduits. The box itself was a meter tall, no more than a half-meter wide, and labeled with a Bajoran identification plate that had been haphazardly attached over a Klingon sign. From what Chief O'Brien had seen of the *Boreth*'s power-distribution system as he was led through the corridors, he had told Odo he was confident that the switching mechanisms in the ship would not have changed significantly since their own time. Odo studied the Bajoran plate more closely, confirming for himself that it did use the same terminology with which he was familiar. Still, when he swung open the access panel, he was relieved to see that the layout of the box's interior was indeed very close to what Rom had described.

At any given time, Odo was aware from experience, a starship generated a constant amount of power for internal use, though the demands on that power varied according to what subsystems—from replicators to sonic showers—were operating from second to second. Thus, a ship's power-distribution system was constantly adjusting the amount of power, available as either basic electricity or the more complex wave-forms of transtator current, that moved through specific sections of the ship's power grid and prevented localized surges, brownouts, and overloads. Odo knew that interfering with that system would, as a matter of course, make such interruptions in the flow of power more likely. And a properly timed interruption that affected engineering could have the desired result of forcing the *Boreth* to drop from warp. That, in fact, was Odo's goal.

Sisko had admitted that it was a risky plan, but the captain had also thought it likely that, given the speed with which the vessels of the other Starfleet had attacked the *Opaka*, if the *Boreth* were to lose warp propulsion in deep space, it would also come under swift attack.

Odo concentrated on transforming his fingers into right-angled wiring grippers in order to disconnect an inline series of transpolar compensators. He trusted that Kira would be as successful with her half of the mission: obtaining a Bajoran combadge from one of the guards watching over the *Defiant*'s rescued crew and passengers. His Deep Space 9 colleague had taken the challenge because, whatever the truth of this future, as Bajorans Kira and Commander Arla were not subject to the same level of scrutiny as the other survivors. Consequently, Kira and Arla had each been given separate staterooms, while the remaining sixteen . . . *prisoners,* Odo decided was the best term for them . . . had been grouped into four main barracks-type rooms, each room featuring enough tiered bunks for twenty-one crew. O'Brien had identified the holding areas as enlisted men's communal quarters—a living area typical of some Klingon warships.

Whatever the barracks' original purpose, Odo had been pleased enough to have been placed in so large a confinement chamber. It had made it easier to move to the back of the room nearest the sanitary facilities and discreetly transform himself into the Klingon insect capable of escaping through the door with the departing guards. While he had originally planned to reach engineering through the ventilation shafts, the Chief had been quick to point out to him that various environmental systems on the ship employed charged grids specifically designed to incinerate unwanted pests.

Odo gave a final twist to the secondary connector ring, and the status lights of the compensators winked out. One down, five to go. By O'Brien's calculations, if he could compromise at least six relay switches within engineering, and then short-circuit a seventh, he'd be able to cause a surge that would interrupt power to the ship's warp generators long enough to trigger an automatic safety shutdown. Although the chief engineer had doubted it would take the crew of the *Boreth* more than ten minutes to bring their ship back into warp, if Kira had her communicator and Rom *was* able to reconfigure it and there *were* real Starfleet vessels nearby, Odo reckoned that ten minutes might be just long enough to bring the *Boreth* under attack.

Whether that attack would result in the rescue of the *Defiant*'s survivors now held prisoner on the *Boreth* was a risk everyone had accepted. Action, in Odo's experience, was always preferable to imprisonment.

First changing the right-angled grippers at the end of his arm back into a hand, he carefully shut the access panel and glanced around his cramped work area. In the dim light, there appeared to be another power-relay switching box four meters along the bulkhead, mounted between two large vertical pipes. Odo approached the switching box, located the release latch for its cover and, just as he was about to open it, heard a soft voice in his ear murmur, "Odo. You can stop now."

Startled, Odo stepped back, unsuccessfully scanning the shadows and darkness for the source of the voice. He couldn't be sure, but it had sounded like Weyoun. Either Weyoun himself was here, or his voice had been relayed through an overhead communications speaker. It was unclear which.

Odo quickly decided against staying long enough to find out. He took a breath, formed a mental image of a vole, and—

—nothing.

Odo tried again.

And again. But his shape appeared to be locked in his half-formed Romulan disguise.

"Such a useful precaution," Weyoun's voice said breathily, from nowhere and from everywhere, "the inhibitor."

Odo simultaneously blinked and stepped back, as a small cylindrical device suddenly appeared to be hovering a few meters in front of him. One end was segmented like a series of stacked golden rings, the other bore a black panel dotted with sequentially flashing lights.

"The original was developed by the Obsidian Order." To Odo, it was as if Weyoun were speaking from the unsupported device, and he wondered if antigravs had actually been miniaturized to such an extent. "A very long and arduous process, as I'm sure you know. Then Damar had it further refined. I believe he was planning on betraying the Founder . . . once the Dominion-Cardassian alliance had proved victorious over the Federation, of course."

And suddenly Weyoun's pale face appeared in midair, smiling with a distracted expression, near the floating inhibitor. Then, with a series of jerky movements, the rest of Weyoun's body came into view.

Odo stared in amazement, as a flurry of small energy discharges revealed the Vorta before him in his entirety, half-dressed in a vedek's robes, half in what could only be an isolation suit with its cloaking field switched off.

"Also a most useful device, wouldn't you agree?" Weyoun said as he stepped neatly out of the bulky red suit and let it fall to the deck. "I'm surprised you people forgot about it. It was a Starfleet invention, after all. Apparently, something called Section 31 reverse-engineered the Romulan cloaking device on the *Defiant*. Quite illegal. It's fascinating what the passage of time brings to the release of secret documents."

Odo had no idea what Weyoun was talking about, and didn't care to know. "Turn off the inhibitor," he said.

Weyoun looked at the device in his hand, shrugged. "I don't think so."

Odo regarded him sternly. "I gave you an order."

"So you did."

Odo was uncomfortable with what he had to say next, but in this one limited case, surely the end justified the means. "Weyoun, I am your god. Do as I say."

Unexpectedly, Weyoun moved toward him, holding out the device as if making an offering of it. "Odo, do you realize you've never spoken to me like that before," the Vorta said as if concerned for his welfare. "I don't believe you know how much it has always troubled me to see you so conflicted, refusing to admit what you are, what you have meant to me."

"Well, I don't refuse to admit it any longer. Turn off the—"

The cylinder struck Odo's face like a club, knocking him to the deck.

Odo held a hand to his all-too-solid face. The pain was intense, and he looked up at Weyoun in shock. The Vorta appeared to be trembling in the throes of nervous excitement.

"I can't tell you how many times in the past twenty-five years I've wondered if I could do that. Did it hurt?"

Slowly, Odo got to his feet, only now recalling Sisko's warning that Weyoun had somehow overcome his genetic imperative to regard changelings as gods. "Yes."

"And that was just a simple blow. Imagine what it must feel like . . . to die."

Odo braced himself. Not only did Weyoun's attack confirm that the Vorta was capable of striking one of the beings he used to worship, it seemed he was preparing himself to kill. Only one explanation was possible. Weyoun was a clone and this one was defective.

"I'm not defective," the Vorta said before Odo could state his conclusion. "I prefer to regard myself as restored. Cured. Freed?" The Vorta shrugged. "The important thing is, I can finally think for myself."

"Perhaps," Odo growled, "you've just been more effectively programmed."

Weyoun merely grinned. "I wondered that myself, Odo, after I returned from the True Temple. After all, if some minor realignment of my amino acids were responsible for my former belief that you and your people were gods, I realized I really couldn't rule out the possibility that some other agency might have made a further modification in my program."

"And what answer did you find?" *As if I don't know,* Odo thought sourly.

As if delighted to share a confidence with one who would truly understand, Weyoun favored him with an intimate smile. "First, I returned to my own homeworld, as it were. To the Dominion cloning facilities on Rondac III. I awoke one of the other Weyouns. And you know, the most sophisticated medical scans showed that there was absolutely no difference between myself and him. Except in our thoughts and beliefs."

"Weyoun Eight believed the Founders were gods."

The Vorta sighed. "To the end, sadly."

Odo snorted. "You mean, you killed him."

Weyoun pursed his mouth, pious. "He was defective, Odo. It was a mercy."

"And what happens when the next Weyoun tracks you down and decides *you're* defective?"

"There is, there will be, *no* next Weyoun," Weyoun said firmly. "*I* am the last. The cloning facility, you see, had . . . outlived its usefulness."

"You mean, you destroyed it."

"You know very well it was in Cardassian territory, so—technically—the Cardassians must take the blame for its loss, because they would not surrender. Believe me, Odo, I would have preferred to have kept at least some other Vorta around to help me through these difficult years."

"You're sure you're the last of your kind?"

Weyoun nodded. "Just as you are the last of yours. At least in the Alpha Quadrant. Isn't that reason enough that we should be united in our purpose?"

"And what purpose would that be?" Odo steeled himself to continue the discussion with the odious creature before him. The more Weyoun babbled on, the more information he would supply that might suggest a way out of this intolerable situation.

"Think of the suffering you've endured, Odo."

Odo loathed the false concern in Weyoun's oily voice, but gave no outward indication of his feelings, waiting to see what the Vorta really wanted from him.

Encouraged, Weyoun warmed to his argument that he and Odo were soulmates. "Cast out by your own people. Forced to become a plaything of Bajoran and Cardassian scientists. Never really belonging to any world, even your own when you returned to the Great Link. But you and I . . . we share so much pain. Isn't it right and proper that we should dedicate our lives to eliminating pain forever?"

"Pain is a necessary part of life," Odo said gruffly. "It enables us to appreciate pleasure."

Weyoun gazed at him thoughtfully. "I never knew you had such a philosophical streak in you."

"Do you really want to end my pain?" Odo asked skeptically. "And the pain of all the others from the *Defiant?*"

Weyoun bowed his head as he had done countless times in Odo's presence, but not this time to Odo. "The cessation of pain, the onset of joy . . . that is the will and the one goal of the True Prophets," he intoned.

"Then free us," Odo said.

Weyoun sighed, lifting his head. "You're not being held prisoner here. You're being protected."

"It seems some words have changed their meanings in the past twenty-five years."

"Not words, Odo. The galaxy has changed. The Federation has become an abomination. Starfleet an organization of brutal murderers. If I gave you a shuttlecraft and sent you to . . . to Vulcan . . . or Andor, do you know how long you'd last?" Weyoun didn't even pause before answering his own question. "They'd shoot you out of space before you finished opening hailing frequencies."

For no distinct reason he could articulate, Odo was beginning to feel that he really wasn't in immediate danger from Weyoun. It was obvious that the Vorta had been changed in some way. Whatever set of neurons in his brain had been programmed to revere changelings had somehow been reconfigured to revere the Pah-wraiths instead. Recalling that once even the Ferengi Grand Nagus Zek had been altered beyond recognition, having entered the first wormhole, only to reemerge as an altruist determined to give away his fortune. As a result, Odo now had little doubt that alteration of fundamental personality traits was well within the capability of wormhole beings.

But still it somehow also appeared to Odo that Weyoun maintained a type of residual respect for him. The Vorta seemed anxious that he talk with him, listen to him, perhaps even come to understand him. And just as Weyoun's worship of him had been advantageous in the past, Odo decided that in this situation, it was still worth capitalizing on any remaining shadow of that behavior, no matter how distasteful it was.

"Weyoun," he began, without a trace of his previous challenging attitude, choosing instead to play along altogether with whatever Weyoun was up to, "I acknowledge there is a great deal about this time I don't understand. But if there is just one question you can answer for me now, then tell me: Why are the people from the *Defiant* so dangerous to the Starfleet of this time that they would kill us on sight?"

Odo was gratified by the effect of his changed tone on Weyoun, who responded by lowering the inhibitor and no longer making a point of threatening him with it. "Rest assured it's not you, Odo. It's Captain Sisko."

Odo kept his surprise to himself. "Why him?"

The Vorta regarded Odo earnestly. "Because he's the False Emissary to the False Prophets. And according to prophecies of Jalbador, the One True Temple cannot be restored until the False Emissary accepts the True Emissary."

Weyoun's face became grave. "There are those in Starfleet who have determined that if they can prevent Captain Sisko from being present when the two halves of the Temple at last open in conjunction, the Day of Ascendancy will be postponed for millennia."

It was beginning to make sense to Odo. "So everyone knew that the *Defiant* hadn't been destroyed along with DS9. That the ship had been caught in a temporal rift."

Weyoun nodded. "Not at once, of course. But as the Ascendancy regained its rightful position of primacy on Bajor—oh, I tell you, Odo, no world has ever seen such a cultural flowering. You would not believe the treasures those Bajoran monks concealed over the centuries, because they contradicted the teachings of the False Prophets. It is only now that ancient texts thought lost forever have been brought out into the light. Together with all of the writings and prophecies that . . . that the world had forgotten even existed, all of them hidden in caverns, walled-up in temples. . . ."

Odo forgot himself for a moment. "And these texts, these writings, described the *Defiant*'s return, did they?"

But Weyoun just smiled, and waggled a finger at him. "I hear that skeptical tone. And, no, the ancient texts didn't say that a twenty-fourth-century starship named the *Defiant* would be caught in a temporal rift only to reappear twenty-five years later."

"Didn't think so."

"Ah, but several texts did say that the False Emissary would arise from those who had perished at the fall of the gateway, just as I explained to Captain Sisko. The three great mystics of Jalbador—Shabren, Eilin, and Naradim—they had to describe their visions in the context of their time, you know."

"Weyoun," Odo said, choosing his words with care, "I have no doubt that ancient mystical texts can be interpreted to support recent events. Humanoids have been doing that for millennia on hundreds of worlds. What I find troubling is that you say Starfleet has also accepted these interpretations."

"What's left of Starfleet. Yes."

"Then what I don't understand is why Starfleet would accept that the writings on which you base your faith are true, yet not then also accept your faith."

Weyoun's smile faded from his face, and for just an instant Odo thought he detected the flash of a red shift in the Vorta's clear gray eyes. "In the final battle to determine the fate of the universe," Weyoun said passionately, "Starfleet, for reasons which no sane mind can comprehend, has chosen to support the wrong side. Could we say they are afraid of that which they don't understand? That they're afraid of change? Or is it something simpler, Odo? Can we simply say that in a universe in which all sentient beings have been given free choice, some, invariably, will choose evil?"

The Vorta paused as if in contact with something or someone of which Odo was unaware, and then disconcertingly began speaking again as if there had been no interruption in his speech. "These same questions have been asked since the True Prophets created sentient beings in their own image, and I doubt we will answer them here in engineering."

Even though he sensed Weyoun becoming threatening again, Odo pushed on.

"Weyoun, all things being equal, how can I know that it's not you who've chosen . . . evil?"

The Vorta studied him for a moment before responding. "You know, if my crew had heard that question come from you, Odo, not even I could have acted fast enough to save your life. If anyone else had asked that question, I would not even try to save him. But you and I . . . ?" Weyoun sighed deeply. "I will make allowances. But just this once. Do you understand?"

Odo nodded. "I understand I'm not to question you like that again."

An appreciative smile touched Weyoun's mouth. "Spoken like a Vorta." And then he was deadly serious again. "If you truly want to know who has allied themselves with the forces of evil, consider this, Odo: *My* forces rescued you and your ship from a Starfleet attack wing."

"Only," Odo interjected, "because you need Captain Sisko to fulfill your prophecy."

"Exactly!" Weyoun said, apparently unoffended by the interruption. "I do need Captain Sisko alive. But the ancient texts say nothing about you, Odo. Or about the others I saved with your captain. If I were serving some evil purpose, would it make sense for me to keep you all alive? Or would I simply have you killed? Just as those Starfleet ships tried to do?"

The Vorta held up his inhibitor device and checked its energy level. "It's time for you to go back to the others now, Odo. Tell them what we've talked about. Be especially sure to tell Captain Sisko that if this ill-conceived escape attempt by some unimaginable set of circumstances had worked, all he would have been escaping from was *my* protection, while at the same time delivering himself up to those whose only goal is to kill him."

Weyoun twisted a control on the inhibitor and, shockingly, Odo felt his outer surface instantly begin to lose its integrity, shifting from his Romulan disguise to his usual humanoid form.

Weyoun waved the inhibitor at him. "I think you would agree, Odo, that my scientists have made a great many advances in the time you've been gone. Just remember I can use this to turn you into a cube of duranium and have you thrown out an airlock if I have to."

Odo shivered in spite of himself. In a way, the experience of forced transformation had been like being in the Great Link. But in *that* surrender of individuality he himself had made the choice. Weyoun's machine had just chosen for him.

Weyoun's voice again filled his ears. "Tell Sisko what I've told you," the Vorta said with finality. "If you want to live, I am the only hope you have."

CHAPTER 11

IT HAD BEEN two years since he had had a new uniform. These days, replicator rations for nonessentials were nearly impossible to obtain. But while the words "nearly impossible" might be a roadblock for some Starfleet captains, to a Ferengi Starfleet captain they were a challenge. So two days ago, beginning with a priceless bottle of Picard champagne—vintage 2382, the last great year before the Earth's destruction—Nog had begun a complex series of trades that had not only resulted in his obtaining enough priority replicator rations to requisition ten new uniforms, but he had also acquired use of one of the last remaining private yachts in Sector 001.

Technically, the *Cerulean Star* was the property of the Andorian trade representative in New Berlin. But since the trade mission didn't have access to adequate civilian antimatter supplies, the yacht had not been used in ten months, and the New Berlin representative was certain that no one at her consulate would miss it—provided Nog returned it in three days and left enough Starfleet antimatter in the ship to reach Andor.

Given his transit time to Starbase 53, that left Nog thirty hours to pick up his passengers and warp back to Mars. There would then be ten days left until the end of the universe.

"But at least I'll face it wearing a new uniform," Nog said aloud.

He stood in the surprisingly large stateroom of the Andorian yacht, in standard orbit of a heavily-shielded Class-B asteroid in the lifeless Largo system, checking his virtual reflection in the holographic mirror that circled him. Over the past year, he had noticed how his old uniforms had begun to fray, but not how the color at his shoulder had faded. This new uniform was an impressively rich black—it showed every speck of dust and lint—and its shoulder was a vivid, saturated crimson. Not quite a dress uniform, but it would do. Because for what he was about to attempt, he was determined to look his best.

Satisfied that the uniform was as perfect as he had time to make it, Nog donned a matching crimson headskirt and tapped his combadge.

"Captain Nog," he said. "One to beam down."

There was no verbal acknowledgment of his request, but he was on schedule, and three seconds later the Andorian stateroom dissolved into light, then reformed as the transporter room in Starbase 53's main ground installation, deep within the asteroid's core.

As Nog had arranged, Captain T'len of the *Augustus* was waiting for him.

"Captain," Nog said as he stepped down from the pad, "it is good to see you again."

T'len kept her hands folded behind her back. "This is most irregular."

Nog hid a smile. He liked Vulcans. They never wasted time—an attribute he had come to appreciate during his Starfleet career. "I agree," he said.

T'len raised an eyebrow. "I refer to your request, not the overall situation."

Nog was ready for that. "If it were not for the overall situation, I wouldn't have made my request."

T'len angled her head slightly in the Vulcan equivalent of a shrug. "Point taken." She gestured to the door, and Nog hung back a step to let her lead the way. Though they shared the same rank, T'len was also a starship commander, and in the subtle, unwritten traditions of the Fleet, that gave her greater privilege.

Nog followed in T'len's wake as she turned left outside the transporter room and walked toward the turbolift. Automatically, he noticed yet discounted the poor state of repair of the walls—sizable dents, repair patches of differing colors, irregular stains from cracked conduits that had leaked in the past. Starfleet had been operating under extreme wartime conditions for more than ten years. Mere appearance, like frayed uniforms, was not at the top of anyone's list of problems to solve.

"How have they adjusted?" Nog asked T'len, as they neared the turbolift alcove.

"Impossible to characterize except on an individual basis."

"So, some of them have adjusted better than others?"

Nog caught T'len's swift sideways glance at him. "If their state of adjustment varies according to each individual, then logic suggests that of course some have adjusted better than others. You will find out for yourself in just a few minutes."

"I'd like to be prepared."

The Vulcan seemed to accept that explanation. "Then you should be prepared for the human civilian Vash. I have recommended that she remain in custody here, until . . . the end of hostilities."

What a euphemism, Nog thought, and he wondered who had first used it. Hostilities would end in less than two weeks, either with Starfleet's being successful in obliterating most of Bajor or with the end of the universe. At the end of hostilities, either Vash would be released, everyone would have new uniforms, walls would be painted, planet-wide celebrations would be held . . . or else nothing would ever matter again.

But the end of the universe was not a topic of conversation in which Starfleet officers engaged. Quite properly, official directives stressed that all personnel were to focus on the mission, not the consequences.

"What's Vash likely to do?" Nog asked. "Escape?"

"In a manner of speaking. She is intent on returning to her own time."

Nog knew better, but couldn't resist. "Would that be so bad?"

T'len stopped and turned to him. "If Vash returned to her time and revealed what she had learned of our time, history would be changed."

"I ask the question again: Would that be so bad?"

Nog was not naive enough to interpret T'len's expression of surprise as evidence of her abandonment of all pretense of Vulcan self-control. "Captain Nog, you are the Integrated Systems Manager for the *Phoenix.*"

Though not quite sure why T'len was stating something so obvious, Nog waited, gambling on her explaining herself without his having to interrupt.

"Thus you understand the logic of time travel," she said.

Nog frowned. "Some would say there is no logic to time travel."

T'len looked away for a moment as if gathering her thoughts—as if a Vulcan ever needed to do that. "If Vash—or indeed, if any of the crew of the *Defiant*—are allowed to return to their present, only two end results are possible. One, Vash changes the past, and we will no longer exist as we are, and the billions of beings born in the past twenty-five years will likely never exist at all. Two, Vash changes the past, and in so doing she creates a new timeline while we remain in ours—exactly as it is, unchanged."

Nog shook his head. "Think of the billions who have died in the past twenty-five years," he said. "Think of Earth. Of Cardassia Prime."

T'len eyed Nog with what Nog felt could only be disappointment. "Captain Nog, in each generation are born a mere handful of great beings. Your Admiral Picard is surely one of them. Perhaps one other starship captain in all of Starfleet's history has matched his accomplishments. But if only one example of his brilliance is required, then we need look no further than Project Phoenix. To change history *without* changing our timeline is a concept as revolutionary as Hawking's normalization of the Heisenberg exceptions."

Suddenly, T'len's attitude, however subtly, seemed to Nog to soften. "Even as a Vulcan," she said, "I do understand what you are about to experience will be fraught with emotion. You are about to open a door to your own past. But do not allow yourself to be trapped by it. Jean-Luc Picard has given us a true phoenix. Trust in him, Captain. As a Starfleet officer, you can do no less."

"Trust *me,* Captain," Nog said emphatically. "I have no intention of doing anything else."

Nog's eyes deliberately met and held the Vulcan's as steadily as if he were negotiating difficult delivery dates with a recalcitrant supplier. And he was certain that Captain T'len in no way detected the lie he had just brazenly uttered.

It's good to be a Ferengi, Nog thought proudly, and not for the first time in his long Starfleet career. His people's four-lobed brains were resistant to most forms of telepathy, and negotiation skills continued to be taught to Ferengi youngsters at an age when most other humanoid babies were only learning to say their first words.

T'len nodded once as she led the way to the turbolift, and they rode the rest of the way to the conference room in silence. It was the Vulcan way. And Nog was glad of it.

In the command conference room of Starbase 53, Jake Sisko knew he was the most nervous of all the temporal refugees from the *Defiant.* Which wasn't to say that tension wasn't high for all the other survivors—officers and civilians, humans and Bajorans alike.

At first, this trip into the future had been just an adventure. High-risk and demanding, but when hadn't space exploration been that way?

But that had all changed only hours after he and the other survivors on the *Augustus* were shown the suspicious briefing tape. Right after viewing that tape, he and the others had been called to another briefing, this time at the request of Worf and Jadzia. The revelations in that second gathering had concerned the past twenty-five years' worth of history in this timeline that they had missed. Suddenly, all that had been left unsaid in the first briefing came into focus for Jake.

In the bluntest of terms, what the people of this time faced was nothing less than the impending end of the universe.

Until the moment Jadzia and Worf and Captain T'len had related this incredible news, almost every pair of captives on board the *Augustus* had already been engaged in planning an escape or an attempt to seize control of the surprisingly deficient ship. Because Worf and Jadzia had been first to take action, they had been the first to learn the truth.

Now no one was planning to escape. Except maybe Vash.

What appeared to be holding the others together at this moment, in Jake's view, was the shared opinion that if the end of the universe were approaching, it was because of what had been done and not done by all present during the last days of Deep Space 9. Although no one was talking about this upsetting conclusion, Jake felt certain that everyone believed in its truth.

Which meant in a way, he realized, that the fifteen temporal refugees from his time were now feeling responsible for everything that had happened in this time during the past twenty-five years, and which was now leading to disaster. How could they not stay here, in this time, to do everything they could to try and reverse what they had set in motion?

"So, you know this big shot?" Vash suddenly asked him.

Jake knew his uncertain smile betrayed his nervousness. He had always known that Nog would do well in Starfleet, and he was gratified to learn that his childhood Ferengi friend was a captain now. But he was having some difficulty thinking of Nog as a "big shot." And it was odder still to think that in just a few moments the doors were going to open and his old friend was going to step through them. *Twenty-five* years older.

"He's—he was—my best friend," Jake told Vash.

"Really." Vash ran her hands along her newly supplied gray-and-black uniform. The gesture was clearly meant to be provocative.

"Nice uniforms, hmm?" she said with a smile, as his eyes involuntarily followed the seductive movement of her hands.

Jake snapped his eyes back to Vash's face with an effort. All fifteen refugees had been given Starfleet uniforms of the day to wear. The Starfleet officers among them had received their equivalent rank and specialty markings. The Bajorans and civilians had been given a variant of the uniform that reminded Jake of what cadets used to wear. Instead of being mostly black, the main uniform was a ribbed gray fabric, leaving only the shoulder section black. The supply officer had explained that the uniform identified them as civilian specialists within the Fleet, subject to Fleet regulations.

Jake had been surprised that the uniforms were issued from a storeroom and not a replicator station, and even more surprised that nothing fit as well as it should—though he supposed that was to be expected when clothes weren't replicated with the benefit of a somatic topography scan.

But whoever had given Vash her specialist uniform must have expended some extra effort in determining her size, because to Jake it fit her to perfection. And she obviously knew it.

"Sorry," Jake stammered, having no idea what to say next. "I . . . yeah, Nog's my best friend." *What an idiot I am,* he thought.

"How old are you?" Vash asked with a frank grin.

"I'll be twenty next month."

"Nineteen . . . what do you think your father would say if we . . ." Vash let her voice trail off suggestively.

Is there even a chance? Jake thought in amazement. He, like everyone else who knew them, had assumed that Vash and Dr. Bashir were . . . He abruptly stopped that line of thought and shifted direction. "Um, I . . . uh, dated a dabo girl once. A couple of years back. That was okay with my dad . . . he even made us dinner."

Vash studied him as if she were really listening to him. "A dabo girl. How educational for you."

Jake nodded, watching her carefully for any signs that she was making fun of him. It actually had been, but not in the way Vash meant. Or did she—

"And after dinner," Vash continued, "was your date arrested, or did she just leave the station?"

Jake frowned. "Uh, Mardah left, yeah. She was accepted at the Regulus Science Academy."

"Let me guess. Your *father* wrote her a great letter of recommendation."

Jake sighed. "Look, I didn't mean to—"

"It's okay, Jake. We'll be friends. We'll go to . . . dinner a couple of years from now. We won't invite your father."

Jake nodded, half-disappointed, half-relieved, then suddenly added, "A couple of years from now. . . . So you think we're going to make it through this?"

Vash pointed to someone standing behind Jake. "Don't ask me. Ask him."

Jake turned to see whom Vash meant. A Ferengi standing in an open doorway beside Captain T'len. A Ferengi who looked like Nog, but wasn't.

This man was about five kilos heavier, with even larger earlobes, and his face seemed drawn, the brown skin weathered and wrinkled around the careworn, sunken eyes and—

"Jake," Nog said in the voice Jake remembered from only four days ago on DS9, "it *is* me."

Jake suddenly felt even more uncomfortable than when Vash had teased him into staring at her. He just knew that a look of shock had swept over his face, with his realization that this grizzled veteran *was* his friend, and that his friend was now so . . . so *old.* In the waves of emotions that broke over him, the strongest was one of sorrow. For all the time passed and not shared.

"Nog. . . ." Jake couldn't say anything else. His throat was suddenly swollen shut.

But Nog shook his head as if in understanding, and stepped forward and hugged him strongly, slapping his back, then looked up at him, beaming. "Just as I remember you. Not a day older. Not a *day* . . ."

Jake saw Nog's old-young eyes begin to glisten as if filling with tears. But then his friend looked away, bared his artfully twisted fangs and called out, "Dr. Bashir! Commander Dax!"

Jake broke away from Nog as his friend greeted all the others, the Ferengi's salutations ending with an awkward pause as he came face-to-face with Worf.

"Commander," Nog said formally, "Starfleet has missed you. And so have I."

"You are a captain," Worf replied gravely. "You do honor to your family and to your father."

And then Starfleet formality between Klingon and Ferengi broke down as Nog spread his arms again and Worf embraced the diminutive officer in a bearhug that Jake knew could fell a *sehlat.*

Finally Worf released his grip, and Nog dropped a few centimeters to the floor, then tugged down on his jacket and turned to face everyone. He cleared his throat noisily. "My friends . . . oh, my friends . . . I almost don't know where to begin."

But Jadzia did. "Captain T'len," the Trill officer said, "has been very efficient in bringing us up to date. We understand the danger threatening . . . everything. And we know that you're here to make a proposal to us about how we can help Starfleet destroy Bajor."

Jake grimaced. Intellectually, he knew he was in a different time, with a much different Starfleet. But emotionally, he was still having a very hard time understanding how anyone from Starfleet could say something like that. His thoughts flew back to when he was a small child in San Francisco and his mother and his father had first explained the Prime Directive to him. He remembered his favorite interactive holobooks, in which Flotter and Trevis had helped children discover the need for the Prime Directive in the Forest of Forever. But in this future—Nog's future—it was as if the Prime Directive had never been issued.

"Still," Jake heard Nog say to Jadzia, "I can imagine how strange, even upsetting all of this must seem to you."

"We are Starfleet officers," Worf said simply. "What is your proposal?"

Nog immediately turned to Captain T'len, and now she stepped all the way into the conference room so that the doors to the corridor slid shut. Then she entered a code into the wall panel, and Jake saw a security condition status light on the panel begin to glow. He had once thought that DS9 had become overly militarized during the course of the Dominion War. But what had happened to the station in no way compared with the battle conditions under which the *Augustus* and Starbase 53 operated.

Nog wasted no time in beginning. "The art of making fancy speeches has declined in the past few years," he said crisply, "so I will state my proposition plainly. You do not belong in this time. Starfleet will not attempt to send you back to your own time. However, given your situation, Starfleet *is* willing to allow whoever among you wishes to volunteer, a chance to make another journey in time."

"That's not possible," Jake blurted out. He looked at Jadzia. "Didn't you say we couldn't establish a second Feynman curve from this time?"

Jadzia nodded to him, but then turned back to look at Nog. It was obvious to Jake that she was interested in what more Nog would say to them.

The Ferengi smiled at him. "Jake, I . . . don't remember you as a scientist," he said.

"Jake and I have had discussions recently," Jadzia said quickly, before Jake could respond, "about the possibilities of going back."

"I see," Nog said. He paused, a thoughtful expression

on his face. "Then—in terms of your using a different time-travel technique to return to your own time—yes, that's right. You could not slingshot around a suitable star and expect to survive a transition back to your starting point in 2375."

"So," Jadzia said, "you're obviously proposing a transition to a different time."

"Correct," Nog agreed.

"But doesn't that entail the same risk to us?" Jadzia asked.

Nog shot a sidelong look at Captain T'len, and Jake could see that twenty-five years older or not, his "old" friend was nervous about what he was going to say next. "Not if the temporal length of your second Feynman curve is sufficiently greater than your initial starting point."

Jake didn't have the slightest idea what that meant. He looked to Jadzia for some explanation. She was nodding her head as if she understood, even if the frown on her face indicated to Jake that she did not agree with Nog's reasoning.

"For what you're suggesting, Nog—Captain—the temporal length of our second transition would have to be longer than our first by a factor of . . ." Jadzia looked up at the conference room's ceiling, as if performing a complex calculation in her head.

"A factor of three," Dr. Bashir unexpectedly said.

Jake felt his stomach tighten. That couldn't be right. "Twenty-five *thousand* years?" He stared at Nog in disbelief.

But his best friend merely shrugged. "That's exactly right."

Now all the temporal refugees around Jake were exchanging looks of unease. Murmurs of protest began to fill the Starbase 53 conference room.

"It's called Project Phoenix," Nog said, waving aside their concerns. "Created by Admiral Jean-Luc Picard."

The name alone brought silence to the group.

"Jean-Luc?" Vash asked. "Is he still . . . ?"

"Yes," Nog confirmed. "He's frail. In poor health. But . . . he has given us hope that the Ascendancy can be stopped before . . . before it's too late."

"Even assuming you have the technology to send us back twenty-five thousand years—" Jadzia began.

"And we do," Nog said, but Jadzia kept talking.

"—any change we make in the timeline to prevent the Ascendancy from arising will either erase this current reality, or create a parallel one, leaving this one unchanged and still facing destruction."

"Ah, but that's where you're wrong," Nog said triumphantly. "There is a *third* solution. Admiral Picard's solution. A way to go back into the past and make a change that will not take effect until *after* the ship has departed, thus *preserving* our timeline."

Dr. Bashir suddenly laughed. The unexpected sound was almost shocking to Jake, as was the observation he so clearly stated next. "A time bomb. You want us to place a literal time bomb."

And Nog confirmed it.

"Basically, that is correct," the Ferengi said. "In the past five years, Starfleet has expended enormous effort on the two critical components of the admiral's plan. The first is the *U.S.S. Phoenix*—the largest Starfleet vessel ever built in your time *or* ours. The second is the deep-time charges, made of a brand-new ultrastable trilithium resin together with advanced timekeeping mechanisms of incredible accuracy."

"So we use the *Phoenix* to go back twenty-five millennia," Bashir said, "plant the deep-time charges on Bajor, and some time after we leave for the past, the charges detonate. Presumably destroying the Ascendancy."

Like everyone in the room, Jake watched and listened as his best friend outlined the unbelievable mission.

"—And also destroying Kai Weyoun, the Red Orbs of Jalbador, and the center of Ascendancy rule," Nog said.

In the utter silence that followed Nog's list of targets, one of the Bajoran civilians gasped, and the following instant Jake understood why. "B'hala . . . ," the civilian said. B'hala was the most sacred city on Bajor. It had vanished from Bajoran knowledge twenty thousand years ago, until Jake's father discovered it buried deep beneath the Ir'Abehr Shield.

"Again, correct," Nog said. "Admiral Picard's first love is archaeology, and he has researched the matter in precise detail."

The Ferengi pressed on, even though the flood of details was beginning to sweep over Jake like a thought-smothering wave, and he knew the overload had to be affecting the other survivors of his time the same way.

"We know," Nog continued, "that the first structures of the city known as B'hala were built approximately twenty-five thousand years ago. Approximately twenty thousand years ago, general knowledge of the city's location was lost for about five thousand years. Then, about fifteen thousand years ago, the last temple was built on the site, and it was swallowed by landslides. Until," Nog nodded at Jake, "Captain Sisko rediscovered it less than thirty years ago.

"According to our latest intelligence estimates, less than one-third of the city has been excavated under the Ascendancy, which means whoever goes back to the city's beginning will know exactly where to hide the deep-time charges in the remaining two-thirds to ensure that they will not be discovered over the millennia to come."

A question broke through the fog of disorientation in Jake. "Nog, why twenty-five thousand years? Why not go back ten years? Or a hundred?"

"A fair question," Nog said. "First of all, the *Phoenix* would have to go back at least a thousand years, to be sure that no early Bajoran space travelers or astronomers detected the ship arriving at warp speed or orbiting the planet for the three weeks it will take for the deployment of the deep-time charges."

"Okay, then go back *fifteen* hundred years," Jake said.

"And you wouldn't need a large starship for that kind of trip," Jadzia added.

Nog shook his head at the both of them. "No. The point is not merely to go back in time and deploy the charges. It's to go back and deploy them without introducing *any* changes in the timeline. That means B'hala must remain a lost city until Captain Sisko finds it in 2373.

"Remember—a team of Starfleet engineers will be working in the Ir'Abehr Shield for three weeks, and they have to be able to do so without attracting *any* attention. Admiral Picard has told us that the only way to be sure that our activities won't inadvertently lead to the early discovery of B'hala is to go back to a time *before* B'hala."

At that, Captain T'len stepped forward as if she were impatient. "The targeted time period is most logical."

"And what about the choice of crew?" Worf asked sternly. "Is that also logical?"

Jake saw something in Worf's eyes that made him think there was more to the question than there appeared to be. Captain T'len's hesitation in answering confirmed his suspicions.

"That argument can be made," she said at last.

Then Bashir again articulated what Worf must already have guessed. "It's a one-way trip, isn't it."

Nog drew himself up, a gesture at once like and unlike the Nog familiar to Jake. "Most likely," the Ferengi said stiffly—but proudly too, Jake thought. "Yes."

"Most likely?" Bashir repeated incredulously.

Nog's voice took on a more determined tone. "The *Phoenix*, Doctor Bashir, is the largest starship ever constructed. It *will* survive a twenty-five-thousand-year temporal slingshot. But all our simulations show that neither her spaceframe nor her warp engines will survive the stresses of a return trip."

That was when Jake saw the logic of it for himself. He and the others from the *Defiant* were already misplaced in time. So what would it matter if they were misplaced somewhere—some*time*—else?

And he wasn't the only one to reach that realization.

"So we're expendable," Vash said angrily. "That's it, isn't it? We're a danger to you in this time, so you want to send us off on some high-risk wild *norp* chase and get rid of us." She leaned forward to jab her finger against Nog's chest. "Well, you can tell your Starfleet admirals that I'm not going."

With a forcefulness Jake knew the Ferengi would

never have attempted in Jake's time, four days ago on DS9, Nog grabbed the anthropologist's hand and pushed it aside. His answer to her was almost a growl. "It is a *volunteer* mission."

"Captain," Jadzia said quickly, diplomatically defusing the sudden increase in tension in the room and returning their attention to what must be faced, "there still has to be more to the mission than what you've described. Once the charges are deployed, what are we . . . what is the crew of this new supership—the *Phoenix*—supposed to do? They certainly can't interact with any culture in the past."

"Absolutely not," Nog agreed, with a grateful glance at the Trill officer. "But Admiral Picard did suggest a course of action that might allow you, or perhaps your children or grandchildren, to return to the present." He looked over at Bashir. "As I said, Doctor, it is *likely* that the mission of the *Phoenix* will be one way. But it is not certain."

Then Jake, together with the others, listened intently as Nog described Picard's plan as confirmed, he said, by extensive studies conducted by the Federation's leading surviving experts in archaeology, biology, and ancient astronomy.

The essence of it, Jake realized, was that almost fifteen hundred years ago—and 7,000 light-years from Earth—a main-sequence star had gone supernova. The expanding gas cloud from that awesome burst of energy became known to Earth astronomers as the Crab Nebula. But to the astronomers of Erelyn IV, that same cosmic explosion was the last thing they or their fellow beings ever saw.

Erelyn IV itself was a Class-M world, home to a race of humanoids that was one of the first to develop interstellar travel—though not warp drive—in the present epoch of the Alpha Quadrant. But—and Nog emphasized this point—the planet was only twelve light-years from the Crab supernova, and the radiation released by that star's explosion had been lethal to all life-bearing planets within *fifty* light-years.

Jake remembered learning about Erelyn IV in school. His instructors had referred to the lifeless, crumbling cities and vast transportation networks of that planet to stress the importance of exploration and discovery. Because the radiation had sterilized Erelyn IV without destroying the buildings, libraries, and technology of its people, the Vulcan archaeologists who had studied the planet for generations had been able to reconstruct Erelynian history in unprecedented detail.

Sadly, the Vulcans also learned that at the time of the supernova, the Erelynians had a prototype warp engine under construction in orbit of their world. Had the funding battles their scientists fought against their world's shortsighted politicians been successful only a few years earlier, faster-than-light probes to the Crab star would have revealed the existence of the supernova before the radiation had reached their world, giving them time to construct underground radiation shelters. Had Erelyn IV's politicians permitted warp research to proceed a mere fifteen years earlier, that would have been enough time for the Erelynians to establish colonies on planets outside the sphere of lethality and to build shelters.

Fifteen lost years. The lesson had been taught to all children in the Federation: that such a short period of time could be all that might stand between planetary extinction and survival. The moral had been clear: Between thinking about one's next term in office and thinking about the next generation was a difference in attitude that could save an entire world—or condemn it.

The people of Erelyn IV had paid the ultimate price for their leaders' lack of vision. But they had left a poignant treasure trove of almost ten thousand years of their history—including, Nog explained, a complete map of the Crab star's solar system as it had existed before the supernova, as charted by sublight robotic probes.

"The Crab star had seven major planets," Nog now explained. "The second from the star was Class-M. The Erelynians' long-range scans showed a standard Gaia-class oxygen atmosphere, indicating a biosphere. But the scans they made also showed no signs of industrial pollutants; nor did they record any electromagnetic or subspace communications."

"So *that's* where you want us to go," Bashir said. He wasn't asking a question, and Nog didn't bother to do more than nod in response.

It was clear to all present that Nog was coming to the final part of the plan.

"The *Phoenix* will be able to make the voyage between Bajor and the Crab star in under two years. The ship is stocked with industrial replicators, nanoconstructors, and complete plans for building a duplicate vessel to bring you home."

"How long?" Worf asked bluntly. "For the nanoconstructors to build a ship without a shipyard and Starfleet work crews."

Jake saw an almost invisible wince twist Nog's features. "Our best estimate is . . . forty-eight years."

Now Jake understood why Nog had said their children or their grandchildren might make it back.

"A great many things can go wrong in forty-eight years," Worf said.

"Which, obviously, is why they picked that world," Bashir said lightly. "If something goes wrong and we can't travel back to this present, then even if our descendants spread out across the world, in the year 1054 A.C.E. everything turns to superheated plasma in any case when the sun explodes. As long as we stay on that world, we will have no interaction with the march of history throughout the rest of the galaxy."

"Exactly," Nog said. He turned to Captain T'len, as if he had said all that was necessary for now.

But Worf had another question. "You have not thought of every eventuality. What if we fail to build a second *Phoenix*, and our descendants first revert to more primitive ways, then develop a spacefaring civilization of their own. Twenty thousand years is more than enough time for that to happen, and for our descendants to travel to Qo'noS or Earth and change history."

"Commander Worf," Nog said with what Jake thought was an odd formality, "I assure you that we *have* thought of every eventuality. And what you describe cannot happen."

Jake didn't understand, but it seemed Bashir felt he did. "There's another bomb in the *Phoenix*," the doctor said. "Set to go off . . . a century . . . ?"

Startled, Jake looked from Bashir to Nog. His friend's face was sad but resigned. Bashir's guess was true.

". . . After we leave," the doctor said slowly as he spoke his thoughts aloud. "Probably something that would set up an energy cascade in the atmosphere of the second planet, killing all higher animal life-forms in that world, but leaving the bulk of the ecosystem unharmed."

But now Jake was thoroughly confused. "But . . . why would we leave the *Phoenix* anywhere near the planet if we knew it could kill us? Or our descendants?" he added.

"Because," Captain T'len said with a stern glance at Nog, "everyone who takes part in this mission will understand and accept the importance of not changing the timeline. As Commander Worf stated, many things can go wrong in forty-eight years. Thus the crew of the *Phoenix* will leave their ship in close orbit of the planet as a fail-safe backup, to ensure that none of their descendants survive to form their own civilization."

The room fell silent once more, and Jake knew that everyone in it was contemplating as he was the enormity of what was being proposed to them.

After a few moments, Nog spoke again. "Admiral Picard set this all in place almost five years ago, and the plans have been continually refined and perfected ever since."

Jake looked over at Bashir, but the doctor seemed not to have anything more to say. Everyone else from the *Defiant*, with the exception of Vash, was making silent eye contact with their fellow temporal refugees. Vash simply glared at Nog and T'len as if they were personally responsible for thwarting her.

"Captain Nog, we would like time to consider your proposal," Worf said.

"I understand," Nog agreed. "But I would ask that you make your decision within the next fifty hours, so we can arrange passage to Utopia Planitia and I can begin your training."

Jake heard something odd in Nog's voice then. "Nog, are you going?"

"On the *Phoenix*? Yes."

"So you think it's going to work."

For the first time in the session, Nog smiled broadly. "I have absolute faith in Admiral Picard. I have reviewed all the operational plans and contingencies. I have no doubt that the mission of the *Phoenix* will succeed, and there will be no need to worry about the safeguard time bombs. I am completely confident that someday I and the crew . . . or our descendants . . . will be able to return to the present and the universe we will have saved."

Nog then said his good-byes, explained that he had meetings to attend, and hoped that he could meet everyone again at 1900 hours for a meal. Then, with the unsmiling Captain T'len at his side, he left.

Instantly a buzz of responses filled with new hope swept through the room. But Jake didn't join in, although Nog's presence on the *Phoenix* did change the equation for him personally.

Jake was in the midst of trying to comprehend the best thing to do.

Because he had seen his Ferengi friend give that same assured smile at least a thousand times in the past. And it had always meant only one thing.

Nog was lying.

So the *Phoenix* was already doomed.

And with her the universe.

CHAPTER 12

"CAPTAIN SISKO! You've been ignoring me!"

Benjamin Sisko snapped out of his reverie and sighed. He was sitting at an uncomfortable Klingon work station in his uncomfortable Klingon quarters on board the uncomfortable Klingon vessel, the *Boreth.* Kasidy Yates was looking out at him from the work station's main display screen. Her image was a stern, unsmiling portrait; it was the one that had been attached to her merchant master's license.

The annoyed voice haranguing him belonged to Quark. It came from the open doorway to Sisko's quarters.

"This isn't the time, Quark," Sisko said quietly, and meant it. Nevertheless he heard the sound of Quark's brisk footsteps as the Ferengi crossed over his threshold.

"In case you haven't noticed, time is what we're running out of." The irate barkeep was now at his side, hands on hips, looking quite ridiculous in his Bajoran penitent's robes of brown and cream.

"Everything will work out," Sisko said, still not raising his voice, surprised at how little irritation he felt at Quark's ill-timed intrusion. Then again, he wondered, was it even possible that he would ever feel anything again?

"How can you say that?!" Quark exclaimed. "The whole universe has been turned upside down! Did you know the entire Ferenginar system has been under an Ascendancy trade blockade for the past seven years? No one on this *frinxing* ship will even let me *try* to get a message through to *anyone* back home."

Sisko bowed his head, took a breath so deep he knew it would strain his chest, but still felt nothing. "Quark, we are all struggling with similar difficulties."

"Ha," Quark said. He pointed to the display. "At least you can access some sort of database to find out about . . ." Quark's verbal assault on Sisko suddenly ceased.

Sisko glanced up at him and saw that the Ferengi was reading the screen.

"I'm . . . sorry," the Ferengi said quietly, all bluster gone from him. "You know, I . . . I always liked Captain Yates."

Sisko nodded. "She was only one of many, Quark. So many people died when Earth was destroyed." He closed his eyes then, but Kasidy's face was still before him. At least, the old report said, she had gone out a hero, during her *fifth* run through Grigari lines to evacuate survivors.

"Captain . . . ?"

Sisko opened his eyes, looked up. "Yes, Quark."

The Ferengi mumbled a few words that were unintelligible before finally getting to the point in a sudden rush. "We need you."

Sisko contemplated Quark, curious. He couldn't remember ever having seen the Ferengi so uncertain, so obviously worried.

"I appreciate the vote of confidence," he told the Ferengi barkeep, "but if you listened to Odo's report about his run-in with Weyoun, I am the one person among us all who you definitely don't want."

Quark rocked back as if surprised by the statement. "Are you saying you *believe* Weyoun about Starfleet wanting to kill you?"

Sisko pushed his chair back from the workstation and stood up, leaving Kasidy's image still on the display. He wasn't yet ready to erase it. The act would carry with it too much finality.

"Starfleet vessels were waiting for us when we reemerged from the timeslip," he said, shifting uncomfortably in his own awkward and confining robes, orange and brown like a vedek's, like Weyoun's. Weyoun. Sisko sighed. He must have been over the Vorta's words to Odo a thousand times in the past two days. "Starfleet vessels attacked us."

"So did Riker in the *Opaka,*" Quark argued.

"The *Opaka* and the *Boreth* chased the Starfleet vessels away."

With that reminder, Quark began to pace back and forth in frustration. "But I talked with Chief O'Brien. He said the Starfleet mines that were beamed onto the *Defiant*'s hull had countdown timers."

Sisko watched as Quark stopped his pacing and stared up at him, challengingly. "If Starfleet really wanted to kill you, then why didn't they use mines that exploded on contact?"

Silent, Sisko gazed at Quark, and the Ferengi slowly nodded, as if satisfied he finally had the *hew-mon*'s undivided attention.

"Captain," Quark said emphatically, as if to a novice who needed remedial training, "there's an old negotiating tactic that's even more basic than the Rules of Acquisition. If you can't convince a customer that your product is better than the competition's, then at least convince the customer that the competition's product is lethal."

Sisko shook his head.

Quark threw up his hands in renewed frustration. "Oh, for—it's like when customers at my bar complain about the menu prices," he sputtered, "and I tell them about the food-poisoning deaths at the Klingon Cafe."

Sisko felt a wry smile tug at the corners of his mouth. Really, the Ferengi barkeep was shameless. "As far as I know, Quark, no one's ever died of food poisoning at the Klingon Cafe."

Quark beamed with relief. "There you go, Captain. I'm so glad we finally understand each other."

Before Sisko could say anything more, the work station buzzed peremptorily. He turned to it in time to see the unsettling transformation of Kasidy's image into that of Weyoun.

"Benjamin," the Vorta simpered, speaking as usual with far too much familiarity, "*may* I call you Benjamin?"

As usual, Sisko ignored the request. "What do you want?"

Weyoun's smooth reaction was as if Sisko's own response had been nothing but a polite exchange in return. "We'll be arriving at Bajor within the next few minutes. I thought you might like to join me on the bridge. To see your adopted world in this glorious new age."

The last thing Sisko wanted to do was to spend more time in Weyoun's company. But he was aware that a chance to examine the bridge might provide useful information about the organization methods and technology used by the Ascendancy . . . or whatever Weyoun's name was for the group that served him and ran this ship.

"Should I wait for an escort?" he asked.

But Weyoun shook his finger as if he'd just heard a clever joke. "Oh, my, no. As I'm sure you've realized by now, my crew has established an exceptionally comprehensive internal sensor system. Someone will be watching you the entire way, to be certain you don't get . . . lost."

"Then I'll be on my way."

Weyoun smiled expansively. "Very good. I do look forward to sharing your company again. Perhaps I can help you see Quark's lies for what they are."

Discovering that Weyoun was aware of the conversation he had just had with Quark was not at all surprising to Sisko. He doubted there was a word any of the people from the *Defiant* had said on this ship that hadn't been recorded by internal security sensors.

With a slow and deeply respectful bow of his head, Weyoun faded from the workstation display, to be replaced by Kasidy.

With a sudden flash of anger, Sisko hit the display controls, turning the screen black. He wished he could weep for Kasidy. That would be the appropriate response to his loss. But his chest felt empty, as if it no longer contained his heart. Only an unfeeling void where love had once reigned.

"If you'll excuse me." Sisko moved past Quark, heading for the open door to the corridor.

But Quark apparently did not feel their conversation was over, and he moved to block his escape. "Captain! I don't care if that puny-eared sycophant heard every word I said *and* every word I thought. He's lying to you about Starfleet and who knows what else!"

Sisko stared down at the Ferengi who stood between him and the door. "Thank you for your input, Quark. I think you should join the others."

"The others," Quark muttered, defiantly holding his ground. "A crazed Cardassian, a frustrated changeling, my idiot brother . . . don't you *get* it, Captain? You're the only one who can get us out of this!"

"Quark, are you aware of the 85th Rule?"

"Of course I am," Quark answered testily. "Never let the . . . oh." His shoulders sagged beneath his robes. "Right. Never mind."

Quark stepped to one side. The way was now clear.

"I'll see you with the others," Sisko said, turning around in the doorway.

"Right," Quark said darkly, shouldering his own way past Sisko and entering the corridor. "Maybe I'll organize a tongo tournament. That should help raise spirits."

Sisko watched the Ferengi stomp off along the dark, rusty-walled Klingon hallway.

Never let the competition know what you're thinking, Sisko thought, completing the 85th Rule.

Perhaps Weyoun *was* lying to him about Starfleet.

Perhaps it was time to fight back with a few lies of his own.

He turned in the direction opposite the one Quark had chosen and headed for the bridge, fully aware that unseen eyes watched him, as always, keeping his thoughts to himself.

The *Boreth*'s bridge was larger than Sisko had expected, at least three times that of even a *Sovereign*-class vessel. Even more unexpected, there was little to it that seemed Klingon. All the sensor screens and status displays he could see were, in fact, Bajoran, as were the muted metallic colors of the wall panels and friction carpet—perhaps the only part of the ship not marred by typical Klingon oxidation stains.

The main viewer, which showed computer reconstructions of stars passing at warp, took up most of the far wall. On the bridge's lower level, at least fifteen duty officers were seated at three rows of consoles facing the screen.

At present, Sisko was on the bridge's upper level where the turbolift had deposited him, and where Weyoun was awaiting him in his command chair, its outlines indistinguishable from those of a command chair that might be found on any Starfleet vessel. Unsurprisingly, Weyoun's throne took center stage. What did surprise Sisko was the fact that he wasn't Weyoun's only guest.

Standing beside the Vorta were Major Kira and Commander Arla. Like everyone else who had been captured with the *Defiant*, the two women were wearing robes typical of a Bajoran religious order. From the collar folds of the white tunics visible beneath their outer robes, Sisko guessed Kira and Arla had been given clothing of the rank of prylar. Their nearly identical expressions of discomfort indicated that neither woman was pleased with the outfit forced upon her, either.

Weyoun turned slowly in his chair, both hands upon its wide arms. Sisko caught the gratified smile that momentarily flashed across his host's face.

"Splendid—just in time." Weyoun gestured for him to come closer. "Please, join us."

Sisko glanced at the wall alongside the turbolift, where three stern Romulans stood, each with a hand on a long-barreled energy weapon holstered at his side. They made no move to stop him, so Sisko went to Weyoun, stopping beside Kira and Arla.

"We have just been having the most *fascinating* conversation about ancient Bajoran beliefs," Weyoun said pleasantly.

"Is that so?" Sisko answered. His eyes kept moving around the bridge stations, finding so much that was familiar, so much that was different in this time.

"Major Kira was describing various punishments that some of the earlier, more . . . strident, shall we say, Bajoran sects would visit upon those whom they viewed as heretics."

"Really," Sisko said, only half listening.

"Really," Weyoun agreed. "And it seems that two or three thousand years ago, at least in some sections of Bajor, I would have had my beating heart cut from my body as I watched. As punishment for professing belief in the True Prophets."

Kira smiled tightly. "In some ways, our ancestors were more advanced than we are."

Weyoun gave Kira a pitying stare. "Really, Major, how droll."

Sisko brought his gaze and attention back to the center of the bridge and Weyoun. "Tell me," he said, "what punishment do *you* inflict on those heretics who profess a belief in the Old Prophets of Bajor?"

Weyoun studied Sisko for a few moments before replying. "This may come as a surprise, Benjamin, but we inflict no punishment at all."

"That is a surprise," Sisko said mildly, "considering that you told Odo your crew would have killed him if they had heard a question he had asked about you choosing—"

Weyoun held up a hand to cut off Sisko before he could finish.

"Really, Benjamin. You should know better. Despite my best intentions, there are always those devoted few who sometimes act in the heat of passion rather than restrain themselves in the cool cloak of the law."

Sisko felt rather than saw Kira bristle at that. Her dynamic presence had always been able to charge a room.

"Oh, really?" she retorted. "So everyone on Bajor is free to follow her own heart in choosing which religion to follow?"

"Of course," Weyoun said testily. "The True Prophets created sentient beings in their own image. That doesn't mean shape or size or number of grasping appendages, it refers to our possessing free will. The one true religion of the True Prophets couldn't very well claim to *represent* the True Prophets if it had to *enforce* its beliefs on everyone, could it?"

"But isn't that what you're doing?" Sisko seized the chance to build on the emotion provoked by Kira. "By destroying whole worlds that don't agree with you?"

Weyoun's lips trembled. Sisko hoped the movement sprang from anger, however tightly controlled. An angry opponent could become vulnerable. "I cannot be responsible for what other people—other worlds—*believe*, Benjamin. By the dictates of my own conscience and the command of the True Prophets, I must allow everyone to come to the right decision—or not—by their own free choice. All I ask in return is that those who don't believe as I do allow my followers and me to adhere to our own faith. A simple request, really." Weyoun's voice became calmer as his own words reassured him if no one else of the truth of his beliefs. "One that fits in nicely with that Prime Directive you used to be so proud of.

"Believe me," the Vorta said piously, "the only time the Bajoran Ascendancy has been forced to prevail against other systems or groups of systems has been when our right to pursue our own beliefs has come under attack. We are quite capable of acting in self-defense."

"Self-defense?!" Sisko said. "Is that what you call the destruction of the entire *Earth?*"

Weyoun sat back in his command chair, frowning as he picked at the skirts of his robe. "That, I fully admit, was a mistake."

Kira snorted in what seemed to be a combination of disbelief and disgust.

"A mistake," Sisko repeated.

"The Grigari trade delegation was not expecting the sensor barrage to which they were subjected. Their commanders thought they were under attack, and . . . they didn't realize that Earth's planetary defense system wasn't able to handle their warning shots. One thing led to another, and . . ." Weyoun held up empty hands. "It wasn't the first time a first contact has gone wrong."

"I don't believe you." Sisko made no attempt to

lower his voice as he challenged Weyoun. He felt it might do some good if the Vorta's crew could hear what others thought of him.

But the Romulan guards gave no reaction, and Weyoun only adopted a look of profound sadness, a false expression like so many he affected. "And that is your right. Though in only ten more days, you—and everyone else in creation—will have the chance to learn the truth."

"Weyoun," Sisko said, "the universe is *not* coming to an end in ten days."

"Of course not," Weyoun agreed. "It will enter a new *beginning.* I knew you'd come to see it my way."

The first thought that came to Sisko then was how much he'd enjoy simply punching Weyoun in his sanctimonious face. *It would feel so good,* Sisko thought. And then he remembered how he had felt when he had read of Kasidy's death, the shocking numbness, and the fear that he might never feel anything again.

Except, it seems, rage, Sisko told himself. Perhaps that was all that was left to him in this era. Rage against those who had caused him such loss, and, perhaps, anger at himself for all that he had left undone.

"Are you all right?" Weyoun inquired.

"What do you think?" Sisko asked.

Just then a voice behind him said, "Emissary?" and Sisko turned to see a Romulan in an ill-fitting Bajoran-style uniform hold up a gleaming metallic padd encased in what appeared to be gold.

"Yes?" Sisko and Weyoun said together.

The Romulan was speaking to Weyoun. *"Emissary,"* he said more emphatically, "we are entering our final approach."

Weyoun smiled at Sisko as he gave his response. "Standard orbit."

The Romulan bowed his head in respect.

Sisko felt his stomach twist.

"Please," Weyoun said with a wave at the main viewer. Then he turned his chair around to face it.

Turning in the same direction, Sisko saw the streaking stars slow. Then a single point of blue light in the center of the viewer suddenly blossomed into an appreciable disk. Next, with only the slightest change in the background hum of the *Boreth*'s engines, the stars abruptly froze in place and the planet Bajor grew until it filled the screen.

Sisko saw Kira's mouth open slightly, and he thought he knew why.

The sphere on the viewer, caught in the full glory of her sun's light, looked little different than it had in their own time. Bright blue oceans sparkled with brilliant light. Elegant swirls of white clouds traced the shores of the northern continent. A dark pinwheel flashing with minuscule bolts of lightning showed a tropical storm building majestically in the South Liran Sea.

And across the continents, verdant forests painted the land in an infinite shifting palette of greens. There was no trace of the dark scars left by the Cardassian Occupation and the final scourging they had inflicted on the Day of Withdrawal.

"Magnificent, isn't it?" Weyoun said. "Bajor restored. Reborn. Unblemished once more."

Sisko wouldn't give the Vorta the satisfaction of a reply. But he was right. Bajor had never looked better, or more compelling.

"Keep watching," Weyoun said.

The terminator passed through the screen, and a dozen cities were called out from the night by the blazing constellations of their streets and buildings. All of them seemed somehow bigger than in Sisko's memory.

"Is that Rhakur?" Kira whispered in amazement.

Sisko saw a sprawling web of light wrap around the distinctive dark shoreline of the inland Rhakur Sea. But the city was twice the size he remembered.

"It is," Weyoun confirmed. "The universities there have attracted scholars from across the two quadrants, and the expansion of facilities has been most gratifying."

Sisko turned his attention from the viewer to Kira. Her eyes glistened with moisture, as if she were about to cry. And again he knew why.

All her life, her world had been crippled and scarred. Yet here it was before her, healed by time itself.

Sisko knew it was the future she had fought for, always dreamed of, yet never really expected to see.

But he refused to let the magnificent vision beguile her. She had to know the price her world had paid for such healing.

"And this is the world you want to destroy," Sisko said to Weyoun.

The Vorta looked over at him, puzzled. "The Prophets will destroy nothing. This world will be transformed, along with all the others of the universe, into a true paradise, and not just a mundane and linear one."

Sisko saw Kira abruptly rub her eyes, and he felt confident he had broken the spell of the moment. He glanced next at Arla, expecting to see a less emotional reaction, since Bajor had never been her home. But to Sisko's surprise, tears streaked the young woman's face.

"I never knew," she said.

Weyoun nodded. "Of course, you didn't. Keep watching."

In the middle of the main viewer, a new source of light slid into view and recaptured Sisko's attention. He squinted at the screen. It was as if a hole had been cut in some vast curtain to let an enormous searchlight bring day to the middle of night.

"Where's that light coming from?" Kira asked before he could.

"Orbital mirrors," Weyoun said smugly. "Bajor-synchronous, tens of kilometers wide, constantly refocused so that the sun will never set on . . ."

"B'hala," Arla breathed.

Weyoun shot a triumphant look at Sisko. "The jewel of Bajor Ascendant," he said. "Home of our culture, the revelation site of the first Orb to be given to the Bajoran people. Lost for millennia, then rediscovered exactly as prophesied, by the Sisko. I hope you appreciate the importance of what you have given the Bajoran people, and the universe, Benjamin. Everything that has happened these past twenty-five years, everything that will happen in the days ahead, is all because of you."

The Vorta inclined his head in Sisko's direction as if worshipping him.

Sisko's hands were balled into fists within the folds of his robes. "I refuse to accept responsibility for your perversion of the Bajoran faith."

Weyoun tried and failed to restrain a sudden fit of amused laughter. "Even your obstinacy in the face of truth was prophesied by the great mystics of Jalbador—Shabren, Eilin, and Naradim. Your life, your deeds, your great accomplishments—an open book, Benjamin.

As if the mystics had stood at your side through all of it. Your protest is quite futile, I assure you."

And then B'hala, bathed in perpetual sunlight, slipped from the viewer, and only a handful of small oases appeared, tiny clusters of lights strung out across the vast stretch of the mountains forming the Ir'Abehr Shield.

"Torse," Weyoun said in a brisk, businesslike voice of command, "that's enough of the surface. Change visual sensors and show our guests our destination."

Sisko looked back over his shoulder to see the Romulan with the golden padd, Torse presumably, obediently turn to a sensor station and make rapid adjustments to the controls. Then Sisko heard both Kira and Arla gasp, and he turned back to face the viewer.

To see Deep Space 9 again.

Ablaze with lights. Surrounded by a cometary halo of spacecraft of all classes. Each docking port filled. Each pylon connected to a different starship. He even recognized one of those ships as Captain Tom Riker's *Opaka*.

Sisko stumbled to voice his swirling thoughts. "The logs . . . on the sensor logs . . . DS9 . . . I saw it destroyed. . . ."

Weyoun stood up and with a flourish freed his arms from his robes. "Never doubt the power of the Ascendancy, Benjamin." His face creased in warning. "Never."

Staring at the home he had shared with his son and with Kasidy, and which he had never expected to see again, Sisko felt Weyoun's light touch on his arm. "As it was written so long ago: Welcome home, Benjamin. We've been waiting for you."

CHAPTER 13

JULIAN BASHIR felt as if he were caught in a dream. The sense of unreality that had begun to envelop him as he had watched the briefing tape on the *Augustus* had become more than a minor sense of unease at the back of his mind. Now that he was on Mars, his apprehension was like a cloak that covered him completely, weighting each breath he took, obscuring his vision, masking his powers of analysis.

Even worse, at times he only felt human.

Of the fifteen temporal refugees who had heard Captain Nog's proposal at Starbase 53, nine had volunteered to join Project Phoenix and lose themselves even more thoroughly in time.

Of the six who had declined, five had been the Bajorans among them—three members of the militia and two civilians. In all good conscience, they had honestly explained that they could not take action against B'hala and their own people, though they understood why Starfleet felt it must. They requested instead that they be allowed to spend the next few weeks in prayer, so that they might put all their trust in the Prophets.

To Bashir's relief, the Bajorans' request had caused no consternation among Nog and his staff. Arrangements would be made, the Bajorans were told. Despite the War of the Prophets, their refusal had been accepted as simply as that. Some sense of Starfleet's original decency, it seemed, still existed in this time.

The last holdout to refuse the mission was—to no one's surprise—Vash. And also to no one's surprise, the volatile archaeologist was not allowed to go anywhere or do anything except accompany the others to Utopia Planitia. Nog informed her that she would not be forced to join the crew of the *Phoenix*, but neither would she be released from custody until the end of "hostilities."

Bashir recalled cringing at that euphemism, though he realized that the Ferengi captain had also felt uncomfortable using it. Under current conditions, such a term could refer to the approaching end of the universe as much as to the end of the great undeclared war against the Ascendancy.

Nog had subsequently left Starbase 53 on the same day he had first met with the temporal refugees, after an oddly tense dinner he shared with them. The spirited, private conversation Jake Sisko had with his aged childhood friend before they were all seated in the officer's mess did not go unobserved by Bashir. Clearly there was some conflict between those two.

By itself, Bashir did not find such discord remarkable. No doubt there would be abandonment issues on both sides of the friendship: Why was it that Nog was left behind on the day that DS9 was destroyed? Why was it that Jake had apparently died, yet now lived again, full of the energy of youth, which Nog as a middle-aged Ferengi no doubt missed?

Yet something more had passed between the two friends and Bashir, for all his intellectual powers, had to admit his frustration that he had no way of determining just what that something more was.

Three days later, everyone had arrived at the Utopia Planitia shipyards aboard Captain T'len's *Augustus*. Like all cadets, Bashir himself had toured the facility in his second year; from Mars orbit, both the constellation of orbital spacedocks and the vast construction fields on the planet's surface were larger than he remembered them being. In the support domes, though, it seemed to Bashir that the corridors and rooms at least were almost identical to his memories of them. Except, of course, for the pervasive and somewhat depressing lack of maintenance and repair.

Upon their arrival at Starbase 53, he and the others were told that fifteen different Starfleet outposts throughout what was left of the Federation had been subjected to terrorist attack on the same day the *Defiant* had reappeared. Reportedly, Utopia Planitia had been one of the hardest hit, with more than 200 personnel injured and 35 dead. When the pressure shield of his habitat dome had been breached, Nog apparently had managed to save both himself and Admiral Picard by taking shelter in a waste-reclamation pumping room that had its own atmospheric forcefield.

Recalling the account they had been given, Bashir couldn't help but feel a bit of pride at how Nog had turned out. Everyone on DS9 had taken a hand in helping mold the youth from the petty juvenile thief he had been at the beginning to the fine officer he had so clearly become.

But to Bashir, a terrorist attack still didn't explain Utopia's torn wallcoverings, out-of-service lifts, cracked and damaged furniture, and a thousand other deviations from the ordered, precise Starfleet way of doing things in which he, like all those in Starfleet, had been trained. Though the operational areas of the shipyards still seemed outwardly as functional and as fully maintained as before, he couldn't help but see how attention to detail was sliding. And that unspoken sense of desperation in this beleaguered version of Starfleet was contributing mightily to the overwhelming unreality of this experience for him.

Which is why, he supposed, on this his second day in the shipyards he wasn't at all shocked when, while going from his quarters to the mess hall, he recognized a familiar figure, unchanged by time, walking toward him.

"Doctor Zimmerman?"

The bald man, whose quick, intelligent eyes were defined by distinct, dark eyebrows, halted a few meters from him. At once, Bashir felt himself subjected to an intense visual inspection. It was as if he were being compared to the contents of some sort of computer library file that only the bald man could see. Suddenly he snapped his fingers and exclaimed, "Julian Bashir! Of the *Defiant!*"

Bashir was puzzled by the way in which Zimmerman chose to identify him. He and the doctor had met on DS9 after all, when the doctor had been developing a long-term medical hologram. Zimmerman, however, didn't appear to have aged at all in the past twenty-five years.

"That's right," Bashir said, and he closed the distance between them to shake Dr. Zimmerman's hand. He checked the Starfleet rank insignia in the middle of the man's chest and smiled politely. "*Admiral* Zimmerman. Very good, sir. And very deserved, I'm sure."

The man before him returned his smile, but it was a rueful one. "Actually, Doctor Bashir, Lewis Zimmerman passed away several years ago."

In his shock, Bashir kept both his hands locked around the bald man's hand. "I beg your pardon?"

"Your confusion is understandable." Still smiling but without real conviction, the admiral who wasn't Dr. Zimmerman pulled his hand free from Bashir's grip. "In appearance, I was modeled after him."

Bashir still felt the heat of the man's hand in his. But if he had heard correctly, there was only one possible explanation for what he was seeing. He looked up to the left and the right of the corridor, where the stained walls met the ceiling.

"There are no holoemitters," the admiral said.

"But . . . are you . . ."

"I *was,*" the admiral said in a tone of resignation. "An EMH. Emergency Medical Hologram."

Bashir took a step back. He had known there would be technological advances in the past twenty-five years, but *this?*

"You are a . . . a . . ."

"Hologram," the admiral said perfunctorily. "Yes. Though obviously a type with which you are not familiar."

"I . . . I am astounded that such an incredible breakthrough has been made in only two and a half decades."

The hologram sighed. "It actually took more like four hundred years, but what's a few centuries among friends? Now, a pleasure to meet you, but I really must be—"

Bashir interrupted him, suddenly intrigued by a construct that was even more than an apparently self-aware, self-generating hologram. The artificial being's comment about "four hundred years" instantly raised a subject of great medical interest. "Excuse me," he said, "but if you meant it took four centuries to develop the technology that's freed you from holoemitters, are you referring to alien technology, or rather to something obtained through time travel?"

The hologram's eyes crinkled not unpleasantly. "My specifications are on-line and, if I might say, make for fascinating bedtime reading. But right now, I am—"

Another voice broke in, completing the hologram's statement. "Doctor, you are late."

"That's what I was just telling this young man."

Bashir turned, looking for whoever it was the hologram was addressing, and his eyes widened as he saw a tall and striking woman, no older than forty, striding purposefully toward him. She had an intense, almost belligerent expression; her pale blonde hair was drawn back severely, and she wore a Starfleet uniform with a blue shoulder and—like the holographic doctor—the rank of admiral.

She also had an unusual biomechanical implant around her left eye, an implant that Bashir was startled to think he recognized.

"They are waiting for us in briefing room 5," the woman said to the hologram.

Bashir couldn't keep his eyes off the ocular implant. He offered his hand. "I'm Julian Bashir of the *Defiant*. Admiral . . . ?"

The woman looked at Bashir's extended hand as if she were Klingon and he was offering her a bowl of dead *gagh.* She made no attempt to offer her own hand in return.

"Seven," she said flatly. "You are one of the temporal refugees."

"That's right," Bashir said. *Could it be possible?* he wondered.

"And you cannot stop staring at my implant," the admiral said.

"I'm . . . I'm sorry," Bashir stammered. "But . . . well, I know I'm twenty-five years out of date, but . . . it looks like Borg technology."

"It does because it is," Admiral Seven said.

Bashir felt as if he were falling down a rabbit hole. "*You* are . . ."

The admiral placed her hands behind her back and stared at Bashir with impatience. "I am Borg. My designation is Seven of Nine. My function is Speaker to the Collective. You must now allow us to continue with our duties. Admiral Janeway does not like to be kept waiting."

Bashir started at the mention of that name. "Admiral Jane—do you mean, *Kathryn* Janeway?"

"Yes," the hologram said as he stood beside the Borg, "and believe me, it doesn't pay to make her angry. So—"

"*Voyager* made it back?" Bashir said.

The Borg frowned at him. "Obviously."

"But . . . how?"

The hologram and the Borg exchanged a look of shared commiseration. Then the hologram said to Bashir, "It's a long story. We really do have to go."

Before Bashir could utter another word, the hologram and the Borg marched off together. And just before they turned the corner into the corridor leading to the briefing rooms, Bashir was stunned to see the Borg reach out to hold the hologram's hand as she leaned over to whisper in his ear as both of them broke out laughing like any young couple in love.

"Oh, brave new world that has such things in it," Bashir said to no one in particular.

Twenty minutes later in the mess hall, Bashir was still mulling over the significance of the beings he had met, and using a padd to review the stunning ten-year-old alliance between the Federation and the Borg Collective as engineered by Admiral Seven of Nine and a Borg whose designation was given only as "Hugh."

Though a great many details of the Treaty of Wolf 359 appeared to be classified, it was becoming apparent to him that technology exchanges were at its core. The Federation had and was providing expertise in nanite-mediated molecular surgery techniques to the Borg, while the Borg were providing transwarp technology which, Bashir concluded from reading between the lines, was the basis of Admiral Picard's *Phoenix*.

"Incredible," Bashir muttered to himself.

"What is?"

Startled, Bashir looked up to see Jake Sisko. How had he missed his approach? Even his enhanced senses seemed to be subject to his bewildering state of confusion these days. "The Borg," he said. "The Borg appear to be our allies now."

Bashir nodded as Jake gestured with the tray of food he held, to ask permission to sit down with him.

"I heard that, too," Jake told him, taking the seat opposite Bashir. The tall youngster leaned forward across the small mess table and dropped his voice. "But I can't get anyone to tell me what happened to the Klingon Empire. Are they part of the Federation now? On the side of the Ascendancy? People either ignore the question or they tell me the information's classified."

Bashir looked around the mess hall. At full capacity, it might hold 300 personnel. But right now, perhaps because it was between shifts, there were only 23 others eating meals or nursing mugs of something hot. Twenty of these other diners were Andorians, the other three Tellarite.

"Have you seen another human here?" Bashir asked Jake.

Now Jake looked around the mess hall. "Well . . . wasn't the lieutenant who showed us our quarters human?"

Bashir shook his head. "Vulcan."

Jake frowned. "At Starbase 53 there were humans. The medical staff."

Bashir held up two fingers. "Two technicians. On a staff of fifteen."

Jake tapped his hands on the sides of his food tray. "So humans *and* Klingons are missing?"

Bashir shrugged and turned off his padd. "There's a lot they aren't telling us about what's going on."

Intriguing to Bashir, Jake immediately dropped his eyes to his collection of reconstituted rations and busily began peeling off their clear tops. When he had first visited the mess hall, Bashir had been interested to notice that what he thought were replicator slots lining one wall were actually small transporter bays with a direct connection to a food-processing facility a few kilometers away. Replicator circuitry and power converters were considered a critical resource and used for only the most important manufacturing needs.

"So, how's Nog?" Bashir asked, trying to keep his tone innocuous, but wondering why Jake had chosen not to react to his statement. He took a sip of the tea he had requisitioned. It was too cold, too sweet, and tasted nothing at all like tea.

"Different," Jake said, frowning at the contents of the containers he had uncovered. Again, it was not clear to Bashir if the frown was directed at the food or at his question.

"To be expected, don't you think?"

Jake gingerly dabbed a finger into the red sauce that covered a brownish square of . . . something, then tentatively licked his finger. He grimaced. "I actually miss the combat rations on the *Augustus.*"

Bashir smiled in commiseration. Vulcan combat rations were logical and not much else. They consisted of tasteless extruded slabs which were mostly vegetable pulp compressed to the consistency of soft wax. Accompanied by packets of distilled water and three uncomfortably large supplement pills to compensate for the differences between Vulcan and human nutrient requirements, 500 grams of pulp were sufficient to maintain a normal adult body for thirty hours. Vulcans were proud of the fact that their rations only had to be ingested once a day, and that the process could be completed in less than two minutes. How much more efficient could eating become? All of the temporal refugees had lost body mass during their voyage on the *Augustus.*

It was also possible, though, that Jake's joke might

have another purpose—to change the subject. Bashir didn't intend to let such a ploy go unchallenged.

"Were you having an argument with Nog?" he asked. "Before we all had dinner at the starbase?"

He saw the answer in Jake's guilty expression. "Jake, it's bad enough that Starfleet is keeping secrets from us. We can't keep them from each other, too." Bashir dropped his own voice to a near whisper. "What did he tell you?"

Jake's shoulders sagged. "It's more what he didn't tell me . . . tell us."

"About what?"

Jake dropped his napkin over his untouched food. "He was lying to us."

Bashir felt the unwelcome touch of alarm. He had considered that possibility himself. "About the *Phoenix?*"

"No . . . I don't think about all that. Like, the *Phoenix* and going back twenty-five thousand years and the deep-time charges in B'hala . . . I really think that's what Starfleet's planning. Or *was* planning. But . . . when he told us he had no doubt that the mission would succeed . . . that was a lie."

Bashir put down his pad. "Considering the rather audacious nature of the mission, I'm not really surprised. It's perfectly understandable that Nog might harbor some doubts about the possibilities for success."

But Jake shook his head emphatically. "I'm not talking about doubts. Or being nervous. I mean . . . look, it's as if Nog already knows the mission *can't* succeed."

"Did he say that to you? Is that what you were arguing about?"

Jake looked right and left, obviously concerned about anyone overhearing their discussion. "That was part of it. But he didn't have to tell me. Not flat out."

"I don't understand."

Jake shifted uncomfortably. "He's been my best friend for . . . well, we *were* best friends for a long time. And I can tell when he's lying. He does this thing with his eyes and . . . his mouth sort of freezes in position."

Jake was obviously developing some skill in observation. "They call it a 'tell.' Or they used to," Bashir corrected himself, "a few centuries ago. In gambling and confidence games, some people develop a nervous habit which gives away the fact that they're bluffing. You're very observant."

Jake shrugged. "Not really. Uh, Nog sort of told me himself. His father and uncle kept giving him a hard time about it. They, uh, they claimed he had picked it up from me . . . a filthy human habit that would hold him back in business." Jake smiled weakly. "He tried to run away from the station a couple of times."

"I didn't know," Bashir said truthfully.

"I . . . talked him out of it. But anyway, he's still doing it. And he was definitely lying to us."

Bashir sat back in the flimsy mess-hall chair and mentally called up a Vulcan behavioral algorithm to try to calculate the odds that Jake was correct in his conclusion of Nog's truthfulness. Once the Vulcans had realized the failure of their early predictions that any species intelligent enough to develop warp drive would of course have embraced logic and peaceful exploration as the guiding principles of their culture, they had developed complex systems for modeling and predicting alien behavior as a form of self-survival. It was a difficult set of equations to master, but one could always count on a Vulcan to figure the odds for just about any eventuality.

Bashir completed his calculations. In the limited way

he had trained himself in the Vulcan technique, he was forced to conclude that given the relationship between Jake and Nog, Jake was more likely than not correct in his assessment of his friend. Since there was nothing to be gained from questioning Jake's conclusion, the only logical course was now to determine the underlying reasons for Nog's behavior.

Bashir began the requisite series of questions. "Did you tell him that you knew he was lying?"

Jake nodded. "That's when he got mad at me."

"But did he deny lying?"

"How could he?"

"Did he say why?"

Jake appeared to be more profoundly unhappy than Bashir ever recalled seeing him before.

"All he told me was that I should keep my . . . my ridiculous *hew-mon* opinions to myself. And then, well, he sort of let me know that it was really important that I not tell anyone what I thought."

"With what you know of him, Jake, is there *any* reason you can think of why Nog would lie to us about the success of the mission?"

Now Jake looked positively haunted. "I . . . I think so."

Bashir leaned forward to hear Jake's theory about how Captain Nog was really going to save the lives of the temporal refugees—and the universe.

And what he heard was utterly fascinating, and at the same time utterly horrifying.

CHAPTER 14

"YOU KNOW HOW stardates work," Commander Arla Rees said.

"Of course." Sisko nodded, distracted, wondering about what was beyond the windowless hull of the small travelpod they were riding in. It reminded him of a two-person escape module, though he could see no indication that it carried emergency supplies or even flight controls. According to Weyoun, transporters were not permitted to operate anywhere within the Bajoran system—though he had provided no explanation why—and all travel here was carried out by pod, runabout, or shuttle. Thus, the survivors from the *Defiant* had been sent off from the *Boreth's* hangar deck two by two, in these tiny pods with no means by which to observe the somehow restored Deep Space 9 as they neared it.

"Seriously?" Arla persisted. "You've actually looked into how the stardate system was devised?"

Sisko looked across the cramped pod—or down the pod, or up it. There was no artificial gravity field, and no inertial dampeners either. Essentially, he and the commander were the only passengers in a gray metal can with two acceleration seats with restraint straps, a pressure door, and four blue-white lights, two at their feet and two at their heads. Sisko even doubted if the simple vessel had its own engines or reaction-control system. He guessed they were being guided from the *Boreth* to DS9 by tractor beam.

"I've studied timekeeping."

Arla frowned. "When? They don't tell you a lot in the Academy."

"Actually, I had reason to take an extension course a few years ago. I even built a few different types of mechanical clocks on my own." Sisko tried to lean back in his acceleration seat, but of course there was no gravity field to aid his maneuver—only the two chest-crossing straps that kept him from floating out of the seat.

"Did your course deal with how the system got started?"

"Some of it. As I understand it, Commander, the impetus behind devising a universal—or, at least, a *galactic*—standard time- and date-keeping system was primarily religious."

From her seat beside him, Arla nodded her head in agreement, though Sisko didn't understand the reason for the odd smile that accompanied that nod.

He continued, not knowing what she was looking for in his answer. "There's certainly precedent for it. Many of the religious festivals and holy days celebrated on Earth are tied to the calendar."

"More often than not the lunar calendar, I believe," Arla said.

"That's right," Sisko said. Though he still didn't know why they were having this conversation, it seemed harmless enough. He decided to run with it. The commander would give him her reasons when she was ready, and that was fine with him. "Now if my memory serves me right, when the first outposts were set up on Earth's moon, since everyone lived underground and the moon is less than a light-second from Earth, timekeeping wasn't a problem. But when the outposts on Mars were established, and it was common for people to spend years there with their families, I recall learning that it became awkward trying to reconcile Martian sols at twenty-four-and-a-half hours with Earth days at just under twenty-four. So a council of religious scholars on Mars came up with the first stardate system—Local Planetary Time—based, I believe, on the look-up tables and charts the Vulcans had been using to reconcile their starships' calendars with their homeworld's."

"The Vulcan system was based in philosophy," Arla said, as if making some important point, "not religion."

"I . . . suppose you could say that," Sisko said amiably. "Now, for most people, once you have a few thousand starships and outposts and a few hundred colonies, it gets too cumbersome to keep using look-up tables and charts. But," Sisko smiled, "not for Vulcans. It's no secret they have no problem keeping forty or fifty different calendar systems in their heads at the same time. But humans, we freely admit, tend to place more cultural and religious importance on specific days."

"Just like Bajorans," Arla said as she turned to him, her eyes filled with a passion Sisko didn't recall having noticed before. She then paused expectantly, as if she had still not heard what she needed to hear.

"Is there some point to this conversation?" Sisko finally asked.

But Arla's answer merely took the form of another question. "What happened next? According to the extension course you took."

Sisko sighed, tiring of their exercise. He wondered how long it would take for the pod to drift over to the station. He was surprising himself with his need to touch the metal walls and feel the decks of DS9 beneath his boots again. And with his desire to have someone tell him how it was that he could have seen DS9 destroyed, and yet see it now restored. Weyoun had been of little help. All he would answer in reply to Sisko's questions was, "In time, Benjamin. All will be explained in time."

Only because there was absolutely nothing else to do at the moment, Sisko continued to humor Arla. This time his answer came straight out of the Academy's first-semester text file. "The underlying principle of the universal stardate system is that of hyperdimensional distance averaging."

"Which is?"

Sisko grimaced. The last time he had had this basic a conversation with anyone about stardates, Jake had been five and sitting on his knee, struggling to get his Flotter Forest Diary program to work on the new padd Sisko had given him for his birthday.

"If you insist." Sisko then rattled off the requisite information. "Any two points in space can be joined by a straight line. The length of that line, divided by two, will yield the midpoint. If the inhabitants of both points convert their local time to the hypothetical time at the midpoint, then they both have an arbitrary yet universally applicable constant time to which they can refer, in order to reconcile their local calendars." He paused before continuing. "You know, of course, it's the exact same principle developed on Earth when an international convention chose to run the zero meridian through Greenwich, establishing Greenwich Mean Time. It was a completely artificial standard, but a standard everyone could use."

"And . . .," Arla prompted.

"And," Sisko sighed. The Bajoran commander's persistence was fully up to Vulcan standards. "Any two points can be joined by a straight line. Go up a dimension, and any three points can be located on a two-dimensional plane. Go up another dimension, and any four points in space can be located on the curved surface of a three-dimensional sphere. Any five points can be found on the surface of a four-dimensional hypersphere, and so on. The standard relationship is that any number of points, *n*, can be mapped onto the surface of a sphere which exists in *n* minus one dimensions. And that means that all of those points are exactly the same distance from the center of the sphere. So, just after the Romulan War, the Starfleet Bureau of Standards and the Vulcan Science Academy arbitrarily chose the center of our galaxy as the center point of a hypersphere with . . . oh, I forget the exact figure . . . something like five hundred million dimensions, okay? So theoretically, every star in our galaxy—along with four hundred million and some starships and outposts—can be located on the surface of the hypersphere and can directly relate their local calendars and clocks to a common standard time that's an equal distance from everywhere. Just as everyone on Earth used to look to Greenwich." Sisko gripped his restraints and pushed himself back into his acceleration couch, trying to compress his spine. The microgravity, not to mention his traveling companion, was giving him a pain in the small of his back, as his spine elongated in the absence of a strong gravity field. "Is that sufficient?" he asked sharply.

"What do you think?" Arla replied.

A sudden shock of pain pulsed through Sisko just above his left kidney. He remembered the sensation from his microgravity training decades ago in the Academy's zero-G gym. He forced his next words out through gritted teeth. "I think it's a damn simple system. One that works independent of position and relativistic velocity. And since it's based on the galactic center it's blessedly free of political overtones." Sisko smiled in relief as his back spasm ended, as suddenly as it had begun, and as he at the same time relived a sudden memory of the one sticking point Jake—like most five-year-olds—had had when it came to learning stardates. "And once a person gets used to the idea that stardates can seem to run backward from place to place, depending on your direction and speed of travel, it becomes an exceedingly simple calculation to convert from local time to stardate anywhere in the galaxy.

"So—if you're asking me if I'm in favor of stardates, Commander, yes, I am. Now what does this have to do with *anything?*"

Arla's expression was maddeningly enigmatic, and Sisko could read no clues in it. "So you consider the system to be completely arbitrary?"

"Any timekeeping system has to be. Because the universe has no absolute time or absolute position. Now would you please answer my question."

"Then how is it—" Arla said, and Sisko's attention was caught by her tone. The commander was finally ready to make her point. "—nine days from now, when the two wormholes are going to open in the Bajoran system only kilometers apart from each other and . . . and supposedly end the universe, or transform it somehow, that that completely arbitrary stardate system is going to roll over to 7700.0 at the same moment that Earth's calendar starts a new century with the first day of 2401 A.C.E.?"

Her question was so incredibly naive, Sisko couldn't believe the Bajoran had even asked it. "Coincidence, Commander." Now it was he who was expectant, waiting for her to say something more, to somehow explain herself.

"Coincidence," she repeated thoughtfully, obviously not accepting his answer. Sisko regarded her with puzzlement.

"Did you know," Arla said, "that an old Klingon calendar system reverts to the Fourth Age of Kahless on that same date? That the Orthodox Andorian Vengeance Cycle begins its 330th iteration then also? That that very same date is the one given in Ferengi tradition when some groups celebrate the day the Great Material River first overflowed its banks among the stars and, in the flood that followed, created Ferenginar and the first Ferengi?"

As Arla recited her list, Sisko observed her gesticulate with one hand to emphasize her words, and was fascinated to see the sudden action in microgravity billow the commander's robes around her like seaweed caught in a tidal current, pulsing back and forth in time with the slow, floating motion of her earring chain.

"*Seventeen* different spacefaring cultures, Captain Sisko. That's how many worlds have calendar systems that either reset or roll over to significant dates or new counting cycles on the *exact* same day the two wormholes come into alignment. Two systems coinciding is a coincidence. I'll give you that. Maybe even three or four. But *seventeen?* There must be some better explanation for that. Wouldn't you agree?"

Sisko took his time replying. He wished he knew the reasons behind the Bajoran commander's sudden obsession with the timing of events and timekeeping systems derived from religious traditions. When he had first met her on DS9, he remembered being impressed by her intensity and by her drive to do the best possible job. True, there had been an awkward moment when he had realized that she was discreetly communicating her interest in getting to know him on a more personal level, but she had responded properly and professionally the moment he had made her aware of his relationship with Kasidy.

He had had no doubt that Arla would make her own mark in Starfleet. Though she had little interest in taking command of a ship and had opted instead for a career track in administration, some of Starfleet's best and most forward-thinking strategic leaders had come from that same background.

But most of all, Sisko knew that Arla had been one of the rare few Bajorans who were completely secular. By her own account, she had no faith in the Prophets. To her, she had maintained to him, they were merely a race of advanced beings who lived in a different dimensional environment, one which rendered communication between themselves and the life-forms of Arla's own dimension very difficult. And she had told him emphatically on more than one occasion that the Celestial Temple was simply a wormhole to her, worthy of study, not for religious reasons, but because it was stable and apparently artificial.

So how did someone like that, he now thought, *suddenly become so interested in comparative religion? And even more intriguingly, why?*

Sisko decided to change tactics. "Do *you* have an explanation?" he asked.

"I don't know," Arla answered simply.

"A theory then? Something that we could put to the test?"

A frown creased Arla's smooth forehead. "A week ago, if you had asked me about the stardate standard, I would have given the same answer you did. That it was an arbitrary timekeeping system. That absolute time didn't exist any more than absolute location." A fleeting smile erased her frown. The smile seemed slightly nervous to Sisko. "What's that old saying, Captain? Everything's relative?"

"That's true, you know," Sisko said.

The Bajoran commander shook her head vehemently in disagreement. "No . . . those other timekeeping systems . . . Terran, Bajoran, Klingon, Andorian . . . they're *not* really arbitrary. They all share a common underpinning—not relative but *related.*"

"Commander." Sisko spoke in his best authoritative tone. "The calendar systems you refer to date back thousands if not tens of thousands of years, to a time before star travel. There is *nothing* to connect them."

"But there is." Arla's voice was rising with an urgency that was beginning to concern Sisko. The source of whatever had upset her was still not clear to him. "Don't you see? They all came out of *religion*. They're all based on some form of creation story. And maybe . . . maybe life arose independently on all those worlds, but maybe it also all arose at the same time—from the same cause."

Sisko's concern changed to indignation. It appeared the Bajoran commander was simply guilty of sloppy thinking. "Commander, for what you're proposing—something for which there is no conclusive empirical proof, by the way—you might as well credit the Preservers with having seeded life throughout the quadrant, as much as invoke a supernatural force. There's about the same amount of evidence for both theories."

Sisko couldn't help noticing Arla's hurt expression, as she came to the correct realization that he considered her idea to be totally without merit. "Captain, I was just trying to explain why I disagreed with the commonly accepted belief that all the timekeeping systems were arbitrary. If they all stem from the same act of creation by the Prophets, then it makes sense that they all come to an end at the same time."

"Then what about stardates?" Sisko asked. "Without question, that's a completely artificial system based in the necessities of interstellar travel."

But Arla was not giving up so easily. "No, sir. You said it yourself. The need for stardates arose in part from the religious need to chart Earth's festivals and holy days on other worlds. How do we know the religious scholars of the time didn't build into their timekeeping system the same hidden knowledge that underlies all the other systems in the quadrant?"

Sisko shifted in his accelerator seat, feeling the restraints securing him in place. He felt trapped in both the conversation and the pod. It was all too obvious that he wasn't going to prevail in this argument. As soon as anyone brought up anything like "hidden knowledge," all possibility of a debate based on available facts flew out the airlock. "I take it your religious views have changed in the past few days," Sisko said in massive understatement.

"I don't know," Arla said, her voice declining in intensity. At last, even she was sounding weary now. Sisko knew how she felt. "What I do know is that there has to be *some* sort of explanation," she said. "And as someone trained in the scientific method, I have to keep my mind open to *all* possible explanations, even the ones I might think are unlikely."

Sisko was aware that the Bajoran commander was chiding him for apparently closing his own mind to the possibility of supernatural intervention in the affairs of the galaxy. But he felt secure in his approach. After all, he had dealt with the Prophets firsthand. And though explanations from them were often difficult to come by, subtlety was not their style. If there had been some sort of connection between the Prophets and worlds other than Bajor, Sisko felt certain that strong evidence for it would have turned up much earlier than now.

"An admirable position," he said in deliberate tones of finality, hoping that Arla would understand and accept that he wanted no more part in this conversation.

Just then the hull of the travelpod creaked, and a slight tremor moved through the small craft.

"Tractor beam?" Arla asked.

"Or docking clamp. Do we seem to be slowing down?"

Immediately, Arla held out both her arms, and watched them as if trying to see if they might respond to a change in delta vee. But except for the undulations of the sleeves of her robe, her arms remained motionless. "Some tractor beams have their own inertial dampening effect," she said. "We could be spinning like a plasma coil right now and not know it."

Sisko knew that was a possibility, though he didn't see the point. From what he'd learned so far, the Ascendancy, for all its apparent capabilities, seemed to be in favor of not expending any effort or supplies unless absolutely necessary.

The lights suddenly flashed with almost blinding intensity, and there was another scrape and a stronger metallic bang, followed by the sound of rushing air. Sisko looked to the pressure door.

"That'll probably be an airlock sealing against the hull," Arla said.

"Not on DS9," Sisko said. "If we were at a docking port on a pylon or the main ring, we'd be within the artificial gravity field."

Arla was looking at him with concern. "Then where did we go? To another ship?"

"I don't know," Sisko said. He braced himself against his restraints and half twisted in his chair to face the door. He debated the wisdom of releasing the restraints, but if a gravity field did switch on suddenly, he couldn't be sure in which direction he might fall.

A new vibration shook the hull—something fast, almost an electrical hum.

"We're changing velocity," Arla said.

Sisko saw the chain of her earring slowly begin to flutter down until it hung beside her neck. But whether it was the effect of acceleration or the beginning of a gravity field there was no way to tell. Einstein had determined that almost five hundred years ago and that, too, was still true.

And then both he and Arla were abruptly shaken as a loud bang erupted in the pod. The sound seemed to come from the direction of the door.

The next bang was even louder but not as startling.

The third deformed the door, and Sisko tensed as he heard a hiss of air indicating that atmospheric integrity had been lost around the door's seal.

But when the pressure within the pod didn't seem to change appreciably, Sisko revised his deduction. They had docked with or somehow been taken aboard another vessel whose atmosphere was slightly different from the pod's.

A fourth bang rocked the pod. The door creaked and swung open.

Beyond the pod's simple portal Sisko glimpsed a pale-yellow light fixture shining within a dark airlock. He could just make out the curve of a Cardassian door wheel in the gloom.

"This *is* the station," he exclaimed. He touched the release tabs on his restraints and pushed himself from the chair. His feet gently made contact with the floor of the pod. Automatically, Sisko estimated gravity at about one-tenth Earth normal.

He nodded at Arla, who then released herself to stand on the floor, still holding the loose restraints to keep herself from bouncing into the pod's low ceiling.

With extreme caution, Sisko began moving toward the open portal. The glare from the single dim light fixture in the airlock prevented him from seeing through the viewport in the far door. All he could be sure of was that whatever was beyond, it was in the dark as well.

He stepped from the pod into the airlock, almost falling as normal gravity suddenly took over.

The moment he regained his footing he took hold of Arla's arm. "Careful. They must be able to focus gravity fields better than we could."

"Who?" Arla asked, as she cautiously entered the more powerful field.

"Knowing Weyoun, this is probably some game he's devised."

"Or a trap."

"He already had us," Sisko reminded her. He pushed his face against the viewport, cupping his hands around his eyes to shield his vision and squinting to see some sort of detail in whatever lay beyond. But the darkness there was absolute.

A sudden mechanical grinding noise caused him to spin around. He saw the other wheel door roll shut, cutting off any chance of their returning to the pod. In any event, with the pressure door damaged—*by what?* Sisko suddenly wondered—the pod would not be the safest place to be.

Another rush of air popped his ears. Oddly enough, the effect made Sisko feel better, because he knew it meant that when the second wheel door opened there would be an atmosphere on the other side.

He turned to check on Arla. "Are you all right?"

Silent, she nodded, slowly raising her hand to point toward the second wheel door, her eyes wide with alarm.

And then just as the second door began to roll Sisko caught sight of what had disturbed her. For just an instant, through the moving viewport, against the darkness of what lay beyond, two eyes glowed red.

"It's Weyoun," Sisko said in disgust. Though what the Vorta was attempting to accomplish with this bit of theater was beyond him.

Then a sudden wind of hot, damp air from beyond the airlock swept over him in a rush, and he gagged at the sweet, fetid stench that accompanied it. Behind him, Arla did the same.

Sisko looked up, eyes watering, the sharp taste of bile in his mouth, knowing that whatever else lay in the darkness, there were organic bodies, rotting.

Then, from out of the darkness, the two red eyes approached him.

Sisko's vision was still blurry in the assault of that terrible smell, but with a sudden tensing of his stomach he realized that the shadowy outlines of the figure who was entering the airlock indicated someone taller than Weyoun. And those shoulders—

It was a Cardassian!

Arla cried out in fear behind him.

A powerful hand closed around Sisko's throat, its cold grip unnaturally strong. Red eyes of fire blazed down at him.

And Sisko recognized the creature who held his life in one gray hand.

It was *Dukat!*

CHAPTER 15

"WHERE ARE MY PEOPLE?" Worf growled.

Normally, Jadzia didn't like to see her husband give himself over to typical Klingon confrontational techniques. But in this case, as Worf glared down at Captain T'len Jadzia was in full agreement. There were too many unanswered questions and too little time to use diplomacy.

T'len stepped back from Worf, her Vulcan features revealing no outward sign of intimidation. Her gaze, however, moved almost imperceptibly to the closed door leading from the planning room to the corridor, as if checking for a path of retreat. *Good,* Jadzia thought. Here was where having three hundred years of experience paid off. And her experience was telling her now that there was seldom a better person to negotiate with than a Vulcan who had a logical reason to cut negotiations short.

She watched as T'len tugged down on her black

tunic. "If you wish to determine the fate of your family members," the Vulcan captain told Worf, "you have been instructed in accessing Starfleet computers for all pertinent personnel records."

Jadzia hid a smile as Worf slammed his massive fist down on the table beside him, causing a large schematic padd to jump several centimeters into the air and spilling a coffee mug onto the floor. Klingons could be so messy. It was one of their most endearing traits, she thought as she regarded her mate with loving pride.

"I am not talking about my family," Worf shouted. "I know my parents have passed on to *Sto-Vo-Kor.* I know my brother died in the evacuation of Lark 53. I am asking, What happened to the Klingon *people?* And I want an answer *now!*"

T'len narrowed her eyes, in what was to Jadzia a rather startling and misguided display of unalloyed Vulcan defiance.

"Or you'll do what, Commander?"

Worf didn't hesitate an instant. Jadzia expected no less of him. Once her mate made up his mind to do something, she knew little could dissuade him.

"Or I will kill you where you stand," Worf said.

T'len raised a dark, sculpted eyebrow. "You wouldn't dare."

"I would rather die battling my enemies than wait passively for the universe to end."

T'len looked past Worf at Jadzia. "Will you talk sense into your husband?"

Jadzia took a moment to enjoy the undercurrent of fear in T'len's voice. It was so satisfying when people had their worldviews turned upside down. As she had discovered in her many different lifetimes, on a personal level few events proved more rewarding. Though it might, of course, take some time for the person caught in such turmoil to realize it.

She shrugged as if completely powerless in this situation, though she and Worf had carefully rehearsed the moment—and this confrontation. "What can I say? You know how willful Klingons can be."

T'len's chin lifted, and she turned again to face Worf. She was backed against a central engineering table that flickered with constantly updating engineering drawings of the *Phoenix*. "Commander, I am not your enemy."

"If you do not tell me the fate of the Klingon Empire in this time period, then I have no choice but to conclude you are somehow responsible for the destruction of the Empire. That makes you my enemy, and deserving of death."

In what Jadzia could only consider a Vulcan's last-ditch retreat into pure desperation, T'len thrust her hand forward in an attempt to give Worf a nerve pinch.

As Jadzia knew he would, Worf caught the Vulcan's hand before it had traveled more than half the distance to his shoulder. Then he began to squeeze it. Hard. "You have attacked me," Worf announced in stentorian tones. "I am now justified in defending myself." At the same time, he began to bend T'len's hand backward.

"I *order* you to release me!" T'len said.

Worf was implacable. He continued without pause. "I do not recognize your right to order me. In my time, the Empire and the Federation were allies. Since you do not support the Empire, to me that makes you an enemy of the Federation. Either explain to me why and how conditions have changed, or prepare to take passage on the Barge of the Dead."

Jadzia could see T'len beginning to tremble in her effort to resist Worf's grip and to control the discomfort she must be feeling in her stressed wrist and hand.

"Vulcans do not believe in Klingon superstition," the captain said, her voice wavering despite her attempts to keep it steady.

"It will not remain a superstition for long," Worf said grimly. "In less than a minute, I guarantee you will have firsthand knowledge."

T'len raised her other hand to try to slap her communicator. But Worf caught that hand, too.

Jadzia judged the time was right. She stepped forward. "Captain, you know we want to help the cause. Isn't it logical that you provide us with the same information that inspires *you* to fight?"

"This is not your concern," Worf snapped at her, exactly as Jadzia had suggested he do. "The Trill homeworld is still within the Federation. But for all the information Starfleet is willing to give me"—he bent down until his fangs and glaring eyes were only a centimeter from T'len's tense features—"the Empire might as well have been destroyed."

"It was!" T'len suddenly exclaimed. "There! Does that satisfy you?!"

Jadzia could see the surprise in Worf's face. Almost as an afterthought he released the Vulcan's hand, and she immediately hugged it to her chest, rubbing at her wrist.

"Why could you not tell me at the beginning?" Worf said accusingly. "Just as you told the humans about the destruction of the Earth."

"Because the Earth was destroyed by the Grigari," T'len said sharply and, Vulcan or not, the bitterness in her was clearly evident. "But the Empire destroyed itself."

At once Jadzia moved to Worf's side then, to keep him grounded in this moment, to prevent his descent into the full rage of battle at T'len's revelation. She put her hands on his arm and his back.

"You—will—tell—me—how." Through the touch that connected them Jadzia felt the visceral struggle each word cost her mate.

T'len's answer was slow in coming. "Project Looking Glass," she said with a wary look at Worf and Jadzia. "The Klingons were so proud of it. While the Federation fought a holding battle against the Ascendancy, the Empire was to prepare a safe haven from the destruction of the universe."

Jadzia stroked her mate's back to calm him. "Isn't that a contradiction in terms?" she asked.

"Not if the safe haven is another universe," T'len said.

As quickly as that, Jadzia understood. "Looking Glass," she said, stepping away from Worf.

Because Worf understood, as well. "The Mirror Universe."

T'len nodded, and Jadzia relaxed, detecting the subtle change in the Vulcan captain's stance in response to Worf's more measured tones.

"In that universe," T'len added with greater assurance, as she sensed that Worf would not respond physically to her unwelcome information, "the Klingon-Cardassian Alliance was in disarray and easy to overcome once the Prime Directive was suspended. The total population was much lower. There were sufficient worlds in which to create new colonies. And the best physicists concluded that the destruction of our own universe would have no effect on the Mirror Universe.

It appears that the Prophets—or the wormhole aliens of Jalbador—don't seem to exist there."

Jadzia knew Worf would not accept T'len's characterization of Klingons, no matter which universe they existed in. And he did not. "It is not like my people to plan for defeat," Worf growled.

T'len promptly deflected his objection. "That was just a contingency plan, Commander. The original intention was to send a Klingon fleet into the Mirror Universe, fight its way to Bajor, then reappear in our universe behind the Ascendancy's lines."

Worf grunted approvingly. "A worthy deception. It sounds like the work of General Martok."

"Chancellor Martok," T'len corrected. "And it *was* his plan."

Jadzia could see from the way Worf's eyes flashed that he already knew how the plan had ended.

"How did it fail?" he asked.

The hesitant manner in which T'len answered suggested to Jadzia that the plan's outcome still baffled the Vulcan captain. "I assure you, Commander Worf, the first exploratory and reconnaissance missions were flawless. Every replicator in the Empire and most of those throughout the Federation were requisitioned to create transporter pads, to transfer goods and warriors to the other side. That effort alone took two years. We still haven't replaced all the replicators we expended. But in time our forces were ready."

T'len's eyes lost their focus and became opaque, as she relived the moment. "The fleet—the Armada—moved out from the Empire in the Mirror Universe, heading for Bajor, while at the same time in our universe, to counter any suspicions, Earth entered into trade and treaty negotiations with the Grigari. But the Grigari fleet attacked Earth without warning, and with so many ships committed to Looking Glass—which we were certain had not been detected by the Ascendancy—there were no reinforcements to save that world."

T'len's eyes cleared, and she looked squarely at Worf. "When word reached the Mirror Universe that the Grigari had attacked *here* before the Klingons could attack *there*, the Fleet turned around to come to Earth's defense. And when it was in that state of confusion as its mission changed, a second Grigari fleet attacked there as well."

Jadzia took an involuntary step forward, then stopped herself as Worf's head bowed in sorrow.

"But how . . . how could the defeat of the Armada lose the *Empire?*" he asked T'len.

"All those transporters," T'len said quietly. "They had been used to send untold trillions of tonnes of supplies and equipment between the universes. Enormous complexes of them were on all the major worlds of the Empire."

"And the Grigari—" T'len paused for a moment before continuing. At that moment, Jadzia realized that in her way the Vulcan captain was trying to be kind to Worf, as she succinctly completed her account with little elaboration of the devastating consequences of the plan's failure.

"The Grigari used those same transporters to move weapons from the Mirror Universe into ours, weapons which detonated in place and tore apart worlds, rendered atmospheres unbreathable and collapsed entire ecosystems.

"The end result . . . was that we learned that the Grigari had known exactly what we had planned and had prepared a perfect series of countermoves against us. According to our best estimates," T'len concluded, "there are slightly more than one million Klingons left alive in this quadrant."

Worf's broad chest heaved, and if not for the presence of the Vulcan Jadzia would have reached out and drawn him close to her, to share his terrible grief.

When he finally spoke, Worf's voice was low but steady. "Why would you not tell me this before?"

"Because Starfleet needs every warrior who can serve. And that includes you, Commander. Also"—Jadzia felt T'len's gaze upon her—"we were concerned that if . . . *when* you found out about the fate of your Empire, you would do what so many other Klingons have done—go off on a suicidal mission to assuage survivor guilt and die in battle. Or that you would attempt to accomplish some great victory, in order to ensure that a relative lost in the destruction of the Armada might find a place in *Sto-Vo-Kor*."

The sounds of Worf's deep breathing intensified, but he did not respond further.

"What will you do, Commander?" T'len asked. "Abandon Starfleet? Abandon the *Phoenix?* Go off and die in glorious battle?"

Jadzia held her breath. This time, not even she knew what Worf's answer would be.

It seemed forever to her before her mate again spoke. "How did Chancellor Martok die?"

"He was with the fleet," T'len said simply, "on the flagship *The Heart of Kahless*. But they were wiped out to the last warrior. I do not know precisely how he died."

"He died with honor," Worf growled fiercely in what

Jadzia knew was a challenge. "Of that you can be certain."

Jadzia tensed. The Vulcan captain stared up at Worf for a moment before making her decision. "I am," the Vulcan said.

Worf nodded once, then said, "I am a Starfleet officer. I see no conflict in fulfilling that duty and behaving honorably as a Klingon warrior. But you must no longer keep secrets from me, or from any of us. Either we are your fellow warriors and your equals, or we will leave you to fight on our own. Is that understood?"

"Yes," T'len said.

Jadzia had a question of her own for T'len. "Why are there so few humans left?"

Once again, T'len's voice betrayed an un-Vulcan-like emotional turmoil, but now Jadzia was realizing that more than just institutions had changed in this time. So had the people. She would have to remember that, and not depend on perhaps irrelevant assumptions derived from centuries of experience in other times. The knowledge gave her an odd feeling of freedom from the past lives she remembered. Whatever she and the others faced in this time would require her to make observations uniquely her own.

"The Klingon colony worlds," T'len explained, "were used to create the Armada in the Mirror Universe. In contrast, human colony worlds were used to establish emergency communities, survival camps really . . . in case Starfleet and the Empire were not successful in stopping the Ascendancy. And the same type of transporter facilities were installed everywhere from Alpha Centauri to Deneva. At sixty percent efficiency, with the facilities we established on fifty colony worlds, we would have had the capacity to transfer up to thirty million people a day into the Mirror Universe. In these past five years, we might have saved—evacuated—almost sixty billion people."

The Trill understood at least one reason for the Vulcan captain's distress. Sixty billion was a vast number, yet it would only have accounted for slightly less than ten percent of the total population of the Federation. And factoring in the populations of the nonaligned systems and all the other beings who must exist elsewhere in the galaxy and throughout the universe, sixty billion was as inconsequential as a raindrop in an ocean.

But there was another possible reason.

"The Grigari used those transporters too, didn't they?" Jadzia asked.

"Nanospores," T'len said with distaste. "Nanites, which exist only to disassemble living cells to make other nanites, which then spread to other life-forms and begin the process again. They can't be screened through biofilters. There are no drugs to which they will respond. Neither are they affected by extremes of temperature. Whole populations were . . . were dissolved. Entire worlds stripped of their biospheres. And Starfleet had to maintain quarantines around all of them, to incinerate any ship that attempted to leave." T'len's dark eyes bore into Jadzia's. "Do you really want to know *more?*"

Jadzia touched Worf's arm, giving it a gentle squeeze. Felt no response in return. "Not now," she said. "I think we need to be alone for a while."

"We tour the *Phoenix* at 0800 hours tomorrow morning," T'len said, by way of agreement.

Jadzia nodded. T'len sighed as she gave a last rub to her strained wrist, then left the planning room.

As soon as the Vulcan captain had moved through the doorway and out of earshot, Worf turned to Jadzia, looked down at her. "This future *cannot* be permitted to happen," he said.

"But it already has, Worf."

Worf shook his head angrily. "We are still connected to our past. To *our* present. We must go back somehow and prevent this."

It was unfortunate, Jadzia thought, that the direct Klingon approach was not always the best—not even in this time, she would wager. And it was always so difficult to explain that to her mate. She put both hands on Worf's shoulders. "Worf, the only way we can go back to our present is by retracing our slingshot trajectory around the red wormhole, and that wormhole is in the middle of the Bajoran system. There's nothing Starfleet can do to get anywhere near it. We *have* to accept that there's nothing more we can do to change the past. But with the *Phoenix*, we do have a chance to change the future."

"I refuse to accept that."

Jadzia made a playful fist and lightly tapped her knuckles against Worf's heavy brow ridges. "Just as I thought," she said. "No evidence of brain matter. Solid bone throughout."

Her mate glared at her. "This is not the time for levity! The universe is trapped in a nightmare and we are the only ones who can restore it!"

"I agree," Jadzia said, drawing her fingers along Worf's cheek. "But what do I always tell you when you make such grand and glorious plans?"

Jadzia hid her smile as Worf's bluster became uncertain.

"I . . . do not remember," he said.

Jadzia didn't believe that for an instant. "We can do anything that we choose to do . . . *say* it. . . ."

Worf grimaced, as if he knew there was no escape this time. And this time, Jadzia thought, she would see that there wasn't.

"We can do anything that we choose to do," he repeated without conviction.

"Very good," Jadzia said, as she lowered her hand to caress his broad chest. "But sometimes, we do not have to choose to do it *now.*"

She looked up at Worf, knowing what it was they both must do to prepare for the battle ahead, just as the first Klingon male and female had done before they had stormed heaven and destroyed the gods who had created them.

"The Empire must be avenged," Worf said.

"I know," Jadzia agreed. "But first we must prepare for battle."

Worf nodded his assent, placed both powerful hands on her arms.

"Computer," Jadzia said clearly, "seal the planning office door. Security request gamma five." She smiled at Worf, glad she had reviewed the security manuals for the shipyards.

Something clicked inside the door, and the security condition light changed from amber to red.

Right at that instant, Worf leaned down and kissed her, his full embrace of her powerful, charged with the emotion of the moment and not tempered by concerns that had gone before or would be faced in the future.

But that was Worf's way, not hers. There was still something that troubled Jadzia. She pulled back from him, but did not look away.

"What?" Worf asked roughly, his voice thick with passion.

"Something Captain T'len said. About . . . getting into *Sto-Vo-Kor.*"

Worf threw back his head proudly. "An easy matter. I have eaten the heart of an enemy."

"There's more to it than that."

"Of course. A warrior must die in glorious battle."

"But T'len said that some Klingons were trying to fight to get their relatives into *Sto-Vo-Kor.*"

Worf sobered, became thoughtful. "There are many qualities a warrior must possess. Among them is the ability to inspire great actions in the hearts of others. So, if a great warrior does not fall in battle, he is not necessarily denied the reward of *Sto-Vo-Kor.* If those who know him dedicate their own great battle to him, then there will be a place for the fallen among the honored dead."

Jadzia felt a wave of thankful relief for her mate's generous nature. In its way, the Klingon religion was also humane, in that there were many chances for personal redemption, even after death.

She gripped Worf's hand tightly in both of hers, and with perfect warrior's inflection she said in Klingon, "Then know this, my husband. That if you should die outside of battle, I will dedicate each battle I fight for the rest of my life to your honor and to your place among the honored dead."

Worf trailed his fingers through her long dark hair. "You are the most romantic female I have ever known," he whispered gruffly.

Jadzia took that hand as well, and lightly bit his fingers. "And will you fight for me if I fall outside of battle?"

Worf kissed her forehead. "That is not your destiny. You will die an old woman with long white hair, secure in your bed, surrounded by your grandchildren, and it will be our sons who will win glorious victories for us both, that we might sit at the table of *Sto-Vo-Kor.*"

Jadzia felt tears well up in her eyes as her love for Worf grew even stronger. She smiled at him, knowing that the time for words, no matter how beautiful, was coming to an end.

"Our *sons?*" she asked teasingly.

"At least ten," Worf murmured as he crushed her in his arms.

"Ten?" Jadzia laughed. "Then we'd better get to work. . . ."

They didn't speak past that, and afterward, content in the arms of her warrior, Jadzia drifted off to sleep, dreaming of sons—and daughters—and scores of grandchildren, and the perfect love she knew would last for decades to come.

Which meant, she dreamily realized, that the universe would *not* end as everyone feared.

She slept soundly, knowing that the future was secure, and that it would be many years before she came to the gates of *Sto-Vo-Kor.*

CHAPTER 16

"Do you BELIEVE?" Gul Dukat shouted, and his voice echoed in the darkness of the charnel house that was Deep Space 9.

Sisko fought to breathe as the Cardassian's deadly chokehold tightened on his throat. He struggled to get a grip on his attacker's arm, but it was as if Dukat's hand were forged from neutronium, and Sisko began to despair of surviving this possessed creature, who was something other than an ordinary life-form.

"DO YOU?" Dukat spat into Sisko's face, his foul breath so much stronger than the malodorous air surrounding them that it seemed to Sisko the Cardassian himself could be the source of the terrible stench. *"Before you are thrown into the Fire Pits to burn for your sins, will you not confess your unworthiness?"*

Sisko flailed uselessly, at last pointing to his gasping

mouth, trying to form the words, "Can't speak," before he lost consciousness.

Dukat's glittering eyes flickered. He angled his head. His hand began to reduce its pressure on Sisko's swollen throat. Sisko's heartbeat no longer thundered in his ears.

And then something dark streaked through the air above Sisko's head, and he heard a thick thud of impact as Dukat's hand released him, and the Cardassian fell back into darkness.

In the same moment, Sisko collapsed to his knees, gulping air, gagging, massaging his bruised throat. In his relief to finally get a breath into his strained lungs, the air no longer seemed as dreadful as it had earlier. Breathing almost normally, he looked up to see Arla at his side, the arm of one of the pod's acceleration chairs balanced in her hand like a club—the weapon she had used against Dukat. She was peering into the dark shadows of the station, the only light on her the backglow from the pale yellow light in the airlock behind them, and beyond that the distant light from their travel pod.

She looked down at Sisko. "Are you all right, Captain?"

Sisko nodded and forced himself to his feet, half-stumbling on the ill-fitting robes he wore.

"Was that Gul Dukat?" Arla asked.

His throat still burning, Sisko shook his head in agreement.

And then a shriek came from the darkness. ". . . *Unbeliever. . . .*"

"Dukat!" Sisko croaked. "We don't want to fight you!"

"Then that makes it much easier for *me!*" Dukat screamed back, and from nowhere a solid fist struck Sisko in the side of the head, knocking him away from Arla, toward the open airlock.

Before Sisko could recover his balance, a shaft of blood-red light sprang from the open palm of Dukat's hand and reached out to engulf Arla, five meters away, in a scarlet corona of energy.

The tall Bajoran cried out as sparks flew from her earring and she was *lifted* into the air, her body writhing, arms swinging, legs kicking furiously.

"Leave her alone!" Sisko jumped to his feet again, commanding Dukat to obey him.

The Cardassian turned and stared at him, head still cocked, its outline framed in a wild frothing spray of white hair in the radiant-red backscatter of energy pulsing from his outstretched hand.

"Emissary," Dukat intoned ominously, "you know I can't do that. She's Bajoran."

"She's no threat to you!"

Dukat drew his hand back and its red halo of energy cut off as if a switch had been thrown. Arla's body fell at once, striking the deck heavily. She moaned, then lay still.

Sisko moved quickly to her side, checked for a pulse, felt it flutter in her neck.

Then he became aware of Dukat towering over him. Sisko looked up, for the first time noticing the red armband the Cardassian wore, and understood what it meant.

"Follow me," Dukat ordered. For now his hollow eyes were shadowed, dark.

"Why?" Sisko said, cradling Arla in his arms.

The white-haired figure shrugged. "Because, Emissary, you have already come back from the dead, just as I have. What more can I do to you that the Prophets have not already done? Yet think what you might *learn. . . .*"

Then, with a flourish of the dark robes he wore, the

Cardassian whirled around and walked into the shadows. The movement caused a rush of evil-smelling air to wash over Sisko, and he swayed back beneath its force. Recovering, he glanced at the open airlock, though he knew the damaged travelpod could not be used again.

He had no choice now.

He lifted up Arla's unconscious form and followed after Dukat, the path taking him deeper into the unknown darkness of a Deep Space 9 he did not know.

Sisko emerged onto what once had been the Promenade, though there was little now that was familiar to him.

In the half-light of a handful of flickering yellow fusion tubes, Sisko could see no sign of any stores or kiosks, only a circular sweep of bare metal deck puddled here and there with dark liquid and framed by empty, open storerooms.

And there were the corpses too, of course. The reason why the air was so awful here and throughout the station.

From what was before him, Sisko guessed at least a hundred had died, more if the scattered, haphazard piles of robed figures were the same in the other sections of the Promenade that he couldn't see.

And the slaughter must have gone on for some time. A few of the bodies were little more than skeletal remains. Some were still covered with flesh, though that was black and shriveled. And others were only a few days old, fresh like those to be found on battlefields, already swelling with the potent gases of decay.

The only thing they shared, other than the silence of the dead, was a thin band of red cloth, tied around each arm—just like Dukat's.

"My congregation," Dukat proclaimed proudly.

He stood on a platform, a pulpit that was little more than a hull plate balanced on top of a battered metal bench and half-covered by a filthy white cloth.

"Can you hear the applause?" Dukat cried as he closed his eyes briefly in bliss. "The cheers and the joy?"

Sisko shifted his dead-weight burden, trying to change Arla's position within his tiring arms, to ease his aching back. The Bajoran was half a head taller than he was, and well muscled. And heavy. She stirred and gave a faint cry, but he didn't want to put her down here. There was no clear space that had not been fouled by the dead.

He called out to Dukat. "Do you follow Weyoun? Or does Wey—"

"SILENCE!" Dukat thundered, and a ruby bolt of fire shot from his hand to scorch the deck at Sisko's feet. In an instant, the dark metal there turned dull red with heat and a nearby puddle of unidentifiable liquid became steam, filling the air with a choking, noxious cloud of what smelled like sewer gas.

"Weyoun." Dukat spat the name out contemptuously. "The Pretender. The Puppet. A mindless plaything of those unfit to dwell within the Temple."

Sisko looked around, confused. Whatever Dukat had been up to here, it had been going on for months at least, if not years. So why had Weyoun brought Sisko and the other survivors from the *Defiant* here? Unless . . .

"Dukat—where are we?"

Dukat gestured grandly to each side of his makeshift pulpit. "In my domain: as it was, as it always shall be, Terok Nor without end. Amojan. Can I hear an Amojan?" He peered down at Sisko, his eyes aflame once more, his terrible gaze stopping on Arla. "Ah, I see you've brought a sacrifice. An innocent. To die like all the others you condemned so long ago, to bless this station."

"No," Sisko said quickly. He nodded at the bodies that surrounded them. "Is that who these people are? What they became? Sacrifices?"

Dukat held out his arms, hands cupped, as if seeking and receiving the adulation of a crowd. "Can you not hear them, Emissary? They have such courage to resist the beguiling promises of the False Prophets. As you well know."

"Which Prophets are those?" Sisko grunted, as he had to let Arla's body slip down, resting it full length against his to support her upright though still unconscious form. "Weyoun's Prophets from the red wormhole? Or those from twenty-five years ago, in the blue wormhole?"

Dukat reeled back, as if startled by the question. Then he leaped down from his platform, advancing on Sisko, his scaly, bare feet splashing through the murky pools of liquid on the metal decking of the Promenade.

"You still don't know, do you?" Dukat crowed in amazement.

"Know what?"

Dukat's gap-toothed smile was almost a leer. This close to his old adversary, Sisko now saw how cruelly the years had treated him, not only turning his hair white but deeply furrowing his skin, whose loose folds now hung from his chin and jowls, emphasizing his gray reptilian knobs and plates.

"I've missed you," Dukat sneered. "Oh, the times we had, the places we've been."

"You were going to tell me something."

Dukat nodded gravely. "I *was* going to kill you. Back then. Before the war was over. I had traveled so far, learned so many things, and then I returned. Did they tell you that? I returned to Damar and Weyoun, determined to obtain from them a simple carving . . . a trifling piece of wood, really. But it had the power to drive the False Prophets from their Temple. To restore Kosst Amojan and the Pah-wraiths to their realm of glory. And to *destroy* you so utterly. . . ." Dukat's grin was terrifying. "So imagine my surprise when Damar told me you were already dead, swallowed by a wormhole. End of story. End of revenge. End of everything.

"Do you understand the irony of that moment?" Dukat snickered, and spittle flew from his open mouth. Sisko turned his face away to avoid breathing the same air. "I came back with plans for my ultimate triumph, but you had already taken it from me, defeating me before you even knew the battle had begun. And then, just to prove that the False Prophets have a sense of humor like no other, since Damar had no other use for me, he had me arrested. For treason."

"But not killed," Sisko said, drawing Arla closer to him. "How merciful."

Dukat reached out to pat Sisko's shoulder and trail a horn-like fingernail along Arla's insensate cheek. "Oh, I've died a thousand times since then, Captain. I'm dead now. In a way, I suppose, I always have been." He frowned at Arla. "Isn't she tiring you? I could take her if you'd like."

"I can manage. Why was Weyoun bringing me to see you?"

Dukat exploded with laughter. This time there was no way to avoid the spray. Sisko closed his eyes just in time. "He was doing no such thing, Emissary! He needs you to end the universe. But I saved you! Brought you here, out of his reach. And as long as you stay here, the universe *cannot* end. It's such a simple plan, don't you think? And all you have to do . . ." And here, Dukat's voice dropped deeper, became louder. "*. . . is remain here forever, like all my congregation.*"

Sisko edged back, keeping Arla close to him, as the red light in Dukat's eyes began to grow in intensity.

"Do not be afraid," Dukat commanded, raising his hands so that Sisko could see the sparks of crimson that were beginning to crackle across his fingers and palms like milling insects of light. *"I have eaten the heart of Kosst Amojan. I have crushed the foul Pah-wraiths who dwelled in the Fire Caves. I am on your side now, Emissary! We serve the same lost Prophets!"*

Then double rays of red light slammed into Sisko and Arla, driving her inert body into his so the two of them fell backward and into a slushy mound of soft bodies.

In the explosion of decomposed tissue and fluids that erupted around them, Arla slipped from Sisko's grasp. But the pungent smell finally awoke her, and she flailed about in the ghastly detritus as, half-conscious and confused, she tried and failed to get to her feet.

Dukat ignored her and held out his fiery hand to Sisko. *"Join me,"* he roared in his demonic voice, *"and the universe shall be saved for all time!"*

And despite the absolute horror of Dukat's temple and the nightmare world that Deep Space 9 had become, Sisko at last heard something in the ghastly Cardassian's entreaty. Something offering hope.

Sisko took a deep breath. Why couldn't he join Dukat? Why couldn't he reach out to the Cardassian's hand and thereby change the fate of the universe?

After all, Sisko thought, *I already know I'm lost.*

Everyone who had come forward in time with him on board the *Defiant* was lost. And if things continued as Weyoun and even Starfleet seemed to believe they would, then all of existence was lost as well.

It would be so simple. So easy. So . . . *worthwhile.*

Sisko got to his feet, took a step forward.

"HERETIC!"

The cry had come from Arla. Sisko had forgotten she was even present. "What are you saying?"

Stained and disheveled but standing once again, the Bajoran pointed a shaking finger at Dukat. "Look at him, Captain," she shouted accusingly. "He's wearing the robes and armband of a Pah-wraith cult."

Sisko stared incredulously at Arla. *He* knew about the Pah-wraith cults because of what had happened to his son when the Reckoning had played out on Deep Space 9. But how did *Arla,* a nonbeliever, know about such things?

"She's a lost child," Dukat crooned. "You don't have to pay any attention to her. Take my hand, Emissary. Take my hand and save existence."

The Reckoning, Sisko thought wildly. So many questions swirled through his mind. Why couldn't he voice at least one of them?

"You'll be able to hear them cheering," Dukat said silkily as he gazed at the bodies around them. "You'll be able to feel their love. . . ." His eyes flashed scarlet, went dark, flashed again.

Love, Sisko thought hazily. He had lost Kasidy. He had lost . . . "My son—what about Jake?"

"He's a lovely boy," Dukat said. "And he's waiting for you. Take my hand. . . . You'll see him for yourself."

"You can't believe him, Captain," Arla warned.

"Whose side are you on?" Sisko demanded of her. He looked at Dukat. "Whose side are *you* on?"

"The side of truth," they both answered together.

Then they both looked at each other and hurled the same word at the same time, *"Liar!"*

Sisko stepped back again, clarity suddenly freeing him. "I know where we are!" he exclaimed. "The wormhole!" He looked from Dukat to Arla. "This is some sort of Orb experience! You're . . . you're both Prophets!"

Dukat howled with scornful laughter. "Really, Emissary. How naive. Can Prophets *die?"*

And then, as if brushing dust from his robes, Dukat lifted his hand and a blast of energy felled Arla. She crumpled with a terrible finality to the floor. A thin trickle of blood trailed from the corner of her mouth.

"No one's had an Orb experience since Weyoun returned from the second Temple," Dukat said in the awful silence. "You must accept the truth, Emissary. It is *now,* and you are very much *here."*

"I don't believe you," Sisko insisted, feeling dazed and doubtful. Arla wasn't dying, *couldn't* be dying, not in the wormhole. "There was a flash of light in the travelpod," he told Dukat. "Like an Orb being opened. That's when all this started."

"True," Dukat agreed. "Except that the light was my transporter, not an Orb."

Sisko fell to his knees and placed a hand on Arla's throat. Nothing. No pulse this time. He struggled to remember something Weyoun had said. "But transporters aren't allowed in the Bajoran system."

"Have you asked yourself why that should be?" Dukat asked. "What Weyoun is really afraid of?"

"He's afraid of attack." Sisko didn't know why he

felt compelled to answer the madman—unless it was the influence of the Prophets.

The light in Dukat's red eyes flared again. "Or is he afraid of escape?"

"Escape to *where,* Dukat?" Sisko asked in frustration. Then Arla's pulse quickened to sudden life under this hand. "You see," he said in triumph, "she's *not* dead!"

"Emissary, I can't believe you're being this obtuse. Look where you are."

"Deep Space 9!"

"Yet that station was destroyed, was it not?"

"The *Defiant* was restored! Obviously the station was too."

Dukat shook his head ponderously. "But it wasn't."

Sisko had had enough. Arla was alive. So was he. Where there was life there was something to fight for. "Then how can we be here?"

Dukat's eyes glowed with insanity. "It's as easy as looking into a mirror and—"

A silver beam sliced through the air, smashing Dukat to one side.

Sisko recognized a directed-energy weapon attack when he saw one, and reflexively he grabbed Arla and pulled her back, to shield her.

But she fought in his grip. "Let go of me! You're no better than—"

Her body stiffened. Her protest ceased. She saw what Sisko saw.

For all around them, in the ruins of what once had been Sisko's Deep Space 9, from every dark shadow and alcove . . .

The dead walked.

CHAPTER 17

IN THE COMPANY of Dr. Bashir, Jake walked along the corridor of the Utopia personnel dome heading for the planning room, where they were to meet Jadzia and Worf.

The doctor had said little since the mess hall, where Jake had told him about Nog's lie. At least what Jake had suspected was a lie.

For once he had seen Bashir's reaction to what he had described, once he had realized the danger they all faced because of it, Jake had gone over his last conversation with his friend, reconsidering, worried that he might have jumped to an unwarranted conclusion.

"What if he's not lying?" Jake asked Bashir.

The doctor kept walking briskly. "I was waiting for you to say that."

"No, really," Jake said as his long legs kept easy pace with Bashir. "What if Nog's changed in the past twenty-five years? What if . . . if I misread the signs?"

"Think of it this way, Jake. There comes a time when each of us has to trust our instincts. And I trust your instincts from a time when you had no idea what the repercussions of your observations would be *more* than I trust your rather predictable second-guessing of yourself now that you're aware of the danger in which you've placed your friend."

Jake was intimidated by Bashir. He knew the man was genetically enhanced, like some latter-day Khan Noonien Singh. How could he argue with someone whose brain was the equivalent of a computer?

But he had to.

"Dr. Bashir, I'm not doing this to save Nog."

Without breaking stride, Bashir shot him an amused smile that let Jake know that was exactly what he was doing.

"Look!" Jake finally said, and for emphasis he stopped dead.

"I'll . . . I'll go tell Nog myself what you're—"

It took a few steps before Bashir realized Jake was no longer beside him. The doctor turned and came back to him, looking irritated. "You will do no such thing!" Bashir hissed. "I know what it's like to lose a friend, Jake. But you have to accept that after twenty-five years you *have* lost Nog. You don't know what pressures he's been exposed to, what compromises he's had to make, all the little capitulations and loss of ideals that accompany adulthood. The fact is, you don't know Nog anymore. You *can't* know him."

Jake felt his face grow hot. "Then why should you accept what I said about his maybe lying to us about the *Phoenix*'s chances?"

"Because that wasn't a conclusion based on friendship," Bashir said. "It was a straight observation, devoid of emotion."

"You mean, like I was a Vulcan," Jake said, depressed at the turn this conversation was taking.

"Say what you will, but Vulcans make the best witnesses. Now—shall we go?"

Jake gave up and then fell into step beside the doctor again. He supposed Bashir had a point, though the guy was awfully cynical about the process of becoming an adult. What sort of compromises would an adult *ever* have to make? Kids—even nineteen-year-olds—were the ones who were trapped by society and convention. Anyone could tell them what to do, force them to go to school, restrict their entertainment choices, and even, on the frontier where it was used, keep hard currency out of their hands.

But adults, it seemed to Jake, had none of these restrictions. Sure, there might be pressures associated with their jobs, but don't forget those pressures were taken on by choice. That choice, in his opinion, was the key difference between someone his age and someone Bashir's.

As they neared the planning room, Jake took a sidelong look at the doctor's face, trying to remember his real age.

Bashir paused beside the door. "What now?"

The guy has eyes in the side of his head, Jake marvelled. "I was just wondering . . . how old are you anyway?"

Bashir sighed. "By our standards, or in this time?"

"By our standards, of course," he said. He knew that technically everyone from the *Defiant* was twenty-five years older than they had been a week ago.

Bashir seemed to hesitate. "How old do you think I am?"

Jake couldn't resist the opportunity the doctor had just given him. "I don't know," he said with a perfectly straight face. "Fifty?"

Bashir's face twisted into an incredulous look. "*Fifty?* I'm thirty-four, Jake."

"I said I didn't know," Jake said innocently. "You made me guess. I guessed."

"Fifty . . ." Bashir rolled his eyes skyward, then punched in his code to open the planning-room door. Jake kept his smile to himself.

The security condition light was still red. It didn't change to either amber or green. Then the computer voice said pleasantly, "This facility is sealed. Operating conditions gamma five."

Bashir flashed a knowing smile at Jake. "Fortunately, I've read the security operations manual. Computer: Permit access to this facility, authorization Bashir, Julian, operating condition beta one."

This time the security light obediently turned from red to amber.

Jake whistled, impressed. "How did you get a security clearance?"

"I'm a physician," Bashir said smugly as the door began to slide open. "It comes with the job. Automatically it seems."

A sudden crash and a strangled cry from inside startled them both.

Bashir didn't wait, so neither did Jake. They both threw themselves at the door before it was fully open and pushed their way into the room where—

—Jake felt his legs threaten to give out as he suddenly found himself facing Lieutenant Commander Worf and Lieutenant Commander Dax, both of whom were, to put it politely, out of uniform.

Bashir instantly spun around and with a quick apology literally leaped back into the corridor.

A second later, open-mouthed, Jake felt Bashir's hand on his arm as he was hauled out as well.

With a thunk, the door slid shut behind them. Only then did Jake risk looking at Bashir.

"Well," Bashir said tersely, and Jake thought it was odd that a medical doctor would be disconcerted by the scene they'd just encountered, "they are married, after all."

"I'll say," Jake added. He wanted to say something more. He wanted to ask if Dr. Bashir had known Jadzia's Trill spots went all the way down to . . . but something in Bashir's face told him that *not* talking about what had just happened was what adults did. If only Nog were still his age and—

The door slid open again.

"You may now enter," Worf growled at them.

Jake set his face on neutral and followed Bashir into the planning room. Worf and Jadzia were both back in uniform, and the large schematic padds were back on the planning table.

"Sorry to have . . . intruded," Bashir murmured.

Jake had a sudden flash of inspiration, as he decided that part of the reason for the palpable tension in the room was that Bashir had always been after Jadzia for himself. Now *that* was a complication of being an adult that was exactly the same as being a teenager—always wanting what couldn't be had. *Maybe there isn't all that much difference between us after all,* Jake thought, as he suppressed the nervous grin that threatened to expose his unseasoned youth. He filed the revelation in his mind for accessing later, when he could more comfortably turn this extraordinary experience into something for a book. He was already full of ideas about how he could incorporate the whole scenario of traveling into the future into *Anslem,* the mostly autobiographical novel he had put aside a few years ago and to which he still returned sporadically when inspiration hit him.

"We have reviewed the schematics of the *Phoenix,*" Worf said stiffly.

A half-dozen different jokes sprang up unbidden in Jake's mind, but he pushed them down, followed Bashir's lead, and said nothing.

"Its weapons systems are impressive and adequate," Worf continued. "However, its propulsion characteristics are . . . unusual."

"They're Borg," Bashir said.

"Transwarp?" Jadzia asked without the slightest trace of embarrassment in her manner or voice. Obviously, being a conjoined Trill had its advantages, Jake thought enviously.

"That's not how the engines were called out in the specs," she said.

"Then maybe it's something beyond transwarp," Bashir suggested. "But believe it or not, an hour ago I met a Borg in the corridor. She's a Starfleet admiral."

"They're our allies," Jake volunteered as he saw Worf's and Jadzia's surprised reactions. "They signed a treaty with the Federation."

"Well," Jadzia said after a moment's thought, "if the *Phoenix*'s warp engines are based on Borg transwarp principles, then from the time they attacked Earth we know they've already demonstrated the ability to channel chronometric particles for propulsion. I would guess the ship is sound."

Then Jadzia looked from Jake to Bashir, as if somehow her Trill senses or experience told her that the two of them could tell her something more about the *Phoenix.* "I'm going to guess you two have data we don't," she said.

Bashir turned to Jake. "Mr. Sisko, tell it to them exactly as you told it to me."

There was no way out, at least none that Jake could think of. So he told the same story he had told Dr. Bashir in the mess hall, about how he could always tell when Nog was lying, how he had sensed Nog was lying about his confidence in the mission of the *Phoenix,* and most importantly, that he thought he knew *why* Nog might have lied.

"And why is that?" Worf asked.

Feeling like a traitor and a turncoat, Jake stared down at the dirty floor of the planning room.

"I think Nog . . . I think Nog actually *believes* that the universe will end."

No one responded to this statement, and after a few moments Jake glanced up to see that they were all waiting for him to go on.

"Just before that dinner we had," he said, "at Starbase 53. I went up to him."

"I remember that," Jadzia said. "I thought you were having an argument."

"We were. Sort of," Jake confirmed. "Anyway, I told him that . . . well . . . that he hadn't really changed all that much in twenty-five years. That he was still the same old Nog—" Jake smiled briefly as he remembered that part of the conversation. "—well, *older* Nog.

And that it was like things hadn't changed—I could still see when he was . . . well, he used to call it adapting the truth to close a sale."

Bashir interrupted. "Jake—you told me that you told him flat out that he was lying."

"I know," Jake said defensively. "Okay, so that's what I told him. I told him I could tell he was lying to us when he said he had confidence in the *Phoenix* completing her mission."

"And his response?" Jadzia prompted.

"I . . . I wish I could remember the exact words, Commander. He kind of got mad at me then."

"Told you to keep your ridiculous *hew-mon* opinions to yourself?" Bashir prompted.

Jake nodded. "Yeah, something like that. And that there was really nothing to worry about. Then something about how he had seen how the river flowed, and that the balance could be restored."

"Was that a reference to the Great Material River of Ferengi myth?" Worf asked sharply.

"I don't think they call it myth," Jake said. "It's more like their religion."

"And in their religion," Jadzia said, "to say someone has seen how the Great Material River *flowed* is the same as saying they've seen the future."

"That's right," Jake said.

"And restoring the balance," Bashir added, "is what happens when the River returns to its source, having completed its course. It's nothing less than the Ferengi apocalypse. The end of time, as it were."

"Maybe . . . ," Jadzia offered. "Maybe Nog's just feeling discouraged."

"It doesn't matter what he's feeling," Jake said

glumly. "It's that he made a prediction, that he claimed to see the future."

"I do not understand," Worf said.

Jake didn't know where to begin. But Jadzia apparently did.

"Everyone knows the Ferengi culture is steeped in business customs," she said to Worf. "Well, part of business is the ability to predict future market trends. So a Ferengi's business prowess—which would be the equivalent of how Klingons judge their own ability in battle—is one of those characteristics that gives him his reputation. As a result, Ferengi usually only make definitive predictions about the future—about how they've seen the 'river' flow—when they're absolutely certain what the outcome will be. And from the Ferengi point of view, the best way to know the outcome is to . . . well, stack the deck."

Worf narrowed his eyes at Jadzia. "You seem to know a great deal about Ferengi culture," he said heavily.

Jadzia shrugged. "So I dated one once. Some of them are kind of . . . cute."

Worf grunted. Then he glared at Jake. "Do you really believe your friend Nog will sabotage the *Phoenix* in order to ensure the universe is destroyed?"

Jake held up his hands as if defending himself from a physical rather than a verbal attack. "Hey, I didn't say anything about sabotage!"

"But that's the only logical conclusion we can draw from what you've said," Bashir said. "If this was one of your stories, Jake, what other motive could Nog have for what he said?"

Jake shook his head. "I . . . I don't know. But sabotage? That's different from just going into something without expecting it to succeed. Isn't it?"

Bashir patted Jake's back. "Look, that's all right. You've told us what you needed to tell us, and . . . if you're uncomfortable, you can go."

All at once, Jake felt as if he were eight years old again and his father was putting him to bed just as the dinner party conversation was getting interesting. He felt his face heat up again, but this time in annoyance, not embarrassment.

"I'm not a kid anymore, Dr. Bashir. I want to get back home or stop this or do *something* as much as the rest of you."

Jadzia put a restraining hand on Bashir's arm, and earned an annoyed look from her mate. "Jake, you do know that we *can't* go home, don't you?"

"Yeah, I know."

"So the *Phoenix* is the best option we have for stopping the Ascendancy's plan," Worf said with a touch of impatience.

"You mean, it might be," Bashir cautioned. "First we have to be absolutely certain about Nog's motives."

Jake rubbed his hands together in frustration. "If all of you are going to talk about motives, then what about this? If Nog had some plan to sabotage the *Phoenix*, why would he go to all the trouble of warping out to Starbase 53 to see us and then invite us onto the ship as its crew? I mean, we're a complication, aren't we?"

"That's a good point." Jadzia looked pointedly at Bashir.

"Unless we are also a good cover for Nog's plans," Worf said.

"We still don't know for sure what those plans are," Bashir countered.

"We could argue about this for hours," Jake said, looking at each of them in turn with frustration. *Adults!*

"We *have* to be certain about our next step," Bashir told him.

"But why waste all this time and effort?" Jake persisted. "Why don't we just *ask* Nog what he's going to do?"

"You said you had already tried that," Worf said.

"No. I said I *thought* he was lying. I didn't ask him why. And even if I had, there was no reason for him to give me a truthful answer."

"If he had no reason to tell the truth to you then," Jadzia asked, "what makes you think he'll tell the truth when you ask him again?"

"Because," Jake said, "if we wait till tomorrow morning we'll be on his ship. And that will give us all the leverage we need. Tell the truth or . . ."

"You would propose to sabotage the ship yourself?" Worf growled.

"Commander," Jake said seriously, "I don't believe that's what Nog is planning to do. So I do believe that he will do everything he can to keep us from damaging the *Phoenix.*"

"Everything he can," Jadzia said thoughtfully. "Even tell the truth?"

"It's like my dad says," Jake told her. "All we can do is hope."

"That is not an inspiring plan to entrust the survival of the universe to," Worf complained.

"No, it isn't," Jadzia said as she slipped an arm around her mate's waist. "But for now, hope is all we have."

Worf grunted again. "If that is true, Jadzia, then the universe is doomed."

CHAPTER 18

IN THE NIGHTMARE of the defiled ruins of Deep Space 9, now more like an ancient decaying fortress of war than an orbital station, Sisko felt Arla shudder in his arms.

He understood why.

The dead of this mad prison were coming to life.

Skeletal creatures emerged from the shadows, their gaunt torsos little more than cages of skin-wrapped bones, curved ribs that swept from a central exposed spine to encompass . . . nothing.

Bone feet clattered on the Promenade deck. Bone joints and bone hands creaked and clicked as the dead came ever closer, trudging over bodies that had not yet stirred.

"Is that the best you can do?" Dukat's voice suddenly echoed.

All the skeletons in Sisko's view stopped at the sound of that challenge. Each of their heads snapped to the side, the dark eye sockets of their inhumanly elongated skulls seeking the source of Dukat's voice.

And then Sisko noticed something that had no place among a walking army of the dead.

The skeletons were carrying weapons—sleek rifles, long and fluid, shining like cooled and captured strands of melted silver.

That was when Sisko realized these beings were not remnants of the dead, nor were they exactly dead.

They were Grigari.

A flash of red light set the shadows aflame, and a Grigari near Sisko flew apart violently. A skeletal arm fell at Sisko's feet, bending and flexing, leaking a thick yellow liquid from a web of coolant tubes—or were they blood vessels? Sisko couldn't be certain.

Whether Grigari were alive or dead, machine or animal—such questions had not been answered in his time, and he doubted they'd been answered in this one.

The remaining Grigari lifted their weapons and fired. Silver lightning pierced the air with high-pitched static. More red bolts sought out white-boned targets, dropping one after another of the walking skeletons in shattering explosions of flying limbs and dripping components.

As the battle raged, Dukat stalked through it, invulnerable, defended by a flickering ovoid of red energy that responded like a starship's shields, intensifying in color wherever Grigari weapons fire connected with it.

Sisko crouched down, and then dragged Arla off with him to find refuge in an alcove on the outer ring of the Promenade. The silver and red blasts of energy flew back and forth nonstop now, illuminating the darkness like lightning, causing the metal to sing in time with their impact strikes.

But the battle was ultimately one-sided. The Grigari weapons could not penetrate Dukat's personal shield, nor did they appear to be weakening it.

"I don't understand," Arla muttered as she huddled by Sisko.

"A minute ago, you seemed to understand everything," Sisko said.

Arla looked at him, confused. "Did I?" She shook her head so that her earring chain swayed. "I remember Dukat attacking you by the airlock . . . I know I swung at him . . . and then . . . we were here. Is this the Promenade?"

Sisko didn't try to explain what he couldn't yet explain. Instead he kept his eyes fixed on Dukat. The Cardassian was now standing in the very center of the Promenade concourse firing energy blasts at the attacking monstrosities as if he were a living phaser cannon. And Sisko still had no idea where he and Arla were, or why Weyoun would deliver him into Dukat's hands.

A familiar glimmer of light at the far curve of the concourse caught his eye. Then another and another. And then Sisko comprehended just where the Grigari were coming from. *Not* from among the piles of dead bodies as he had first thought. They were being *beamed* into the station. But from where?

Sisko involuntarily blinked as a second intense source of crimson energy joined the Grigari fusillade of silver beams, and Dukat was blasted from behind by a meter-thick shaft of translucent fire that deformed the ovoid shield surrounding him.

The Cardassian stumbled forward, recovered, spun around, reached out both hands and shot his own energy blasts back toward the source of new attack.

Weyoun.

The Vorta was striding purposefully along the concourse, encased in the same type of flickering personal forcefield that protected Dukat and firing the same type of red energy bursts from each outstretched hand.

"*BETRAYER!*" Dukat screamed, as he seemed to gather his strength to withstand Weyoun's onslaught.

"*MADMAN!*" Weyoun shouted in reply.

Like sorcerers of legend, the two beings advanced on each other on an unstoppable collision course, energy shields blazing with power, energy beams crisscrossing the air in spectacular bursts.

And the eyes of both Vorta and Cardassian glowed with the red madness of the Pah-wraiths.

Ricocheting shafts of energy leaped from the two forcefields—searing piles of corpses, setting still-fleshed bodies on fire, and mowing down the relentlessly marching rows of Grigari, whose weapons' silver fire embroidered the air of the red-blasted battleground.

Dense smoke began to fill the Promenade, replacing the breathable atmosphere. Sisko knew he and Arla had to make their move now. Their eyes met in complete understanding, though each knew there was nowhere to go on the station.

A new glimmer of light appeared behind Arla, and two Grigari materialized. Sisko pushed her aside, tensing, ready to leap, stopping only in shock as he recognized a third figure now joining the Grigari.

Tom Riker.

But he was a surprise that Sisko did not intend to question.

"Come with me!" Riker shouted.

Sisko could barely hear the words above the lightning-like crackle and sizzle of the energy exchange on the concourse, but he had heard enough. He yanked Arla around to show her Riker and gestured for her to run ahead of him, behind the two Grigari guards. Then, before he followed after her, Sisko took one last look back at the concourse.

Now Dukat and Weyoun were locked in physical combat, encased within the *same* ovoid shield of red energy, both bodies inexplicably rippling and distorted by intermingling layers of flame. Their tangled bodies tumbled and spun like an airborne gyroscope, as if gravity were no longer of any importance to them. Their single shield trailed bright cascades of sparks and oily smoke wherever it struck the walls and decks of the Promenade.

Sisko called out to Riker ahead of him. Perhaps he would have the answers. "What's happening?"

The answer that floated back to him was less than satisfying. "That fight's been going on for millennia, Captain. It won't end here." Riker stopped to allow Arla and Sisko to catch up to him and his Grigari guards. Then he reached down to his side, and Sisko saw a slender silver tube attached to Riker's belt. "Take hold of me," Riker instructed. "Both of you."

Immediately Sisko gripped one of Riker's arms, Arla the other; Riker nodded at the two Grigari, and the guards marched forward like machines, adding the fire of their own weapons to the lethal struggle still continuing undiminished.

Now it seemed to Sisko that half the infrastructure of the Promenade was melting, coagulating into glowing pools of superheated hull metal, reflecting blazing pyramids of corpses. Yet the joined forms of Dukat and Weyoun were still locked in battle, glowing hands around each other's throats, the two opposing forces oblivious to the destruction they were causing.

"Has *this* happened before?" Sisko asked, tightening his grip on Riker's arm.

Riker tapped a control on the silver cylinder. Lights on it began to flash, slowly at first, then faster. "Not here," Riker said cryptically. "We were surprised that Dukat had actually brought this station within range. It seems you were the perfect bait to force his hand."

"What do you mean, bait?"

But before Riker could answer, everything flashed around them, and then Sisko and Arla and Riker were standing on—

—the Promenade again.

A different one.

Brightly lit. Carpeted. With clean, breathable air.

Storefronts lined the outer and inner rings. Customers—all Bajoran—walked slowly by the storefronts, looking at Sisko, Riker, and Arla, curious but not breaking their pattern, as if strangers beamed into their view every day.

And then Sisko remembered Dukat's words about looking into a mirror.

"That other station," he said to Riker, who was paying close attention to what appeared to be the small medical scanner he held close to Sisko, then to Arla. "It was in the *Mirror* Universe."

"That's right," Riker said, distracted, reacting with surprise to something he evidently saw on the scanner's small screen. "Dukat used his energy beam against you?"

Arla, still groggy, frowned at Riker's question. "Yes. Is there long-term—" But she didn't have a chance to finish her own question. Riker had touched the medical scanner to her neck, and after a soft hissing noise, she at once fell backwards.

Sisko caught the Bajoran before she could hit the deck of the Promenade. He glared at Riker. "Hasn't she been through enough?"

Riker slipped the scanner back into his belt. "We take possession very seriously around here. She wasn't showing signs of being currently inhabited by a Pah-wraith. But she has been. Quite recently. Probably a low-level transference when Dukat attacked her."

Sisko rubbed at his temples, as if by doing so he could rid his brain of the disturbing thoughts Riker's news provoked in him. Possession. "I thought you people *worship* the Pah-wraiths."

Riker regarded him with surprise. "Not the ones from the Fire Caves. There was a reason why Kosst Amojan and those who followed him were expelled from the True Temple."

"And that would be?" Sisko asked wearily, angrily. Would no one tell him what was going on here?

Riker declined to enlighten him. "Something for you to discuss with the Emissary." He nodded at Arla, supported once again in Sisko's arms. "Let's get her to the Infirmary."

Sisko struggled to control his impatience as he followed Riker along the concourse, distracting himself by trying to identify landmarks from his past. But the layout had completely changed from his day. The Infirmary was where Garak's tailor shop had been, and all the equipment within it was Bajoran. In fact, except for the basic architecture, *everything* about the station now was Bajoran in design and color.

Riker had Sisko put Arla on a diagnostic bed, then

turned her over to the care of a young Bajoran physician.

"Now what?" Sisko asked, as he followed Riker to an office area near the Infirmary's entrance.

"We wait for the Emissary."

"If he survives."

Riker smiled grimly. "He always does. The struggle among the Pah-wraiths is as old as the war between the Pahwraiths and the False Prophets. It won't end until the universe ends."

Sisko wanted to grab Riker by his white beard and shove his face against the closest wall. Weyoun's followers were insufferable. This entire situation was insufferable. He longed for his own time. His son. Kasidy. His station. His life.

Riker appeared to sense Sisko's mood. "You have a problem with that?"

"I didn't think the universe was ending," Sisko said bluntly. "I thought it was being . . . transfigured."

Riker kept his eyes locked with Sisko's. "You've spent time with the Emissary. What do you believe?"

"I believe the Emissary is insane."

Riker appeared to consider Sisko's statement for a few moments, as if trying to uncover hidden subtleties, then he withdrew his medical scanner again and moved it around Sisko's face, then around the sides of his head.

"What are you looking for now?" Sisko demanded.

To his surprise, Riker leaned closer as if to read the scanner's display screen, and whispered, "I'm working for Starfleet. The *real* one."

Sisko's anger vanished at once. He caught Riker's eyes, and in an instant an unspoken, blessedly sane, and understandable communication had flashed between them.

Tom Riker had just placed his life in his hands. And Sisko knew he wouldn't—couldn't—betray that trust.

After an awkward moment, Sisko looked at the small medical scanner. "Is everything all right?"

"No sign of possession," Riker said loudly. "Of any kind."

"Good to know." Sisko waited before saying anything else, hoping Riker would give some clue as to how they were to proceed.

But Riker gave none.

Sisko gestured at the station around them, not knowing what else to say. "Can I ask how the station was restored?"

Riker looked puzzled.

"Deep Space 9," Sisko said.

"Oh! No, no," Riker answered. "This isn't Terok Nor. It's Empok Nor. The Emissary had it towed here from the Trivas system. One of the prophecies of . . . I believe it was Eilin, was that the True Emissary would restore the Gateway. So . . ."

Sisko needed to act on what Riker had told him, but it was clear that Riker felt they were under some type of surveillance.

"I'm not familiar with the prophecies of Eilin," he said carefully.

Riker didn't seem to think that was too important. "How about Shabren?"

Sisko nodded. Shabren's Fifth Prophecy was one with which he was especially familiar.

"Eilin was a contemporary of Shabren. And of Naradim. The three great mystics of Jalbador. Though

Eilin and Naradim were considered apocryphal by the religious leaders of your time. Until recently, most of what they wrote was known only to scholars."

Despite his earlier relief, Sisko felt now as if he were drowning in a sea of small talk. He looked around the Infirmary, trying to see where surreptitious sensors might be hidden. "But not Shabren."

Riker smiled. "People used to say that Shabren's writings were never censored because no one could be certain what he was saying."

Sisko didn't want this to go on any longer. "When will Arla be released?"

"That will be up to the Emissary."

"Where are the rest of my crew and the people from the *Defiant?*"

"The Emissary has made arrangements for them all to be quartered here, until . . . the ceremony."

Sisko stared at Riker until Riker acknowledged the unspoken question.

"At the end. When both halves of the Temple will open their doors at the same time and in the same place, and . . . they will be rejoined, praise be to the True Prophets of the One True Temple."

"In what now—nine days?"

Riker nodded.

"How'd you come to work for Weyoun?" Sisko asked. "And not Starfleet?"

"When Cardassia fell, the camp I was imprisoned in at Lazon II was liberated by the Grigari. It was Starfleet that abandoned me to that camp. Starfleet cowardice and—"

"As I recall," Sisko interrupted, "you willingly sacrificed your freedom to save your crew and the *Defiant.*"

Riker's eyes flickered in warning. "That's not how it happened and you know it. Starfleet tricked me into that camp, and the Emissary freed me. And the more I studied the Bajoran texts, the more I realized that the Emissary was right. I owe him everything. We all do," he said emphatically.

From Riker's overly intense response, Sisko realized that the man must have created an elaborate cover story to gain Weyoun's trust. And if Weyoun's supporters had undertaken any efforts to double-check that story, then it must be that Starfleet had altered its records of Tom Riker's attempt to hijack the *Defiant* from DS9 and his subsequent selfless surrender, in order to confirm his story. To Sisko, that suggested that Riker was supported by the highest levels of Starfleet.

Sisko looked past Riker to Arla. She was still unconscious. The Bajoran physician was in the midst of meticulously arranging blinking neural stimulators on Arla's forehead and temples. "Where's your . . . your brother, I suppose you'd call him these days?"

"You mean my transporter duplicate," Riker said. "He made captain finally. The *Enterprise*. Took over from Picard."

"The *Enterprise* is a fine ship."

Riker frowned. "It's probably not the one you're thinking of. The E was lost in the Battle of Rigel VII. An unknown terrorist group attempted to alter the gravitational balance between Rigel and its moon. Caused them to collide. Starfleet claimed it was agents of the Ascendancy, but we don't do that kind of thing. It was probably Starfleet agents attempting to make us look bad.

"Anyway, no one told Picard about Starfleet's involvement, and he sacrificed his ship to destroy the gravity generator. Reconfigured the deflector dish or something, so that the ship and the generator together formed an artificial black hole."

Riker cleared his throat. "Starfleet held another hearing—three starships is an awful number to have lost—but there were precedents, so they gave Picard the *Enterprise*-F. First of its class, for once. Incredible ship. Think of the *Defiant* to the tenth power. Multivector assault capability. Built specifically to fight the Grigari. Fired the first shot in the . . . unfortunate miscommunication incident that resulted in the Sector 001 disaster—"

"You mean the destruction of Earth," Sisko said, appalled that such a hideous event should be referred to as an "incident."

"Completely avoidable," Riker said. "But my transporter duplicate seemed to be looking for a fight that day. First hint of trouble he went to battle stations, fired at the Grigari flagship, and—the *Enterprise*-F lasted all of three minutes in battle."

"So . . . he's dead," Sisko said.

"They all are. Troi. La Forge. Krueger. Paris. My duplicate's wife. End of an era."

"End of a world, you mean."

Riker nodded almost subliminally, as if to let Sisko know that he shared the captain's outrage, though he could not admit it publicly.

Sisko knew he and Riker had to talk free of surveillance. "I want to find out more about what happened on Earth," he said. "Is there a time we could talk again?"

Again, Riker's signal to him was barely perceptible. "There'll be time enough for study after the Ascension," Riker said. "Every being will have all questions answered then. I think a better use of your remaining time in the linear realm would be to visit B'hala."

"Would that be permitted?"

"I believe it's demanded." Riker held Sisko's gaze. "Portions of the city have been restored to what they were tens of thousands of years ago, exact in every way. No computers, no communications systems . . ."

No surveillance, Sisko thought, understanding. "I'd like to see that," he said.

"I think the Emissary has already started making plans."

Frustration swept over Sisko again, because there seemed to be nothing more to say. Yet if Riker was telling the truth with his revelation about working for Starfleet, then both he and Riker were committed to stopping Weyoun before the Vorta could merge the wormholes.

After a few minutes of silent waiting, the Bajoran physician joined them to let them know that Arla would recover from Dukat's attack. And then he asked them to turn their backs, because a new patient was arriving.

Riker complied with the physician's instruction at once. After a moment, Sisko followed his lead. Then the glow of a transporter filled the room, and Sisko detected the sounds of quick movement among the medical staff along with the irregular, rasping exhalations of someone having difficulty breathing.

Sisko risked a quick, surreptitious glance over his shoulder in time to see Weyoun—floating in an antigrav field, his naked body in a glistening coat of blood, his flesh disfigured with gaping wounds and charred patches of tissue. As his face turned to one side, Sisko saw that one of Weyoun's long ear ridges was missing, ripped out of place.

Frantic Bajoran physicians clustered round the Vorta's body, working rapidly, their huddle preventing Sisko from seeing exactly what treatment they were attempting to apply, though he caught glimpses of them cleaning out the gashes, abrading crusted skin, and wiping off blood.

Sisko felt Riker tap his arm, saw him shake his head in warning, as if he shouldn't be watching. But just then the physicians stepped back, and Sisko clearly saw Weyoun's most damaging wounds decrease in size until they were little more than minor skin scrapes any home protoplaser could heal.

And then even those signs of battle damage faded. Weyoun had been *restored.*

To Sisko, what he had witnessed was like watching Starfleet sensor logs of Borg ships undergoing self-repair.

He suddenly became aware that even Weyoun's hoarse breathing had eased. And with that realization, he saw the Vorta's head slowly turn in his direction. Then Weyoun's eyelids fluttered opened, and the Vorta looked at him—into him—as a soft red glow pulsed once in his eyes.

Sisko didn't look away.

Weyoun smiled.

"What is he?" Sisko asked Riker.

"No one knows," Riker replied in a low voice, "unless he's like the Grigari."

Riker's words made sudden, terrible sense to Sisko.

Defeating Weyoun had just become much harder.

Because how could Sisko stop an enemy who was already dead?

CHAPTER 19

NOG ADJUSTED his tunic, checked to see that his combadge was on straight, then—out of habit—turned to the automated transporter console and said "Energize," as if the *U.S.S. Phoenix* actually needed a transporter technician for such a simple task.

Ten columns of light swirled into life on the elevated transporter pad, then coalesced into the temporal refugees snatched from the *Defiant*, including his friends: Jake. Lieutenant Commander Worf. Lieutenant Commander Dax. Dr. Bashir. Nog also noticed three others in the group who were unfamiliar to him—a young Centaurian ensign and two other Starfleet officers—as well as two *hew-mon* civilians. And, of course, Vash.

He wasn't at all surprised that it was Vash who spoke first, complaining as always.

"I said I didn't want to volunteer for this stupid mission!"

Nog watched, amused, as the archaeologist angrily pulled away from Bashir, who was vainly trying to calm her. But then Vash jumped off the pad to confront *him.*

"You!" she snapped. "Who's in charge up here?"

Nog resigned himself to the confusion someone like Vash could bring to a ship as complex as the *Phoenix.* As he saw it, he really had no choice. Even the conscientious objectors from Bajor who thought they'd be spending the rest of their lives—and the life of the universe—in prayer chambers on Mars would be brought aboard this ship soon enough. And they wouldn't be any happier about it than Vash was.

"I am," he told her.

Vash laughed mockingly. *"You.* In charge of all this?"

"As far as you are concerned, yes." Nog regarded her with some annoyance. His schedule didn't allow for annoyance. By now, T'len might already know the refugees were missing.

"Well, I want off." Vash said.

"That is not going to happen."

"You can't kidnap me like this!"

Nog sighed. The universe was scheduled to end in a little over seven days. "It's not as if you have time to lodge a formal complaint."

Vash made a threatening fist. "Then I guess I'll just have to lodge this up your—"

"Enough!"

Worf's commanding voice froze every movement in the transporter room. Though the Klingon stepped down to a position beside the belligerent archaeologist, he still towered over her. "As we agreed with Captain T'len, you are in our custody until we depart on the *Phoenix.* You will then be held in your quarters in the personnel dome until . . ." Worf stopped speaking, as if embarrassed to continue.

"Yeah, right," Vash sneered. "Until the 'end of hostilities.' " She glared at Nog. "Don't think I don't know what's going on in that swollen little skull of yours. You have no intention of letting me off this ship, do you?"

Nog kept his expression completely neutral. "Of course I'll let you off. Everyone will return to Mars today for further training. The *Phoenix* is not due to depart for another forty hours."

And then, knowing he had delivered another adaptation of the truth, Nog couldn't stop himself from glancing at Jake.

He saw the frown on Jake's face. Did he know? Had he guessed?

Nog turned away. He *knew* he wasn't that transparent. How could he have succeeded as a Ferengi if any . . . manipulation of the facts he resorted to was that easy to detect? No, there wasn't anything wrong with *him*. It was Jake. Had to be. Either Jake was upset about something completely unrelated to Nog's action, or his frown, if it indicated he was on to Nog, was the result of some non-*hew-mon* blood in the Siskos' family history. Something that could give Jake some kind of . . . of telepathy. *That's it!* Nog thought. The only way Jake could know for sure what Nog was doing was if Jake were a mind reader—even of Ferengi minds. And that was just impossible.

Feeling much better already, Nog clapped his hands, motioned toward the door. "Well, let's get this tour under way. I'm sure you'll find the *Phoenix* is a most impressive vessel."

The doors slid open to reveal the wide corridor beyond. Like every other habitable area on the *Phoenix*, the bulkheads, deck, and ceiling were unfinished, in keeping with Starfleet's wartime priorities.

"We already know the ship's impressive," Jake said, hanging back as the refugees entered the corridor. "We've seen the schematics, remember?"

Vash halted beside Jake, folded her arms defiantly. "Yeah, the kid's right. Why do we even need this tour anyway?"

Nog sympathized with Jake as he saw the resentful look that had settled on his friend's face at that "kid" reference. But being no kid himself, Nog addressed Vash sternly. "In case you haven't noticed, all the shipyard's holodecks are off-line. To understand this ship, you have to see it firsthand."

It didn't matter to Nog that neither Vash nor Jake believed his explanation. The important thing was that Jake, for whatever reason, had yet to challenge anything he had said so far.

But if he really is a mind reader, Nog thought, *then at least he'll understand why I* have *to do this.*

Vash, on her part, was whining so much about everything that no one was even listening to her anymore. Nog wished he didn't have to, either.

"Let's join the others," he suggested in a firm voice, and led the way without waiting for a response.

As they made their way toward a bank of turbolifts, Nog told his followers about the ship's construction. For all its great size, interestingly enough, the *Phoenix* had less habitable space than the *Defiant.* In fact, eighty-two percent of the ship's volume was taken up by its power generators, including an unprecedented array of forty-eight linked transwarp engines, any thirty-six of which would be sufficient for their voyage into the past.

As he and his party waited for the lift cars to arrive, Nog heard Bashir say, "I find it difficult to believe that a ship with forty-eight engines could even get out of spacedock with a crew of only twenty-two."

Nog smiled expansively. This was something he could explain. "Actually, Doctor, the *operational* crew is even smaller—fourteen. The other eight crew members are the engineers who will deploy the deep-time charges at B'hala. Or at the site of what eventually will become B'hala."

"Fourteen," Bashir said. "Even with full automation, how is that possible?"

The lifts arrived. "It's possible," Nog said, "because forty-four of the engines are designed to be used only once. Repairs and maintenance won't be necessary, so neither is an engineering crew."

Nog ushered the refugees into two different cars, joining Jake and four others in one of them. "Bridge," he said. The doors closed, and with a sudden jolt the car began to move.

"Don't you have inertial dampeners?" Jadzia asked him.

Nog coughed nervously. "The structural integrity field is still being aligned," he said. "So the dampeners are off for the moment." This time, he didn't dare look at Jake.

With another jolt, the car stopped and the doors opened onto the bridge of the *Phoenix*.

Nog stepped out, and though it was so familiar to him, he tried to see the bridge through the eyes of the temporal refugees. Certainly, he thought, they would recognize its near-circular layout, despite the fact that most of the wall stations were still obscured by tacked-up plastic sheets and dust shields. And there was a main viewer dead ahead, switched off for now, providing a central focus for the overall layout.

But the chairs and workstations would be different to old eyes, he knew. Almost alien, in fact.

There were fourteen chairs in total on the bridge, one for each of the operational crew, arranged in wide rows facing the viewer. Unlike the simple seats his guests would remember from their starship duties, these were enclosed units, with curving sides and tops, full body-web restraints, fold-down consoles, and holographic displays.

Worf was the first to deliver his assessment of the design. "This is not a ship built for battle."

Nog knew that the Klingon meant that by confining the crew within those chairs, he could see there was little chance for carrying out the swift replacement of injured personnel.

"But twenty-five thousand years in the past," Nog told Worf, "there will be no one for us to fight."

Worf didn't look at all convinced. "We must still get to Bajor in *this* time."

"And to do that, we will be protected by the largest task force Starfleet has ever assembled," Nog said.

"Hold it," Jake said suddenly. "I don't understand. If this ship can take us into the past, why don't we just slingshot around *Earth's* sun, go back twenty-five thousand years, and *then* go to Bajor without having to fight *anyone?*"

"It's a question of temporal accuracy," Nog said stiffly to his childhood friend, who was still so close to childhood. "The farther we are from Bajor when we travel back in time, the greater the error factor we introduce into our final temporal coordinates at Bajor itself. Stardates aside, time really is relative to different inertial frames of reference. If we were to follow exactly a twenty-five-thousand-year slingshot trajectory around Earth's sun, we might only travel back twenty thousand years in regard to Bajor—and land when Bajorans had already settled the B'hala region."

"Then let's go back *fifty* thousand years," Jake said. "A twenty percent error would still bring us to a time before the site was settled."

As Nog tried to think of the best way to answer, Jadzia came to his rescue. "Jake, I think they're facing two difficulties with that idea," the Trill said helpfully. "First, I don't think anyone could build a ship capable of going back much more than thirty thousand years. Not without a radical new theory of temporal physics. And second, just from the geological data I've seen describing the proposed placement of the deep-time charges, I'd say the B'hala area was subjected to severe earthquakes or volcanic disruptions a thousand years or so before it was settled, significantly disturbing all the underlying strata. Is that right, Captain Nog?"

"Exactly," Nog said. He held his hands together as he took over the explanation for Jake. "You see, Jake, we're actually trying to arrive within a very narrow *window* of time. We can't arrive any later than twenty-five thousand years, because someone might see us. But we can't arrive any earlier than twenty-*six* thousand years, because before that there *were* a series of powerful crustal upheavals that would probably destroy the deep-time charges. That means we're attempting to achieve an error factor of plus or minus two percent on our first try. To even have a chance at that level of accuracy, we have no choice but to slingshot around *Bajor's* sun—and no other."

"You people are just crazy," Vash muttered.

"Excuse me, but we are attempting to save the universe," Nog said.

"Yeah, in the most bureaucratic, bungling Starfleet way you can." Vash threw her arms in the air. "What's wrong with you people?! Don't any of you get it? Do you know how many things have to go right for this ridiculous scheme to work?"

"It is not ridiculous!" Nog said.

Vash stared at him long and hard. "You know what, Captain? I don't believe you. Your heart—or your lobes or whatever it is you Ferengi invest with meaning—just isn't in it."

Nog was terrified. Was Vash a mind reader, too? Or could *everyone* tell what he was thinking? "I suppose Q gave you the power to read my mind," he said sarcastically.

"No one can read what passes for a Ferengi mind," Vash said with a rude smirk. "And I don't *have* to be a mind reader to know that you're not on the level. Oh, I've negotiated my share of deals with Ferengi. I know how you operate."

Thoroughly rattled though he was, Nog knew he had to act quickly. He couldn't risk any of the others following Vash's line of reasoning, even if there didn't seem to be much reason to it for now.

"Vash. Please. I understand what's really upsetting you and I guarantee you'll be able to leave the ship."

Then Nog was aware of Jake stepping to his side. "Nog," his friend said in a low voice. "We have to talk."

"Frinx," Nog sputtered. "What's wrong with you people?!"

"That's what I said!" Vash chimed in.

"STOP IT!"

Everyone stopped talking and stared at Nog.

Nog felt the sweet rush of power. He had given an order and had it obeyed. Instantly. Just like Worf.

"Much better," he said. "Now, to continue our tour, I'd like everyone to take a chair." He directed Worf to tactical, Jadzia to main sensors, Bashir to life-support, his chest swelling with pride as all three complied without protest. He then quickly polled the Starfleet personnel on their specialties and assigned them also to appropriate chairs.

Soon only Vash, Jake, and the three civilians were left without places.

"Can we go home now?" Vash asked without much conviction.

Nog pointed to the back of the bridge, where a series of padded half-cylinders were inset into the bulkhead.

"There's an awful lot of crash-padding on this ship," Vash said darkly as she backed into one cylinder, then jerked as autorestraints snaked around her. "What the hell's going on, Captain?"

"Our trajectory around Bajor's sun will be very rough. I want everyone to get a chance to try out the restraint devices."

Vash glared at him, but she was firmly secured against the bulkhead.

Nog looked around the bridge. Now he was the only one standing. It was going to work.

"Don't worry. We'll have plenty of time to talk later," he said to Jake as Jake adjusted his cylinder's restraint harness. Then he said "Very good" to everyone else as he walked around to the front of the bridge, where they'd be able to see him. "Now we're going to try out the holographic displays. You'll be able to see the status of any station on the bridge without leaving your—"

With a rush of static and a sudden glare of light, the main viewer came on behind Nog.

Nog felt his lobes shrivel. It could only be one person.

"Captain Nog, what are you doing on the *Phoenix?*"

As Nog expected, T'len's face filled the viewer. Judging from the equipment behind her, she was in the main flight-control center deep below the nanoassembler facilities on the surface. Nog took that as a good sign. She'd be on the bridge of the *Augustus* soon enough.

"I'm conducting a familiarization tour for the crew."

"They'll have two days for that en route to Bajor. Why have you pulled the work crews from engineering bay four?"

"Their work was done," Nog said, with what he hoped was the proper amount of surprise.

"Not according to the computer records," T'len said.

"It's not unusual for the records to lag," Nog pointed out.

"Report to me at ground control at once."

He held up his hand. "May I finish the tour first?"

"At *once,*" T'len repeated. She reached for something out of sight, and the viewer went dark.

Nog turned back to face his crew. "Well, I think that brings this part of the tour to a close."

He braced himself for the first complaints.

"Captain Nog!" Worf said indignantly. "The restraints will not release."

"That's odd," Nog said in what he hoped was an offhand manner. "Let me check with the master control."

Nog walked quickly to the side of the bridge, straight to the transporter control station. The small clusters of transporter pads to either side of the bridge had been his contribution to the design of the *Phoenix*. He'd remembered how convenient it was to have similar facilities in Ops at Deep Space Nine. So much time had been saved. Like now.

Nog put his hand on the control station's security plate. "Computer, run Nog Five and Nog Alpha. Command authority Alpha Alpha One."

The starboard pads came to life first, and the five Bajorans from the past suddenly appeared. Civilians and militia alike, they were all in believers' robes. Two were kneeling in prayer. Everyone looked confused by what had happened.

"Quickly!" Nog commanded. "Go back to the crash cylinders!"

The other temporal refugees, who by now could have no doubt that Nog was acting on his own, started calling out to the Bajorans to release them.

But Nog slapped a red panel on a tactical station, and instantly a siren sounded and red lights flashed as the ship went to General Quarters.

"Hurry!" Nog shouted at the Bajorans. "We're under attack!"

Then the port pad flashed into life, and Nog was running for it, even before the frail form of Admiral Picard had fully materialized.

"My word," the Old Man said, as he half-stumbled from the pad. He was in his uniform, but it was wrinkled, as if he'd been asleep in a chair. "Is everything all right, Will?"

"Perfect," Nog said. He looked up at the graceful sweep of the illumination ceiling. "Computer: activate all shields. Rotating pattern Nog One." Gently he guided Picard to the captain's chair and helped him settle in. Nog also took the precaution of disabling the control console.

Now everyone was secure, and the *Phoenix* was impenetrable to attack. Nog knew that there was no turning back.

He was stealing a starship.

The only starship that might save the universe.

He ran back across the bridge, ignoring the clamor of the sirens and the shouted protests of those trapped inside their crash chairs. According to a time readout on the navigation substation, he had three minutes left to clear the spacedock and go to transwarp. In three minutes and one second, every simulation he had run for this operation had ended with the arrival of a Starfleet task force that could keep the *Phoenix* pinned in position until commandos came aboard.

Nog swiftly checked to see that the shields were still flashing off and on in the preset pattern, then began overriding the security codes on the transwarp station. He gave fervent thanks that given his position as Integrated Systems Manager it was not a difficult procedure—merely a time-consuming one.

Then the navigation displays came up, free of security blocks. Nog checked the time. Ninety seconds. He was going to make it. All he had to do now was wait for—

Nog squealed, as a large hand gripped his shoulder and yanked him away from the bridge station. He tumbled head-over-heels and came to a stop, sprawled on his stomach, watching as Worf's huge boots clomped toward him.

"No!" Nog gasped. "You don't understand!" He looked over at the chair Worf had been confined to and saw smoke rising from its cracked protective covering. Obviously a redesign would be in order.

But Nog's protests did no good, because Worf's powerful hand was already crushing his right ear, dragging him back to his feet as he squealed again.

"For your betrayal, you have brought dishonor not only to your house, but to your species," Worf thundered at him.

"I haven't betrayed anyone!" Nog squeaked. "You really *don't* understand!"

"Do you deny that you have joined the Ascendancy?"

"No-o!" Nog's hands scrabbled ineffectually at Worf's, vainly trying to dislodge the Klingon's brutally painful grip on his sensitive lobe. His entire head throbbed with agony. The intense pain robbed him of all reason.

"Then why are you attempting to steal this starship?"

"I can explain later! I *will* explain later!"

Without even seeming to expend any physical effort, Worf lifted him high in the air until their faces were a centimeter apart. "You will explain *now.*"

Even to his own ear, Nog's voice was reduced to the high-pitched yowl of a cat. "Commander, please, you have to put me down before—" Nog started gagging, the pain was becoming unbearable.

"Before *what?*" Worf bellowed deafeningly.

And before Nog could answer, before Nog could warn Worf about what was about to happen—

It happened.

Nog saw three flashes of light flicker in the Klingon's dark, enraged eyes. He saw Worf look up, past the Ferengi in hand, and react in shock.

Then three more flashes reflected from Worf's sweat-covered skin. The odd rhythm of the light's appearance, Nog knew, was matched with the pattern of the rotating shields, timed to create transporter windows every few seconds.

Worf looked at Nog with unbridled disgust, then threw him to the deck.

Nog shivered with relief as he rubbed his crushed ear. He saw Worf slowly raise his hands as if in response to an unspoken order.

"I'm sorry," Nog croaked, but his throat was too raw for his voice to be heard over the GQ sirens that continued to blare.

And then Worf pivoted suddenly and launched himself to the side and—

—was hit on three sides by disruptor beams.

The Klingon fell heavily to the deck, his massive body motionless, smoke curling from each beam's impact on his uniform.

Nog shuddered. Everything was all wrong. It wasn't supposed to have happened like this.

Another hand took hold of his arm, pulled him to his feet.

Nog looked up. He was getting tired of this. Everyone tugging him one way, then another.

Then he recognized the person who stood before him.

Centurion Karon.

Three more Romulans beamed in behind her. They quickly ran to join the five others scattered around the bridge.

"How much time?" Nog gasped.

"Twenty seconds to spare," Karon said. "Congratulations, Captain. By turning over this vessel to the New Romulan Star Empire, you have guaranteed there will be a future."

Nog nodded, dazed. Then he felt a sudden drop in the deck as the inertial dampeners came on.

"Transwarp is enabled," a Romulan called out over the sirens.

"Activate," Karon ordered. "Transfactor twelve."

A deep rumbling came through the deck and reverberated through the bridge.

"Screen on," Karon said, as if she had flown this ship for years.

The main viewer came back to life, and on it stars flew past in stuttering flashes of color, too fast for the ship's computers to render in smooth lines.

"We have decided to call this vessel the *Alth'Indor.*" The Romulan centurion smiled at Nog again. "It means 'phoenix.' We have the same story in our mythology."

Nog no longer cared—and he was sure his expression showed it.

"Don't worry," Karon said briskly, as if she also had no trouble reading his mood, if not his mind. "You have done the right thing."

That sentiment Nog could agree with, even though he knew his reasons were not the same as hers.

The stars sped by even faster.

The ship sped toward its journey through time.

Some of those on board the *Phoenix* would survive, Nog knew. That much was inarguable.

But not even Nog knew who those few would be.

CHAPTER 20

GARAK SAVORED the satisfying crunch his boots made as they crushed the ancient stones of B'hala. They had something of the same consistency as sun-bleached bones. At least so he had heard, and now, happily, he could confirm it for himself.

In this future, he thought, Bajoran boots had very likely walked through the rubble of Cardassia Prime, as the Bajorans had reveled in the destruction of his world. Somehow, that made his sense of anticipation for the coming destruction of everything else more reasonable. Especially this holy city, which had unleashed on the universe the ultimate means to the ultimate end.

"Garak? Are you all right?"

Garak turned and held up his hand to shield his eyes from the excruciating glare of the space mirror, which was low on the horizon and in his line of sight. At any given time, he recalled being told, there were two of those mirrors illuminating B'hala, making the city always appear as if it were high noon on a world with binary suns, even in the dead of night. The double shadows were disconcerting, giving as they did to everything the unreal look of artificiality. There was, however, another apparition that was even more unusual.

Garak smiled at the sight of Odo in penitent's robes. "Tell me, Odo. Are those robes part of you? Or did our charming hosts make you put them on like the rest of us?"

Odo adjusted his robes with impatience. "The ones I formed weren't proper, I was told. I am actually wearing these. I don't know how you solids stand it."

"Ah, if I had known you were amenable to wearing clothes, I would have offered you a discount at my shop. Believe me, there is nothing like the kiss of Argelian silk to soothe the troubles of the day."

Odo folded his arms—an oddly bulky gesture, Garak observed, given what the changeling was wearing. "Don't think I haven't noticed that you've changed the subject," Odo said gruffly.

Garak bowed his head in a sign of respect. And he did respect Odo. In a way, as an adversary, more often than not. Though sometimes as an ally. The apparent contradiction did not trouble Garak. He was quite comfortable with the fact that his relationships with others were often as fluid as the politics of Cardassia. What was life, after all, but change?

"I am fine, Constable. And I do appreciate your concern in asking."

Garak could see that Odo was unlikely to accept his statement as the final word in the matter. While he waited patiently for whatever it was that Odo would decide to do next, Garak turned his attention to the surrounding restored buildings of heavily-eroded stone blocks, noting that no structure appeared to be more than two or three stories high, and that most were still supported by crude wooden scaffolding lashed together by vegetable-fiber rope. Intriguingly, it was as if he and Odo were thousands of years in the past. Except for the weapons carried by their Grigari guards, who had taken up positions far in the distance, Garak could detect no sign of technology or any other indication that this city was the wellspring of an interstellar movement that had brought the Federation to its figurative knees.

Odo coughed. From experience, Garak knew the awkward gesture was the changeling's way of changing the subject. Odo wasn't much of a conversationalist.

"Garak, I really don't know any way of saying this that doesn't sound completely inadequate, but I am sorry for your loss."

Garak felt quite sure that Odo's statement was false. The Cardassians had never been a friend to Odo. But social discourse did require the lubrication of lies.

"Thank you, Odo. I appreciate your good wishes, as well."

Odo cleared his throat. "If I had heard my world had been destroyed, I don't think I'd be taking it like you."

"What would you have me do, Odo? We're all terminal cases. Even our cultures. Even our worlds. A hundred years for an individual and he's gone, only a memory for a hundred more, at most. Perhaps longer if he's someone to whom they build statues. But after a thousand years, whom do we really remember? Garak shrugged, enjoying the rustle of the robes he wore. On some backward worlds of his acquaintance, such garments would be considered quite fashionable.

"You must remember that as nation states rise and fall, each one is always eager to erase its predecessor from the records. I doubt if Cardassian historians even knew the names of more than a few of the warlords who ruled our world, or parts of it, at least, one after the other. And each of those worthy souls fought mighty battles, brought death to tens of thousands, gave life to tens of thousands more. Yet their empires are gone, their deeds forgotten.

"And worlds, my dear Odo, are no different from people or countries. Had the universe continued, Cardassia's sun would have swollen into a red giant, or gone nova someday. And then the whole planet, the sum total of every pre-spaceflight Cardassian who had ever lived, warlords and rabble alike, would have returned to the elemental gas from which the planet had condensed in the first place. Five billion years from now, perhaps some of my parents' atoms would come back to life in the bodies of aliens we can't imagine. Aliens who would never know of the glories of Cardassia, because they would be too busy fighting mighty battles of their own. The same would happen to Earth. And to Vulcan. Even to your Great Link."

Garak smiled at the changeling. "Death is never a surprise, Odo. Only the timing of it."

Odo snorted. "I wish I had your blunt outlook on life."

"No you don't," Garak said amiably. He pointed ahead, to where the others were gathering around an excavation site with Sisko and Weyoun. "Shall we continue? The Emissary did say he had something of interest to show us. I can't imagine what it might be."

"We'll continue," Odo said. "For a while at least."

Garak appreciated the changeling's flair for the dramatic. So many people lacked it these days.

As they walked on together, Garak decided that Odo would be an ally today. At the same time as he made that decision, he found himself idly wondering which number was greater—the grains of sand that covered B'hala or the number of stars in the sky, somewhere beyond those infernal space mirrors.

He took a moment to contemplate, in honest wonder, the idea that something—some physical process as yet unknown and undefined—might actually have the power to erase every star from the heavens.

The very concept was astounding.

And to be present, to see it actually take place . . .

In truth, the possibility was making him feel privileged, even humble.

And considering how few things had actually had that effect on him in his lifetime, the experience was novel, and one he fully intended to enjoy exploring.

As far as exploring other things, however, it appeared Weyoun had been a busy Vorta.

He had obviously invited all eighteen prisoners from the *Defiant* to see B'hala before the end. Garak recalled that back in his present, B'hala had been merely a series of tunnels deep beneath the mountains. But here and now, the great lost city was exposed to the sky—at least, according to the briefing they had been given, a third of it was exposed. The rest apparently was still buried, and was destined to stay that way until the end of time.

Despite the fact that the end of time was only seven days and some few hours away, Garak couldn't help being fascinated, as he and Odo approached the other prisoners who stood beside Weyoun, that the Bajoran workers under the Vorta's command were diligently continuing their digging and tunneling, and recording every detail of the flayed site—as if any of it would or could matter anymore.

But the latest excavation in B'hala was a very special one, or so Weyoun had said when he had offered his invitation.

Right now, in fact, the Emissary to the True Prophets was crouched down at the lip of the deep pit—its opening was almost twenty meters across—peering with great interest into its depths, which were crisscrossed by wooden ladders and catwalks and only dimly lit by flickering combustion torches. The angles of the space mirrors appeared to be set too low to provide any appreciable downward illumination.

Behind the kneeling figure of Weyoun, Garak recognized Captain Sisko, Major Kira, and Commander Arla. Their only apparent guard was Captain Tom Riker. He was also the only member of this gathering who was not wearing religious robes. Instead he was dressed in what Garak considered to be a most inelegant uniform, a hodgepodge of Starfleet severity and Bajoran pomp.

All it would take is one gentle push, Garak mused to himself, as he and Odo joined the outer edges of the group. A simple nudge and Weyoun would tumble into the depths faster than Riker could run forward to save him. In his mind's eye, Garak watched the Vorta's arms thrashing, heard his wheedling voice receding in a doppler shift of death.

If Weyoun could only be removed from the events to come, it was entirely possible the universe could be saved.

Garak was familiar enough with Sisko and Kira to know that both possessed the courage to take such action—even if it meant immediate death. So the fact that they were choosing not to take advantage of their opportunity revealed to Garak that the two knew something he didn't. Most probably, that Weyoun *couldn't* be stopped by a fall.

"Such a fascinating time," Garak said aloud.

"I'm sorry?" Odo asked.

"A private musing, Odo. Not important. What do you suppose is down there?" Garak gestured to the yawning pit.

"With our luck," Odo grumbled, "more red orbs."

Garak nodded. How interesting. He himself hadn't thought of that. "Now that would be a delightful complication."

Beside him he heard Odo sigh.

Then a shout echoed up from the excavation floor. Someone reporting that "it" was under way.

As Odo leaned forward to stare downward, frowning, Garak amused himself by turning to study the other prisoners clustered beside them. People had always been of more interest to him than things.

And the most interesting grouping was that of the two Ferengi—Quark and Rom—with the human engineer, O'Brien. These three had single-handedly come up with the plot to escape from the *Boreth,* sending Odo out on his fool's errand to overload the ship's powergrid. Garak had tried to explain that no one in their right minds would put all of their hostages in one location *without* arranging surveillance. But humans had this hopeless notion, that if they whispered softly enough no one would overhear what they were saying.

Surprisingly, Odo had not been executed. In fact, Weyoun had taken no reprisals against the prisoners at all. In Garak's experience, that was a sign of a sloppy leader, or perhaps of someone who could not conceive of anyone's challenging his authority. From events that had transpired since, Garak was leaning towards presuming Weyoun to be one of the latter. No one who could command Grigari could be considered sloppy.

Someone in the crowd jostled Garak, as several of the prisoners edged forward to the lip of the excavation and began pointing down. With a sigh, Garak pushed forward to look down into the gloom as well.

And saw Weyoun staring down at a large object, perhaps four meters long and two meters across, that was rising from the depths. Given the absence of ropes and pulleys, Garak concluded that the Vorta had relaxed the rules of B'hala's restoration to allow the use of antigrav lifters.

A few meters down from the lip of the excavation, it became apparent that the object was nothing more than a large boulder, the same pale color as the sand and stones that surrounded everything here.

"It must have some special significance," Odo said expectantly.

"After all this work, I should hope so," Garak said.

They watched with the others, as the enormous rock floated easily upward from the excavation, then shifted sideways through the air to a barren clearing to one side of the spectators. By the time the boulder had settled—without the slightest disturbance of the dry soil beneath it—Weyoun had scaled its summit so that he could speak to his audience.

As he did so, Bajoran workers swarmed the base of the rock, detaching from it blue devices the size of Garak's forearm—obviously the antigravs.

"My *dear* friends," Weyoun said. "What we are gathered here to witness today—or should I say, tonight—is the last preparation we must undertake before the ceremony of the Ascension can begin. Now, I know this rock doesn't look like much. It's certainly not a sacred stone, and there are no mystical carvings upon it. But it has fulfilled a very special function for us all.

"You see, the events that will lead to the transformation of the universe are—and always have been—very well known to Bajoran scholars. True, in the past those scholars made misguided attempts to censor the revealed truths of the True Prophets, and were reluctant to share their knowledge of the transformation with the people who trusted in them.

"But we have changed all that. Now we know the steps that must be undertaken before the transformation can begin."

Here Weyoun pointed down at Sisko. "First, the False Emissary must rise from the dead who fell when the Gateway vanished—and I'm so glad to have your own Captain Benjamin Lafayette Sisko with us here today." In a moment which Garak felt was amusingly surreal, Weyoun began to applaud, gesturing for his audience to join in. But no one did.

Weyoun made a show of adjusting his robes before continuing. "In the days ahead, I can promise you all that there will be further ceremonial activities conducted here in B'hala, and eventually up on the Gateway—and then at the doors of the sundered Temple itself." The Vorta smiled broadly, and Garak could see he was trying to make eye contact with every prisoner. Garak nodded in acknowledgment when Weyoun's gaze fell upon him. But he heard Odo's harrumph of disapproval, and saw the changeling look down when the Vorta's attention settled on him.

Garak caught the flicker of disappointment that touched Weyoun's face at Odo's dismissal of him. How strange that someone with such power could still want for something.

"In these troubled times," Weyoun began again, "we of the Ascendancy must admit that we have enemies. Doubters we can accept. Nonbelievers we can coexist with. But enemies . . . they're not interested in either our acceptance or coexistence, only in destruction. *Our* destruction, my dear friends.

"To date, I can tell you that our enemies have tried to destroy our ships, our worlds, our places of prayer. So we have fought back, as is our right. While our enemies have used their most sophisticated weapons against us, filled subspace with their lies, even tried to subvert us from within."

Garak was intrigued to see that at this point in his speech Weyoun bestowed a most meaningful look on Sisko, although even Garak could not understand how anyone could accuse the captain of duplicity. Sisko had never made any effort to disguise his fierce opposition to Weyoun and the Ascendants.

"But, dear friends, we have withstood their assaults, and in only seven days we will never have to endure them again." The Vorta paused, as if allowing time for his audience to cheer his words, but again there was no response.

"However," Weyoun said after a moment, "these next seven days bring special risks. Because the enemy will now be provoked into using its most fearsome weapons against us. And one of their greatest perversions of technology is the ability to travel through time itself."

A current of reaction raced through the gathering. It seemed to Garak that all but Sisko, Kira, and Arla were whispering to each other. He himself glanced at Odo, and the two of them silently shared their sudden interest in whatever it was Weyoun was building up to.

"In fact," Weyoun said, his voice ringing across the excavation site, "the scientists of the Ascendancy have said that it is even possible that our enemies would go so far as to travel *back* in time to before any of *this* existed." He spread his arms wide, and Garak knew the Vorta's reference was to the city of B'hala, revealed and unrevealed.

"And there and then," Weyoun said, "they could bury bombs of immense destructive power . . . bombs that would be hidden through the ages among the lost treasures of B'hala . . . bombs that would not detonate until *after* their timeships had set off on their blasphemous journey, so that our enemies could falsely claim that they had not wreaked havoc with the timeline."

"What an absolutely splendid concept," Garak murmured admiringly to Odo. "To change the past without changing the present . . . only the future. I'm truly taken aback with admiration. I wish I had had a chance to employ a similar technique when—"

"Be quiet," Odo hissed.

Undeterred, Garak cast his eye across the group again, wondering who the specific audience for Weyoun's performance was. Because that's exactly what this invitation to the excavation was—a performance, pure and simple, for the benefit of one or two of the prisoners.

His eye fell on Rom. Certainly the midlevel Ferengi technician had astounded everyone with his *savant* abilities in engineering. In fact, after Rom had come up with the audacious technology of self-replicating mines, seemingly in defiance of the laws of physics, Garak himself had even gone so far as to risk contacting some of his old . . . business acquaintances. He'd been curious to find out if any brilliant Ferengi scientists had disappeared in the past decade, perhaps predisposed to find a new and simpler life in some kind of disguise.

But this investigation had turned up no evidence regarding the possibility that Rom was something other than what he claimed to be, though Garak still had his suspicions.

However, he reminded himself, even if it was Rom who had conceived of the delayed temporal warfare Weyoun had described, it still seemed improbable that Starfleet could have moved on the idea so quickly, or that someone as lowly placed as Rom could have passed word to the correct authorities to begin with.

And that problem of communication likely ruled out Chief O'Brien as well. A stolid, boring sort of fellow to be sure, but also dedicated and forthright. Just the sort to have under one's command in case a grenade someday came through a window and required someone to throw his body upon it and save his betters. People like O'Brien had their uses.

But not in this case.

Which meant, Garak reasoned, that Weyoun's performance could only be intended for the one person present who could have had ample opportunity to be in contact with Starfleet—the *real* Starfleet—in time either to suggest preparing an attack in the past or to have learned that such an attack was planned.

Captain Thomas Riker.

Someone who—beyond any doubt—would be dead before this gathering was over.

Garak straightened his robes, pleased with the realization that of all the people here, only he knew what Weyoun was thinking.

Garak's attention returned to the Vorta, who was still emoting up there on his rock. Effortlessly picking up the thread of Weyoun's speech in progress, Garak wondered precisely how many heartbeats Riker had left. Such a fragile thing, life.

"Of course," Weyoun whined self-righteously, "knowing our enemies' plans, we had to take action. Yes, we could have sent our own forces into the past, to set up a shield of justice around our world. But the possibility that some unforeseen accident might change the past made us rule against it. Instead, our scientists concluded that we should let our enemies do their worst: Let them stand revealed as the monsters that they are.

"Let them take their sordid voyage into our history, plant their bombs, and be done with them, but"—Weyoun broke off unexpectedly to wave to a group of workers who had been waiting at the far edge of the excavation—"be certain that whatever cowardly action they take in our past cannot be hidden from the eyes of the Prophets."

The Vorta's smile was smug. "Which brings us to this rock." He stamped his foot against it. In seeming response to Weyoun's action, a few of the workers below him gathered around one end. They all held small tools, whose purpose Garak couldn't quite make out.

"A year ago, dear friends, our scientists constructed this rock—that's right, *constructed*. And then a group of brave believers traveled back through the Orb of Time to an age before the founding of B'hala, and there buried this rock in stable ground."

Suddenly the workers jumped back from Weyoun's

pulpit rock, as a section of it fell off with a loud pop as if something under pressure had just opened. Garak leaned forward with the others to see the hollowed-out area now visible in the boulder.

"You don't suppose . . ."

"Will you be *quiet,*" Odo said.

Weyoun was still atop his pulpit. "As you can see, this is not just a rock. Instead, our scientists carved into it with microtransporters and then installed within it the most stable and precise passive sensors. Sensors that could not be detected by our enemies' scans. Sensors that for almost twenty-six thousand years have waited patiently for us to reclaim them."

Weyoun slid down the artificial boulder to join the workers at its open end. He glanced over at Sisko, and then spoke loudly enough for the rest of the prisoners to hear. "Now, I can tell what you're worried about, Benjamin. What if *we're* altering the timeline by opening this prematurely? Could we be setting a predestination paradox in motion?" The Vorta shook his head. "Of course not. The Ascendancy has far more respect for the natural order of things than does your Starfleet."

Weyoun's workers busied themselves removing long, metallic cylinders from the boulder's interior. The silver objects gleamed in the blinding light from the space mirrors, as if they were freshly minted and not millennia old.

Garak was exhilarated by the spectacle the Vorta had provided for their enjoyment. But he decided against sharing his delight with Odo. Really, the changeling just had no idea how to enjoy the moment.

"No, Benjamin," Weyoun proclaimed. "The reason

we are opening the deep-time sensors today is because *yesterday,* Starfleet's timeship began its voyage. And interestingly enough, your son was on it. Jake. Should give him something interesting to write about, don't you agree?"

It was impressive to Garak just how well Captain Sisko was controlling his anger. The human had never appreciated his offspring's involvement with the more difficult events on Deep Space 9. Garak wondered if he would have an opportunity to remind Sisko that perhaps it was for the best that Jake escaped the coming end of everything by being safely ensconced in the past.

"So," Weyoun said triumphantly; Garak was relieved to sense the Vorta was finally coming to his conclusion—despots so rarely understood there were a few occasions on which less was more. "What Starfleet has done, was done long ago, and because of our patience the timeline is intact. And as we play back the sensor records of the past, we will be able to chart the location of each bomb the crew of that ship placed beneath us—here, in the unexplored regions of B'hala. And though Starfleet's plan was undoubtedly to ignite those bombs during the final ceremony to be held here, destroying half of Bajor in the process, even now ships of our own Ascendant Starfleet are in orbit above us, waiting to transport each bomb away and disperse it into deep space."

Weyoun bowed his head in pride. Held his fists to his shoulders. "Praise be to the True Prophets, may they show our enemies the errors of their ways." He looked up and nodded at the workers with the sensors. "You may examine them now."

"This should be very interesting," Garak said to Odo.

"Why? Because Weyoun has figured out a way to stop a last-ditch plan to save us all?"

"The plan's not ruined yet," Garak admonished the changeling. "After all, if *I* had designed the bombs Weyoun is looking for, I'd have buried them in pairs so that any chance observation would make someone think there was only one to each location. And then I'd make certain they were *all* set to go off the instant any of them was hit by a transporter beam. This entire city could be reduced to molten slag any moment now—a bracing thought, wouldn't you agree?"

Garak relished the sudden look of consternation that disturbed Odo's smooth features.

"Oh, relax, Constable. If we do go up in a fireball of apocalyptic proportions, at least you'll have the satisfaction of knowing that the universe has been saved."

"You're right," Odo muttered acidly. "I feel so much better."

"That's the spirit." Garak beamed as he watched Weyoun's workers hold all manner of tricorders and other devices near the deep-time sensor arrays. From time to time, he glanced over to see Sisko in intense conversation with Kira and Arla.

Rom and O'Brien were also engaged in a fevered conversation, no doubt reverse-engineering the sensors just from their appearance and Weyoun's description of their capabilities. But Quark was looking positively bored and stood to one side, alone.

"What a remarkable day," Garak said aloud, not intending the words for anyone but himself. "What a remarkable life."

"Has anyone ever told you how obnoxious you are?" Odo asked.

"Often," Garak conceded. "Though after we've discussed it in private, it turns out they always have meant it in jest. Interesting how people can be persuaded to change their minds, wouldn't you say?"

Odo rolled his eyes, obviously not willing to be baited. Garak joined him in watching the work on the sensors.

It was over in less than twenty minutes.

And then Weyoun turned to Sisko with an expression of sadness, and again spoke loud and clear for posterity. "Oh, dear Benjamin, I am so sorry. But the sensors show that no bombs were ever planted here. There are no transporter traces, no residual tractor-beam radiation trails, no sudden alterations in the gravimetric structure of the region, . . . nothing. It appears that Starfleet's mission has failed, and your son Jake . . . well, I *am* so sorry. But the wages of disbelief are—"

Sisko threw himself at Weyoun, and Garak's pulse quickened. There was nothing quite so uplifting as seeing what a parent would do for its child.

But before Sisko could reach the Vorta, Riker had tackled the captain, bringing him down in a cloud of dry dust.

The two humans wrestled for a few moments on the edge of the excavation, but it soon became disappointingly apparent to Garak that Sisko was merely venting anger, and that Riker had no desire to make an example of him.

In less than a minute, Riker was back on his feet again, brushing sand from his atrocious uniform. Sisko sat still on the ground for a moment.

And then, quite unexpectedly—or so Garak thought—Weyoun went to Sisko and offered him his hand.

It also appeared that Weyoun was saying something to the captain, but this time the Vorta's words were intended only for Sisko. And most unfortunately, the angle of Weyoun's face was such that Garak couldn't read his lips.

"What a charming gesture," Garak said, annoyed. The Vorta was playing by the rules.

But then, predictably, Sisko rebuffed Weyoun's offer of help and pushed himself to his feet without assistance, in a whirl of dancing dust.

Garak's eyes narrowed as the Vorta reacted graciously by simply clasping his hands to his chest and bowing to Sisko, as if to say no offense had been taken.

But just then a giant gasp arose from all the prisoners and the workers, as Captain Tom Riker threw himself across the two-meter distance between himself and Weyoun and propelled the Vorta howling into the pit—

"Well done!" Garak exclaimed. He'd underestimated Riker.

Transporter hums filled the air, and waves of Grigari soldiers suddenly materialized, surrounding the area. Their bone-spur claws dug into the prisoners' robes, forcing all back from the pit that had claimed Weyoun and Riker.

"So much for Ragnarok," Odo said.

"A bit anticlimactic, though," Garak observed critically.

And then Weyoun rose up from the depths of the excavation, floating, arms outstretched, supported, it seemed, only by a softly glowing halo of red light.

"What is that?" Odo asked in shock.

Garak frowned. "What else? A Pah-wraith inhabiting the vessel of a linear being. Riker should have anticipated that."

Predictably, Odo glared at him. "A good man has died trying to save us!"

Garak was hardly in the mood for an argument. But then, neither did he intend to let Odo have the last word. "That 'good man' once worked for the Maquis. And knowing what I know about the Pah-wraiths, he is not dead yet."

As if on cue—a happy accident of timing but which Garak much appreciated all the same—Weyoun then dropped a hand to the pit below, gesturing as if giving a command for something else to arise.

That something was Tom Riker. Breathing hard. The bright blood streaming from a long gash on his head turning his white beard red.

Riker's left leg was also not hanging straight, and Garak could see a small, sharp glimmer of white against his dark, red-stained trousers.

"Compound fracture of the femur," Garak explained helpfully to Odo, who of course lacked any bones whatsoever. "Quite painful, I believe."

Weyoun drifted to the side of the pit and stepped gracefully onto solid ground. Riker remained suspended in midair, above the pit, his body in spasms, bubbles of blood forming at the corners of his mouth. A possible punctured lung, Garak thought. He turned to share this observation with Odo, but the changeling was looking elsewhere.

Sisko had his hands on Weyoun and they were having a heated conversation. At least, the human was heated. The Vorta looked detached.

But it seemed even a Pah-wraith did not have unlimited patience, and finally Weyoun flicked his hand at the human and a blinding flash of red light sent Sisko flying backward into the sand.

Then Weyoun imperiously gestured again into the

pit, and a moment later a red strand of rope shot up and coiled out of it like the unfurling tongue of an immense unseen amphibian. Another rapid hand movement from the Vorta, and the sinuous rope snaked around Riker's neck.

The floating human grabbed at the rope, tore at its tightening coils, his one good leg kicking out for freedom.

A gasp from the horrified onlookers caught Garak's ear and he turned to see Quark suddenly stagger back, hands at his own neck. The Ferengi was obviously reliving some unpleasant memory. Garak frowned. An interesting development to be sure, but not in the end as intriguing as the one featuring Weyoun and Captain Riker. He turned his back on Quark.

To see Weyoun raise his hand high and Riker float higher, his struggles lessening, the mysterious rope looping in the air beside him.

Weyoun dropped his hand, and Riker dropped but the rope did not. It flexed and snapped tight, breaking only as its burden was sundered at its weakest point, and Riker's head and body plunged into darkness—separately.

"Showy, but no subtlety," Garak murmured.

Odo's face leaned menacingly into Garak's. "I don't want to hear another word out of you!"

Garak sighed. He had been intimidated by experts, rarely successfully, and certainly never by a mere changeling sworn to uphold justice. Swearing such an oath, in fact, had worked to undercut a great deal of Odo's authority, Garak had always believed.

"What I meant, Constable, is that there was no need for Weyoun to behave so crudely. After all, he has won.

He can't be killed. And Starfleet's attempt to travel through time has obviously failed. He could have left Riker at the bottom of the pit to bleed to death in a dignified fashion. Instead, we've all been treated to a quite unnecessary look inside a troubled mind."

Odo stared at Garak in disgust. "You see something like . . . like *that* and *analyze* it?"

"Someone has to," Garak said. "And I do think it might be worth pointing out to Captain Sisko that Weyoun clearly has a weak spot in his personality. One that might conceivably be exploited to our benefit."

"And what weak spot would that be?" Odo growled, as if he couldn't believe he was engaged in this conversation.

"I think it might be wise to let the emotions of the moment dissipate," Garak said kindly. "You've been through a considerable strain."

Odo drew back as if he'd been slapped. "And you haven't, I suppose?"

Garak was tired of being questioned in this way. Tired of Odo's attitude. He looked from side to side and put on his best bland face—the kind that struck such terror into poor, sweet, gullible Dr. Bashir. "Odo . . . whatever we saw here today, remember this. I've seen worse."

Odo clenched his jaw, clearly wanting to say something more but just as clearly unable to bring himself to.

And Garak, oddly, found himself struggling not to add the words, *And so have you—on the Day of Withdrawal.*

Now, why would I think that? he wondered. There was no way *he* could know what Odo might have seen or not seen when the Cardassians had withdrawn from Bajor. *Unless . . .*

"No," Garak said aloud.

Odo looked at him, not understanding.

But even Garak didn't understand this time.

The universe was coming to an end.

Nothing mattered anymore.

Not the death of Tom Riker.

Nor the Day of Withdrawal.

Nor even how his own lost memories from that final day on Terok Nor—

—when the Obsidian Order had come for him . . .

—when Terrell had taken him to the room . . .

—where . . .

"Garak?"

Garak stared at Odo, and for a moment it was as if the changeling was wearing his old clothes, the short cape and rough fabric from the time before he had donned the uniform of the militia, from the time before . . .

"Garak? What's wrong?"

"Nothing." Garak forced himself to smile. "A touch of vertigo. Nothing a good apocalypse can't extinguish."

Odo's eyes narrowed. "It seems you're not as tough as you let on."

"I'm not," Garak said firmly. "I'm tougher."

And then Weyoun summoned the Grigari guards to come for them and the other prisoners, to lead them away from the pit back to the shuttle that would return them to Empok Nor, the restored Gateway.

And Garak, who knew there was no point in thinking of the future, and who could not think of the past, devoted himself to thinking about only the moment and the glorious view of Bajor, as the shuttle climbed above the clouds and into space.

There might well be many good things in this universe, he knew. But in his experience, bad things had far outweighed them.

The end of everything would be a good thing.

He would finally be free of the horrors of his past.

Maybe he wouldn't tell Sisko about Weyoun's weak spot after all.

CHAPTER 21

NOG DROPPED a battered piece of metal onto the table in the unfinished conference room of the *Phoenix.*

It was a dedication plaque.

Its significance was lost on Jake, who looked at Jadzia and Bashir to see if they understood.

From the expressions on their faces, they apparently did.

Jadzia was the first to pick up the plaque and study it closely.

Jake noticed that Karon, the Romulan centurion at the head of the table and the leader of the team that had taken control of the *Phoenix,* was studying Jadzia just as intently, as if she expected some type of treachery.

After a few moments, the Trill passed the damaged rectangle of metal to Bashir, then looked at Nog. "I take it you've run a complete molecular scan to be certain it's not simply a replicated copy."

"I studied it atom by atom," Nog said. "It is the same plaque that is now on display on the bridge of this ship, *except* it is 25,627 years older. And, of course, its condition has been somewhat altered by . . . a variety of mishaps."

Nog's hesitation raised in Jake the desire to know exactly what those mishaps had been. He looked quickly at Centurion Karon, but she didn't seem to have noticed the pause in Nog's delivery.

"So the *Phoenix* crashes on a moon in the Bajoran system," Bashir said angrily. "That could mean this ship was damaged *after* we deployed the deep-time charges and we scuttled it where no one would find it."

Nog laid his hands on the tabletop and spoke forcefully. "Doctor, the Romulans have recovered almost forty percent of the ship. There are components from *all* of the deep-time charges we're currently carrying. That means we did not deploy the charges. And that means our mission will be a failure—because it already was."

"And you believe the Romulans?" Bashir asked, his sarcasm leaving no doubt as to what he thought the answer was.

Centurion Karon responded before Nog could. "Dr. Bashir, I understand your reluctance to trust us. If you were Vulcan, I would call upon your logic. But as it is, I shall ask you to employ that human characteristic known as 'common sense.'

"The mission of the *Phoenix* as planned makes good sense—to stop the Ascendancy without changing the timeline. Surely it is to all our advantages for it to succeed. The Star Empire—old or new—would embrace that result.

"The facts, however, indicate that this mission will

fail. That suggests that sometime in the next six standard days the universe will end, as the Ascendancy plans. Our position then becomes, why waste this resource, this magnificent vessel? As much as it distresses us, changing the timeline is preferable to allowing the universe to die."

Jake wasn't an expert, but he had heard his father discuss the terrible equations of the Dominion War with Admiral Ross. And he had come to believe as his father did: There was no escaping the fact that in order to accomplish good, sometimes bad things had to happen.

In the case of the war to save the Federation, that had meant that soldiers had to die. And Jake could see the same inescapable equation at work here. "It makes sense to me," he said quietly, and was suddenly aware of everyone in the room staring at him. "I mean, if I had the chance to take back some tragedy by changing time, I'd do it."

"Even if it meant wiping yourself from existence?" Bashir asked.

"If the tragedy was big enough, I'd have to, wouldn't I? Wouldn't all of us?"

Karon nodded approvingly at him. "This young man is correct. What we are proposing is no different from sending a group of Imperial Commandos on a one-way mission to inflict terrible damage on an enemy and thereby win a war. Perhaps we will die, but billions more will live because of our sacrifice. Perhaps trillions."

Jake didn't understand why Jadzia hadn't yet offered her opinion, and why Bashir now seemed unwilling to say more.

Karon tried to prompt a reaction from them. "Dr. Bashir, Commander Dax, you and your fellow travelers through time were willing to risk your lives for the mission of the *Phoenix*. Why are you not willing to risk your lives on a plan that has a *real* chance of success?"

"Maybe because it's a *Romulan* plan," Bashir said. "And I'm just not comfortable with taking this ship back twenty-five years into the past and laying waste to an entire world."

At that, Karon rose abruptly from the table, the sound of her chair echoing harshly in the unfinished room, and Jake could see her hands were clenched into fists at her side. "I apologize for being Romulan. But I invite you to work through the problem yourselves. One world and twenty-five years balanced against the universe and infinity. Which would you choose if I had been human, Doctor? Or Andorian, or Klingon?" Obviously upset, the Romulan centurion inclined her head briefly in a nod of leave-taking. "I suggest you discuss your options. Because one way or another, this ship *is* on a new mission, with or without her crew."

Karon headed for the doors, where, as the doors to the corridor slid open, Jake saw two Romulans with disruptors standing to either side of the doorway. Then the doors closed and they were alone.

"What were you thinking?" Bashir snapped at Nog.

"Me? You insulted her." Nog said. "Besides, the mission fails. It doesn't need thinking about. The facts are the facts!"

"The Romulans almost killed Worf!" Jadzia said heatedly.

Jake knew that Jadzia's mate was in the ship's sickbay being tended to by an entire holographic medical team, even though they weren't programmed for

Klingon physiology. Fortunately for Worf, his disruptor burns were superficial.

Jadzia's accusation hung in the air. But strangely enough, Nog did not fight back. More than anything, Jake thought, the Ferengi looked sad.

"I am truly sorry for the commander," Nog said, "but I know I did the right thing. If this ship had been taken out on her mission as planned, we would have accomplished nothing. It's as simple as that."

Jake hated seeing his friend so beleaguered, so defensive. Nog was looking twice as old as he had on Starbase 53. Jake tried to remember what Bashir had said about the little capitulations and loss of ideals that accompanied adulthood. How many small defeats had Nog had to endure in the years they had been apart? What had brought him to this state—a troubling and troubled person who had sold out every ideal he had ever believed in?

Unless, Jake suddenly thought, *Nog hasn't changed at all. . . .*

"Nog," Jake said, reaching out for the plaque and holding it up, "what other mishaps?"

Nog looked down the table at him and Jake saw in the Ferengi's sudden wariness that he had hit on something.

The plaque. The plaque was the key. Somehow.

Jake put the plaque down on the table and ran his fingers over its raised lettering. He felt excitement bubbling up in him.

"When you said you conducted tests on this, you said it showed signs of various 'mishaps.' That's an odd word to use."

Nog took a deep breath, and if his friend had still been only nineteen, Jake would have sworn he was gathering his strength to confess some transgression of youth to his father. Then Nog glanced at the closed door, and Jake leaned forward, on the alert. Nog had something he was *hiding* from the Romulans.

Maybe his friend wasn't the traitor, the loser he seemed to have become.

Maybe there was still some of the old Nog—the *young* Nog—locked up in that middle-aged Ferengi's body.

Now Nog leaned forward and dropped his voice to a low whisper.

"Do you know *how* the Ascendancy plans to bring on the end of the universe?" he asked the three before him.

"By merging the two wormholes," Bashir said.

"Yes, but how?" Nog asked. "I mean, really—by what technique can you actually *move* two energy phenomena held in place by verteron pressure?"

Jake, Bashir, and Jadzia all shook their heads.

"Well, Starfleet doesn't know, either. That's one of the reasons we were so slow to react to the Ascendancy's plans. The best scientists just didn't think what they planned to do was possible."

"But . . . ," Jake said, grasping for enlightenment, "it *is?*"

"Yesss!" Nog hissed. "Most certainly. And I know what they plan to do, because the evidence is all right here. . . ." He patted the dedication plaque. "My friends, I needed the Romulans to help me steal this ship from Starfleet, but now I need your help to steal it back."

"Yess!" Jake thought. *That's* my *Nog.* Then he sat forward even closer to listen to Nog's plan.

CHAPTER 22

"WE'VE LOST, haven't we?" Kira asked.

Sisko stared up at the night sky from his cell. Its narrow window faced north, and the beams from B'hala's space mirrors did not interfere with his view of the stars.

"We're still breathing," he said. As the stars appeared from Bajor, they were almost as familiar to him as the stars of Earth.

Kira didn't sound convinced. "For how much longer?"

"Maybe . . . we shouldn't fight this anymore," Arla said from her corner of the cell.

The enclosure imprisoning them, its walls made of the ancient stones of B'hala, was small, with only three small piles of old rags for beds and a bucket for all other physical needs. But Sisko and the two Bajorans had had no trouble sharing it. There were bigger concerns facing them than mere physical discomfort and lack of privacy.

Sisko turned away from the stars in time to see the look of shock on Kira's face, but felt none himself. After witnessing Tom Riker's appalling death last night, he felt numb to further surprise.

"You can't be serious," Kira said hotly.

"You believe in the Prophets, don't you?" Arla asked.

"Of course I do!"

Arla slowly got to her feet in one fluid, athletic movement, and smoothed her robes around her. "Then isn't what's going to happen here what you've wanted all your life?" she asked.

Kira's head bobbed forward in amazement. "The end of *everything?* Why would you believe that *I* would want that?"

Any other time, Sisko might have thought that the secular Arla was merely baiting the religious Kira, and might have intervened. But he recognized a new undercurrent to Arla's questions, and understood that she was trying to comprehend something that had never been part of her own life.

"Isn't it part of your religion that at some time good and evil will fight a final battle?" Arla asked.

"So?" Kira answered.

"So isn't this it? When the two halves of the Temple are rejoined, the Pah-wraiths and the Prophets will fight that final battle and existence will end. That's what it says in your texts, isn't it?"

Kira exhaled noisily as if indignant at Arla's ignorance, but Sisko knew her well enough to sense that she was stalling for time. "Yes. My religion says that sometime there will be a final battle between good and evil. But it doesn't say anything about there being *two* Temples!"

Arla folded her arms inside her robes like a monk. Sisko thought it was an odd gesture for a non-believing Bajoran to have picked up.

"Major, I mean no disrespect, but are you really surprised that your side—the good—has a slightly different version of events than the bad side? Doesn't it make sense that alternate versions of the texts were written to . . . to sow confusion, to lead people from the righteous path?"

Kira narrowed her eyes in suspicion. "Are you saying you *believe* the texts? That you accept the Prophets as gods?"

Arla shook her head, not defiantly, Sisko saw, but in confusion.

"I honestly don't know," she said slowly. "But I saw Dukat and Weyoun fight like . . . like nothing natural should fight. I saw what Weyoun did to poor Captain Riker. I can't deny that there is something going on here that goes beyond any science or history or folklore I know. So . . . so I'm just trying to understand it from a different hypothesis."

"And that would be?" Kira asked.

"That you're right. That the Prophets are gods, not aliens. That the Temples are their dwelling place and not wormholes. That among the texts of Bajor's religions are those that truly are inspired by gods and correctly foretell the future."

Sisko interrupted the uncomfortable silence that followed.

"And is it working?" he asked Arla. "Does it help you accept what's happening?"

The tall Bajoran shook her head again. "What I don't understand is that if everything that's going on *is* what was prophesied in the Bajoran religion . . ." She looked at Kira. "Allowing for some technical discrepancies introduced by purely mortal error in the transcription of the texts through the millennia, or by the deliberate, malevolent interference of the Pah-wraiths . . ." She turned back to Sisko. "Why is everyone against it?"

"The end of the universe?" Kira demanded, as if she still couldn't believe the question.

"But is it really the end, Major? If *your* religion is right, isn't this actually the transformation that Weyoun claims it will be? Isn't this only the end result of linear existence? The ultimate proof of your beliefs?"

Sisko saw Kira's chin tremble in anger. "*I* believe that *when* the real Prophets choose to change the nature of existence, it will be when every being has reached a state of understanding. It will *not* be forced upon us. It will *not* involve war or murder. It will be something that everyone will see coming and will embrace, because they have come to know the Prophets and the time is right."

Arla's calm seemed only to deepen as Kira's temper rose. "Is that what it says in your texts?" she asked. "Or is that just what you'd *like* to believe?"

"It's in the texts!" Kira insisted.

"Where?" Arla asked.

Kira looked dismayed. "I . . . I don't have them here. Weyoun's probably burned all of the real texts, anyway." She turned away from Arla, to end the conversation.

Sisko studied the commander, wondering if she could have some ulterior motive for upsetting Kira, something he'd overlooked. But he knew nothing that disturbed him. Other than the fact that her questions had merit.

Because as far as he knew, there *were* no passages in

any of the mainstream texts of Bajor describing the end of time as Kira had.

Time and existence would end for Bajor as it would for the cultures of a thousand different worlds—in a final battle between good and evil, light and dark, blue and red.

"I'm right, aren't I?" Arla asked quietly of Kira and Sisko. "We shouldn't be fighting this."

Kira offered no other answer.

Sisko considered Arla's challenge. "It all . . . it all comes down to free choice," he said at last. "I suppose that we each have to make our own decision in our own way."

"Well said, Benjamin!"

Weyoun was back.

He was standing on the other side of the heavy wooden door to their cell, peering in through its small, barred window.

"I'm *so* glad to see that you're all exploring such important religious issues," the Vorta said. He backed away from the window, and Sisko heard the rattling of the chain that kept it closed. "But if you'll just be patient a few more days, you won't have to trouble yourselves with trying to second-guess the True Prophets. I suggest you do what Commander Arla suggests. Embrace the coming transformation."

Then the heavy door swung open to reveal the Vorta and his five Grigari guards.

"After all," Weyoun said beneficently, "this impending battle is described both in my texts and yours, Major Kira. The only real difference between them is which of us is on the winning side. And since the hallmark of any religion is that the forces of good shall always triumph in the end, I think it's safe to say that whatever we believe now, we'll all be pleasantly surprised then." He pursed his lips in a mischievous smile directed squarely at Sisko. "Wouldn't you say, Benjamin?"

Sisko laughed in spite of himself. "What *I* say is that if the True Prophets are so powerful, so righteous, why do they need to wait so long—and why do they need *you* to restore the Temple? If they're gods, shouldn't they be able to snap their cosmic fingers and reorder reality to their liking?"

Weyoun made a tsk-tsk sound as he wagged a finger back and forth at Sisko. "*That*, my dear Benjamin, is a philosophical conundrum that has puzzled scholars for centuries. If I were you I'd keep it in mind to ask the True Prophets when you next see them, because I'm certain there's a perfectly good explanation." Weyoun bowed deeply and gestured toward the door. "And now . . ."

"Now what?" Sisko said.

"It's time to prepare."

"For what?"

Weyoun rolled his eyes. "Really, Benjamin. Why else are you here?" The Vorta's eyes flickered with just a flash of red light. "Why else have I kept you alive?"

Sisko gathered his robes around him, glanced once at Kira and Arla, then stepped through the doorway and out of the cell.

Weyoun was right.

It was time for the end to begin.

CHAPTER 23

BASHIR WALKED onto the bridge of the *Phoenix*, hands behind his back, whistling tunelessly. He had been chosen for this role because his genetically-enhanced capabilities were thought to give him an edge at remaining calm.

Certainly Nog didn't want to risk telling any more lies to the Romulans, not given his track record with Jake.

And besides, Bashir thought, I'm a physician. Which makes what I have to say all the more believable.

Aware of Romulan eyes watching every move he made, Bashir sauntered casually over to Centurion Karon's command chair. On the main viewer, only a computer navigation chart was displayed. Watching the strobing stars passing at transwarp velocities had been too disorienting, for humans and Romulans alike.

The route that was charted took the *Phoenix*—or the *Alth'Indor,* as the Romulans had rechristened her—on a wide galactic curve away from Bajor and into what had once been Cardassian space. This would enable the ship to make her final run toward Bajor from an unexpected direction, and at transwarp speeds even a two-minute lead could translate into a ten-light-year advantage.

Karon looked up from her holographic display as Bashir stopped beside her.

"Any sign of pursuit?" Bashir asked her.

"The alarms would have sounded," Karon said crisply. "In transwarp, we are virtually undetectable, just as the Borg are."

Bashir nodded and looked around, hands still behind his back.

"There is something else?" Karon asked, appearing a touch more impatient, exactly as Bashir and the others had hoped.

"Well, it will be four days till we reach our objective . . ."

"Correct."

". . . and I'd like to fill the time with something worthwhile."

"I suggest meditation."

"I was thinking more along the lines of medical research."

Karon stared at him, waiting for him to continue.

"No one's ever traveled through time in this ship," Bashir explained. "There is a slight possibility that there could be some . . . novel physical disruptions in bodily processes. Indigestion. Gas. Diarrhea. Vomiting."

"I am aware of bodily processes," Karon said coldly.

"Well, in order for me to treat these symptoms—if they occur—I'd like to have a baseline medical file on all crew members. So I can compare their readings before and after the—"

"I am also aware of the purpose of baseline readings, Doctor. Get to the point."

"I want to give physicals to your crew."

Karon considered Bashir, her dark eyes unblinking.

Bashir did his best to look innocent, then puzzled, then alarmed.

"Have I said something wrong, Centurion?"

"You really don't expect me to let you take my crew, one by one, into sickbay, where you will be free to inject them with drugs, neural implants, who knows what."

Bashir let his mouth drop open, as in shock. "Centurion, no! I just want to—"

"I know what you want to do, Doctor. This truce between us is strained enough as it is. Don't make it worse by attempting to gain the upper hand."

Bashir affected an air of disappointment and defeat. "If that's what you think, I apologize. It wasn't at all what I was—"

"Is there anything else, Doctor?"

Bashir acted perplexed, then spoke as if he had just had a thought. "Would it be all right if I ran baseline tests on just the humans and Bajorans?"

"You may vivisect them, if it will keep you off my bridge."

"It . . . won't be that drastic—but thank you." Bashir looked back at the other crew chairs. There were five temporal refugees among the Romulans. "I'll start with them, may I?"

"Just leave."

Bashir gave a deliberately calculated half-bow, then

gestured to the humans and Bajorans to accompany him to sickbay.

The Romulan standing guard at the turbolift alcove immediately questioned the fact that the refugees were leaving, but Centurion Karon instructed him to let the doctor proceed with his patients.

Bashir and his party entered the lift. Bashir nodded at the guard and smiled warmly. The guard turned away with a grunt of disapproval.

Then Bashir completed the final, most important act of his deception. As the lift doors began to close, he reached out his hand to make them open again, stepped out into the alcove, and firmly grasped the edges of the ship's dedication plaque and *pulled.*

He felt as if he had sliced open half his fingers, but Nog had been right. The metal plaque released from its mag connectors with a pop.

The Romulan guard turned in time to see Bashir step back into the lift with the gleaming metal plate.

"We're going to make you a new one," Bashir said. "So it says *Alth'Indor.*"

The guard frowned but made no move to stop them as the lift doors closed a second time.

Bashir kept his smile in place until he felt the jolt of the lift car beginning to move. He was no longer startled by it, now that Nog had explained why the dampening fields had been tuned to a slow response time.

When they had descended four decks, Bashir tapped his commbadge. "We're on our way to sickbay. I have all the patients."

A moment later, Worf's voice said, "Acknowledged."

Bashir grinned, and this time he meant it.

When the lift stopped on deck 8, Bashir rushed out,

heading for engineering, leaving his confused patients to follow on their own. One of them even called out that this wasn't the deck for sickbay.

Bashir burst into engineering, hoping he was in time.

He was. Just.

On the systems wall a large display showed a schematic of the *Phoenix*, all three kilometers of her, a sleek shape most resembling a pumpkin seed bristling with transwarp pods on its aft hulls, ventral and dorsal.

"Here goes," Nog said, with a tense nod at Bashir.

He tapped some controls on the main engineering table. Instantly, a set of system displays turned red and the computer voice said, "Warning: Initiating multivector attack mode while in—" Nog silenced the voice with a sharp jab at the controls.

Also at the main engineering table, Jadzia looked up in alarm. "Would they hear that on the bridge?"

"Doesn't matter," Nog said quickly as his fingers flew over the controls. "They're not going anywhere."

On the schematic, Bashir saw all the turbolift shafts turn red.

Then a communications screen opened on the table and a holographic image of Centurion Karon took shape. "Captain Nog!" she shouted. "You will cease your attempts to override bridge authority and return the ship's dedication plaque at once!"

"Actually," Nog muttered, "that's exactly what I'm *not* going to do." He held a finger over one final, flashing red control. "Hold on to your lobes, everyone," he said, then pressed it.

Instantly the engineering workroom filled with sirens and flashing lights and on the main schematic Bashir watched as a small section of the forward ventral hull become outlined in red.

"Partial multivector mode established," the computer reported. "Prepare for bridge-segment jettison."

The deck shuddered, as the red-outlined section of the schematic suddenly vanished from the board.

"All control transferred to battle bridge," the computer said.

The computer was immediately followed by Worf's triumphant voice. "We are the *Phoenix* once again."

Bashir cheered along with Jadzia. Jake pounded Nog on the back.

Then Worf asked over the comm link, "What are your orders, Captain Nog?"

The doctor heard the passion in the Ferengi's swift reply. "We're going to Bajor."

Bashir relaxed.

The universe had one last chance.

CHAPTER 24

WEYOUN STEPPED OUT onto the balcony of the temple in the center of B'hala and held out his arms as if to show off his new robes of intense, saturated red.

"The blood of innocents?" Sisko asked.

"The flame of faith," Weyoun answered.

Sisko turned back to B'hala, concentrating on the heat of the morning sun, the dry scent of dust, and the silence.

The silence was absolute.

This last day of existence, as reports of riots on other worlds spread across the subspace channels, Bajor was still. Its population had long since been winnowed by expulsion and execution until it was only a home for believers. And this day, even the believers had been sent home, to pray and to wait for their Ascension.

Sisko wondered how many Bajorans were huddled in the stone buildings within his view. He wondered how many were whispering the prayers of the Pah-wraiths and how many were clinging fearfully to the prayers of the Prophets, trusting without trust in one last miracle, one last tear as the Prophets wept for their people.

"Still hoping there might be a bomb or two hidden down there?" Weyoun asked, as he came to stand by Sisko's side as if, somehow, they were equals.

"It would be a nice surprise," Sisko said.

"Ah, but if Starfleet's brave chrononauts *had* managed to plant them and fool our sensors, they would have gone off by now, don't you think?"

"Maybe Starfleet sank a planet buster near the core," Sisko said, baring his teeth in a facsimile of a smile. "Take out the whole planet any time now."

"Benjamin, you know that's not Starfleet's style. Destroy an entire world, just to stop one man?"

"You're not a man, Weyoun. But I am glad to hear the lies have stopped. Starfleet wouldn't destroy a world. Wouldn't start a war. Wouldn't spread lies."

"I wouldn't advise you to take that as a sign of moral rectitude. You should look at it as I do: as a sign of their weakness. *Your* weakness, Benjamin."

"Starfleet's not weak," Sisko said. "There's still time to stop you."

Weyoun's laugh was derisive. "In twenty hours? No. Every attempt has failed—and failed miserably. Operation Looking Glass? That pathetic attempt to attack us in the Mirror Universe—a fiasco. Operation Phoenix? It literally fell apart—a Grigari ship found the *bridge* of the *Phoenix* adrift near the Vulcan frontier, filled with a crew of terrified Romulans. Don't you see, Benjamin? You people wasted too much energy fighting each other. That is your greatest weakness. No self-control."

Sisko refused to be provoked. "Twenty hours. Twenty seconds. I won't give up."

"And that's your weakness, too—refusing to accept the inevitable."

Sisko concentrated on the smooth texture of the worn rock that formed the balcony's edge. This couldn't end. This *wouldn't* end. "You will be stopped, Weyoun."

"Did I mention Operation Guardian?" Weyoun asked.

Sisko shrugged, uninterested.

"Fascinating plan. A sure sign of the sheer desperation rampant in what was left of the Federation." Weyoun leaned forward to be sure Sisko could both see and hear him. "It called for a combined force of Starfleet vessels and Borg cubeships! Can you imagine? The Federation and the Borg acting together?"

Sisko was dismissive of Weyoun and his gloating. "What of it? It's our way to make our enemies our allies. Always has been. Always will be."

"The combined force—fifty, sixty ships at least—were trying to regain a small planetoid with a strange alien device built into it. Have you ever heard of the Guardian of Forever?"

Surprised, Sisko studied Weyoun. *That might work,* he thought.

Weyoun smiled. "But they failed, of course. The Grigari were ready for them. To Starfleet's credit, or perhaps it was the Borg's—it doesn't really matter which," the Vorta said, "the battle lasted for days. And then, when that noble Admiral Janeway finally managed to get her troops on the ground and within sight of the device—"

Sisko closed his eyes, willing Weyoun to vanish. Willing Bajor to be consumed by a bomb planted a billion years ago. Anything to end Weyoun's vicious prattling.

"—You really should pay attention to this, Benjamin . . . I assure you it is quite amusing. Just at that moment when Janeway thought she had won—*knew* she had won—the Grigari activated a singularity bomb." Weyoun snapped his fingers. "Instant black hole. Borg. Starfleet. The Guardian. Even the Grigari. Sucked out of the universe just like that. A taste of what's to come for all of us, hmm?"

"I *could* throw myself off this balcony," Sisko said, looking down on the silent city far below.

"You could," Weyoun agreed. "In fact, I'm a little surprised you haven't tried it by now. Don't let me stop you."

"If I fall and die, would you just bring me back to life? Or would I just not fall?"

"Why not try it? And I'll surprise you."

Sisko turned around, his back to the city, leaned against the balcony wall. "Tell me, Weyoun. Do you really need me here to . . . to accomplish something? Or are you just desperate for an audience?"

Red sparks danced in Weyoun's eyes. "Oh, I do need you, Benjamin. Two Temples. Two groups of Prophets. Two Emissaries. It all has to be brought into balance."

"How?" The question Sisko had wanted answered for so long hung in the air between them.

Weyoun looked up at the brilliant blue sky and to Sisko, it was almost as if the Vorta were staring directly into Bajor's sun. "Oh, the Temples are easy. And when they come together, the Prophets will know what to do. But the role of the Emissaries . . . you know, that's a puzzle."

Sisko tensed, alert to the first admission from Weyoun that his power and knowledge were not absolute.

"There's something that's not written in your texts?" Sisko asked carefully.

Weyoun shook his head. "That's what's so intriguing, Benjamin. *Everything* is in the texts. Even your name—the Sisko. Your discovery of B'hala. The False Reckoning on your old station. The fall of the Gateway. Your return in time for the joining of the Temples.

"The texts make it very clear that whoever wrote them knew about you. And that you are an absolute requirement for the Ascension to take place as prophesied. But . . . just before the end . . . the text stops—not as if there's a missing page—the narrative simply ends, as if whoever saw this future didn't see its end either."

"Then maybe it doesn't," Sisko said.

Weyoun waved a hand in the air. "Admittedly there are a few theological loose ends. But, really, physics is physics. Whatever you think about what might be in them, when those two wormholes come together these eleven dimensions of space-time around us will unravel instantaneously and irretrievably."

"What kind of god would want that fate for creation?" Sisko asked.

As if in answer to Sisko's question, an intense red glow flared and then faded in Weyoun's eyes. Then the Vorta reached out to take his arm.

"What do you want of me?" Sisko demanded, drawing back.

Weyoun smiled and shook his head. Then firmly holding on to Sisko, he tapped his chest as if something were hidden beneath his robes.

"Two to beam up," he said.

B'hala dissolved into light as once again, Sisko was transported.

CHAPTER 25

THE *PHOENIX* ripped through a realm of space not even Zefram Cochrane had imagined.

Her engines had the power to change the course of stars and turn planets into glittering nebulae of atomic gas just by passing too close to them. But that power was contained and channeled by technology—technology assimilated from a thousand different cultures, from trillions of different individuals, representing as it did the sum total of Borg knowledge.

But now, only seventeen beings rode within the *Phoenix* as she began her final run. Fifteen of her passengers were already displaced in time. Two others were willing to face the same risks.

The ship's destination was fifty light-years away. But with the incomprehensible power she controlled, she would reach it within the hour.

And that hour might be the last the beings within her would ever know.

"Come with us," Jake said.

But Nog shook his head, his attention riveted on the main viewer of the battle bridge. "The *Phoenix* has to end up on Syladdo, fourth moon of Ba'Syladon," he said.

Without taking his eyes from the viewer, Nog brandished the gleaming dedication plaque he was holding. "Along with this."

"Nog, you can't do this!" Jake said, alarmed by his friend's intentions. "The wreckage wasn't found until *after* we disappeared. You won't be changing the timeline."

Nog stared straight ahead, undeterred. "If the wreckage isn't there, the timeline *will* be changed. I've gone over it with Jadzia and Dr. Bashir."

"Then . . . ," Jake struggled to find the right words, the right argument. "Then program the computer to crash the damn thing!"

"No, Jake. There's no guarantee the computers will function after the slingshot maneuver. If they need any significant time to reset themselves, the *Phoenix* could crash somewhere else in the meantime. Maybe even on Bajor. Wipe out a city."

"Come on, Nog. You *can't* kill yourself!"

"I don't plan to. The Romulans' charts of the crash site were very detailed. And as I told you before, they only found forty percent of the ship." Nog flashed a quick grin at Jake over his shoulder, before turning back to the viewer. "Remember, the *Phoenix* is a multivector ship. Not counting the bridge we jettisoned, that means two segments *didn't* crash. I'll be able to go anywhere. Even Erelyn IV."

"Anywhere except home," Jake said. Because that was Nog's plan for the rest of them. Starfleet Intelligence knew that Ascendancy starships would be keeping station at the coordinates where the wormholes would open and merge. Nog was going to beam Jake and the others to the bridge of one of those starships so that it could instantly warp into a slingshot trajectory around the mouth of the *blue* wormhole. The precise temporal heading would be unimportant, because wherever in the past the ship emerged, Jadzia would have more than enough time to calculate a precise trajectory to bring them back to their own time, *before* the Red Orbs of Jalbador were discovered.

It would be an alternate timeline. The past twenty-five years could not be erased. But at least *one* universe would survive. Perhaps.

Jake couldn't hold his emotions in any longer. He and Nog had been through too much together. "I'm going to miss you," he said.

Nog suddenly turned his back on the viewer. "Me too, Jake. But there'll be another me back in your time." He reached out and gave Jake's shoulder a squeeze.

Jake felt a lump tighten his throat. "Bet he'll be surprised when I tell him how things turned out here."

But Nog shook his head. "Don't tell him. Please."

"Why not?"

"Back then I was just a kid, Jake. I wasn't sure what I wanted. I liked Starfleet. I thought maybe I had a career. But part of me still wanted to go into business. When things got bad after the station was destroyed, that's when I decided to stick it out in the Fleet. But if things are different when you go back . . . well, I wouldn't want some version of myself sticking with Starfleet just because that's what I did. I'd like to think I had a second chance along with the rest of the universe. Okay?"

Jake nodded. He understood. At least he thought he did. "I'm still going to put this all in a book," he told Nog.

"Just make sure it's fiction."

"Absolutely."

"And make sure the brave Ferengi captain has really crooked teeth and spectacularly *big* lobes."

"Gigantic!" Jake had to smile in spite of the way he felt.

"And put in a scene like in *Vulcan Love Slave*—" Nog giggled, just the way Jake remembered he used to.

"Part Two!" Jake laughed out loud as Nog's giggles became contagious.

"The Revenge!" both young men, both little boys, shouted in unison.

"Only this time, the *Ferengi* gets the girls! And they're all . . . fully clothed!"

They collapsed against each other then, gasping in hilarity, laughing as they hadn't laughed in twenty-five years, Jake realized.

Suddenly serious, Jake looked at his friend. "I promise," he said.

"I know. You're a good man, Jake."

Then the door to the battle bridge slid open. Quickly composing themselves, Jake and Nog turned together to see—

Vash.

And Admiral Picard at her side.

"Where's Q when you need him? That's what I want to know," Vash said as she guided Admiral Picard onto the battle bridge, while gently holding on to his arm. The admiral was smiling happily.

"Will! Geordi! Where have you two been hiding?"

Everyone on the *Phoenix* knew the Old Man had his good times and his bad, easily distinguished by the names by which he addressed those he met. So both Jake and Nog respectfully greeted the admiral in turn without correcting him, and Vash helped Picard to his chair, from which all operational controls had carefully been removed.

"Seriously," Vash said to Nog as she joined him by the viewer, "does anyone know what's happened to Q?"

"The admiral's been telling you about him?" Nog asked.

Vash nodded. "He says Q comes to see him almost every day. Is that right?"

"No," Nog said. "I wish it were. A few years ago when all this started, there was a whole division at Starfleet that was trying to make contact with the Q continuum. Q helped out the Old Man once before with time travel. We thought maybe we could ask him to help again. But no one's seen him for . . . well, since DS9 was destroyed. Except for the Old Man's stories, that is."

"And you're really sure Q *isn't* in contact with him?"

"Positive," Nog said. "At the shipyards, we even tried putting the Old Man under constant surveillance. He'd have conversations with an empty chair, then tell us that Q had visited him. Or Data. Sometimes it was Worf. Sorry."

Jake saw how Vash watched Picard in his chair, saw the sudden liquid brightening her eyes. "So am I," she said. Then she squared her shoulders and looked down at Nog. "Okay, Hotshot, listen up. I'm coming with you."

"No, you're not!" Nog sputtered in surprise.

"Yes I am, and you can't stop me because you need me."

"I do not!"

Vash pointed to the admiral. "But *he* does!" She held up a small medkit. "When was the last time you checked his peridaxon levels?"

Jake was surprised by how flustered Nog became under Vash's stern scrutiny. "I've . . . been busy. I was just going to."

"And because you've been so busy," Vash said, "the greatest starship commander in Starfleet history has been calling *you* Will Riker and *him* Geordi La Forge. He deserves better treatment, *Captain* Nog."

"And what makes you think he can get it from you?"

In the midst of this heated exchange, Jake saw Vash become unexpectedly quiet. And the only reason for her change in mood that he could see was that she was again gazing at Picard.

"I owe that man," she said, without anger or hostility.

"You *knew* him?" Nog asked. "I mean . . ."

Vash nodded. "I know what you mean. Ever hear of Dr. Samuel Estragon?"

Nog hadn't. Neither had Jake.

"Doesn't matter. But I'm not leaving Jean-Luc. And I don't care if I have to chew your precious lobes off to make you agree."

Jake saw Nog flush. "Do you know what you're getting yourself into?"

"I do," Vash said simply. "An act of loyalty for one.

An appreciation of a great man." She looked deep into Nog's eyes. "Maybe even a chance to help you out because I just know you're going to need all the help you can get."

"You're also risking getting trapped more than two and half millennia in the past."

"I'm an archaeologist, Hotshot. I should be so lucky." Then she tapped Nog's chest with her finger. "And just for the record, I've already been farther back in the past, farther forward in the future, and farther away than this two-credit quadrant."

Nog stared at Vash in disbelief, but Jake thought he knew what she meant.

"How is that even possible?" Nog asked.

Vash grinned. "Jean-Luc and me, let's just say we've got a friend in high places. And maybe he hasn't shown up in this timeline 'cause he knows it doesn't amount to anything. And maybe when we show up a few dozen centuries out of place he'll look in on us again."

"Q," Nog said, distrustful. "And what if he doesn't?"

Vash rolled her shoulders. "I speak and write ancient Bajoran. Maybe we can put on a traveling show."

Nog was wary. "If I do let you accompany us on our mission, I will expect you to behave like a member of my crew and treat me with respect."

"And I'll expect you to act in such a way that you'll deserve my respect."

Vash and Nog stared at each other for a long moment, and Jake could tell that neither one of them wanted to be the first to give in.

So Jake took the initiative.

"I think it's a good deal," he said. "I think you should shake on it before you change your minds." He put his hand on Nog's shoulder. "Think of the admiral. She's got a point."

Nog grudgingly held out his hand. "All right. For the Old Man's sake. But don't make me regret taking you."

Vash's smile was dazzling, and instead of taking Nog's hand she ran two fingers lightly around the outer curve of his ear, ending with a small scratch at his sensitive lower lobe. "Regret taking me? Are you kidding?"

Jake thought Nog's eyes would roll up permanently in his head.

Vash fluttered her long, slim fingers at him, then turned away and went back to Picard.

"What have I done?" Nog marveled.

"I think you've made the best decision of your life," Jake said heartily, not sure at all about what he was saying. But then Nog had never been able to tell when *he* was bluffing.

"Really?"

"Look at it this way," Jake told his friend. "With Vash along, whatever else happens she's going to keep things . . . interesting."

Nog sighed heavily. "That's what I'm afraid of."

Then Jake looked at the time display on the main viewer.

The universe had forty-seven minutes left.

CHAPTER 26

"IT WON'T WORK," Miles O'Brien said.

"Uh . . . I agree," Rom added.

Quark leaned forward and banged his broad forehead against the stone wall of the cell in B'hala. "Perfect, just perfect. Half the galaxy's convinced the universe is going to end in less than an hour, and my idiot brother just *happens* to figure out that this whole War of the Prophets is a big mistake." He banged his head again. "Why not call up Weyoun? See if he'll let us go home now?" Bang.

"Uh, maybe you shouldn't be doing that, Brother. You might hurt yourself."

At that, Quark opened his mouth and screamed and flung himself at Rom with arms outstretched, and for a second it seemed nothing could stop one Ferengi from crashing the other into solid rock.

Except me, Odo sighed to himself, as he reluctantly

changed his humanoid arms into tentacles that snaked out across the length of the room to snag Quark.

"Will you settle down!" he said, as he deposited a squirming Quark on the side of the cell opposite Rom. "Maybe the Chief is onto something. What are they going to do? Lock me up? Kill me?"

"We can only hope," Quark said darkly.

Odo grunted, more concerned about the grasping tentacles he'd formed so quickly, which were now becoming tangled in the robes he'd been forced to wear. He swiftly solved the situation by puddling faster than his robes could fall, then surging to the side and reforming in his humanoid shape again, his outer layer now a perfect reproduction of a Bajoran militia uniform, circa 2374. "That's better," he said emphatically.

"Good for you," Quark groused. "Now why don't you change into a balloon and float us all out of here? Wouldn't want to be late for *the end of the universe!*"

Quark, however annoying a cellmate for the past seven days they had been incarcerated together, was not the real problem, Odo thought. What was truly unfortunate was that their cell in this partially restored B'hala structure was ringed by the same type of polymorphic inhibitor Weyoun had used against him on the *Boreth*. Behind these walls and barred windows, Odo was as caged as any solid.

But he refused to give in to self-centered neuroticism as Quark had done, though. Instead, he walked over to the wall where O'Brien and Rom had been scratching equations and diagrams into the soft stone for the past two days.

"Why won't it work?" the changeling asked O'Brien. He had to. Somehow, he had to believe there was still hope in this universe, that somehow he would be rejoined with Kira. Because to find love and lose it in so short a time . . . Odo refused to believe that Kira's Prophets would allow such agony.

"In the simplest terms," O'Brien said, "it's inertia." Odo watched as the Chief used a long stick he had peeled off one of the timbers of a bunk to point to a diagram of the Bajoran solar system and explain the orbits marked upon it.

Apparently, the entrance region of the blue wormhole of the Prophets maintained a nearly circular orbit around Bajor's sun, just at the edges of the Denorios Belt. And sometimes the wormhole actually crossed into it.

The Chief indicated the entrance region of the red wormhole which, in contrast to that of the blue wormhole, had a more eccentric orbit. Reminiscent, he said, of a comet's, travelling from the system's outer reaches and plunging past Bajor's own orbit before it returned to the realm of the gas giants.

On the Chief's diagram Odo noticed that the red wormhole actually crossed the orbit of the Denorios Belt and the blue wormhole four times each orbit. And in less than an hour, O'Brien said, for the first time since the red wormhole had been reestablished by the three Red Orbs of Jalbador twenty-five years ago in Quark's bar, the orbital harmonics of the Bajoran system were finally going to bring the two wormhole entrance regions to their closest possible approach.

"But that closest approach," the Chief emphasized, "is still going to leave the entrance regions approximately five hundred kilometers apart."

"Uh, four hundred and sixty-three kilometers," Rom corrected him. "More or less."

From the other side of the cell, Quark moaned loudly. He was again leaning his head against the cell wall.

"What's the difficulty presented by that distance?" Odo asked, deliberately shutting out the sound of Quark's complaining. "It doesn't seem very far, cosmically speaking."

"The entrance effect of a wormhole is very constrained, Odo," O'Brien said. "I mean, that's one of the reasons it took so long for the blue wormhole to be discovered. If you're not within a kilometer or so of it when it opens, there's no force acting on you to pull you in. If this thing had been swallowing hunks of the Denorios Belt for the past few thousand years, someone would have noticed pretty early on. But its effect on normal space is very limited. That's why we have to pilot a ship toward it with great precision to actually travel through it."

"In other words," Rom added hesitantly but eagerly, "even if both wormholes open at the precise moment of their closest approach, they're both too far away from each other to have any attractive effect."

From his corner, Quark called out to them. "Before you pay too much attention to that lobeless wonder, did I ever tell you how Rom once stuck a toy whip from my Marauder Mo playset into his ear? He was eight years old, and he was *always* playing with his ears. I was so embarrassed. But here he took this little—"

"Shut up, Quark!" Odo, O'Brien, and Rom said it all together.

"I'm just saying he's not right," Quark said loudly. "Always with the ears. Stop it or you'll go deaf, Moogie kept telling him. But did he listen? Ha? How could he? He had half my toys shoved up his ear canal!"

"No one's listening, Quark," Odo growled. "Please, Rom, Chief O'Brien—go on."

Rom's cheeks were flushed red. "There's, uh, not much more to tell. The wormholes won't move through space. So they won't join. So . . . the universe won't come to an end. That's about it."

"Why didn't Starfleet scientists discover this?" Odo asked.

"Well, it's difficult to chart wormhole orbits accurately," O'Brien said. "They respond to interior verteron forces, as well as to the number of times they open and close in a given orbit. I'm guessing that Starfleet's first reaction was that the wormholes would never come close enough to represent a threat. What do you think, Rom?"

Obviously pleased to have the Chief consult him, especially after such abuse from his brother, Rom quickly nodded his support for this theory.

"Further observations," O'Brien continued, "suggested that the two wormholes *would* open close enough to merge today. But from what the Ascendants told us during those interminable briefings they kept giving us, the orbits are fairly well known for the next few months. And according to their own figures, they just won't be close enough."

"Are you certain there's no way to move them?" Odo asked. "Tow them somehow? Use a tractor beam? Connect them by a charged particle web?"

O'Brien and Rom glanced at each other and both shook their heads. Odo saw little beads of sweat fall from their foreheads.

"You see, Odo, most wormhole entrances are created by verteron particles impinging on weakened areas of space-time," O'Brien explained as Odo listened intently, doing his best to follow the technical language.

"The opening they form is bound by *negative* matter, and it's kept open by negative energy, just as they suspected back in the twenty-first century. But not even the Iconians had the ability to manipulate negative matter. It would be like . . ." The Chief frowned as he tried to come up with the most helpful comparison ". . . like trying to outrun your shadow."

Odo stared at the scratchings on the wall. "Then why do you suppose Weyoun's people are so convinced that today's the day the wormholes merge? They're going to look awfully foolish tomorrow."

Quark's indignant voice sounded from just behind him. Odo turned to see the Ferengi pulling out on his robes like a small child about to curtsey. "*They're* going to look foolish?"

They all said it again. Only this time more emphatically. "SHUT UP, QUARK!"

Rom giggled as his brother stomped off with a curse, then recovered himself. "Uh, maybe Weyoun will claim that he interceded with the Prophets on behalf of the people of the universe," he said. "That way, he can take credit for . . . saving us all."

O'Brien nodded. "That makes sense, Rom. The easiest disaster to prevent is the one that could never happen. High priests and shamans have been doing it forever—driving off the dragon that eats the moon, bringing summer back after the solstice."

Odo was feeling buoyed by this revelation. Perhaps he *would* hold Kira's hand again, mold his lips to hers once more. But still, he thought, surely there were easier ways for Weyoun to gain the respect of the galaxy than to manufacture a doomsday scenario that could be disproved by a few lines of mathematics.

"Are you certain there's no way to move 'negative' matter?" he asked O'Brien.

The chief engineer was adamant. "The wormholes are fixed in the space-time metric, Odo, like rocks in cement. Nothing's going to move them. It just won't work."

"Well, then," Odo said with new enthusiasm, "we'd better start thinking what we'd like for dinner tonight."

"There's nothing like an idiot's death," Quark muttered from his corner. "Happy to the end."

Odo walked over to the barred window, felt the warning tingle of the inhibitor field. He looked out at the blazing sun. He wondered if Kira was looking at it, too. He wished he could reassure her that there was nothing to worry about, after all. But Weyoun had been keeping both Kira and Arla with Sisko.

Odo turned away from the window. "I wonder when our jailers will come back," he said to O'Brien. The Bajoran guards that had been posted for them had not arrived this morning. Even the loathsome Grigari were gone.

"I wonder when you'll face the inevitable," Quark snapped.

Odo had just about had it with the Ferengi. "Trust in physics, Quark."

"Ha!" Quark exclaimed. "If I trusted in physics I'd be paying out twice as many dabos and—" He shut his mouth with an audible smack. "Forget I said that." He turned away, face as red as his brother's.

In fact, Odo noticed even O'Brien was more flushed than usual. "Are you all right, Chief?"

"I could use a nice cold beer," O'Brien said with a weary grin. He moved to the window and held up a hand next to it. "That's odd. The breeze doesn't feel all that hot."

"Because it's the wall," Rom said.

Odo and O'Brien shared the same puzzled reaction, and stared at the wall Rom pointed to. It was made of typical B'hala building stones, half a meter square, badly eroded, set without mortar. The only thing beyond it was the outside.

But as Odo watched, the stone wall seemed to waver, as if seen through a raging fire.

"Stand back," Odo cautioned.

O'Brien, Rom, and Odo began retreating from the rippling wall, not taking their eyes off it.

"Here it comes," Quark sniped from his corner position where the rippling wall met the far wall. "Reality's dissolving. I'd say I told you so but what would be the point?"

Odo motioned to the Ferengi. "I'd get over here if I were you, Quark."

But Quark didn't budge. "If I were you," he said, mimicking Odo's way of speaking. "You know what I've always wanted to say to you, Odo?" he announced.

"No," Odo told him.

The rippling wall resembled liquid now, and an oval shape was forming in its center as the heat in the cell air increased.

Quark cleared his throat. "I've always wanted to say, Why don't you turn yourself into a two-pronged Mandorian gutter snail and go—"

A high-pitched squeal rang out as the liquid-like wall exploded inward with a flash of near-blinding red light. Odo and Rom and O'Brien stumbled forward as a rush of cool air blasted *into* the wall opening, kicking up a cloud of sand from the floor and sucking the bunk, the buckets, and Quark all in the same direction.

And then, without warning, the wind ended. The bunks and the buckets and Quark stopped moving.

The sand on the floor lay as still and undisturbed as if in a vacuum.

But Quark wasn't abhorring a vacuum as much as anything else in nature.

"*That* was the end of the universe?" he crowed, hopping on one foot to shake the sand from his ears. "After all that buildup?"

This time not even Odo bothered to tell Quark to shut up.

Because Odo saw through the opening in the wall that someone else was about to join them.

A humanoid shape was walking toward them from a dark room that Odo *knew* was *not* beyond the shattered wall.

The stench of putrefaction swept into the small cell and infected every molecule of air. O'Brien gagged, Rom whimpered, and Quark protested in disgust.

Then Odo saw a pair of glowing red eyes just like Weyoun's.

"Oh, *frinx,*" Quark said. "Not another one."

"No," a deep voice answered. *"Not another one. The* first *one."*

Odo stepped back as Dukat entered the cell. But the Cardassian's eyes were normal and he was normal, except for the soiled robes he wore and his halo of wild dead-white hair.

"My dear, dear friends," he said. "How good to see you once again."

"How did you get here?" Odo asked Dukat. He had seen enough strange things in this future to not waste time questioning them.

Dukat held up a silver cylinder a bit larger than Weyoun's inhibitor, and looked at it lovingly. "A multidimensional transporter device. A toy, really."

O'Brien stared at Dukat. "The Mirror Universe?"

Dukat lowered the cylinder. "And like all mirrors, what it contains is only a reflection. So when this universe ends, so shall it."

"But this universe isn't ending," O'Brien argued. "The wormholes won't open close enough to each other. And there's no way they can be moved."

Dukat looked at O'Brien as if the Chief were no more than a babbling child. "Miles, that's not very imaginative of you. Of course the wormhole entrances can't be moved through space. But what if *space* were moved. What you might even call a *warp*."

"Dear God," O'Brien said. "Rom, they're going to change the space-time metric."

"Great River," Rom squeaked. "There's only one way to do that."

"I *knew* it," Quark added. "Um, whatever it is."

"But you have a way out, don't you, Dukat?" Odo said. He for one was not willing to give up just yet.

Dukat beamed. "Odo . . . I always knew there was a reason why I liked you." He held out his hand. "And there is exactly that. A way out. A way to escape the destruction of everything. And all I ask is for one small favor in return . . ."

Odo stared at Dukat's hand as if it were a gray-scaled snake poised to strike. He looked up at Dukat's eyes—at Weyoun's eyes—saw the red sparks ignite.

The universe had thirty minutes left.

It was not as if they had a choice.

CHAPTER 27

THEY WERE ALL on the battle bridge now: Captain Nog, Admiral Picard, Vash, Jake, and the thirteen other temporal refugees.

"Computer," Nog said. "Go to long-range transfactor sensors. Image Bajor-B'hava'el.

Bashir observed the computer navigation graphic vanish from the main viewer, to be replaced by a real-time representation of Bajor's sun. He noted a small solar flare frozen in a graceful arc from its northwestern hemisphere, and a string of small sunspots scattered at its equator. As far as he could tell, it was to all appearances a typical type-G star, securely in the middle of the main sequence.

"What's the time lag with this system?" Jadzia asked.

"With transfactor imaging at this distance? We're seeing the sun as it existed less than half a second ago." Nog's hand moved through a holographic control panel and a spectrographic display of the sun appeared at the bottom of the viewer. Even Bashir was able to see that there were no anomalies present.

"You're sure about this?" Jadzia asked. "Stars don't get much more stable than that."

Bashir could tell the Trill was worried, and about more than Nog's planned maneuver. Jadzia's spotting stood out in high contrast to her pale, drawn face, and the reason for her concern was standing beside her: Worf, his shoulders rounded, restricted by the pressure bandages the holographic medical team had applied to his disruptor wounds. The problem was that this ship had no medical equipment set for Klingon physiology, and what would have required a simple fifteen-minute treatment in Bashir's infirmary on DS9 had become a week-long ordeal of daily bandage-changings and the constant threat of infection. Jadzia was clearly worried that in his weakened condition Worf might not survive what Nog had in mind. And Bashir had been unable to say much to reassure her. As Vash had earlier pointed out, there were just too many things that could go wrong.

But Nog was a study in confidence. "I'm positive," the Ferengi answered. Then he adjusted more holographic controls, until the image of Bajor's sun shrank to the upper-right-hand corner of the viewer and a new image window opened. Now they were looking at a closeup of the *Phoenix*'s twenty-five-thousand-year-old dedication plate recovered by the Romulans. "Look at the atomic tracings," he said.

Thin lines of artificial color appeared over the plaque. Most of the lines were dead straight. A very few, Bashir noticed, curved and looped like the trail of subatomic particles in a child's cloud chamber.

"Read the isotope numbers, too," Nog urged Jadzia. "And the energy matrix."

This was a more difficult piece of evidence for Bashir to understand. But from what Nog had already told them, it apparently showed incontrovertible evidence that the plaque had been in close proximity to a supernova. In addition, Nog said, to having been subjected to an intense burst of chronometric particles, which suggested it had traveled along a temporal slingshot trajectory.

Furthermore, the Ferengi maintained, the distinctive mix of elements and isotopes that had left their trails through the plaque's metal structure were an exact match for Bajor-B'hava'el—a sun that should not be at risk for even a simple nova reaction for more than a billion years.

Which apparently left room for only one conclusion.

The Ascendancy was going to deliberately trigger the sun's explosion.

And the reason was, again according to Nog, perfectly logical: When the two wormholes opened at their closest approach to each other—something which would happen in just over fifteen minutes, relative time—the portals would be too far away from each other to interact.

The supernova detonation of Bajor's sun, however, provided it was properly timed, would create a high-density, faster-than-light subspace pressure wave. And that pressure wave would be followed minutes later by a near-light-speed physical wall of superheated gas thrown off from the surface of the collapsing sun.

As far as Bashir had been able to understand from Nog's explanation, the combined effect of the two near-simultaneous concussions in real space and subspace—when added to the gravity waves generated by the sudden disappearance of the Bajoran gravity well around which the wormholes orbited—would actually cause the underlying structure of space-time to warp.

Nog told them that the effect would be a natural version of what a Cochrane engine did on an ongoing and far more focused basis in every starship that had ever flown. And then the Ferengi had shown the math to Jadzia that described an incredible event. For approximately four seconds, the space between the two wormhole openings would relativistically decrease from almost five hundred kilometers to less than five hundred meters.

And, Nog insisted, there was nothing in the universe that could keep the two wormholes apart at that distance.

Thus would the Ascendancy end the universe.

"Commander Dax," the Ferengi captain said with finality. "Like it or not, we're running out of time. We'll be at our first insertion point in . . . seven minutes."

"Are you certain you don't want to attempt to place the deep-time charges?" Jadzia asked.

"If we had planted them, they would have detonated by now," Nog said. "There's only one more thing we can do."

Bashir could see that Jadzia's concern was now shared by everyone else who would be beaming from the *Phoenix* at . . . at transfactor twelve, whatever that meant in recalibrated warp factors.

And with Nog claiming that modern transporters could handle the task by using something called "micropacket-burst-transmission," who among the temporal refugees from the past could argue with something so incomprehensible? Certainly *he* himself couldn't, Bashir thought.

Nog turned from the viewer to address his apprehensive passengers. "Trust in the River," he said. "It might not take you where you want to go, but have faith that it will always take you where you *need* to go. Good profits to you all. Now please report to your assigned transporter pads."

Having faced death many times on this strange journey, Bashir himself felt rather unconcerned about soon facing it again. Besides, if anything went wrong with Nog's plan in the past, he and all the others simply wouldn't exist. So they wouldn't even be dead.

As the others left the battle bridge he approached Nog, who was in the middle of saying his farewell to Jake, at least that's what it seemed to Bashir that the Ferengi was doing. What he overheard of their exchange did not make much sense to him.

"Remember," Nog warned his friend, "don't tell 'me.' "

Jake's answering smile was rather mournful, Bashir thought. "But I'll make sure you get all the girls," Jake said. "Fully clothed."

As Jake stepped back, he bumped into Bashir, awkwardly pinning Vash between the two of them.

"Don't look so glum, boys," she said, separating them with a playful push. "This is going to work. I know it." The archaeologist manifested none of the nervousness possessing everyone else.

"How can you be so sure?" Bashir asked her, curious, and rather envious of her upbeat, invigorated mood.

She winked at him. "Let's just say I've seen how the River flowed."

Bashir frowned at her. What did she mean? Had Vash learned something—about the past? Frustratingly, there was however no time left for questions—no time even to express his regret that he and she had not had the opportunity to follow up on the promise of that kiss they had shared on the *Augustus*. More than anything else—if only to bring completion to his time with her—Bashir wished he could kiss Vash again.

The woman was a mind reader. But it seemed she had read the wrong mind. She pushed past Bashir to grab *Jake's* face between her hands and kissed Jake with a passion that could have melted duranium.

When she released him, Jake looked dizzy, and shocked, and pleased—incredibly pleased—all at the same time. And incapable of coherent speech. Horridly jealous, Bashir felt a hundred years old. He remembered feeling that way himself. And hoped he would again.

"You know," Bashir heard Vash say to Jake, "people are going to tell you that you always remember your first love."

Jake nodded silently, still dazed.

"But you know what the truth is?" Vash didn't wait for an answer. "The truth is, the one you really never forget is your *best* love."

Then she looked past Jake at Bashir, who felt his heart skip a beat. But then he too was dismissed by her gaze, which now settled on another: Admiral Picard, sheltered in his command chair.

Vash flicked her finger under Jake's nose. "And what I want *you* to remember is your twenty-fifth birthday. I'm buying."

"Okay," Jake mumbled hoarsely, "I'll be there."

Then Jake left, and Bashir felt uncomfortable staying in Vash's presence without him. He crossed quickly to Picard's side, unwilling to leave without one last chance to speak to the living legend.

"Dr. Bashir!" Picard said as Bashir approached his chair.

Bashir was startled at Picard's recognition of him. Through most of his time on the *Phoenix,* the admiral had thought he was someone called Wesley.

"You remember me," Bashir said, pleased, as he shook the admiral's hand.

"How could I forget? Between you and Admiral McCoy, I lived in constant fear that my wife was going to leave me for either one of her heroes. She was a doctor, too, you know."

"I didn't know you had married," Bashir said.

"Damned Grigari took her. Battle of Earth. Good thing we can stop them with this bloody marvelous ship, eh?"

"A very good thing," Bashir agreed. He looked up to see that he was the last of the passengers in the battle bridge. It was time to go. "A real pleasure to meet you again, Admiral Picard. I hope—"

"Oh, don't call me that, young man. I'm not Admiral Jean-Luc Picard anymore."

Bashir blinked in confusion. He felt Nog's hands on his back.

"Doctor," Nog said, with some urgency, "you really have to get to your transporter."

"We're going undercover!" Picard called after Bashir. "A critical mission!"

"Are you sure his medication is under control?" Bashir asked Vash, as she took over from Nog and pushed him toward the doors.

"Absolutely," Vash said. "You have to hurry."

"My new name is Shabren!" Picard shouted proudly.

Bashir stared at Vash in horror. "You can't be serious! You three?"

Vash patted his arm. "Don't know if we have to yet. But who else is gonna know how to spell the Sisko's name twenty-five thousand years ago? Now *run!*"

The battle bridge doors slid shut before Bashir could say another word. So he ran as instructed. And as he did, he tried not to picture the convoluted timeline that might emerge if the archaeologist actually carried out what it seemed she was planning.

For the truth was, unless Nog could accomplish the first part of his mission in the next three minutes, its second part would mean nothing at all.

Because none of this would ever have happened.

And nothing would ever happen again.

The universe now had ten minutes left.

CHAPTER 28

"DOES IT FEEL LIKE coming home?" Weyoun asked.

Sisko looked around the restored bridge of the *Defiant,* almost unable to believe he was really here. It had been a shock when the transporter effect had faded and he had realized where he was. And the shock wasn't fading. He had never expected to see this ship again.

But he refused to accept returning here under any conditions but his own. "I won't play your games," he warned Weyoun.

The Vorta slipped into the command chair, examined the controls on either arm. "I wish I knew what games those might be," he said. "I'm certain they'd be amusing."

Sisko could feel his heartbeat quickening, nearly to the point of euphoria. Two weeks ago, O'Brien had clearly explained that there was only one way back to their own present, and that was by taking the *Defiant*—

and only the *Defiant*—on a reverse slingshot trajectory around the the mouth of the red wormhole.

Two weeks ago, with the *Defiant* battered and being towed by the *Boreth*, even the possibility of such a return trip had been unthinkable.

Yet here was a chance. It didn't matter how slight.

In only minutes, he knew, the red wormhole would open again. So a reverse flight *could* be attempted. And even if he had to face the terrible prospect of leaving his crew behind, if he *could* return to his present, then there *was* a chance he could slingshot back to this future with a full task force to rescue them in the minutes remaining.

Sisko shot a glance across the bridge to the engineering station, trying to see if—

"I know what you're doing," Weyoun said. "I know what you're thinking. What you're planning. What you're hoping. And I assure you, none of it is going to happen."

Sisko faced facing the Vorta, hating the way his own robes dragged on the *Defiant*'s carpet, wanting more than anything to be in uniform again. He wanted to belong on this bridge as a Starfleet officer, as he was meant to be.

Apparently untroubled by his own red robes, Weyoun steepled his hands, elbows on the arms of the chair. "Benjamin, I know you'd like nothing better than to go back to the past. To stop the Orbs of Jalbador from ever being brought together. And I know that this vessel following a reverse temporal trajectory is your only way of doing that. So, not being the fool you take me for, when I had this ship repaired I gave specific orders that her warp engines were to be . . . gutted."

Weyoun leaned forward. "Go ahead, check the engine status. You'll find you don't have any."

Sisko crossed quickly to the engineering station, called up the status screens, to make his own confirmation.

Weyoun was right.

No impulse engines. No dilithium. The warp core had been jettisoned.

The *Defiant* had as much chance of traveling at warp as a falling rock.

"No going back," Weyoun said. "Only forward." He glanced over at a time display on the science station. "At least for about the next sixteen minutes."

Sisko's pulse continue to pound, but with rage now. "Damn you, Weyoun! Why are we here?"

Weyoun seemed genuinely surprised by the sudden show of emotion. "In the absence of any definitive guidance, I thought it would be fitting—somehow in keeping with this all-important theme of balance that runs through the texts of the True Prophets. The *Defiant* after all was the first ship to enter their Temple. I thought there would be a certain poetry in having it be the last, as well. Surely you of all people see that?"

Sisko strode off to Weyoun's left, swinging his arms, shaking his head, struggling to keep his mind clear.

"I asked you a question, Benjamin."

Sisko strode back, turned, then whirled around, and abandoning all thought he lunged at Weyoun and smashed his fist into the Vorta's placid, hateful face.

Weyoun was thrown back in the command chair, then sat forward, looking down at the carpet, a small drop of blood escaping from his nose.

Sisko caught his breath, expecting to be consumed by endless fire any moment.

He would welcome it.

But nothing happened.

After a few moments, Weyoun sat back again and rubbed his face, that was all.

"There," the Vorta said as if nothing of much importance had just happened. "Did that help? Do you feel better?"

Pulse still pounding, Sisko checked the time readout. Fourteen minutes. How could he or anyone else have anything to lose at this point, so close to the end of everything? What was to stop anyone from doing *anything?*

"Yes," he said. "And I'm sure I can feel even better!"

He swung at Weyoun again and the Vorta didn't dodge his blow. There was a loud crack, a gasp, and Sisko saw blood gush forth from the Vorta's nose.

"You . . . you broke it," Weyoun said thickly, his fingers gripping the bloody bridge of his nose.

"Then kill me," Sisko taunted.

Weyoun used the back of his hand to wipe the bright red liquid that dripped down his upper lip, held out his blood-smeared hand and looked at it with a bemused expression. "It's not my decision."

"Then whose is it?" Sisko demanded.

"As you would say," Weyoun replied, "your fate is now . . . in the hands of the Prophets."

"Which ones?"

Weyoun pursed his lips as if Sisko had asked a trick question. "Why, the winners, of course."

Then he tapped a bloody finger against the comm control. "*Defiant* to *Boreth.* I believe we are ready to depart." He looked ahead. "Screen on, please."

The *Defiant*'s main viewer came to life. On it, Sisko saw the *Boreth* slide into view just as a shifting purple tractor beam shot out from it.

Then the image on the screen changed, as the *Defiant*

was realigned in space. Bajor appeared, most of it in darkness, only a thin crescent showing the light of day.

Next, slowly, the planet began to recede as the *Defiant* was towed at warp.

"A lovely planet," Weyoun said wistfully. "Would you like to say good-bye?"

Sisko checked the time display again. "Not for twelve minutes."

"Oh, no," Weyoun said. "It's not for Bajor to see the end of the universe. Watch."

And then Sisko cried out in shock as on the viewer the crescent limb of his adopted world blazed with blinding light and what seemed to be a vast wind of white steam shot all around the planet and the atmosphere on the dark side glowed with fire and the oceans boiled and the continents rose and—

—in a flash of light that hurt his eyes despite the safety overrides in the viewer, Bajor became . . . dust and . . .

. . . disappeared.

"Bajor . . . what . . ."

"Supernova," Weyoun said matter-of-factly. "Don't worry though. I understand the first pulse of radiation is enough to instantly kill any living being before the shockwave hits. Your crew felt no pain. I know that was important to you."

With a roar of primal rage that startled even him, Sisko threw himself at Weyoun and was suddenly flat on his back by the science station chair, each breath he took stabbing him.

Weyoun's eyes glowed. Red. "We've played that game, I believe. And I don't like it anymore."

Sisko got to his feet. Started for Weyoun again. "You have no choice!"

A bolt of red struck Sisko's chest.

Sisko froze in place. He could not move. The lance had come from Weyoun's hand.

"Neither do you," the Vorta said. "Now be still. And perhaps . . . perhaps . . ." For a single heartbeat, the red light in Weyoun's eyes flickered, then vanished. "Perhaps we can both find out what's supposed to happen next."

Sisko stood transfixed on the bridge of his starship. There was a bigger conflict here than he had ever imagined.

Not only was the universe about to be destroyed, the one person responsible didn't even know why.

The real adversaries were still in hiding.

The universe now had nine minutes left.

CHAPTER 29

GRIGARI WERE deactivated by the millions, and equal numbers of living beings died in those final minutes, as a thousand battles raged through space in the vast cubic-parsec sphere that surrounded the Bajoran system.

But the Grigari lines held.

The last Starfleet vessel attempting to reach Bajor—to destroy whatever remained of the Ascendancy—was blown apart with less than eight minutes left.

The loss of that ship marked the Federation's end.

And with such a glorious dream lost forever, perhaps the universe no longer deserved to exist.

Inward from the chaos of those battles, at the center of the calm eye of the galactic storm, the *Boreth* towed the tiny *Defiant* at warp factor five. Easily outpacing the protomatter-induced supernova of Bajor-B'hava'el, both in real- and subspace.

Total transit time from Bajor to the required coordinates near the Denorios Belt was three minutes, twelve seconds.

The universe had just over five minutes of existence left.

It was then that the *Boreth* came to relative rest and fired a small impulse probe at the exact coordinates of the Bajoran wormhole, and for the first time in twenty-five years the doorway to the Celestial Temple blossomed in a majestic display of energies unknown to normal space-time.

Soft blue light bathed the pale hull of the *Defiant.* And in that same radiance, five hundred kilometers distant, a trio of hourglass-shaped orbs of a translucent red substance equally alien to this realm orbited together, sparkling from within as they responded to that first verteron bloom, then matched it.

A second opening appeared against the stars and the shifting Denorios plasma ribbons. Radiating red energy as if every wavelength from the first wormhole had just been reversed.

And then, with only two minutes remaining until there would be no time at all, exactly as had been prophesied by the three great mystics of Jalbador, the doors to the Temples opened together.

Both Temples.

One Temple.

The reason why the Prophets wept.

Still immobile, in place, Sisko struggled for breath as he saw both wormholes expanding on the *Defiant*'s main viewer. Weyoun had left the command chair to stand closer to the screen, his weak Vorta eyesight robbing him of the grandeur of the spectacle before him.

"*Defiant* to *Boreth*," the Vorta breathed. "You may release us now." He turned back to Sisko. "Almost time." He open his mouth in a soundless laugh. "Almost *no* time."

The ship's collision alarms sounded abruptly.

"What is it? What's happening?" the Vorta exclaimed, cringing, his hands over his ears.

"Let . . . me . . . go. . . ." Sisko's words were little more than a rasp.

Weyoun gestured impatiently and whatever cord of energy had kept Sisko bound, he was suddenly released. He ran.

Toward the tactical station, where he saw a reading that he didn't understand.

"It looks like a Borg ship," he said to Weyoun, his voice stronger, freer by the moment. "Coming in at transwarp velocities."

"Is it headed for us?" Weyoun gasped in alarm.

Sisko did an instant, rough analysis of the vessel's trajectory. A slingshot. *Good,* he thought.

"Are we in danger?" Weyoun cried.

"No," Sisko lied. "It looks like it's out of control."

Weyoun had turned back to the viewer. The two wormholes remained open as a subspace distortion wave made them ripple. Fine filaments of energy tentatively splashed out toward each other, but still too far away to connect.

"Why aren't we moving?" Weyoun wailed.

"Where to?" Sisko asked. Why should any location matter now?

"We have to get inside the Temple," Weyoun explained despairingly. "That's the only place to escape what will happen." He looked up again. "*Defiant* to *Boreth.* This is Weyoun. Release the tractor beam."

And then, finally, a voice replied from the *Boreth.*

"Never."

Weyoun's white face betrayed his utter shock.

"Who is that? Identify yourself."

The viewer switched to a new image, and both Sisko and Weyoun flinched back as Dukat's features overwhelmed them, red eyes glowing, thin-lipped gray mouth twisted in a terrifying grimace of victory.

"You?!" Weyoun cried out in disbelief.

"You lost before, you'll lose again," Dukat gloated. "The true War of the Prophets is not your fight. It is *ours!"*

Suddenly, the *Defiant*'s bridge rang with even more collision alarms, weapons-lock sirens, and intruder alerts—all sounding at once as Weyoun twisted back and forth, his hands pressed tightly over his sensitive ears.

And then the bridge pulsed with multiple flashes of light as three brilliant starbursts exploded around Sisko, and from each of them a human figure seemed to unfold.

Sisko shouted out in recognition.

It was Worf and Bashir—and a young ensign who had just arrived at DS9 only a few days before the station's destruction. All three looked disoriented. They gestured at him, urgent, their mouths open in entreaty. But Sisko couldn't hear a word they said over the blaring alarms.

He ran to join Worf who staggered over to tactical, hampered by thick bandages wound around his torso. As soon as he was by his side, Sisko heard Worf's voice clear and victorious: "They all made it!"

"Jake?" Sisko cried out, his only thought. His only hope.

Worf nodded vigorously. "All of them! All through the ship!"

Then Sisko saw the time readout. Only a minute remained.

"We have to get into the wormhole!" he shouted to Worf.

Worf stared down at his station. "We have no engines!"

But Sisko refused to be beaten. Could no longer be beaten. Not when his son had been returned to him. Not when the Prophets were finally showing he was right to have hope.

"The tractor beam!" he yelled at Worf. "Steal momentum from the *Boreth!* Use all the station-keeping thrusters at once!"

Then the alarms cut off and Sisko saw Bashir. At the conn. Frantically trying to call up any set of controls that might let him guide the ship.

"Now can you hear oblivion approaching?" Dukat declared, triumphant, from the screen.

"Madman!" Weyoun screeched.

"Loser," Dukat cackled. "Remember that, pretender . . . remember that, *forever.*"

Then, laughing maniacally, Dukat vanished from the viewer, and Sisko looked up to see the two wormholes again, both wavering as space shifted around them.

Then the *Boreth* appeared, heading toward the blue wormhole.

"Worf!" Sisko commanded. "Everything we've got! *Now!"*

A shaft of purple light sprang forward and gripped the Klingon ship.

"He is attempting to use shields to disengage us," Worf said.

"Keep us attached as long as you can," Sisko urged.

"Nooo!" Weyoun screamed as the view of the

wormholes began to shift and the *Defiant* was pulled forward by the ship it had caught.

"Dr. Bashir!" Sisko ordered. Commanded. Demanded. "Stand by on thrusters. Get us into that wormhole!"

Sisko checked the time readout.

Thirty seconds.

Worf reported. "The *Boreth* is swinging off course."

"Are we going with it?"

"Not if we detach . . . *NOW!*"

On the viewer, the *Boreth* tumbled toward the red wormhole.

As the blue wormhole grew larger.

". . . *No* . . . ," Weyoun sobbed. "This wasn't supposed to happen."

Twenty seconds.

"Full thrusters, Doctor!"

"Hydrazine is exhausted," Bashir cried. "All we've got now is momentum."

Dazed, crazed, Sisko checked their rate of approach. Checked the time.

They weren't going to make it.

Fifteen seconds.

"DAD!"

Heart soaring, Sisko wheeled. Saw Jake run for him.

Caught him in a wordless embrace, stricken with horror at what he had brought to his child, felt the same inexpressible feelings in his son.

Jake.

Ten seconds.

Worf reported again. "Supernova shockwave approaching."

The *Defiant* trembled.

Sisko looked up. "What was that?"

The young ensign—at the science station. "Subspace pressure wave! It's caught us."

Sisko heard Worf's voice. "Distance to wormhole is decreasing."

Five seconds.

On the viewer, long tendrils of red energy. Snaking. Twisting. Engaging blue tendrils.

Sisko heard Worf again. "The wormholes are merging as predicted."

"The Temple!" Weyoun was raising his red-robed arms to the ceiling. "The Temple is restored!"

Three seconds.

Sisko appealed to everyone. And no one. "Are we going to make it?"

Two seconds.

"Are we—"

Worf said, "Impact."

Weyoun screamed.

One second.

The bridge went dark, the viewer died.

Gravity shut down.

Sisko felt the *Defiant* fall away from him. Felt Jake fall away from him.

Felt everything and everyone and nothing and no one in the universe streak away as if he and they and it had plunged from an infinite cliff and were tumbling toward the infinite—nothingness—never to land.

"I did everything I could," Sisko cried into the silence that engulfed him.

But everything he had ever done was for nothing.

For everything that had ever been was for nothing.

Zero seconds.

It was over.

$t = \Omega$

IT WAS SO SIMPLE a reaction, the equation describing it could fit on a leisure shirt.

What had been broken was made whole again.

The dimensional wound—upon whose fractal edges something called reality had grown like random frost—closed seamlessly in an instant. Healed at last.

And where there had been eleven dimensions of existence, there now were none.

Perfect unity had been achieved again.

In that last eternal moment before the illusion called time ceased to be, the expansion of what had been called space-time abruptly stopped. All at once. Throughout the full extent of its reach.

Some sentient intelligences might have been aware of something gone awry, a sudden slowing of the worlds around them, a sluggishness to the atmosphere or the liquid from which they drew life. But that moment of disquiet was all that they would know. For there was no more time left to explore the reason for the slowing.

If a vantage point had been possible within another realm, then the cessation of expansion would have been apparent. Followed not by an explosion from the point at which the ripped dimension had been rejoined, but by a sudden condensation. A condensation of existence.

Matter did not move through space. Nor did energy change over time. But space-time itself shrank.

Instantly.

A bubble bursting.

A dream vanishing upon awakening.

Not even a black hole extinguished existence as swiftly, as absolute as the effect of total nothingness.

There was not even a place for there to be an absence of anything.

There was not even a place for nothing to exist.

The human adventure had come to its end.

The universe was gone.

EPILOGUE

At the Doors of the Temple

SISKO OPENED HIS EYES, half expecting to see nothing, half expecting to see white light.

Instead he saw a room.

Familiar.

Comforting.

An observation lounge. On a starship.

He shook his head, clearing it of the disturbing dream he had had.

That's it, he thought with relief. It was all a dream. A simple disruption in his sleep during the journey out here. The journey to . . .

He looked out the curved viewports of the room.

Bajor.

A beautiful planet, he had to admit. Though he didn't want to stay here. Not really. A space station was not the place to raise his son.

But his eyes kept turning back to Bajor, so perfect and green and blue.

A dream . . . ?

Had he even had a dream?

He closed his eyes a moment, rubbed them, saw again the disastrous ruin of the Promenade of Deep Space 9.

He had just been on it, touring his new command.

He had been awake twenty hours, between reviewing reports and briefings, even to squeeze in an hour with Jake at the fishing hole.

So when had he managed to have a dream? Let alone a nightmare?

The door slid open. Another man entered.

Or maybe he had been there all along.

"Commander, come in," the man said. "Welcome to Bajor."

He pronounced it in the old way, with a soft *j*.

Sisko reached out to shake the man's hand, thought the man looked better than he had just a few . . .

Sisko recognized him.

"It's been a long time, Captain."

Picard! Sisko thought. *Of course . . .*

Picard looked at Sisko with a puzzled expression. "Have we met before?"

Sisko grinned with relief, all the pieces coming together.

"That depends," he said to Picard. "What does 'before' mean in nonlinear time?"

Picard did not answer the question, said what he had said before. "I assume you've been briefed on the events leading to the Cardassian withdrawal."

"It's all right," Sisko insisted. "I know what's happened. I know where we are. This is the Celestial Temple. We've met before, or will meet, or have always known each other."

It isn't over, Sisko thought in excitement. Some realm beyond the universe still existed. There was still hope. . . .

"Incorrect," Picard said. "Even here, there's a first time for everything. . . ."

Through the viewports, Bajor suddenly dissolved like a child's sandcastle, flying into billions of fragments as the shockwave of the sun's detonation hit.

Sisko shrank back from the heat of that destruction. The viewports cracked. The top surface of the conference table curled up and ignited.

Sisko looked for Picard, saw him at that table leaning forward, appearing to be falling—but no—he was—

—growing.

—transforming.

Eyes now afire with the same flames that were consuming the ashes of Bajor.

Sisko stepped back, hit something, turned to see—

—his command chair.

He was back on the *Defiant.*

The bodies of his crew around him.

All dead.

Because of him.

Everything—everyone—dead because of him.

The thing that had been Picard loomed over him, and whether it was the admiral or Grigari or Weyoun or Dukat, Sisko had no way of knowing.

All he did know was that it was coming for him, its eyes ablaze with the insane fury of the Pah-wraiths.

The creature leered down at him, slime dripping

from its yawning maw. "Welcome to Hell, *Emissary!*"

The flames reached out for Sisko and their heat seared his flesh.

The universe had ended.

But in the Temple of the Pah-wraiths, his punishment had just begun.

TO BE CONTINUED IN . . .

DEEP SPACE NINE®
MILLENNIUM
BOOK III of III
INFERNO

ACKNOWLEDGMENTS

When Rick Berman and Michael Piller created the *Deep Space Nine* television series, they accomplished an almost impossible twofold task. Not only did they successfully expand the *Star Trek* paradigm beyond the limits of stand-alone stories centered around a ship that traveled from place to place, they set in place an arena and an initial set of characters so full of possibilities they fueled 176 hours of a series that even in its seventh and final season showed no signs of running out of creative energy and new directions.

But simply providing fertile starting conditions is not enough to guarantee success, and Berman and Piller also deserve the highest regard for the way in which they set in place an ongoing creative team—to say nothing of their top-notch production team—that took those starting conditions and lived up to the series' promise, constantly making it even richer and more satisfying.

Dozens if not hundreds of dedicated people need to be thanked for their ongoing contributions to the series throughout its seven-year run, and fortunately, in the soon-to-be-published *Star Trek: Deep Space Nine Companion* by Terry J. Erdmann with Paula M. Block the full story of all those contributors through every season will be told in detail.

But because we're limited to just these few words, we must call out only one additional star of that galaxy of talent for special acknowledgment: Just as *Deep Space Nine* would not exist without Berman and Piller, it would not have developed so magnificently without Ira Steven Behr.

Our thanks to all, for a series still rich, compelling, and full of promise, even seven years into its mission.

When do the movies start?

—J&G

THE CHRONICLES OF GALEN SWORD #2: NIGHTFEEDER

Galen Sword is an aimless New York twenty-something with no friends, no family, and a multimillion-dollar trust fund. After a night of indulgence he crashes his sportscar, and the doctors in emergency write him off, as his injuries are too extensive for him to survive. Then a mysterious man with blue glowing hands heals Galen, and as Galen's body is restored, so are long-buried memories of his early childhood, a childhood he appears to have spent in another world of exotic beings and magical forces. Filled with new purpose, Galen uses his wealth to become an investigator of the unknown and the unexplainable—not to disprove such things, but to find his way home.

NIGHTFEEDER, *the second book in the series, continues the story of Galen's first encounter with the beings and forces of his home: a world torn apart by violent intrigue, now made even more volatile by*

Galen's interference in the impending war between the two Greater Clans, the shapeshifers of Arkady and the formless Seyshen. Key to this conflict—and to Galen's future—is Orion, a being who has an equal chance of becoming Galen's greatest ally or his deadliest enemy. In the First World, Orion is the last survivor of Clan Isis. But in the Second World—our world—he is a terrifying creature of legend . . .

ONE

Alone and unprotected on the deserted beach, the vampire waited for the sun to rise.

It was his ritual, its origin lost in the mist of too many centuries of memories—his own and those whose lives had nourished him, now bound within his heart and soul forever. And because he was a vampire, he knew what forever truly was.

There on the beach, the surf calm in the still air before dawn, the slate sky to the east slowly brightening as the far western stars glimmered in the last deep blue of night, the vampire felt his body resonate with the conflicting echoes of lives consumed beyond his ability to count. Each lost name called out to him, struggling to be his own. Each hidden voice cried to tell its story. But the vampire knew there were only three truths within the chaos. Three truths above all.

His name *was* Orion.

The sun was his enemy.

And he would survive again.

A lance of white fire erupted from the rounded crest of the coastal mountains before him, and Orion clenched his fists at his sides as he bore the first brunt of the sun's assault. His olive eyes narrowed in the brilliant glare, but he did not—would not—look away.

The sun rose and Orion called out his challenge to it.

A full third of the sun's disk blazed above the mountains now, and the vampire's shadow stretched out behind him to the rising waves of the Pacific. Gusts of wind rose up to blow his long brown hair away from the hard and handsome planes of his face and flap his loose white shirt and pants against his straining muscles.

His war was not just with the sun.

It was with nature.

Orion's hoarse cry of defiance became a bellow of torment as the searing rays of sunlight enveloped him. His bare toes dug into the moist sand like talons. Dark scarlet blood dripped from the wounds his own nails dug within the palms of his clenched fists. Instinctively, his razorsharp feeding incisors slid from their hidden sockets behind his human teeth and extended to their full fighting length. His vision clouded with overwhelming rage.

Then, in his challenge to the sun, in his cry to nature, suddenly one word was clear above all else.

"Iiiiisis!"

This was his agony, worse than any the sun could inflict, for his Clan was Isis and he was the last adept to carry its name.

Now, half the killing disk bulged above the mountains and Orion knew he had won enough of his battle for today. He turned his stinging, tearing eyes from the fierce face of his enemy and ran forward from the beach to the small white clapboard house that waited silently for him, set back from the Malibu beach—his refuge from the day and those who would destroy him.

Even with the force of the light still burning on his skin and in his flesh, he ran faster than the sun could rise to stop him, swifter than the scorching wind that poured forth from the morning's approach, more silently than the smallest drops of water that fell from frothing waves upon the beach's sand. He had survived again and, as he did from all that gave him life, he had taken from nature those powers with which she had tried to crush him.

Within moments Orion was safe within the shade of the beach house's old and sand-scarred porch. He paused then, one hand braced against a thick wooden pillar, filling his lungs with cool air, feeling the hideous flush still fading from his golden skin, watching the sun's glimmer spread on the rising waves as a general watches the enemy's troops regroup to attack again. Someday he knew, he would see the sun's full disk rise into the terrible blue sky, and he would stand beneath its glare at noon. On that day he would be invincible—and those who had destroyed Clan Isis would at last be repaid for their treachery.

But until that day Orion had other, more compelling concerns, and if those vampires who had passed successfully through the centuries had learned anything from their immortality, it was that patience was always rewarded. *Always.*

Secure within the shadows, Orion's eyes slowly

cleared and the full range of his hypersensitive vision was restored. He focused on the tangle of scrub and twisted trees that surrounded the isolated beach house, probing for the flowing black forms of those who guarded him during the day. Perhaps alone of all the creatures of the First and Second Worlds, only the Seyshen could match a vampire's prowess—though it was not a battle Orion would seek out. For now, by the terms of the treaty, their presence around his refuge gave him sanctuary from the assassins of Tepesh and the constant threat of dark hunters.

But nothing moved within the scrub, no shadows flowed.

Orion's lips parted as he began his search again, eyes tracking through the landscape with the precision of a hawk's, his mouth gently drawing in the air to taste for the presence of his guards.

Nothing.

He had been abandoned. Protection lifted. After thirty-eight cycles, without warning, the treaty had been abrogated.

Orion's hand gripped the porch pillar he rested against and, without his awareness, the solid timber splintered beneath his fingers. Burning now with swift anger instead of pain, he turned his back on the day and pushed into the shuttered depths of the beach house. There was a telephone inside, a human toy which required no wires or connections. He had been given a number he could call—if there were any left who would answer. The telephone had been part of the treaty that had brought him here.

The door to the porch slammed shut behind him, encasing him in life-giving blackness. He halted abruptly, commanding his heart to stop its pounding, willing himself to calmness. He was in danger.

Something moved to his side. He heard the ripple of wooden louvers covering a window, just as a dozen parallel shafts of sunlight sprang into the room, striping the wooden floor at his feet.

The vampire remained still, inches from the threatening light, and squinted through the swaths it sliced through the dust-filled air. A backlit figure sat in an armchair by the window, swinging the louver cord idly in its hand.

"A thousand apologies, vampire." The figure's voice was soft and whispery, and had a distinct British accent, bred in the highest circles. "I did not expect you to be out of your pod so late in the morning." The louvers remained open, and Orion had no doubt whom he faced—*what* he faced—past the cloaking glare of the sun.

The vampire reached out without looking to the light switch on the wall behind him, knowing exactly where it would be. An overhead fixture came on, and it lessened the contrast between daylight and darkness with a dull tungsten glow.

For an instant in the added light it seemed as if in the chair by the window a shadow twisted, like oil on water, but by the time Orion's eyes had adjusted to the new light level in the room the Seyshen had reformed in its open aspect, a perfect human male. Orion recognized the creature. It was Gérard.

"Where are the sentinels?" Orion asked. It was a simple matter to keep his voice even, but keeping his fangs retracted required great effort.

Gérard smiled. In his open aspect the Seyshen's teeth

were shockingly white, precisely even, framed by lips full and soft. His face was narrow but exquisitely balanced, his eyes dark, intelligent, quick. His black hair slicked back tight against his skull.

"Have they been withdrawn so soon?" the Seyshen replied. He reached within his white linen jacket and withdrew a black enameled cigarette case, snapping it open without taking his eyes from Orion. He slid a thin white cigarette from the case.

"We have an arrangement," Orion said. "The sentinels are to be present always during daylight."

"The period of your greatest vulnerability," Gérard agreed consolingly, drawing out the final word. He dabbed the end of the cigarette's tip against his tongue and the slender white cylinder came away glowing red and smoking. The Seyshen turned the cigarette elegantly in his fingers and took a long draw from it.

Orion flicked his eyes around the parts of the beach house he could see, listening intently for sounds from those other parts he could not, trying to determine if he and the Seyshen were alone. "Am I to assume that the conditions of our arrangement have been changed somehow? Without discussion?" The small house seemed empty to Orion's heightened senses, though if other Seyshen were present in their closed aspect he knew it would be difficult for even a vampire to be certain.

Gérard sensually rolled the smoke from his mouth. "What could there possibly be to discuss, vampire?"

At least a vampire was direct, Orion thought bitterly. At least a vampire, having chosen a nourisher, took that nourisher cleanly and quickly. But the Seyshen were like cats with mice. They lived for the hunt and not its culmination.

"The war with the Clan Arkady, for one," Orion said. He knew that conflict had been brewing for years, ever since the elemental adept, Tomas Roth, Regent to the Clan Pendragon, had become consort to Arkady's Victor, Morgana LaVey. The Seyshen were determined to prevent the shapeshifters of Arkady from amassing any more power within the First World, and Clan Arkady had clearly known that the Seyshen would be assembled against it. An open war between the two clans had been inevitable for years, for thirty-eight cycles.

But Gérard raised his eyebrows. "War with . . . Arkady?"

Orion felt a chill of uncertainty. Could Arkady have been defeated so quickly? Before the war had even begun? "That is why Clan Seyshen concluded its treaty with Clan Isis," Orion said. He was to have been a living weapon in the Seyshen arsenal. They would keep him safe during daylight, holding him in reserve until the war was declared. In the First World, no shifter dared take on a vampire by choice. With his presence alone enough to change the tide of battle, Orion was as close as the Seyshen could come to a guaranteed victory over Arkady.

"Times change, vampire," Gérard said lightly. "What is true one day, is . . . open . . . the next." A perfect ring of smoke rolled from his rounded lips, appearing to pulsate as it flared and dimmed and flared again, moving through the bands of light streaming through the shutters.

Orion knew then that he truly had been abandoned. Once more he was alone. But how had it happened? And why?

Orion fought to keep the icy chill he felt from his

voice. "Last night was to have been Arkady's Ceremony of the Change. Your strategists had expected the entire Clan would go to shifter form in preparation for the war." Gérard maintained his expression of bland amusement. Orion pressed on. "I do not believe that even the Seyshen could have defeated the entire Clan Arkady in one night, by themselves."

"Perhaps . . . we had help," Gérard suggested, taking a final draw from his cigarette. The smoke from it swept away from the Seyshen, as if being repulsed by an electric charge in the air surrounding him.

"*I* was to have been your help, Gérard. And even with my help, you could not have defeated an entire clan of shifters in one night. Nothing in the First World is that powerful."

Gérard rolled the stub of his cigarette between his palms. When he took his hands apart, the stub was gone. "Perhaps . . . our help was not First World."

Orion frowned. He had no knowledge of any within the Shadow World with substance enough to alter the balance of power between the Clans. "A *halfling* gave you the advantage you needed?" But the question was absurd. Since only one of a halfling's parents was an adept, a halfling's substance could only be less—not more—than what would be found in the First World.

"A halfling?" Gérard repeated. Then he smiled silkily again. "Whatever made you think our help came from the *Shadow* World?"

For an instant, Orion stopped breathing, so great was his surprise. "The *Second* World?" he asked.

Gérard's smile grew.

"A *human* helped you *defeat* Arkady during the Ceremony of the Change?"

The Seyshen could not resist, and let a bit of its true self slip out into its open aspect. The smile Gérard wore grew even broader, stretching across the full width of his face, angling up to his ears, gleaming teeth appearing in even rows behind the splitting skin of the Seyshen's human disguise.

"Impossible," Orion said flatly, ignoring how the Seyshen's head was bisected by its gaping grin. He had seen far worse sights in his centuries.

"Then where are your sentinels, vampire?" Gérard's mouth melted back into something more human. "Arkady is no longer a threat." He twirled the louver cord around one long finger. "And Orion is no longer protected by Seyshen."

"How did it happen?" Orion persisted, still disbelieving the creature's story. "What kind of human could face an Arkady shifter and live? What kind of human could face the massed clan?" The very concept was madness. "Who was it?"

Gérard tugged aimlessly on the louver cord. "Galen Sword," he said, angling his eyes to stare at Orion, checking for the vampire's reaction.

But Orion had none. He had expected the name of a general, or a politician, or a mad killer. "The name means nothing to me."

"Even a vampire must have heard of the Swords," Gérard said mockingly. "The Swords of Pendragon?"

Orion was thoroughly disconcerted now. Pendragon was a Greater Clan of elementals. One of the oldest. In that context, the name Sword belonged to the history of the First World. "But you said this . . . Galen Sword . . . was a human."

With his free hand, Gérard adjusted his white jacket.

"Alas, to the great and lasting shame of his illustrious line . . . he *is* human. Only human." The Seyshen laughed without humor.

Then Orion remembered. "*That* Sword?"

The Seyshen stared at Orion, not bothering to answer such a senseless question.

"But," Orion protested, "that . . . that's just a Softwind tale. That Sword is only a legend."

Gérard's finger tightened on the cord one final time. "Ah, but then you must remember, clanless one, that in the Second World, in which the legendary Galen Sword now lives, so are . . . vampires."

The shutters instantly clacked shut, and the overhead fixture sparked and was extinguished, plunging the room into darkness.

Orion caught only the merest glimpse of the dark form of the Seyshen's closed aspect as it re-formed out of its disguise but he heard the clatter of its undulating claws move swiftly to the front door. Then the bottom of the door burst outward into shards as the Seyshen passed through without slowing.

Unprepared for the sudden entry of so much daylight, Orion leaped backward, squinting as his eyes adjusted once again. But by the time he had gathered himself to face the renewed threat of the sun the Seyshen was gone, and all was silent except for the rhythmic pulse of the distant surf on the deserted beach.

Orion stayed motionless in the shadows, as he rapidly calculated the most probable next step to be taken by the Clan Seyshen. For thirty-eight cycles he had been under its protection. Now he was a marked target again. But since none of his enemies would have risked tracking him when he was surrounded by Seyshen, there was a good chance that for the moment his whereabouts were unknown. The Seyshen, of course, would trade that information within days, if not hours. Not for any gain the information might bring them, but simply to start a dark hunt in motion—to keep the Worlds in the disarray the Seyshen thrived upon.

But for now, Orion concluded, he was safe. Through all his long lifetime it had always been this way—despite immortality, his survival could only be measured from one instant to the next. Thus—treaty or no treaty, Seyshen ally or foe—nothing had changed. Orion was alone again, the last of his clan, without friend or future, with only his vow of revenge to keep him alive from one night to the next.

The situation was nothing he had not faced before, and thinking that, he smiled at what the Seyshen itself had said. His life *was* the stuff from which legends were made, in the First World of adepts as well as in the Second World of humans. Even in the shifting Shadow World that lay between, where humans and adepts made business and sport and, sometimes, halfling progeny cursed to belong to neither world, the fear of the vampire held sway.

But vampires belonged to the First World, and Orion was sworn to regain full status there. Though without the Seyshen to aid him, he knew that his chances for victory were as ephemeral as moonlight.

Unless, he decided, he could find another to take the Seyshen's place.

Moving as soundlessly as the darkness that was his home, Orion stepped into the bedroom of the beach house, where he kept his pod. The dim sheen of the hibernaculum's brushed stainless-steel finish was comforting to him, and he yawned, so ingrained was the association of his pod's presence and the promise of undisturbed sleep.

Another to help him, he mused, as he tapped his fingers over the pod's number pad, inputting the proper code. Then he stood back as the pod's armored lid puffed up on its pneumatic hinges. Someone fearless enough to join with a vampire. A fighter powerful enough to face an entire Clan of shifters. And win.

Perhaps there was a warrior worthy of a legend, Orion thought as he lay back within his pod and armed its detectors and defenses, watching as the lid descended and its seals engaged and locked.

If what the treacherous Seyshen had said was true, there might be one more chance for him. As quickly as possible, he must find the warrior who was both a human in the Second World and a legend in the First. The warrior who, if the Softwind tales were true, held the fates of all the Worlds in his hands. The warrior a vampire could turn to for help, even if he was only human.

The legend named Galen Sword.

Presenting, one chapter per month . . .

The very beginning of the
Starfleet Adventure . . .

OUR FIRST SERIAL NOVEL!

STAR TREK®
STARFLEET: YEAR ONE

A Novel in Twelve Parts®

by
Michael Jan Friedman

Chapter Eight

When Captain Bryce Shumar materialized in the transporter room of the Tellarite trading vessel, he did so with his laser pistol drawn and leveled in front of him.

As it turned out, his concern was unfounded. Outside of Shumar, Kelly, and the three armed crewmen they had brought with them, there was only one other humanoid in the room—a Tellarite transporter operator.

"Come with me," he said.

"It would be my pleasure," said the captain.

He gestured with his weapon for his team to follow. Then he stepped down from the transporter disc and fell in line behind their guide.

The corridors of the vessel were stark and poorly illuminated, but very wide. It wasn't surprising, Shumar reflected, considering the girth of the average Tellarite.

Before long, they came to a cargo bay. As luck would have it, it was on the same level as the transporter room. The Tellarite opened the door for them and plodded off.

Broj, the vessel's captain, was waiting for them inside. He wasn't alone, either. There was a tall, green-skinned Orion with a sour expression standing next to him.

Not that there was anything unusual about that. Tellarite traders often took on financial backers from other species, and there never seemed to be a shortage of willing Orions.

However, this particular Orion didn't look like a financier. He looked more like a mercenary—which inclined Shumar to be that much more careful in his dealings here.

In addition to Broj and his green-skinned associate, the cargo bay contained perhaps two dozen metal containers. None of them were labeled. They could have contained apricots or antibiotics, though Shumar wasn't looking for either of those.

Shumar nodded. "Captain Broj."

"This is an outrage," the Tellarite rumbled.

Shumar didn't answer him. He simply turned to Kelly and said, "Keep an eye on these gentlemen."

"Aye, sir," she assured him, the barrel of her laser pistol moving from the Tellarite to the Orion and back again.

Tucking his weapon inside his belt, Shumar crossed the room and worked the lid off a container at random. Then, still eyeing Broj, he reached inside. His fingers closed on something dry and granular.

Extracting a handful of the stuff, he held it out in front of him. It looked like rice—except for the blood-red color.

"D'saako seeds," said the Tellarite.

"I know what they are," Shumar told him. "When you run a starbase, you encounter every kind of cargo imaginable."

Taking out his laser, he pointed it at the bottom half of the container. Then he activated its bright blue beam.

Not even titanium could stand that kind of point-blank assault. The metal puckered and gave way, leaving a hole the size of a man's fist.

"What are you doing?" bellowed Broj, taking a step forward. He looked ready to charge Shumar, but couldn't because of the lasers trained on him. "I paid good money for that grain!"

"No doubt," the human responded, deactivating the beam and putting his pistol away again. "But I'm willing to bet there's more than d'saako seeds in this container."

After waiting a moment longer for the metal to cool, Shumar reached inside. What he found was most definitely not seeds. They were too big and hard. Smiling, he removed some.

"Gold?" asked Kelly.

"Gold," the captain confirmed.

There were perhaps a dozen shiny, irregularly shaped orange nuggets in his open hand, ranging in size from that of a pea to that of an acorn. Shumar showed them to Broj.

"Our informants say this gold is from Ornathia Prime."

The smuggler grunted disdainfully. "I don't know where it came from. I only know I was paid to take a cargo from one place to another."

"According to our informants," said Shumar, "that's a lie. You mined this gold yourself, ignoring the fact that you had no right to do so. Then you set out for the Magabenthus system in the hope of peddling it."

The Tellarite puffed out his chest. "Your informants are the ones who are lying," he huffed.

"In that case," said the captain, "you won't mind our checking your other cargo bay. You know, the one a couple of decks below us? I'll bet you we find some gold-mining equipment."

The smuggler scowled disdainfully. "Go ahead and check. Then you can apologize to my government for waylaying an honest businessman."

Shumar knew he would need the mining equipment as evidence, so he tilted his head in the direction of the exit. "Come on," he told Kelly and his other crewmen. "Let's take a look at that other bay."

"Aye, sir," said Kelly. She gestured with her laser for the Tellarite to lead the way.

But before Shumar had made it halfway to the exit, something occurred to him. He stopped dead—and his weapons officer noticed.

"What is it?" Kelly asked him.

The captain turned to Broj. "Where did those d'saako seeds come from?"

The Tellarite regarded him. "Ekkenda Four. Why?"

Why indeed, Shumar thought. *Because an immunologist at the University of Pennsylvania, back on Earth, is trying to cure Vegan choriomeningitis using the DNA of certain Ekkendan lizards—creatures whose entire diets seem to consist of adult sun-ripened d'saako plants.*

If Shumar could find some lizard cells among the d'saako seeds, he might be able to conduct some experiments of his own. Maybe he could even expedite the discovery of a cure. It was the kind of work that would make people sit up and take notice. . . .

And see the possibilities inherent in a science-driven Starfleet.

"Captain?" said Kelly, sounding annoyed at the delay.

"Hang on a moment," Shumar told her.

Returning to the open, laser-punctured container, he zipped down the front of his uniform almost to his waist. Then he scooped up a healthy handful of d'saako seeds, poured them carefully into an inside pocket and zipped up his uniform again.

If there were lizard cells present, his science officers would be able to detect them and pull them out. And if there weren't, the captain mused, he hadn't lost anything.

That's when he felt the business end of a laser pistol poke him in the small of his back.

"No one move," rasped the Orion.

Apparently, he had had a concealed weapon on him. Shumar's detour had given him an opening to use it—but he would eventually have used it anyway. At least, that was what the captain chose to believe.

"I'll kill him if I have to," the Orion vowed.

Shumar didn't doubt it. "Easy," he said. "Stay calm."

"Don't tell me how to feel," the Orion snapped. "Don't tell me anything. Just tell *them* to move out of our way."

"*Our* way?" the captain echoed.

"That's right," said his captor. "You and I are going to take a little trip in an escape pod."

"What about me?" asked Broj.

"You're on your own," the Orion told him.

So much for honor among thieves, Shumar thought. Feeling the prod of the laser pistol, he began to move toward the exit.

Then he saw Kelly raise her weapon and fire.

The flash of blue light blinded him, so he couldn't tell what effect the beam had had. But a moment later, it occurred to him that the pistol in his back was gone.

"Are you all right?" asked a feminine voice, amid the scrape of boots and the barking of a warning.

The captain blinked a few times and made out Kelly through the haze of after-images. Then he looked down and saw the Orion lying unconscious on the deck. Broj had his hands up, kept in line by Shumar's crewmen.

"Fine," he told Kelly, "thanks to you. I was surprised you were able to get a clear shot at him."

The weapons officer grunted. "I didn't."

Shumar's vision had improved enough for him to see her face. It confirmed that she wasn't kidding.

"What would I do without you?" he asked sotto voce.

"I don't know," Kelly said in the same soft voice. "Exercise a little more care, maybe?"

"Come on," said the captain, understanding exactly what she was talking about. "There was no way I could have known the Orion was armed."

"All the more reason not to leave yourself open."

Shumar wanted to argue the point further. And he would have, except he knew that the woman was right.

Taking out his communicator, he flipped it open and contacted his ship. "Commander Mullen?"

"Aye, sir. Did you find what you were looking for?"

The captain glanced at the Orion, who was still sprawled on the floor. His actions were all the justification Shumar needed to seize the *Prosperous.*

"That and more," he told Mullen. "Send a couple of teams over. We've got a smuggling vessel to secure."

Daniel Hagedorn watched the cottony, violet-colored walls slide by on every side of his vessel, missing his titanium hull by less than thirty meters in any direction.

He and his crew were traveling the main corridor of a nebular maze—a gargantuan cloud of dust and destructive high-energy plasma that dominated this part of space. Unlike other nebulae of its kind discovered over the last thirty years, this one was rife with a network of corridors and subcorridors, the largest of which allowed a ship like Hagedorn's to make its way through unscathed.

Hence the term "maze."

The captain's orders called for him to remain in the phenomenon's main passageway, where he would gather as much data as possible. Normally, he was the kind of officer who followed such instructions to the letter. Today however, he planned to diverge from that policy.

For the last several minutes he had been scanning the cottony wall on his right for an offshoot that could give him some clearance. Unfortunately, that offshoot hadn't materialized.

Until now.

"Lieutenant Kendall," Hagedorn told his helm officer, "we're going to change course. Take the next corridor to starboard." He consulted the readout in his armrest. "Heading two-four-two mark six."

Kendall glanced at the captain, his confusion evident. "Sir," he said, "that's not the way out."

"It is now," Hagedorn told him.

For a moment, the helmsman looked as if he were about to object to the course change. Then he turned to his console and dutifully put the captain's order into effect.

Instantly, the *Christopher* veered to starboard and entered the passageway, which was substantially narrower than the main corridor but still navigable. Satisfied, Hagedorn leaned back in his seat—and saw that his executive officer was standing beside him.

Her name was Corspa Zenar. She was an Andorian, tall and willowy, with blue skin and white hair. Her antennae were bent forward at the moment—which could have signified a lot of things, disapproval among them.

"You'd like an explanation," the captain guessed.

Zenar shrugged her bony shoulders. "That won't be necessary."

"And why is that?" Hagedorn asked, intrigued.

"Because I know what you have in mind," she said. "You're going to try to find the exit that will let us out near the Kryannen system."

He eyed her. "For what purpose?"

"During the war, the Pelidossians aided the Romulans. They sold them supplies, even helped them with repairs. Earth Command returned the favor by destroying a couple of Pelidossian ships."

The captain was impressed. "And now?"

"Now you want to reconnoiter—and you don't know when you'll again be in a position to do so." Zenar glanced at the viewscreen. "Of course, our orders call for us to chart the main corridor only. But if you're waiting for me to object, you'll be waiting a long time."

It didn't take him long to figure out why. "Because you're a scientist first and foremost, and the more prodding around we do in these tunnels the better you'll like it."

The first officer nodded. "Something like that."

Hagedorn grunted. "I believe you and I are going to work well together, Commander Zenar."

The Andorian allowed herself a hint of a smile. "Nothing would please me more, sir."

Hiro Matsura had never fought the Shayal'brun, but he knew some captains who had. They were said to be a vicious species, capable of unpredictable and devastatingly effective violence whenever they perceived that their borders had been violated.

The problem, as Matsura understood it, was that their borders seemed to change constantly—at least from the Shayal'brun's point of view. As a result, Earth Command had felt compelled to monitor the aliens' movements every few months, sending patrols out to the Shayal'brun's part of space even at the height of the Romulan Wars.

But now, with Earth Command turning so many of its activities over to Starfleet, responsibility for keeping track of the Shayal'brun had fallen to Matsura. That was why he was slicing through the void at warp one, scanning the aliens' farthest-flung holdings for signs of hostile intent.

"Anything?" asked Matsura, hovering over his navigator's console.

Williams shook her head from side to side. "Not yet, sir," she reported, continuing to consult her monitor. "No new colonies, no new sensor platforms, no new supply depots. . . ."

"And no sign of the Shayal'brun fleet," said Jezzelis, Matsura's long-tusked Vobilite first officer.

"Looks pretty quiet to me," Williams concluded.

Matsura straightened. "Then let's get out of here. The last thing we want to do is start an incident."

It was a real concern. The Shayal'brun were no doubt scanning them even as they scanned the Shayal'brun. The aliens would likely overlook a fly-by, as long as the ship remained outside their perceived borders.

But if the *Yellowjacket* lingered long enough, the Shayal'brun would attack. That much was certain.

"Mr. McCallum," said the captain, "bring us about and—"

Before Matsura could finish, his ship bucked and veered to starboard. The captain grabbed wildly for the back of Williams' chair and found a handhold there, or he would surely have lost his feet.

"What was *that?*" asked Jezzelis.

Williams examined her monitor again, hoping to give him an answer. But McCallum beat her to it.

"It's a subspace chute," said the helmsman.

Matsura looked at him. "A *what?*"

"A chute, sir," McCallum repeated, his fingers dancing across his control panel. The man looked excited, to say the least. "We ran into one on the *Pasteur* about a year ago."

"And what did you find out?" asked the captain.

"Not much, sir," said the helmsman. "Our instruments weren't nearly as powerful as the *Yellowjacket*'s." He looked up suddenly. "If I may say so, sir, this is a rare opportunity."

"You mean to turn back and study the chute?"

"Yes, sir." McCallum looked almost feverish in his desire to retrace their steps. "We may never come across one again."

Matsura frowned and turned to the viewscreen, where the stars burned brightly against the black velvet of space. He couldn't ignore the fact that some of those stars belonged to the Shayal'brun.

On the other hand, every captain in the fleet wanted to get a better handle on subspace anomalies, regardless of his background. Lives had been lost during the war because they hadn't known enough about such things.

And here was an opportunity to rectify that problem.

Jezzelis, who had enjoyed both military and scientific

careers, didn't say anything. But his expression spoke volumes.

"All right," Matsura told his helmsman. "You've got ten minutes—not a second more."

McCallum started to argue, to say that ten minutes might not be enough for the kind of analysis he had in mind. Then he saw the captain's eyes and seemed to think better of it.

"Yes, sir," said the helmsman. "Ten minutes. Thank you, sir." And he brought the ship about.

Matsura glanced at the viewscreen again and bit his lip. With luck, he thought, their little detour wouldn't be a bloody one.

Sitting at the compact computer station in his quarters, Aaron Stiles called up the message he had received a few minutes earlier.

Normally, he waited until the end of his shift before he left the bridge to read his personal messages. But this one was different. This one had come from Big Ed Walker.

The first thing Stiles noticed was that the admiral was smiling. It was a good sign, he told himself.

"Hello, Aaron," said Walker. "I hope you're well. I've been doing my best to keep track of your exploits. It sounds like you're doing good work, considering the adverse circumstances."

Naturally, the admiral was referring to the butterfly catchers. He just didn't want to mention them by name, in case his message accidentally fell into the wrong hands.

"I just wanted you to know that everything is looking good back here on Earth," Walker continued. "Our side is gaining the upper hand. It's looking more and more like one of us will get that brass ring they've been dangling in front of you."

The brass ring, of course, was the *Daedalus*. The upper hand was control of the fleet. And if the Earth Command camp was winning the battle, Stiles wouldn't have to worry about Darigghi and his ilk much longer.

In the captain's opinion, it couldn't happen soon enough.

"Stay well, son," said the admiral. "Walker out."

Stiles saw the Earth Command insignia replace the man's image. Tapping out a command on his padd, he dumped the message. Then he returned to his bridge, his step just a little lighter than before.

Bryce Shumar regarded the image of Daniel Hagedorn on the computer monitor outside his bedroom.

"So," said Shumar, "Councillor Sammak arrived safely?"

The esteemed Sammak of Vulcan was returning to his homeworld for his daughter's wedding ceremony. He had left San Francisco on an Earth Command vessel, which had transferred him to the *Peregrine* two days earlier. Now the *Peregrine* was transferring the councillor to the *Horatio*.

"He's being shown to his quarters now," Hagedorn told him.

"How are your missions going?" asked Shumar, because he had to say *something*.

"Well enough," said his counterpart. "And yours?"

"We're getting by."

Neither of them spoke for a moment. After all, if it was a war they were fighting over the future of the fleet, neither of them wanted to give away any strategic information.

It was a shame that it had to be that way, Shumar told himself. Hagedorn wasn't a bad sort of guy. And he had taken Cobaryn's side in that brawl back in San Francisco.

Maybe the time he had spent with a crew half full of scientists had softened his position a little. Maybe with a little urging he could be made to see the other side of the issue.

There was only one way to find out.

"Actually," Shumar remarked, "I'm glad we've got a chance to compare notes. I think you and I are a lot alike."

"In what way?" Hagedorn asked, his expression giving away nothing.

"We're reasonable men, I'd say."

The other man's eyes narrowed ever so slightly. "Reasonable . . . ?"

"We can see the other fellow's side of the story," Shumar elaborated. "Certainly I can."

"And what side is the *other* side?" Hagedorn inquired. He was beginning to look wary.

Shumar smiled in an attempt to put the man at ease. "I think you know what I'm going to say. That a strictly military-minded Starfleet would miss out on all kinds of scientific opportunities. That it would fail to embrace all the benefits the universe has to offer."

Hagedorn hadn't lodged an objection yet. Shumar interpreted that as his cue to go on.

"Mind you," he said, "there's a lot to be said for combat smarts. I've learned that first-hand. But two hundred years ago, when man went out into space it was to expand his store of knowledge. It would be a shame if we were compelled to abandon that philosophy now."

Hagedorn regarded him. "In other words, you would like me to rethink my position on the nature of Starfleet."

"I would," Shumar admitted, "yes. And believe me, not because I want to win this little internecine war of ours. That doesn't matter to me one bit. All that matters is that the Federation doesn't get cheated out of the advancements it deserves."

The other man leaned back in his chair. "You know," he said, in a surprisingly tired voice, "I like you. What's more, I respect you. And I sure as hell won't try to tell you that you don't have a point."

Shumar's hopes fell as he heard a "but" coming. Clearly, the other shoe was about to fall.

"But," Hagedorn went on, "I believe that this fleet has to

be a military organization first and foremost, and I can't tell you I'd ever advocate anything else. Not even for a nanosecond."

The scientist accepted the defeat. "Well," he responded in the same spirit of candidness, "it was worth a try."

The other man just looked at him. He seemed at a loss as to how to respond.

Shumar could see there was nothing to be gained by further conversation. "I ought to be getting on to my next assignment, I suppose. I'll see you around, no doubt."

Hagedorn nodded. "No doubt."

"Shumar out."

He was about to break the connection when the other captain said something. It was low, under his breath—as if it had escaped without his wanting it to.

"I didn't catch that," Shumar told him.

Hagedorn looked sympathetic. "I said it wasn't. Worth a try, I mean. The competition is already over."

Shumar felt his cheeks grow hot. "What are you talking about?"

"I mean it's over," Hagedorn said soberly. "I'd tell you more, but I've probably said too much already."

Shumar saw the undiluted honesty in the man's eyes. Hagedorn wasn't maneuvering, he realized. He really meant it.

"Thank you," Shumar replied. "I think."

For a moment it looked as if his colleague was going to say something else. Then he must have thought better of it.

"Hagedorn out," he said. And with that, his image vanished from the monitor and was replaced with the Starfleet insignia.

Suddenly, Shumar thought, he had a lot to think about.

Connor Dane made his decision and turned to his helmsman. "Take us out of orbit, Mr. Dolgin."

Dolgin shot a glance at him, his surprise evident on his florid, red-bearded face. "Sir?"

"Out of orbit," the captain repeated, with just a hint of derision. "That means *away.* More specifically, away from *here.*"

The helmsman blushed. "Yes, sir," he said with an undercurrent of indignation, and got to work.

"Captain Dane?" said Nasir, his tall, dark-skinned blade of a first officer. He moved to Dane's side and leaned over to speak with him. "Would you say it's wise to move off so quickly?"

The captain looked up at his exec. "*Quickly?* We've been here for two entire days. If the Nurstim are going to take note of us, I'd say they've probably done it already."

Nasir frowned. "Begging your pardon," he said, "but the Nurstim may simply be waiting for us to move off."

"At which point they'll attack the Arbazans?"

"Precisely, sir."

"In that case," said Dane, "maybe we should stay here forever. Then we can be *sure* the Nurstim won't start anything."

Nasir smiled thinly. "Another day—" he began.

"Is a day too many," the captain told him. "Our orders called for us to stay two days—no longer."

His first officer nodded. "That's certainly true. But I assure you, anyone with a military background—"

"Can go straight to hell," said Dane.

That brought Nasir up short. "All I meant—"

"I *know* what you meant," the captain declared. "That I didn't wear black and gold during the war, so I can't possibly have the slightest idea of what I'm doing. Right?"

The first officer shook his head. "Not at all, sir. I just—"

Dane held his hand up. "Spare me the denials, Commander. I'm not in the mood." He turned to the science console, which was situated behind him and to his right. "Mr. Hudlin?"

Hudlin, who was hanging around the bridge as usual, looked up from his monitors. "Sir?"

"Didn't we pass something on the way here that you wanted to investigate? Some kind of cloud or something?"

The white-haired man smiled. "An ionized gas torus," he said. "It was trailing one of the moons around the seventh planet."

"Sounds intriguing," said Dane, though it didn't really sound intriguing to him at all. "Let's look into it."

Hudlin looked at him askance. "What about the Arbazans?"

"The Arbazans are as safe as they're going to be," the captain told him. He addressed his helmsman again. "Mr. Dolgin, head for the seventh planet. Three-quarters impulse."

"Aye, sir," came the faintly grudging response.

Next, Dane turned to his navigator. "Chart a course for the eighth and ninth planets as well, Lieutenant Ideko. They might have some interesting moons too."

Ideko, a slender, graceful Dedderac, nodded her black-and-white-striped head. "Aye, sir."

Hudlin seemed unable to believe his ears. "If I may ask, sir . . . why the sudden interest in moons?"

The captain shrugged. "I've always been interested in moons, Mr. Hudlin. It's the scientist in me."

For Nasir, that appeared to be the last straw. He straightened and looked down at Dane with undisguised hostility. "It's only fair to inform you that I'll be lodging a formal protest."

The captain nodded. "Thanks for being fair, Commander. It's one of the things I like best about you."

The first officer didn't say anything more. He just moved away from the center seat and took up a position near the engineering console.

Inwardly, Dane cursed himself. Nasir was a strutting know-it-all he should never have hired in the first place—but still, he didn't deserve that kind of tongue-lashing. It wasn't his fault that his captain was a walking tinderbox lately.

It was Big Ed Walker's.

Dane's uncle was the one who had notified him that the Earth Command faction had carried the day. As if I were one of them, he reflected bitterly. As if I had come around, just the way Big Ed always knew I would.

Truth be told, Dane hadn't considered himself an ally of Shumar and Cobaryn either. But his uncle's message had sparked something inside him—and not just resentment.

It had made him realize that he had to take a stand in this war sooner or later. He had to choose between the cowboys and the butterfly catchers, or someone else would make the choice for him.

All his life, he had denied his family's glorious military history—but he hadn't embraced anything else in its place. Maybe it was time to make a commitment to something, Dane told himself.

Maybe it was time to start chasing butterflies.

Bryce Shumar watched the small, slender woman take a seat in the anteroom of his quarters.

"Well," said Clarisse Dumont, "here I am. I hope this is as important as you made it out to be."

The *Peregrine* had been nearly a trillion kilometers from Earth when Shumar had asked to speak with Dumont. Of course, it would have been a lot more convenient for them to send messages back and forth through subspace, but the captain had wanted to see his patron in person.

So Dumont had pulled some strings. She had made it to the nearest Earth base via commercial vessels. And now she was waiting to hear why she had made such a long and arduous trip.

Shumar found himself in the mood to be blunt. He yielded to it. "What's going on?" he asked unceremoniously.

Dumont's brow puckered. "What exactly do you mean?"

Shumar felt a surge of anger constrict his throat. "Don't play games with me," he said with forced calm. "I spoke with Hagedorn. He told me that the war for the fleet is over—that his side has already won."

He wanted Dumont to tell him he was crazy. He wanted her to say that Hagedorn didn't know what he was talking about. But she didn't do either of those things.

The only response she could muster was, "Is that so?"

"Was he right?" the captain pressed, feeling he knew the answer already. "Is the war already over?"

Dumont sighed. "Honestly, not yet. But it's getting there. Unless something changes—and quickly—Starfleet's going to be nothing more than Earth Command with a different name."

Shumar frowned. "You could have told me," he said.

"I could have," she agreed. "But then, you might have stopped fighting—and whatever slim chance we had would have been gone."

It made sense in a heavy-handed, presumptuous kind of way. He asked himself what he would have done if he had been Clarisse Dumont. It didn't take him long to come up with an answer.

"You should have left that up to me," the captain told her. "I deserved to know the truth."

Dumont smiled a bitter smile. "We seldom get what we deserve." She paused. "So now what, Captain? Are you going to pack it in, as I feared? Or are you going to keep fighting?"

Shumar grunted. "Do I have a choice?"

She nodded. "Always."

The woman was glib—he had to give her that. But then, she hadn't risen to such prominence by being shy.

"In that case," he told her, "I'll have to give it some thought."

"I hope you'll do that," said Dumont. "And I hope you'll come to the same conclusion you did before, odds or no odds."

He didn't pick up the gauntlet she had thrown down. Instead, he changed the subject. "Can I get you something to eat?"

She shook her head. "Thank you, but no. I should be getting back to the base. As always, I've got work to do." She smiled again. "Miles to go before I sleep and all that."

The captain nodded. "I understand."

He and Dumont talked about something on their way back to the transporter room—though afterward, he wasn't sure what. And he must have given the order for his transporter operator to return her to Earth Base 12, but he didn't remember issuing it.

All Shumar remembered was what Dumont had said. *Unless something changes—and quickly—Starfleet's going to be nothing more than Earth Command with a different name.*

It was a depressing thought, to say the least.

In the privacy of his tiny suite on the *Cheyenne*, Alonis Cobaryn viewed a recorded message from his friend and colleague Captain Shumar. It didn't appear to be good news.

"Dumont confirmed it," said Shumar, his brow creased with concern. "Our side is losing the war for the *Daedalus*."

Cobaryn eased himself back into his chair. He was sorry to hear such a thing. He was sorry indeed.

"She asked me whether I intended to stop fighting," Shumar continued, "since our cause was all but lost." He chuckled bitterly. "I told her I'd give it some thought."

And what decision did you make? the Rigelian wondered.

Shumar shrugged. "What could I do except stick it out? I made a commitment, Alonis. I can't give up now."

Cobaryn nodded. *Bravo,* he thought.

"I'll expect the worst, of course," the Earthman told him. "But that doesn't mean I'll stop hoping for the best."

Cobaryn smiled. "And they call *me* a cockeyed optimist," he said out loud.

Shumar sighed. "Pathetic, isn't it?"

If it is, the Rigelian reflected, *then we are both pathetic. Like you, I will see this venture through to its conclusion.*

He had barely completed the thought when a light began to blink in the upper quadrant of his screen, signaling an incoming message. Responding to it, he saw that it was from Earth.

From Director Abute . . .

Aaron Stiles was peering at the tiny screen of a handheld computer, going over the results of his science section's analysis of the asteroid belt, when his navigator spoke up.

"Sir," said Rosten, a tall woman with long, dark hair, "I have a message for you from Director Abute."

Stiles turned in his seat to acknowledge her, glad for the opportunity to put the asteroid data aside. "Put it on-screen, Lieutenant."

"Aye, sir," said Rosten.

A moment later, the starfield on the forward viewer was replaced by Abute's dark, hawk-nosed visage. The man looked positively grim.

"Good morning, Captain Stiles," said the Starfleet administrator. "I have a mission for you."

Judging from the seriousness of the man's tone, Stiles guessed that it was a *real* mission this time. He certainly hoped so. He'd had enough asteroid-watching to last him several Vulcan lifetimes.

"I trust you're familiar with the Oreias system," Abute continued. "It's not far from your present position."

In fact, the captain *was* familiar with Oreias. A girl he had dated for a while had gone there to help establish an Earth colony.

"We have four scientific installations there, one on each of Oreias's class-M planets," the director noted. "Late yesterday, the Oreias Five colony was attacked by an unknown aggressor."

Unknown? thought Stiles. He felt his jaw clench.

"I know what you're thinking," said Abute. "That it may be the Romulans again. Frankly, I can't imagine what they would have to gain by such an action, but I concede that we cannot rule out the possibility."

Seeing a shadow fall across his lap, the captain traced it to its source. He found Darigghi standing next to him, his tiny Osadjani eyes focused on the Earthman's message.

"Fortunately," the director remarked, "no one died in the attack. However, the place is a bloody shambles and the colonists are scared to death—those on the other worlds as well as on Oreias Five. After all, whoever did this could be targeting the other colonies as well."

True, Stiles reflected. And if it *was* the Romulans, if he found even a hint that they were back on the warpath . . .

"Which is why we need a Starfleet presence there as quickly as possible," Abute declared, "to stabilize the situation, defend against further attacks, and try to determine who was responsible. Your vessel is the one closest to Oreias, Captain—"

Stiles smiled to himself. So I'll be the one who gets to check it out, he concluded. He was already beginning to savor the challenge when Abute completed his sentence.

"—so it looks as though you will be the first to arrive.

However, I am deploying the remainder of the fleet to the Oreias system as well. A threat of this potential magnitude clearly dictates a team effort."

The captain slumped in his seat. Six ships . . . to investigate a single sneak attack? If they had worked that way during the war they would never have had time to launch an attack of their own.

"Good luck," said the director. "I look forward to the report of your initial findings. Abute out."

Abruptly, the man's image was replaced with a starfield. Stiles frowned and turned to his navigator. "Lieutenant Rosten," he sighed, "set a course for Oreias Five. Top cruising speed."

"Aye, sir," said the navigator, applying herself to the task.

The captain leaned back in his seat. Then he looked up at Darigghi. "I don't suppose you've ever been in battle before?" he asked.

The Osadjani shook his head. "I have not."

"Well," said Stiles, "this may be your chance."

Look for STAR TREK fiction from Pocket Books

Star Trek®: The Original Series

Enterprise: The First Adventure • Vonda N. McIntyre
Final Frontier • Diane Carey
Strangers from the Sky • Margaret Wander Bonanno
Spock's World • Diane Duane
The Lost Years • J.M. Dillard
Probe • Margaret Wander Bonanno
Prime Directive • Judith and Garfield Reeves-Stevens
Best Destiny • Diane Carey
Shadows on the Sun • Michael Jan Friedman
Sarek • A.C. Crispin
Federation • Judith and Garfield Reeves-Stevens
Vulcan's Forge • Josepha Sherman & Susan Shwartz
Mission to Horatius • Mack Reynolds
Vulcan's Heart • Josepha Sherman & Susan Shwartz

Novelizations

Star Trek: The Motion Picture • Gene Roddenberry
Star Trek II: The Wrath of Khan • Vonda N. McIntyre
Star Trek III: The Search for Spock • Vonda N. McIntyre
Star Trek IV: The Voyage Home • Vonda N. McIntyre
Star Trek V: The Final Frontier • J.M. Dillard
Star Trek VI: The Undiscovered Country • J.M. Dillard
Star Trek Generations • J.M. Dillard
Starfleet Academy • Diane Carey

Star Trek books by William Shatner with Judith and Garfield Reeves-Stevens

The Ashes of Eden
The Return
Avenger
Star Trek: Odyssey (contains *The Ashes of Eden*, *The Return*, and *Avenger)*
Spectre
Dark Victory

#1 • *Star Trek: The Motion Picture* • Gene Roddenberry
#2 • *The Entropy Effect* • Vonda N. McIntyre
#3 • *The Klingon Gambit* • Robert E. Vardeman
#4 • *The Covenant of the Crown* • Howard Weinstein
#5 • *The Prometheus Design* • Sondra Marshak & Myrna Culbreath

#6 • *The Abode of Life* • Lee Correy
#7 • *Star Trek II: The Wrath of Khan* • Vonda N. McIntyre
#8 • *Black Fire* • Sonni Cooper
#9 • *Triangle* • Sondra Marshak & Myrna Culbreath
#10 • *Web of the Romulans* • M.S. Murdock
#11 • *Yesterday's Son* • A.C. Crispin
#12 • *Mutiny on the Enterprise* • Robert E. Vardeman
#13 • *The Wounded Sky* • Diane Duane
#14 • *The Trellisane Confrontation* • David Dvorkin
#15 • *Corona* • Greg Bear
#16 • *The Final Reflection* • John M. Ford
#17 • *Star Trek III: The Search for Spock* • Vonda N. McIntyre
#18 • *My Enemy, My Ally* • Diane Duane
#19 • *The Tears of the Singers* • Melinda Snodgrass
#20 • *The Vulcan Academy Murders* • Jean Lorrah
#21 • *Uhura's Song* • Janet Kagan
#22 • *Shadow Land* • Laurence Yep
#23 • *Ishmael* • Barbara Hambly
#24 • *Killing Time* • Della Van Hise
#25 • *Dwellers in the Crucible* • Margaret Wander Bonanno
#26 • *Pawns and Symbols* • Majiliss Larson
#27 • *Mindshadow* • J.M. Dillard
#28 • *Crisis on Centaurus* • Brad Ferguson
#29 • *Dreadnought!* • Diane Carey
#30 • *Demons* • J.M. Dillard
#31 • *Battlestations!* • Diane Carey
#32 • *Chain of Attack* • Gene DeWeese
#33 • *Deep Domain* • Howard Weinstein
#34 • *Dreams of the Raven* • Carmen Carter
#35 • *The Romulan Way* • Diane Duane & Peter Morwood
#36 • *How Much for Just the Planet?* • John M. Ford
#37 • *Bloodthirst* • J.M. Dillard
#38 • *The IDIC Epidemic* • Jean Lorrah
#39 • *Time for Yesterday* • A.C. Crispin
#40 • *Timetrap* • David Dvorkin
#41 • *The Three-Minute Universe* • Barbara Paul
#42 • *Memory Prime* • Judith and Garfield Reeves-Stevens
#43 • *The Final Nexus* • Gene DeWeese
#44 • *Vulcan's Glory* • D.C. Fontana
#45 • *Double, Double* • Michael Jan Friedman
#46 • *The Cry of the Onlies* • Judy Klass
#47 • *The Kobayashi Maru* • Julia Ecklar

#48 • *Rules of Engagement* • Peter Morwood
#49 • *The Pandora Principle* • Carolyn Clowes
#50 • *Doctor's Orders* • Diane Duane
#51 • *Unseen Enemy* • V.E. Mitchell
#52 • *Home Is the Hunter* • Dana Kramer Rolls
#53 • *Ghost-Walker* • Barbara Hambly
#54 • *A Flag Full of Stars* • Brad Ferguson
#55 • *Renegade* • Gene DeWeese
#56 • *Legacy* • Michael Jan Friedman
#57 • *The Rift* • Peter David
#58 • *Face of Fire* • Michael Jan Friedman
#59 • *The Disinherited* • Peter David
#60 • *Ice Trap* • L.A. Graf
#61 • *Sanctuary* • John Vornholt
#62 • *Death Count* • L.A. Graf
#63 • *Shell Game* • Melissa Crandall
#64 • *The Starship Trap* • Mel Gilden
#65 • *Windows on a Lost World* • V.E. Mitchell
#66 • *From the Depths* • Victor Milan
#67 • *The Great Starship Race* • Diane Carey
#68 • *Firestorm* • L.A. Graf
#69 • *The Patrian Transgression* • Simon Hawke
#70 • *Traitor Winds* • L.A. Graf
#71 • *Crossroad* • Barbara Hambly
#72 • *The Better Man* • Howard Weinstein
#73 • *Recovery* • J.M. Dillard
#74 • *The Fearful Summons* • Denny Martin Flynn
#75 • *First Frontier* • Diane Carey & Dr. James I. Kirkland
#76 • *The Captain's Daughter* • Peter David
#77 • *Twilight's End* • Jerry Oltion
#78 • *The Rings of Tautee* • Dean Wesley Smith & Kristine Kathryn Rusch
#79 • *Invasion!* #1: *First Strike* • Diane Carey
#80 • *The Joy Machine* • James Gunn
#81 • *Mudd in Your Eye* • Jerry Oltion
#82 • *Mind Meld* • John Vornholt
#83 • *Heart of the Sun* • Pamela Sargent & George Zebrowski
#84 • *Assignment: Eternity* • Greg Cox
#85-87 • *My Brother's Keeper* • Michael Jan Friedman
    #85 • *Republic*
    #86 • *Constitution*
    #87 • *Enterprise*
#88 • *Across the Universe* • Pamela Sargent & George Zebrowski

Star Trek: The Next Generation®

Metamorphosis • Jean Lorrah
Vendetta • Peter David
Reunion • Michael Jan Friedman
Imzadi • Peter David
The Devil's Heart • Carmen Carter
Dark Mirror • Diane Duane
Q-Squared • Peter David
Crossover • Michael Jan Friedman
Kahless • Michael Jan Friedman
Ship of the Line • Diane Carey
The Best and the Brightest • Susan Wright
Planet X • Michael Jan Friedman
Imzadi II: Triangle • Peter David
I, Q • Peter David & John de Lancie

Novelizations

Encounter at Farpoint • David Gerrold
Unification • Jeri Taylor
Relics • Michael Jan Friedman
Descent • Diane Carey
All Good Things... • Michael Jan Friedman
Star Trek: Klingon • Dean Wesley Smith & Kristine Kathryn Rusch
Star Trek Generations • J.M. Dillard
Star Trek: First Contact • J.M. Dillard
Star Trek: Insurrection • J.M. Dillard

#1 • *Ghost Ship* • Diane Carey
#2 • *The Peacekeepers* • Gene DeWeese
#3 • *The Children of Hamlin* • Carmen Carter
#4 • *Survivors* • Jean Lorrah
#5 • *Strike Zone* • Peter David
#6 • *Power Hungry* • Howard Weinstein
#7 • *Masks* • John Vornholt
#8 • *The Captain's Honor* • David and Daniel Dvorkin
#9 • *A Call to Darkness* • Michael Jan Friedman
#10 • *A Rock and a Hard Place* • Peter David
#11 • *Gulliver's Fugitives* • Keith Sharee
#12 • *Doomsday World* • David, Carter, Friedman & Greenberger
#13 • *The Eyes of the Beholders* • A.C. Crispin
#14 • *Exiles* • Howard Weinstein
#15 • *Fortune's Light* • Michael Jan Friedman

#16 • *Contamination* • John Vornholt
#17 • *Boogeymen* • Mel Gilden
#18 • *Q-in-Law* • Peter David
#19 • *Perchance to Dream* • Howard Weinstein
#20 • *Spartacus* • T.L. Mancour
#21 • *Chains of Command* • W.A. McCoy & E.L. Flood
#22 • *Imbalance* • V.E. Mitchell
#23 • *War Drums* • John Vornholt
#24 • *Nightshade* • Laurell K. Hamilton
#25 • *Grounded* • David Bischoff
#26 • *The Romulan Prize* • Simon Hawke
#27 • *Guises of the Mind* • Rebecca Neason
#28 • *Here There Be Dragons* • John Peel
#29 • *Sins of Commission* • Susan Wright
#30 • *Debtor's Planet* • W.R. Thompson
#31 • *Foreign Foes* • Dave Galanter & Greg Brodeur
#32 • *Requiem* • Michael Jan Friedman & Kevin Ryan
#33 • *Balance of Power* • Dafydd ab Hugh
#34 • *Blaze of Glory* • Simon Hawke
#35 • *The Romulan Stratagem* • Robert Greenberger
#36 • *Into the Nebula* • Gene DeWeese
#37 • *The Last Stand* • Brad Ferguson
#38 • *Dragon's Honor* • Kij Johnson & Greg Cox
#39 • *Rogue Saucer* • John Vornholt
#40 • *Possession* • J.M. Dillard & Kathleen O'Malley
#41 • *Invasion! #2: The Soldiers of Fear* • Dean Wesley Smith & Kristine Kathryn Rusch
#42 • *Infiltrator* • W.R. Thompson
#43 • *A Fury Scorned* • Pamela Sargent & George Zebrowski
#44 • *The Death of Princes* • John Peel
#45 • *Intellivore* • Diane Duane
#46 • *To Storm Heaven* • Esther Friesner
#47-49 • *The Q Continuum* • Greg Cox
  #47 • *Q-Space*
  #48 • *Q-Zone*
  #49 • *Q-Strike*
#50 • *Dyson Sphere* • Charles Pellegrino & George Zebrowski
#51-56 • *Double Helix*
  #51 • *Infection* • John Gregory Betancourt
  #52 • *Vectors* • Dean Wesley Smith & Kristine Kathryn Rusch
  #53 • *Red Sector* • Diane Carey
  #54 • *Quarantine* • John Vornholt

#55 • *Double or Nothing* • Peter David
#56 • *The First Virtue* • Michael Jan Friedman & Christie Golden
#57 • *The Forgotten War* • William Fortschen
#58-59 • *Gemworld* • John Vornholt
#58 • *Gemworld #1*
#59 • *Gemworld #2*

Star Trek: Deep Space Nine®

Warped • K.W. Jeter
Legends of the Ferengi • Ira Steven Behr & Robert Hewitt Wolfe
The Lives of Dax • Marco Palmieri, ed.

Novelizations
Emissary • J.M. Dillard
The Search • Diane Carey
The Way of the Warrior • Diane Carey
Star Trek: Klingon • Dean Wesley Smith & Kristine Kathryn Rusch
Trials and Tribble-ations • Diane Carey
Far Beyond the Stars • Steve Barnes
What You Leave Behind • Diane Carey

#1 • *Emissary* • J.M. Dillard
#2 • *The Siege* • Peter David
#3 • *Bloodletter* • K.W. Jeter
#4 • *The Big Game* • Sandy Schofield
#5 • *Fallen Heroes* • Dafydd ab Hugh
#6 • *Betrayal* • Lois Tilton
#7 • *Warchild* • Esther Friesner
#8 • *Antimatter* • John Vornholt
#9 • *Proud Helios* • Melissa Scott
#10 • *Valhalla* • Nathan Archer
#11 • *Devil in the Sky* • Greg Cox & John Gregory Betancourt
#12 • *The Laertian Gamble* • Robert Sheckley
#13 • *Station Rage* • Diane Carey
#14 • *The Long Night* • Dean Wesley Smith & Kristine Kathryn Rusch
#15 • *Objective: Bajor* • John Peel
#16 • *Invasion! #3: Time's Enemy* • L.A. Graf
#17 • *The Heart of the Warrior* • John Gregory Betancourt
#18 • *Saratoga* • Michael Jan Friedman
#19 • *The Tempest* • Susan Wright
#20 • *Wrath of the Prophets* • David, Friedman & Greenberger
#21 • *Trial by Error* • Mark Garland

#22 • *Vengeance* • Dafydd ab Hugh
#23 • *The 34th Rule* • Armin Shimerman & David R. George III
#24-26 • *Rebels* • Dafydd ab Hugh
#24 • *The Conquered*
#25 • *The Courageous*
#26 • *The Liberated*

Star Trek: Voyager®

Mosaic • Jeri Taylor
Pathways • Jeri Taylor
Captain Proton! • Dean Wesley Smith
Novelizations
Caretaker • L.A. Graf
Flashback • Diane Carey
Day of Honor • Michael Jan Friedman
Equinox • Diane Carey

#1 • *Caretaker* • L.A. Graf
#2 • *The Escape* • Dean Wesley Smith & Kristine Kathryn Rusch
#3 • *Ragnarok* • Nathan Archer
#4 • *Violations* • Susan Wright
#5 • *Incident at Arbuk* • John Gregory Betancourt
#6 • *The Murdered Sun* • Christie Golden
#7 • *Ghost of a Chance* • Mark A. Garland & Charles G. McGraw
#8 • *Cybersong* • S.N. Lewitt
#9 • *Invasion! #4: Final Fury* • Dafydd ab Hugh
#10 • *Bless the Beasts* • Karen Haber
#11 • *The Garden* • Melissa Scott
#12 • *Chrysalis* • David Niall Wilson
#13 • *The Black Shore* • Greg Cox
#14 • *Marooned* • Christie Golden
#15 • *Echoes* • Dean Wesley Smith, Kristine Kathryn Rusch & Nina Kiriki Hoffman
#16 • *Seven of Nine* • Christie Golden
#17 • *Death of a Neutron Star* • Eric Kotani
#18 • *Battle Lines* • Dave Galanter & Greg Brodeur

Star Trek®: New Frontier

New Frontier #1-4 Collector's Edition • Peter David
#1 • *House of Cards* • Peter David

#2 • *Into the Void* • Peter David
#3 • *The Two-Front War* • Peter David
#4 • *End Game* • Peter David
#5 • *Martyr* • Peter David
#6 • *Fire on High* • Peter David
The Captain's Table #5 • *Once Burned* • Peter David
Double Helix #5 • *Double or Nothing* • Peter David
#7 • *The Quiet Place* • Peter David
#8 • *Dark Allies* • Peter David

Star Trek®: Invasion!

#1 • *First Strike* • Diane Carey
#2 • *The Soldiers of Fear* • Dean Wesley Smith & Kristine Kathryn Rusch
#3 • *Time's Enemy* • L.A. Graf
#4 • *Final Fury* • Dafydd ab Hugh
Invasion! Omnibus • various

Star Trek®: Day of Honor

#1 • *Ancient Blood* • Diane Carey
#2 • *Armageddon Sky* • L.A. Graf
#3 • *Her Klingon Soul* • Michael Jan Friedman
#4 • *Treaty's Law* • Dean Wesley Smith & Kristine Kathryn Rusch
The Television Episode • Michael Jan Friedman
Day of Honor Omnibus • various

Star Trek®: The Captain's Table

#1 • *War Dragons* • L.A. Graf
#2 • *Dujonian's Hoard* • Michael Jan Friedman
#3 • *The Mist* • Dean Wesley Smith & Kristine Kathryn Rusch
#4 • *Fire Ship* • Diane Carey
#5 • *Once Burned* • Peter David
#6 • *Where Sea Meets Sky* • Jerry Oltion

Star Trek®: The Dominion War

#1 • *Behind Enemy Lines* • John Vornholt
#2 • *Call to Arms...* • Diane Carey
#3 • *Tunnel Through the Stars* • John Vornholt
#4 • *...Sacrifice of Angels* • Diane Carey

Star Trek® Books available in Trade Paperback

Omnibus Editions

Invasion! Omnibus • various

Day of Honor Omnibus • various

Star Trek: Odyssey • William Shatner with Judith and Garfield Reeves-Stevens

Other Books

Legends of the Ferengi • Ira Steven Behr & Robert Hewitt Wolfe

Strange New Worlds, vol. I and II • Dean Wesley Smith, ed.

Adventures in Time and Space • Mary Taylor

The Lives of Dax • Marco Palmieri, ed.

Captain Proton! • Dean Wesley Smith